THE EXPATRIATE

CHARLES BROWNSON

TEMPE ARIZONA
OCOTILLO ARTS
2013

Brownson, Charles, 1945-
    The Expatriate. 2nd ed
I. Title.
PS3552.R788X   813.54

ISBN 978-0-9893492-3-9 (print)
ISBN 978-0-9893472-4-6 (e-book)

This version of *The Expatriate* is the text of an artists book published by Ocotillo Arts 1n 2012 in an edition of three. A first edition was published in 2009. ISBN 978-0-578-03681-6

Contents

Monuments

Hostages

Refugees

BREAD

A crust of bread is marvelous at first sight because of that almost panoramic impression which it makes: as if one had under one's hand the Alps, the Taurus, or the Cordilleras of the Andean.

So it was that an amorphous exploding mass was slid for us into the celestial oven where upon hardening was fashioned into valleys, rolling hills, crevasses… And all this fretwork so neatly articulated, this fine filigree on which the light lies so carefully — covers up that disgusting feminine softness which lies beneath.

That flabby and cold stuff which we call the crumb is a tissue like that of sponges: foliage and flowers all mashed together like Siamese sisters. When bread goes stale these flowers wither and curl up: they detach themselves one from another and the mass becomes crumbly…

But break it: because bread when it is put into our mouths is not so much an object of respect as it is something to be used up.

Francis Ponge, *Le Parti pris des choses*
(Gallimard, 1946)
Translated by Charles Brownson

JAKE

Do not think to put the gods to work for your own purpose. Their ends are greater than yours.
— Some Greek, probably

He had been a tall man, and taller still in appearance because of the high-crowned Western hat which he wore summer and winter, a hat which face-on completed the long oval of his head, divided in two by the line of the hat brim. The effect was a bit cartoon-like. It was part of his charm.

He was called Jake now by most of those who knew him. At first it had been Christof. After a few years and some gravitas it became Dr Greidel, or Professor by students meaning to be familiar without knowing that was the more honorable form of address.

Saleem didn't like the name Jake. He said it had mostly negative connotations.

Jake himself didn't know how the name had originated. Some boy's father had started calling him that when Jake was himself a boy, with mysterious and probably derisory intent. That would be Saleem's view if he had had one. Saleem kept to himself, and even Jake wouldn't have known much about him beyond the typical graduate student's proclivity for niggling.

Saleem was on everyone's mind, of course.

Jake had had a prominent jaw and large blue eyes deep in bony sockets, an appearance which made unobservant people wonder if he had Indian blood. He habitually wore Western boots, too, well-polished but humble, and unlike the other elderly professors, seldom a tie. Winter and summer a long-sleeved dress shirt, dark gabardines, and when it was cold enough also a dark green goretex parka.

That was the way he was dressed when we found him collapsed across his desk one Friday morning late in the term. Reiva Derwent had come to collect for the department's staff presents.

Dead.

The next week it came out he'd put something poisonous into his coffee. Some kindly drug, not sleeping pills which so many use when they're not certain, nor anything painful like arsenic. How they knew it was him that put it into his coffee was not explained.

Nor was it ever, but Reiva knew it by instinct the moment she saw him.

Of course.

Jake's office was the usual clutter of books and papers stacked everywhere, shelves full of pedestrian editions of the texts he taught picked up second-hand in shops as suitable for lending to undergraduates. A disused typewriter heaped with file folders, relegated there by an old but not antiquated desktop computer. Jake had sent a couple of e-mails before having coffee, something after midnight. But they were only department business and gave away nothing beyond the time of death. The earliest time.

Reiva hadn't been especially close to Jake, and it was just happenstance that she was the one to find him. What happened after that would have happened in any case. People said otherwise, of course. People are hungry for reasons, and will speculate as necessary on the behavior of others.

Jake had not, in fact, been close to anyone in the department. For maybe for thirty years now (only the Chair went back that far) he had taught his classes and attended meetings carrying a faint and slightly distanced smile as a wrapping paper around his private self which no one wanted to tear. Malicious people said the box was empty anyway. He'd been married, to all appearances happily, to a woman somewhat like Jago's wife, so it was fortunate he'd never had the ambition of Snow's protagonist in that novel. She was left behind now. No one knew how she was taking it (we didn't even know her name) until it was too late to decently find out. Jake's two grown children were equally inaccessible.

Reiva remarked that if it had been her husband she would have thrown herself on the ground — well, on the floor — and thrashed about, with much gnashing and wailing. But that remained a conjecture, as she wasn't married and wasn't likely to be.

Jake had published a couple of well-enough regarded books that his death was noted in the *Chronicle* a month or so afterward. Just about the last thing to do with that kindly inconsiderable man was a nasty squabble in a department meeting between Reiva and the Chair.

It had to do with a memorial scholarship which Tor had proposed.

No one at the table had any inkling that Reiva was about to go off the rails. She had been a little odd all through the first weeks of spring term, it was true. Perhaps the holidays had not gone well for her. Of course, propriety being what it is under Tor, an incipient breakdown is not likely to be spotted, but nevertheless an alert colleague in a nearby seat might have noticed certain signs. Tor made his suggestion concerning the memorial scholarship in Jake's name and passed on to other business. At this point Reiva rose slowly from her seat and said in an unusually alto voice something no one quite heard and walked out, leaving behind on the table two file folders and a plastic glass of water.

Of course the theory immediately proposed was that there had been something between them. The most obviously desirable something was a liason, of course, and this theory went on for some time sprouting newly baroque elaborations and glosses (somewhat akin to Saleem's perennially unfinished dissertation) until it fell of its own weight. But the taste of it remained on the tongue, of something unseemly which was to be kept off the table. Since nothing stuck to the ever-smiling and unflappably benign Jake Greidel the whatever-it-was lay on Reiva's plate like a booger.

She was, at that point, doomed.

It was a fine sunny day in late March, a week after spring break, that the big dust-up finally came. The pretext was Saleem's dissertation. With Jake gone, no one else was willing to supervise the thing. Reiva herself was too junior to take it on so, to Tor's evident satisfaction, Saleem would be hustled out of the program. No one except Reiva minded that, but she minded very much. It was an injustice, she fumed, and said some unforgivable things. As the Chair would not repeat them, gossip was again rife, but the nature of Reiva's accusations was not hard to guess.

And that was it. In a little less than an hour, about the space of a senior seminar, one career was unmade and another cancelled, and events were set afoot which would lead who knew where.

And so the path of Saleem Singh though life left two more victims in the ditch. A couple of years later someone at a conference at UCLA reported that Saleem was teaching at a community college in southern California somewhere. So that turned out all right, more or less.

Reiva moved on to a college in upstate New York, near her parents, where she found work as an instructor on a year-to-year contract and as far as any of us knows she's still there.

Requiscat in pace.

Jake closed the front door of his house slowly, feeling the wedge of the latch slide across the plate and then snick liquidly home. Cool. High forties. He took a slow breath, released it slowly.

The intersection with 3rd was quiet this morning. A couple of students on bicycles, their fat sticky tires sounding like tape peeled up. Jake sucked on his tongue, imitating the sound, and smiled wanly. The scuffed leather valise felt heavy in his left hand, though there wasn't much in it but a piece of bread and cheese for lunch, a planner, and a magazine which he intended to read during office hours. The nine o'clock winter sun pushed in under the brim of his hat, which he tilted back a little so as to better shade his neck where Mrs. Jake was always trying to slather sunblock. He ran his hand in under the collar of his shirt, scratching among the coarse gray hairs as if something in the sheets had bitten him, but the probe was only speculative.

Wattled old skin. An image that suggested nothing to most people. Wattle and daub — who knew what that was?

Skin like eroded adobe.

Ariel's boy, she said, was bitten by a brown recluse sleeping in a rental place in Lake Havasu over Thanksgiving. Why he would want to go to Lake Havasu. Serve him right, Ol' Ed would say. If Ol' Ed were still around. Got it down to the bone and he had to have it looked at finally.

Couple of weeks down the jake-hole for that. Then kaput. Quick. Mercifully quick Mrs. Jake would say, as if she took mercy seriously. Believed there was such a thing.

He walked slowly, strolling almost, having an hour now, soaking in the lizard sun and sweating a little in his nylon-colored jacket, slowly taking the unwarmed air into his lungs. Letting it seep back out as a sighing breeze which said wuwei, wuwei.

On the mall more bicycles. Foot traffic disrupted by construction fences between the traffic circle and the union where a hole was being dug for a library. For more of the library. Library and pizza reaching out for each other like breeding amoeba. Mud still from the rain of a week ago, along the wood-paved path from one side of the mall to the other.

Halfway across, Jake waited while men in yellow plastic hats opened a gate in the wire fence to let a dump truck through. The peak of the professor's hat stood out above the knot of student hairdos, gray felt among the mostly spiky light brown stuff, with here and there a slick of Asian black. Classes were changing. The bright-colored student mob surged forward and dispersed on the other side of the excavation, down the sidewalks between the stone buildings. Jake started out too, just as another chattering stream flowed around the yellow hard-hats and then himself. Still smiling distantly, he passed around a corner of the union and into the side door of the building where his seminar was scheduled this semester.

A metal door, mostly glass with embedded chicken wire, heavy with hydraulic resistance but nevertheless clanking shut too quickly, swatting petite scholars to the floor, books flying, cellphones skittering off under the water fountain. The hallway smelled like college the way college smelled when Jake was eight years old and spent the hours after school in his mother's lab. It was a psychology lab but it smelled of chemicals anyway. The whole college smelled of formaldehyde. That and linoleum. A gray linoleum smell compounded with the janitor's rag used for wiping out water fountains.

The linoleum in the dentist's hallway was green, and smelled different.

People's garages smelled dark and oily then because they were made of wood which somehow was soaked with dirty crankcase oil. The neighbors' garage burned spectacularly one winter night but they got it out, leaving a powerful campground odor which the undergraduate Jake could still smell through his open window when it rained. A fabled occurrence, that fire. Old as Ur.

The hallway was empty. His leather soles cracked on the bare floor. Some yards along he turned into the open doorway of a classroom, which he closed softly behind him. Inside, twenty or so chairs with tablet arms were scattered around the room, most of them pushed into a shoal under the windows that ran most of the length of the long wall opposite the door. Five students occupied the other seats, which they had taken without forming up into a row or any other pattern.

Good morning.

The prof's voice was quiet, slow. He stashed his battered valise on a shelf of the lectern and took another of the chairs for himself.

The two women met his greeting. Of the three men, one was a middle-aged and businesslike and the other two were science nerds who despite their apparent twinship seemed never to have noticed each other.

Nevertheless, discussions in this seminar were frequently lively. Jake laid his hat on the floor. The room was as cold as a cave.

Shall we begin?

The middle-aged man's name was Bill, and it was his turn to present. He'd taken the last time slot in order to see what the rules were. Risk averse. After four years still outside the academic culture. Ex-military, mindful of the proprieties. Bill had chosen the Rwandan genocide topic, and Jake guessed he might have been in Somalia at the time, or some such place. Bill wasn't likely to let anyone know his sore spots.

In a low uninflected voice, Bill read his paper. Predictably, his concerns were all for the issue of international intervention. There was a dry rehearsal of preliminary events, a catalog of those in a position to interfere, reasons given, some rather good capsule policy analyses. He avoided entirely any questions of right and wrong, and all grisly stories of actual events on the ground, until in the wrapup on the aftermath he slipped in some details about refugee camps.

Bill's suppressed affect only stoked the smoldering dudgeon in Claire, whose opening paper on terrorism and the Huntington/Fukuyama diad had set the bar way too high for everyone else. James — nerd two, the microbiologist who'd bitten off Nazi antisemitism, and really had done quite well with that immense subject — and Mia, who had been very firm with her Vietnamese self and probably regretted her paper on that war, sat between them and in the line of fire. Nerd one had chosen to apart Hobbes and Machiavelli on custom and public duty. Thorough and dead-on, he was the perfect damper after Claire, so dominating his material that he precluded discussion and put everyone to sleep.

In a department meeting earlier in the semester Jake remarked, apropos of Reiva's complaint about unruly classroom behavior, that students' thinking is seated in the hippocampus, not the frontal cortex. He'd been thinking of nerd one, who could make a drink of soda into a standoff between the jackals and the vultures. Actually, he was a sweet, shy boy whose eyes registered the constant bewilderment and pain of other people's mysterious unfathomable behavior toward him. Jake saw it easily — did no one else? — but nerd one gave no opening.

He would do well, though, if he were lucky. Everyone has a test they cannot pass. Maybe nerd one would never face his particular nemesis. Better to be duped by Kafka's doorman than that. It had been a better seminar than some. Of course, within the department people were speculating on why a course on the Problem Of Evil in 20th century politics and thought had not, a year after the destruction of the World Trade Center, attracted more enrollment.

A transparent smile floated off the corners of Jake's mouth, but characteristically he made no other response nor offered any hypothesis, leaving his colleagues free to finger any number of faults and character flaws as the source of the problem.

It's all common knowledge among the students, of course, that Dr Greidel has lost it. Over the hill.

Reiva lifted one eyebrow like the lid on a pot starting to bubble. She'd read some of the work which came out of Jake's seminar, and it was good. There was a paper on Hobbes —

The Chair would let Jake have the senior seminar, but the survey courses which made up the rest of his assignment were no more popular. Students don't like intellectual history. The old boy would be retiring in a couple of years, Tor observed, and take the problem away with him. Why make an issue of it?

That's cruel, said Reiva quietly.

You'll defend Singh's dissertation, too, I suppose, Tor cut in testily, which always put an end to these exchanges since no one cared to be tarred with that brush.

Had he heard it, this exchange would have sent the manic Pakistani on a coracle through riffs of cultural imagery on guilt by association, probably with data on the relatively frequency of black to red, the original connection with tar, Greek fire, and who knew what else. Incorrigible.

The dissertation will never be finished, of course.

Especially now that Jake was dead.

When the students had gone, Jake retrieved his hat and valise and went himself, leaving the classroom door open and the lights on. His constant smile, always when his face was relaxed, sat faintly now on his lips — a little wrinkle at the right side — and the tiniest lifting of the hoodedness of his eyes. Really the expression was more of rue than satisfaction. Reiva and Saleem were agreed that Jake was a melancholy man — not bitter, just tired. If not, why would he choose to offer a seminar on atrocities?

Jake's office was in a nondescript brick building opposite Old Main not far away. He cut across the mall lawn, made time for a cup from the department pot, and went up for office hours.

Jake had never made much of an effort to make his office cozy. There were rugs and soft chairs, In the Chairman's suite Tor had a stereo, lights of various degrees of hush, thickets of photographs and framed prints. Jake had had an office plant sometimes, but it usually ended up a foundling in the reception area somewhere. He didn't like to hear it always screaming, he said.

During the seminar discussion after Bill's paper, Mia had remarked on an obscure source she thought had something to say, but Jake was sure she'd got it wrong. As he rattled the old lock it came to him finally. Pushing through some piles on the window ledge (which were keeping the blinds rucked up) he extracted a photocopy with two yellow wedges along one corner where it had been sticking out from the pile into the light. Jake fingered this darkened area regretfully and then rubbed the finger against the ball of his thumb as if testing the coarseness of some grit found there. Plugging in the kettle he sat down on a corner of his office chair to read, breaking off after a moment to find the cafétière, then a teabag. Then a mug.

Mia had indeed got it backwards. More curious was that she had discovered this particular document at all. It was a State Department internal memorandum which had found its way into the Congressional Record as an intrusion into a speech on highway construction. Adding raisins and bits of candied ginger to the loaf after it was already kneaded up was a way of taking the least possible official notice of something. Izzy Stone made his reputation picking these things out of the dough, but Mia Hong wasn't made of that stuff.

Or was she? Jake sighed, anticipating a plagiarism controversy, something which had troubled Jake himself at times. Some internal associational logic would velcro together two bits of information hiding in his piles of stuff. It wasn't a mysterious process, but because it wasn't syllogistic or documentable the results were often regarded with suspicion, as if Jake had neglected to mention Causubon's monograph on the subject as the real source of this tidbit. Then Saleem Singh turned up in the doctoral program with his unusual proposal and for the first time Jake encountered another mind which worked as his did. A riff, Saleem called it. Riffs were the reason why Jake had been drawn to intellectual history in the first place. But that discipline has seen better days and Jake, who was never thought to be particularly disciplined anyway, stayed on mostly by staying on.

Some people in the department, and some editors too, weren't about to dignify Jake's thinking with a methodology. Ditziness, they said.

Saleem used Talmudic structure as a metaphor for what he as up to. Jake would have thought the equally brambly and concentric Rigveda commentary was one a Pakistani Muslim would have would have been more familiar with, which only exposed another painful stereotype in Jake. Just because Saleem was an ethnic Pakistani, after three generations he was no more Hindu or Jew than Jake was, or had been. Saleem was mum about that, but did let it slip once that it was a something that had dogged him since high school. Psychic scar from the Partition, maybe. Or not — two beers had not been enough to find out.

A diffident knock on the open door caused Jake to look up. The diffident one was a student from Jake's sophomore survey course looking for advance intelligence on the final exam, or confirming time, perhaps verifying the place where the oracle was expected, would it be this or that rule of ceremony, really just hoping for some clue, perhaps inadvertent, as to what this unusually incomprehensible professor might be up to. Jake's students inclined to be fond of him in a distant way, but also regarded him as a little scary. Aside from being inscrutable on life and death issues like grades he was likely to refer to ideas hatched in the sixties or the twenties as if they were still alive, or speak in phrases out of old novels like the donnish Latin tags of yore, or to greet a student newly risen from the flu with a peering, sepulchral remark like "So, you've passed down the long road?"

Definitely scary.

Jake was able to put his student at ease and returned to his reading. But during the conversation his tea had gone cold, so he broke off again to carry the mug down the hall to the microwave in the workroom. While there he picked a wad of mail out of the slot marked for him and on which, juggling the mug and the photocopy too, his spilled his tea. But a momentary glance was sufficient and he dropped the entire tea-stained wad in the big recycling can on his way out.

Reiva Derwent's office was across the hall from his own, and on the way back with his now-empty mug he encountered her coming out, a stack of paperbacks, planners, and notebooks clutched to her chest like a schoolgirl. One of the advantages Jake had in the department, a reason why he had survived to become the senior man, was a certain whimsical deprecating humor and a self-detachment which made him impervious to innuendo or insinuation. Since these were his colleagues' only means of asserting anything from this coffee tastes bad to your mother's a goat, Jake seldom knew what anyone else was trying to get at.

But he was not unobservant. Reiva, he had found out, was often incapacitated by shyness and self-doubt. That, he thought, accounted for her pugnacious ways.

The practice of history is not one to foster confidence. You read as many of the primary documents as you have time and money for, you cite the evidence and segregate it rigidly from opinion — except of course artifacts and attitudes aren't so easy to pry apart as that; you will have to be clever — but still, it's not as if any of us stand in a relation of serious bad faith, it's just these little slips, though whether marking Creon down as a "politically obtuse chucklehead" only interested in power and face-saving might be a "little slip" in open to comment.

This Sophoclean allegory was Saleem's, too. Sometimes it seemed as if all of it were his invention, as if everyone else's dharma were his, projected or translated by him, a kind of ventriloquism using puppets, Commedia people with masks front and back, Reiva on side and Antigone on the other, except of course for the suchness of one's experience which remains despite its exploitation by the world's explainers, its expropriation as the material for tales, its citation as evidence.

Or would remain, if our spiritual education were any good.

Reiva grinned uncertainly and skittered away, leaving her door open. Jake reached across and pulled it almost to.

In her role as Antigone, Reiva would have had to repudiate the Bismarckian questions raised that morning in Jake's seminar, if she had known herself to be playing that part. That was Saleem's work again, translating her into a scheme of moral politics. Antigone would not, Jake thought, have made a distinction between Bismarck and Machiavelli. Niccolo had not been a ruthless man, merely intent. Realistic we could say if the term were not anachronistic before Bismarck changed its meaning. Nothing in Bismarck's sordid aspirations would correspond to the renaissance conception of *virtu*. It was all Creonism to her, and equally hateful.

As his rather pitiful office hour was now over and he had no reason to stay longer, Jake pulled his own door shut and left by the other stairway so as not to be seen frequenting a female colleague. Too late he remembered the teakettle and had to return to unplug it, fortunately not yet boiled dry but breathing a strong mineral smell.

She was not in the department office. Jake stopped to talk to Ariel Trent.

The question to be answered was what were the rules for posting grades after term now that social security numbers could not be used. There was no reason to ask, really, since he knew that Ariel would advise him to post his grades on the secure server. Jake was no luddite, but still — trekking around to one's professors' offices to consult sheets or scraps of paper taped, pinned, or stapled to their doors, or to the dirty wall, some grade lists crisply printed and some scratched out with a pencil end, in ossuarious hallways already unheated, empty, smelling of ... well, it was a necessary part of the ritual of taking leave, wasn't it?

Of what does one take leave? Of the past, of a respected elder, or the hope to be respected, of the process of grieving. Taking leave is not to be foregone, no more foregone than sitting on the hallway floor waiting for the door to open, waiting to be admitted to...

But Jake discovered that in fact he could still post a paper list using the last four digits of the student's ID.

And how's your son getting on, Mrs Trent?

What a cognomen. Slip of a woman no more than forty, elvish face, spiky hair of some beige color. But still, Prospero's minion, accommodating if henchpersonal.

Good of him to ask. The bite on the boy's leg had festered down to the bone and will take a while to heal. He won't, she supposed, be out of long pants this summer.

Tcha. I'm sorry.

His sympathetic grimace was not so much over the spider, which was surely an inoffensive being, as over suppurations and unhealing wounds. Ariel Trent had been the history department factotum for ten years now, but so far as Jake knew she had never shown any familiarity with grailwork, wastelands, Frazier, Eliade, or anything of that sort, so his gesture of concern was not likely to be misinterpreted.

On the way home Jake stopped at Breugger's for some coffee and a toasted sesame-seed bagel. It was, he noticed, becoming harder to buy bagels, which were now apparently to be classified with yoghurt, croissants, and innumerable other ordinary objects which had proved to be fashionable after all and hence liable to be unfashioned.

Lickery was there, diffident no longer but talking at a good working rate to two others, a man and a woman, about something on his laptop. Jake hoped that Lickery wasn't selling insurance, that this meeting was about the intellectual enterprise rather than making ends meet.

Jake's gaze retreated lest he draw attention to himself, and he slipped away through the other door into the parking lot. Perhaps he regretted all those intense discussions about such questions, thought in his youth to be unfathomably profound, as what Sartre's remodeling of Heidegger's phenomenology had really accomplished, and why was it was so necessary to wear red canvas high-tops?

It was getting hot. Perhaps it was the coffee. Jake stopped in the middle of the sidewalk to set down his valise, which slumped tiredly on the cracked pavement. He shucked off his jacket and threaded it through the handles. Then he went on, hatbrim still shading the back of his neck as it had done since morning.

Jake's house was only two blocks more. This had been a neighborhood of professors' houses once, after the war, about the time when Existentialism had not yet been discovered to be a fashion. Young faculty couldn't afford it now, though the houses were small. Or had been originally small. Jake had paid his house off twenty years ago — that was another benefit of never having amounted to anything more than senior man. It was a very satisfactory neighborhood, still not ostentatious, pleasing in its variety of structure and vegetation, though if one looked closely one could see that they had been tract homes in fact, wherever there was a row of three or four which had retained a family resemblance despite repeated reoccupation. Not all of them were sand-colored, nor did they look anything like the suburbs of San Diego being reproduced in the mountains to the north, all white plaster and terracotta.

He did miss having neighbors like himself, neighbors who were not such a struggle to find something polite to say to when he encountered them of a morning, getting his newspaper from the driveway. Those people had died off. Now it was joggers, not to speak to at all.

Jake pushed forward the finger of his key into the lock, feeling warmly for that spot, pulling back very slightly at the moment when the worn tumblers admitted him and the bolt could be withdrawn, scraping against the plate. Slowly, the door opened. The cool breath of morning greeted him, having been asleep inside since he left, like a cat.

I just think you need to be a little more circumspect here, Jake was saying. About making the connection between —

No listen — ! Saleem paced back and forth in Jake's office, adroitly sidestepping the piles of books and folders, unwilling to settle in the chair which had been cleared for him. He was in the grip of some enthusiasm, as he so often was in Jake's company. The opportunity to talk loosed it in him. The weekly meeting left him exhausted, but also frequently fired by new ideas and he would type furiously all weekend, his laptop tethered to its transformer because the poor battery could not keep up. Minute by minute he would break away to pace the margins of his two rooms, pounce on the keyboard again, or stumble back as if weak from dehydration, to slake the brain and finally, on Sunday night or Monday morning, fall comatose.

With no perchance to dream.

Saleem had a mattress on the floor, with a sheet which he tried to remember to wash. The computer, which he never turned off, waited through the hot hours for him to wake again. Saleem imagined his computer to be, at these times, the little fellow in the comics with his fat legs lotus-pretzeled and sitting on the wryly condescending patience of an immortal.

Usually he threw all that out. Or most of it. But new things, left hanging like mosquito larvae on the underside of an algae coat, would hatch and swarm out in a few days

But for some reason, today Jake wanted to break the cycle. He got to his feet and towed Saleem, still gesticulating and waving his hands and elbows inside his cloud of bugs, out of the office to a bar a few blocks away where he ordered two drafts and a basket of wings.

You're getting worse, Saleem, he said, when the man had at last come a moment's silence. You're not like this with everyone now, only me. But you will be. And then what will you do?

Saleem took a long breath. He picked up a chicken wing, experimentally, but the barbecue sauce smeared his fingers and he put it back. Jake had taken none of them either. Saleem gulped down some of the beer. The unaccustomed silence stretched out until it was acknowledged that Saleem would offer no reply.

I used to talk to myself, Jake mused. Then I started noticing people in the street who were doing that — this was before cell phones, you understand. I saw that we had the same gestural language, the crazy people and I. We were always pushing someone to the side, a persistent imaginary beggar. That means, you know, that you don't want to talk, you only want to get by. Get past. Who was this beggar? A personal demon, yes. For a while I studied these crazy people carefully, trying to spot their demons. No luck.

Do I do that? Shoo people away?

No, not yet. You still have the energy for the game. You don't want to be left alone.

I get caught up, Dr Greidel.

Saleem had never been able to call

There's so much that's interesting, he said. I have no one to talk to. No one else seems to care. They're all dead.

Jake put out his hand, covering Saleem's.

Saleem, he said. If you will do the dissertation I will find you a place somewhere. We will find a place where there are one or two sympathetic colleagues, maybe even someone who has himself looked into these things.

Silence, exile, cunning. Saleem intoned the words with plain distaste. And who here but Jake would know the reference? he thought bitterly. Of what worth was such a strategy if not taken up freely? Otherwise you were just a stupid, dumb refugee, herded uncomprehendingly from this camp to that still more squalid camp until you died of dysentery or something worse.

Have a wing, Jake said.

They both eyed the greasy basket uneasily. Saleem thought again, despairingly, of Daedalus.

But he hadn't done it, had he? Despite Jake's offer, and the encouragement of perpetual years. He couldn't finish it. The thing was beyond him, put beyond him by his own manic, excessive, neurotic curiosity.

At midnight the building was quiet. The sash of Jake's office window was propped open about six inches with a volume of Herodotus even though it was thirty degrees outside. Jake had always counted himself fortunate as one of the very few to have a window that opened, and so he opened it whenever he could. Traffic hissed in the distance; the sound might have been the ghostly old steam radiator. The marks of its feet remained in the linoleum.

The traffic was growing lighter. Despite half a million people this was still a small college town, sensitive to the coming and going of its students who were just now in chrysalis, not to hatch out for another two weeks. So the building was quiet. Lamps on stalks stood up haloed and bleary through the smeared glass along with some blue assault callboxes here and there among the network of deserted walkways on the mall. Squat dark brick buildings loomed up on either side like tenements enclosing a river. At the other end of the mall cranes had gathered around a pit where a computer commons was being dug under the library — Jake had had to pick his way around that earlier in the evening. The planks had been already slippery with dew. Now the midnight sky was lit by urban glow despite the laws on light pollution, a dirty tan color on which the black tangled lines of the construction machinery appeared as brush strokes in a Chinese landscape.

Jake took a deep breath of the moist air. It smelled of nothing, merely cold and wet. A cup of coffee steamed a little on the corner of his desk, pushed in precariously among the stacks of paper and books which were always there.

It was many years since he saw fit to put away these piles. Not since he had been a person who thinks to take a towel to the beach. His early work had been as methodical as a combustion engine. That was the way to get tenure and to be elected or appointed to this and that. Jake was grateful that his career had not been organized the other way round, wasting the energy of youth trying to be wise and then discovering ambition when it was too late. A lot of men his age or a little younger had been victimized that way, he thought, by the romantic idealism prevalent then, just at the time when they began to come into their inheritance.

Jake's thoughts drifted toward his wife, presumably asleep in bed. He took a slow sip of coffee and fitted the cup back onto the corner of the desk.

Saleem's imagination began to falter. Jake had put something into his coffee, they said. Drunk it. Then waited peacefully. For what?

Had he had second thoughts? Jake was not a man for dithering or recriminations. His mind would find out by itself what was going to happen next and then this discovery would float up into the world of knowledge. It was like waking up on Sunday morning.

Or so Saleem guessed. For himself, in the morning he was either drugged or electrocuted.

He tried to imagine that dispersal of himself into the being of the world which Jake had believed in, which is supposed to be the legacy, or desire, of the religious, and failed. He might as well have been standing with his nose on a wall.

Jake took another sip of coffee. It was staying hot a long time. Another blessing. He had once had a mug made of some mysterious ceramic which dispersed the heat out of everything put into it in a few seconds. A fact which it had taken Jake several years to remember long enough to do anything about it. The mug had been blue and had had something to do with Nebraska. Time and again he would drink the cold coffee from that mug and then put it away uneasily at the back of the drawer, and somehow he would always pick it out again the next day. Was it maybe a good color?

Jake remembered about the unpaired sock which always contrives to crawl hopefully atop the pile. He also remembered a story he read once about evil coathangers multiplying in closets everywhere, plotting to take over the world.

He chuckled softly. Fondly.

That would be good advice to Saleem. Study the coathangers. Befriend them if you can. The world is full of wonders. Drink your coffee.

But not just yet.

The Doodah Man

Poor Grendel's had an accident, I whisper.
So may you all.
                    — John Gardner

The ruckus afterwards was caused firstly by Tor's decision to appoint no one to succeed Jake Greidel. Since Reiva had insisted publicly that the department needed a cultural or intellectual historian she took this personally as a repudiation of herself as well as a reproof of her politics, and so the collapse began.

The Chairman had, already during the semester break when few people were about, made the first move by circulating a memo proposing to hire an Asian historian. This fiat (in effect) was tacitly opposed by a coterie of the untenured on grounds which were unpleasantly reminiscent to the older faculty of the battles twenty-five years earlier over Middle Eastern history. "Oriental" it was called then, in a time when students were foreign, not international. Tor's feint was successful. Everyone but Reiva agreed on a historian of science.

The most imperialist and hegemonic possible topic in the history of ideas, she muttered, a little too loudly.

Reiva's position was really too extreme — in fact, as the only female, any position she might have taken would have been considered extreme. Ismene-like, her colleagues abandoned the field, supposedly validating her position by abstention but actually leaving her exposed on the killing field beyond the battlements. Even those who felt that cultural history (as practiced, anyway) was trendy nonsense objected to Tor's hijacking of their voice in establishing the direction of the department's growth. That the department was not growing was overlooked, and the supposed consensus concerning the history of science was allowed to stand so that the whole business might make more loaves of their daily bread. The manna of complaint, someone said with comfortable humor.

And anyway, students don't want to learn the succession of kings, they want to know about the common people. Information, not the legacy of the *Nichomachean Ethics*. Greidel had been out of touch.

Old, in other words.

By some years.

Reiva could hardly benefit by association with a dotty geezer and a doctoral student with attention deficit disorder.

.

Anyway, since the Reiva woman persisted in her opposition, Tor was able to exploit that to seek no one, to leave Jake's position vacant, crippling the department and exposing his recalcitrant Assistant Professor to the annoyance of her colleagues.

It's too late in the hiring cycle, he advised the search committee. Advertise in the fall, he suggested. Give ourselves plenty of time to sort things out.

Of course, Saleem was no boy. He was as old as she, nearly forty, but he had spent ten years or so doing other things, rather than living as she had done hand to mouth, a peripatetic instructor mostly in community colleges for just enough to keep her from getting welfare. Five or six survey courses a semester. No benefits, of course. She'd had to be sterilized on public health. No vacation either — that meant no pay. Who knew what Saleem lived on other than his assistantship, $9500 a year, which fortunately was not a perk and couldn't be taken away, though if department funding declined any further it would be hard to attract even the half-dozen doctoral students they had now with such a pittance. And then who would teach the bloody survey courses that Jake had always taken on? For the bloody engineers who needed bloody humanities credits to graduate and didn't give a damn about Bloody Mary and the bloody Scottish independence or for that matter the poor bloody crofters either?

Probably Jake had known about those other things Saleem was up to before making that eccentric and reckless decision to get a doctorate in history.

After the ruckus over her reappointment Reiva, who felt somewhat responsible for Saleem, bereft as he now was of his champion, exposed to a hostile department, invited him out to dinner at a Mexican restaurant on 4th where they were not likely to be seen by anyone but their own students. She had wanted to say something about Saleem's future, but found that Saleem wanted to talk more about her own future. He was developing this metaphor concerning Sophocles's Antigone, you see, which to his mind explained everything.

Reiva, to her annoyance as a feminist historian, found herself being instructed in this by a Pakistani male, an embarrassing display of intolerance on her part when the poor fellow only wanted, perhaps, to get out of the light. Wanted not to be mothered. By her.

In his enthusiasm to expound his views Saleem was a little messy with the chips and salsa, spraying crunchy bits from his mouth as he talked and getting tomatoes on his shirt front, which he dabbed away hastily with a napkin as he went on talking. Really he was infectious. His monolog overbore Reiva's ordinary fastidiousness, for otherwise her ears would have been closed.

The restaurant was unpretentious. They had gotten a table along the front window, although not in the corner where there would have been more room and fewer neighbors, but at least not right by the door. Both her bag and Saleem's were stuffed promiscuously on the third chair, covered by the dark fleece pullovers they had both worn. There was a persistent cold draft which made Reiva, with her back to the door, shiver every time it banged to. There was an unlit candle on the table, and under that a black and white plaid oilcloth. Reiva had ordered a Dos-X amber for herself. Saleem was drinking Bud Lite. Halfway through the chips a waitress dropped off a pair of menus but neither Reiva nor Saleem looked at them. Chicken taco and green corn enchilada for him, chimi with carnitas and red sauce for her. Beans and rice, and another Dos-X. The waitress was a pudgy good-natured woman who Reiva knew had been an undergraduate in cultural anthropology a couple of years earlier but had dropped out with a child. She'd gone two or three times to a women's reading group that Reiva was part of. Had been part of.

The food came. Saleem talked on, filling up all the space, which in any case Reiva by this time had no interest in taking back. She was tired, disgusted. She should not have drunk two beers. The door banged shut behind her with an irritating frequency not quite regular. She left her rice untouched, most of the beans, and one end of the chimichanga. The waitress brought the bill, which Reiva took charge of with her credit card before Saleem could make an issue of it.

Saleem Singh, named after two cricket players in a confused gesture of nostalgia for an imperial past which had departed even quicker than his grandparents' mother tongue, his parents' ethnic loyalties, and his own history. Reiva guessed that his family's emigration must have occurred at the time of the Partition when they were all Delhi Muslims, and Saleem had never been, in fact, Pakistani. Or Muslim either, for that matter. Just a tall, dark-skinned man from somewhere in California whose first exposure to politics was not Syed Ahmed Khan but Governor Ronald Reagan. As a teenager he'd listened to... well, Reiva had no idea. She wasn't paying attention to popular music then.

As it happened, in college she won the role of Antigone in Anouilh's version of the play. Saleem seemed to be unaware of this French rewrite despite his encyclopedic compendium of factoids about the whereabouts of Parisian pocket theaters during and immediately after the war and similar lines of inquiry of relevance to that endless dissertation. There was, certainly, some sense to Tor's prating about rigor and focus and his contempt for Saleem's "pack rat" methods.

The boy who played opposite her, in the role of Creon, hadn't had a clue as to the significance of his lines. Reiva thought maybe he hadn't known that Paris was occupied by the Germans when the play premiered. He'd managed as good an approximation of gravitas as might be expected from an eighteen-year-old, and spoke his part with a plodding and unflinching progress that made Anouilh's point after all. But then, Reiva herself had not been a lot sharper about what was going on in the play. Perhaps that was why she'd retained a sort of fondness for the feckless Creon of her youth. But he disappeared back into the college of engineering or wherever he came from and she never saw him again.

This was the sort of boy who'd populated Jake's survey courses and who Jake was supposed to have been out of touch with. Out of touch because he wore a tie to class sometimes, and been a little unworldly or eccentric. Distant.

Saleem's allegory was based on a reading of Sophocles which she later traced to a book by Tyrrell and Bennett from which at least, to his credit, he'd borrowed with decent accuracy. Provoked by her memory of being Antigone for two weekends she read up the commentary over the weekend. As a feminist historian it was something she was obliged to get right, anyhow.

As she reviewed this material, and what she remembered of her own lines in Anouilh, the logic of Saleem's notion insinuated itself and it wasn't long before she found herself parsing her argument with Tor in Antigonish terms, constructing herself as Antigone, keeping an eye out for ways of casting familiar people in the vacant roles.

That was the way with Saleem. There *was* a logic to his seemingly demented thinking, if one had the patience to let it insinuate itself. As Jake had had. As none of the others did.

How frustrating was that, then? To be willfully made inarticulate. Deliberately misunderstood. She hoped Saleem had at least the good sense to avoid being victimized by his own narrative, but from what she knew he was not long on good sense. To play the Haemon and immolate himself.

As she read Sophocles and Anouilh and something of the history and scholarship she began to understand that this was not about Antigone. Reiva had not, in fact, had the starring role. Antigone's behavior is easily understood, identical and consistent in both Sophocles and Anouilh. Her mantra is personal responsibility and natural morality (the Thoreauvian position justifying civil disobedience) and she suffers the same end in both plays. But Creon now. Sophocles' Creon sides with the legislators on matters of public order. Likewise Anhouilh's, but the French Creon, a stand-in for the pack of Germans and Vichy collabos, tries to absolve himself as being only the agent of higher law. Aside from the chutzpah of self-absolution, this new Creon is claiming the law is transcendental when his audience knew perfectly well that it was only German. Antigone was a straight-ahead existential moralist and her defiance was as inevitable as a Victorian novel. Creon was more complicated.

Reiva had never been able to read Austen, nor the others. Too many of these plots stood up only because the characters enmeshed in them persisted in keeping secrets from each other.

The Greek Creon was plain wrong. He thought so himself. He suffered his punishment for it and that was that.

The French Creon was not wrong, evidently, as he suffered nothing, but blithely continued on his way as an agent of the State with no consequences other than an unfortunate death in the family. The French Creon acknowledged only the meaninglessness of human action. There is nothing to repent. It is merely a question of acting as events require, or not so acting and being destroyed by those same events. Why this pointless self-immolation? Antigone is not *wrong* either. Only naive.

This put Saleem-Haemon in the position, insofar as he wanted that ill-fated PhD, of working for Tor-Creon's ends. Or he could give up the PhD and join Antigone in her grave.

When he was alive Jake had insulated him from these quandaries. Presumably insulated.

When the paparazzi have gone, Tor said calmly (speaking ex-cathedra facilitates calm), we will appoint a sensible historian of science to Professor Greidel's vacancy and this messy-mindedness will be done with.

The messy-minded Reiva would be got rid of for her making a scene and ABD Singh would be got rid of for playing out his old public rituals of Dionysius and tragedy, and both of them would go willingly in the interest of furthering right behavior.

What Jake had thought he was doing was a mystery.

Saleem was dozing in a Berkeley café, his laptop open on the table beside the cups and plates. He had been in the library all morning and had gone out for coffee and perhaps a cinnamon bun, but the buns were all gone so he'd had a pannini with cheese, which had made him sleepy. The Berkeley air was warm even in January. Not so warm as at home, though.

He had come back for a few days to plaster a hole in his research but now wished he hadn't. The brickwork could have been left exposed in that spot, or if necessary a picture hung over it. The trouble was that he liked it here, and he didn't like it at home, and when he came here he didn't want to go home again. It hadn't been so bad in Paris. His French was no good and his appearance allowed the ethnic locals to take him for an Algerian and any thoughts of living there were clearly fantastic. So he hid out in Belleville among the North Africans and the blacks whose liquid French was utterly unintelligible and spent Jake's money on lamb and bread and espresso and bad oranges from Israel and went home happily.

Vienna was about the same except that there he was a Turk and had had to take a pension with a lot of loud Germans, hostelish folk who didn't eat breakfast. There were two pairs. The women were the more objectionable — as tall as Saleem was, smelly and hairy and as thick as porridge.

Saleem wondered whether, if he should finish his degree, he could work here in Berkeley. Aside from his being a Turk or an Algerian or whatever he was, if he would be good enough. Jake thought so, but Jake was always quick to say that *good enough* wasn't everything. One needed help. He could arrange for Saleem to study with ... this person or that. Such moments were as close as Saleem got to being angry with Jake. How was he, Saleem, supposed to go to that man who Jake said was needful when his utmost efforts had brought him only here? What reason would that man have to listen to the Turk Saleem? What work could he bring to show when no work was done? When there was only Jake's good word? Who was supposed to believe in him when even Jake sometimes did not? Saleem was a man in a refugee camp — in

Palestine or wherever — who is making his way from day to day as best he can. Someone — Eleanor Roosevelt or whoever — looks about the camp and says what's wrong with these people? Why do they put up with this squalor and filth? Why do they allow themselves to be treated like beasts? Why do the old women know nothing but to wail about their murdered sons and why do the living ones show off their wounds like marks of honor?

Why don't they just walk?

Because they *are* beasts, of course.

Saleem thought about his life at home. Why hadn't he just walked, left all that squalor and torture and intellectual violence and gone somewhere he would not be a pariah, a savage, a Grendel, an over-intellectual Caliban who knows the words but not the sense?

Yes, he should just walk out and go to America.

It was enough to make one snort.

Saleem! Saleem!

A dusty boy was running across the square towards him, skipping with eight-year old agility across the shell holes and the blocks of broken concrete. A balloon popped somewhere maybe. The boy disappeared into a crater. Saleem woke from his doze. His elbow had jostled the glass of tea, thick tea, sweet and viscous, almost green —

The glass had smashed on the floor...

Saleem had left his laptop on, still connected to the café's wireless zone.

There was mail.

Jake had killed himself.

So He.

The refrain of Browning's *Caliban Upon Setebos*. The complaint of poor Caliban, victimized by the arbitrary and cruel being who does as do I. Kind of whiny, but he has a point. What has this Prospero done to deserve the sunshine when Caliban has none?

That said there is little more. Caliban gets stiffed because every system of thought requires someone for that role — Marxist underclasses, Christian sinners and Jewish exiles, Freudian sons and Jungian others — Tor liked the Fascist explanation best, perversely for its simplicity and purity: Caliban is ugly. Short and ugly would be better if it could be managed but in this case it can't. Caliban is not short but bent or crushed, the objective correlative of the hidden claim of blood, that you are not of my tribe.

So he.

For a while Saleem was angry with Jake for having abandoned him. Working with Tor was so much more difficult. With his propriety, his reserve. It was never about what you said and always about whether you should say it *that* way or indeed whether it would be better or safer not to say it at all. Tor's ideal dissertation was a perverse mirror of Balzac's unknown masterpiece. Saleem stamped his foot in frustration and wondered what Tor saw in his mirror in the morning. It was no wonder the man had never married. Saleem was indeed angry with Jake.

Saleem's tendency to break out and flood the surrounding countryside was perhaps not convenient but in Jake's view it was the natural consequence of carrying so much water and that you don't get grand canyons or a river of dynasties stretching back to the Old One by building a dam across it. Whereas Tor's view was more the view of the tessellated Baghdadi of the Marsh Arab, or of the little brown men who every year are washed into the sea by the Brahmaputra, that such will never be civilized.

Saleem was always inclined to make a dyad out of any conflict. For a while he was in the habit of opposing the Taoists to the

Confucians until Jake asked him to swot that up, to learn something about The Middle Way.

Saleem waved his hand before his face palm outwards, as if to wipe away the mist.

Tor never asked him to swot up anything.

Saleem confided at times, after Jake's death had made him lose his way, to Prospero's minion. It was her name, of course — Ariel — which had suggested the whole allegory to Saleem in the first place. He was making a fool of himself now, sniveling to this distant almost elderly woman who absorbed his troubles as so much morning e-mail while she typed and filed and scheduled.

Ariel Trent was too well-bred to say so to his wretched, sweaty face, of course. He felt he was sweating. His skin felt greasy as if he had been eating meat. Mrs Trent only went on with what she was doing, indicating with a motion of her fingers when he needed to scuttle out lest he be overheard, discovered by some expected visitor.

Saleem never said anything coherent anyway. What could she have betrayed to Prospero? He talked because he had to, as when he was a boy who had just learned to read and every word had the same weight and savor — bread wrappers, newspapers, billboards — and he would read them all because he must, because nothing must go unread.

All boys, he supposed, were like that. But he had known no boys. And who was he to talk to now? No one had ears.

He felt suffocated.

After Professor Reiva left the taqueria Saleem sat on, pondering what to do. His long fingers played with the shaker of hot pepper flakes until finally it tipped over and rolled into his lap. He sighed, brushed the spilled flakes into his hand, and threw them over his shoulder. His fingers retrieved the jar and set it twirling again on its thick bottom rim.

There was probably a name, he thought, for the geometric figure described by a point on a hula hoop as it walks across the lawn and decays, settles —

He remembered the lawn, but hula hoops were of his parents' generation. His mother had had one. Saleem found it in the attic and she showed him how, not a difficult trick for one as lithe and long-waisted as he was. But it was not a trick whose pleasure lasted. Bored, he let it roll away and settle under the hydrangea bush.

Both dead. Because they had been in their late thirties before beginning and because this writing of Saleem's was taking so long to come to an end.

He should not have said "whose pleasure." Pleasure is not a person. Is it?

Gilles Tor's name exposed his origins as did Saleem's. He was a collabo child. His mother had emigrated to Quebec and lived under her own name, which was Genevieve Leroy. She had given him instead this one which he had kept maybe out of annoyance with her. She was a podgy woman of country background, from Arras. Tor père or rather *der Papa*, he supposed — *der Vati* — Gilles had several theories, none of them provided with facts. His mother had been affectionate enough, but not disposed to talk about her feelings. He, too, had had a hula hoop, and a coonskin cap, and other American toys which were entirely useless among the French-speaking boys at school. The young Gilles Tor sat on the side of his bed, swinging his legs, one sandaled toe scraping the floor in a metronomic tic, wearing his cap of plastic fur.

Had it been plastic? Surely not. Neither raccoon of course. Rabbit. Though nowadays it would be plastic.

As a boy Gilles had not been inclined to resent the behavior of his Papa Gott toward himself, until he was older and for a time suffered for not having something the others did, like a certain sort of shoe, or money. The arbitrariness of circumstances impressed itself early on him by this means. So he had lived quietly with his mother waiting his chance.

Just the two of them. Gilles had chosen to work in the history of mining in the Southwest to get as far away from that claustrophobic childhood as he could. But was it so far from the coonskin to the Stetson, the flintlock to the six-shooter? It was maddening, this inability to remake oneself even by the smallest amount. Genevieve Leroy had not been a repressed woman. All through Tor's childhood there had been one or another therapeutic man about the house Man and boy had kept a mutual distance. There was not a lot to learn from each other.

No scholar, she had said.

Jake had been one in his day, though not lately.

Tor's view was that Saleem would have to begin again. Start over from the beginning. Cut away all this discussion of historiography, all this intellectual scene-setting, the metaphysics of nostalgia, the sociology of community, and the rest of it. Focus. The generation of 1950 perhaps. Not in New York: it's been done. And San Francisco or Paris were much too obvious.

Chicago. Saul Bellow.

Some of the boys in the neighborhood had built a clubhouse in the areaway, a narrow passage that ran between their two buildings. It was a little shack of less than two square meters made out of scraps salvaged from a vacant lot and held up by the building it leaned against. This clubhouse had a second story only a meter high, just big enough for two, a sort of high council with a trap door. The entrance below was by pushing aside a heavy canvas flap, a discarded mailbag someone's father brought home. The canvas was full of dust and loosed an acrid, choking cloud whenever anyone went in or out.

There was a girl in the club whose only purpose was to be, after a time, drummed out of it. You can't have a club otherwise, without drumming someone out. There was a kangaroo court. She was supposed to have made off with some of the club's rubbish.

It was hot, and the heat brought out a sort of dead cat smell from the walls of the area. No one went there but the boys. One could lurk in the mouth of it, beyond the smell where it opened into the sunlit court formed by the backs of the buildings. These were red brick buildings of four (or five) stories which looked down over their shoulders like suspicious teachers with more important boys to look after than you. It was hot in the courtyard in the sun. Acrid dust puffed up from the bare patches between the walks and there was a dry drain in the center covered by a grating which led down through the area passage was where the cat was.

There was not room in the clubhouse for a proper trial so the boys of the club gathered outside, at a spot in the area just out of sight of the courtyard windows. The girl wore a neat shift and canvas shoes and at her trial made no use of the rhetorical tools available to her, choosing to play neither the spitfire nor the queen nor the weeping victim. She had only listened to what they had to say, her round green eyes a little inward as she waited for them to be done with their mysterious business, and then walked slowly away.

Among the boys' part there had been some talk about panties and other punishments. It was only talk, it seemed.

Gilles went away to sit at home on the side of his bed, swinging his feet and listening to the shouts of the children in the courtyard, wearing his fake coonskin cap and feeling alternately angry and nauseous without knowing why.

And so He.

One day Saleem had lunch on the Place de la Contrescarpe, in a bistro a few steps off the Place on the rue du Cardinal Lemoine. Eighty years ago this was the neighborhood of Hemingway's first apartment in Paris, a mattress on the floor for him and Hadley. An apache neighborhood, he said it was then. Hardly that now. Quaint, rather. The rue Mouffetard's pedestrian markets, a painter's street even recently. Well-off student painters. Saleem had a photograph of the rue Mouffetard which made it look like the lower east side, but perhaps Papa had exaggerated a little, in the service of the Code.

The bistro was a local place. People were coming in who ate there every day, with each other, talking between tables and calling the waitress by name, which was Marie. There were two rooms — a bar through which one entered, and a side room of ten or so tables with small-paned windows running along the street side. Saleem sat by an open window, out of the way and enjoying the light breeze. The waitress served him a delicious onion soup boiling hot, and then a thick beef stew. Contentedly he lifted his spoon and gazed about him, out the little window, listening to the half-intelligible talk which flowed through the close room.

These were cheerful people. Marie was a dumpy woman with an inner smile, strongly built, calm and unhurried, willing to serve mumbling Algerian Americans and Frenchmen alike. The customers were a man resembling a superior mechanic, a couple of car salesmen, a store clerk perhaps, office workers. Saleem paid at the bar, a bit generously, reluctant to leave.

On the Place he hesitated, tempted by some sidewalk tables and the thought of espresso and a brioche. But a gust raised some gritty dust jus then, and the sunlight seemed harsh, and he went away, crossing into the street opposite, making for the Luxembourg gardens. At the Boulevard St Michel he turned left and walked down to Montparnasse and the Pont Royal metro stop.

Here was the bottom of the rue Henri Barbusse where Mason Hoffenberg had lived, from 1948.

Turning the corner, Saleem stopped to stare, non-plussed. It was nothing like what he had expected, but rather a long, slightly bent nondescript line of five-story bourgeois apartment buildings. Here had lived the rackety bohemian with a child, a wife who went off to work every morning at the United Nations, marketing for dinner, lunching at some neighborhood place on onion soup brought by another one of those chunky square well-rubbed Parisian women who have been here at least since Heloise.

Saleem sighed and unzipped the pocket of his jacket where the camera was. His hopeful nostalgia had taken another blow, not unexpected really, but it was hard to know, with the modern Paris around him now, how it was at the time and what construction to put on the stories people told. So he walked about taking pictures and making notes of where he had been, consulted a sheaf of photocopied scenes from illustrated memoirs and histories and the remarks of people who were there recorded as cocktail party chat, and tried to make of it what he could.

He sat for a long while on a low wall in the springtime Paris sunshine writing in a thick spiral-bound notebook. He drew a little street plan at the bottom of the page, noted the exposure numbers on his camera, and packed everything away in the big canvas bag which he carried everywhere, here and at home, squishing the end of baguette he had saved from breakfast.

He didn't want to walk up the rue Henri Barbusse. There was nothing to see but these blocks of flats and farther along a lycée and an "institute" just as blankly dignified.

Instead, he turned the other way, toward Montparnasse and the now imaginary Café Sélect.

And so Saleem sat where the others in their turn had sat, not with poets or raucous Existentialist trumpeters but with Dr Tor, to drink green tea. But then what else? Certainly not beer or Absolut. He'd worn his best clothes, a pair of dark pants which hung loosely on him, falling over his crossed legs like newspaper, and a blue dress shirt open at the neck, done up by the laundry for him for a dollar. He'd neglected the shoes, of necessity. Some polish. Carefully rubbed so as to keep his nails clean.

He lifted the tea bowl delicately to his lips.

So perhaps he would begin again. Though as to Dr Tor's advice he would demur. Chicago was not a congenial place after Reed and Anderson left. Not now.

Saleem had never been good at small talk. Fortunately his purpose now was to listen while Tor indicated this and that feature of what was to be Saleem's new life. Saleem studied the rim of his porcelain tea bowl. There had been raku and stoneware bowls also to choose from among the group huddled on the tray at the end of the credenza. Some sort of aesthetic test.

Saleem disliked connoisseurs, as he did puzzles and attempts at correcting his English, a working-class idiom.

He adjusted his legs, a futile attempt at preserving the crease in his trousers.

Such an old conflict, Gilgamesh-old, so old as to be stupid to spend blood on as it would never be resolved. This was Prospero's island and the good government of it required a Middle Way. Crazy Taoists seeking immortality should go into the mountains. Should paint scrolls with little figures in black standing on mountain tops peering into the mist.

Hobbit Confucians with their wizarding assistants and their minion hordes hold the plains and all the mountain tops are occupied by Saurons. Buddhist Ishmaels everywhere, but no English popes.

He was so tired.

Of what religion are you, Saleem? Perhaps I shouldn't ask. It's so easy to give offense nowadays.

Startled, Saleem could not reply at once. My mother was a Methodist, he said after a rather long pause, unintentionally discomfiting. Low Methodist.

And your father?

I suppose you would say he was an unbeliever. Nothing so definite as an atheist, you see. It was not a subject which interested him. His parents emigrated before the Partition, and I believe that violence had something to do with his hatred of causes. A distaste for strife. Religions make war, he would say, and make this sort of walking motion with his fingers as if shooing along toast crumbs...

Saleem's voice trailed off into the Grimpen Mire of enthusiasm and sank.

You are Catholic, I suppose? Saleem began again quietly after another discomfiture.

Tor nodded imperceptibly. My mother was.

Why do we say "imperceptibly" when we mean "very slightly" or something not actually imperceptible which if it really were ... ? Saleem longed for the unselfconscious insouciance of Wallace who never imagines any significance in Gromit's amused little sneer.

Tor made a few more remarks on the direction which he felt Saleem's dissertation ought to take. His tea bowl came to rest on his desk with a slight click, releasing an acerbic odor of tea into the room. He rose. Ariel Trent intruded into the room with a yellow file folder, somehow deflecting the need, or the urge, for the two men to clasp hands. Saleem scuttled out.

How, he wondered, did the two of them co-ordinate that routine so precisely? Concerted it must be else how would Tor stand for her breaking in that way? But then, Ariel was a sprite. She it was who brought Prospero into being, just as Grendel created Beowulf and Antigone, Creon. And all these associations create Saleem, compounded of Ishmael and Gromit and Jake, without whom he would be... well, nothing. Ideas are the dust which makes the devil Saleem visible in the world, and now he was being asked not to whirl about so, to let the dust settle. To disappear.

Not a cold place. Somewhere in California, in Los Angeles.

What an odd young man, said Ariel Trent as she took back the yellow folder from Tor's hand. There was nothing in it, of course.

Indeed. Though not young, I think. Few doctoral students are, these days. He worked some years in an insurance agency, I believe. Comptroller's office. It's hard to imagine such a volatile person...

He must have felt quite stifled, Mrs Trent offered. She began to clear away the tea things.

Yes. And then of course the degree is so long. One envies the scientists at times. Two years, they do. A blink, hardly noticeable. But then, years as a post-doc living on grants. And for what? Two or three papers in obscure journals which will never be cited, years of bloviating to children who are only interested in making money.

Mrs Trent cocked her ear at the unusual colloquialism.

Indeed, he repeated to himself when she had gone. Sotto voce. Indeed.

Saleem possessed a rickety old car, the sort of car which survives only in a dry climate. He didn't like to take it anywhere out of the way for fear it would break down, but he was becoming restless with the routines of research and writing. Formerly there would have been the weekly conferences with Jake. Even before that he had been seeing fewer and fewer people. Now he saw no one.

On the wall over his bed he had pinned a large world map. Not a political map, but geological, with Japan more or less in the middle. The jagged vertical of the international date line divided the social world into unequal halves, and at the bottom was a small striped inset of time zones which conveyed more information about how human folly and tribal glue will scramble a neat scheme than it did about what time it actually is in Calcutta. The map was mostly shades of blue and green with a filigree of brown mountains and one large white region in Tibet and southwestern China.

Omphalos.

Of course, every people thinks it lives at the center of the world. Just as the word for itself in the native language is usually The People.

Saleem spent a lot of time looking at this map when he wasn't working. Himself gregarious, he found the map's attitude a bit mysterious, even creepy, like those pictures of people without skins, showing the layers of muscle and always the round white eyes staring, shocked.

He needed to get out. He needed to break this morbid solitude.

He would treat himself. That was always his first thought. Go to a cafe somewhere for coffee and perhaps pie or a pecan roll.

But of late, since Jake's death, he had begun to realize that this urge was an indicator of something lacking inside himself and that maybe sticky buns were not the best stuff to be filling it with.

Something more permanent. Eat concrete and jump into the river. If there were a river. The locally available sticky bun was a close approximation to cement, however.

He had been reading an old sociology book by Rollo May, from 1950, as part of his endless background study, this struggle for "thick description." He had found there a discussion of apathy which worried him. Of course he would be worried in any case. He had always been a little hypochondriac. As a boy he read articles on rare or curious diseases in his parents' magazines and imagined himself to have all of them, just as he was prone to serial love affairs with the philosophers, infatuated by whoever he happened to be reading. It was something Jake had cautioned him about. But then Jake, only somewhat less distractible than Saleem, would admit that this ability always to be falling in love and never to be disappointed lent an attractive intensity...

It was just that nothing even came of it. There was nothing it build on. It was all mud.

Clay. Dust.

And now Saleem's attention had wandered off and he had forgotten what it was about apathy to begin with.

Jake hadn't had a funeral. Mrs Jake had taken the ashes with her. Saleem supposed there were ashes. Put them in the basement probably. Next to the peaches.

People don't can fruit and vegetables any more, do they?

The thought of his body being put into a vault in the ground to melt slowly, very slowly, into a puddle made Saleem nauseous. Being cast to the winds in the mountains somewhere would have been more attractive if there were any place he thought enough of to want to be cast away there, to — what, *blend* with? But really that was too benign an end. A public burning, or exposure in a high place as the Indians do (did?) or their American namesakes. Best a pine box and the clods of earth thrown in by one or two mourners, thoughtfully somber, quick to molder unseen, disappearing cleanly. Just enough solemnity to close, to acknowledge the horror without letting it get out of hand.

Saleem decided that what he had was a *condition,* and he didn't have to read far to find a program to deal with it, in so many simple stages. This one had four: apathy, withdrawal from the active world, impatience, hopelessness and despair, and ending in numbness, an alienated morbidness which can release the irrational violence always present in that limbic swamp on which human nature is built.

Saleem's sensitive cultural ear heard the bedtime story of fifties alienation, the old existential song of beatniks and the Ionescos and Camuses which good children were once warned against. Twenty years after, its counter-cultural obverse would explain away the mousketeering reprise. More years passed and now the grannies were singing it again, constructing again the same ancient fears. This Saleem's ear heard, but he knew he was slipping away just as described and he watched himself, scandalized by his failure, giving himself up to the will to believe.

. He needed to rouse himself, to get out, away from this grinding research for which absolutely everything was grist. He needed to get away from the world of thought to that other, green and blue world, the flayed world of the staring naked eye.

But not too far away. There was his rackety old car to consider.

A little ways north of the city was a mountain preserve. He could go as far as the parking lot at the foot of the mountain and ride the shuttle bus up into the canyon, where he would go walking and enjoy the view.

Yet he did not want to go alone. It was a measure of his isolation that the only person he felt able to ask was Reiva Derwent.

Perhaps she too was at loose ends. And what did that mean? Saleem wondered. Unsecured ship's ropes, perhaps, or broken knitting. At any rate, though sounding startled, she agreed to come. Without breakfast yet, however — suppose they meet at the bagel shop near her house, just east of campus?

He knew the shop of course, and was grateful to avoid the awkwardness of any domestic hospitality. Reiva was standing by the door when he cluttered up to park in the lot behind. She had a partly munched toasted bagel in one hand and in the other a large paper cup of coffee which she set on the roof of the car while she fitted herself into the seat, then reached up to retrieve the coffee, swapping hands and closing the door with her elbow on the bagel side. A choreography which made her laugh self-consciously, but to Saleem's mind in its present morbidity this was all because she hadn't wanted to let her food touch his dirty car and he was uncharacteristically silent all the way to the Sabino Canyon parking lot.

Even on the shuttle bus he kept quiet, and he sensed that Reiva was watching out of the corner of her eye, non-plussed perhaps but willing to wait, willing to be the vessel of another purpose.

They got out of the bus at the first viewpoint overlooking the city. Red tile roofs covered the foothills below, breaking up into a more ploughed earth of shingles and asphalt in the older part farther off. There was a breeze, strong enough to ruffle Reiva's spiky hair. And still she waited.

Saleem felt strangled or choked, unable to croak out any words which were in any case mostly mysterious to him, unmeaning.

You will need to move on, Saleem, she said, somehow striking exactly to the center of the wound. I think it is hard for you to accept death.

He made an inarticulate noise.

It's all right to stare, Saleem, at dead people.

Saleem's hand twitched involuntarily, a sort of shooing or shushing motion which Reiva read correctly at once, and a flush of anger spread over Saleem, a warmth that started in his stomach and rose to his ears. He did not like to be so transparent. He did not like to be so lacking in empathy in comparison to her. So self-centered. What business had she to be kind? And how did she manage it when he could not?

Eventually he found his voice and the familiar words began to crawl out into the light. It helped him to be walking, as if there were a rod in his spine that moved up and down with his legs and made his mouth work. So they set off up the paved road.

There have been some attacks by mountain lions here recently I think, he began.

Yes. I've heard so.

A pause. Saleem was walking on the gravel verge and his shoes crunched the stones. He tried to lay his foot down more quietly but finally stepped up companionably onto the pavement.

When I was in Berkeley, he said, I heard that there are something like seven thousand deer living in the hills. Or some large number. Is that a great many deer?

It does seem rather a lot. In the city.

Yes, right among the houses. Eating people's lettuce and geraniums you see. I was told that a city deer has a range of about five square blocks.

They live their whole lives there, do they?

Yes.

A pause.

I find that bizarre, he said.

More so than a coyote dipping into your back yard and snatching away little Fluffy to eat?

No. No, not *more* bizarre.

But you yourself grew up in the suburbs, Saleem.

Yes. Well — he stopped walking in order to listen to the wind — I suppose...

There was a hot dusty smell in the air already, a precursor of summer. He should have brought a hat, because the sun had begun to be warm and his head ached from it.

Where are *you* from? he asked.

Syracuse, she said. Leafy urban, you might say. College town. My neighborhood was, anyway. Not like Columbia or NYU.

I've been wondering whether I might get into Edinburgh somehow.

Reiva said nothing to this fantasy, but he could see that was what she thought it was and lapsed again into wretched silence.

I'm told, he was able to say eventually, after walking a little distance, that if you meet a mountain lion you ought to make yourself as big as you can by waving your arms or something, and scream.

Mm. Successful lions pounce on you from behind.

Saleem shuddered at the thought of being eaten alive.

A common experience among animals, he observed, trying to remain calm. And ourselves at one time.

When we were animals, eh? said Reiva with a wry smile.

But she had misjudged, this time. That was more truth than he could bear.

Saleem kept still, his face turned toward the sky and his eyes squeezed shut with fear and regret, tears starting from under the lids.

After a while the shuttle bus came by. They got on and rode back down to the parking lot where Saleem went off to the men's privy to dispose of what little remained inside him. There was a dirty mirror there which he looked into when he had cleaned up. Always skinny, he was becoming almost gaunt.

He would treat himself, he decided. To kebabs and apple pie.

THE RIVER DERWENT

Sosen painted nothing but monkeys. He was living with monkeys in his house, he was living like a monkey, and finally he understood the thought of monkeys. At last, when he took his brush in hand to paint monkeys, all the monkeys came and stood behind him and criticized him.
— Sokei-an

At the beginning of that year, the final year as it proved, Jake had taken Reiva to lunch at an upscale Mexican place downtown, in a hotel. The story was of the elder professor squiring the department's youngest through the last two years of becoming tenured. Jake drove. It was early September, still too hot to walk anywhere, but of course there was nowhere to walk other than the bagel shop. At one time there had been a hamburger joint on the north side of campus, one of those old-time student places so intense with ambience it was hard to swallow your food. But that was gone, swept away by newly invented sciences needing new buildings, and that wasn't the north side of campus anymore, either.

What with driving and reservations it was a two hour lunch. Reiva assumed the department paid, but now she thought maybe it was simply Jake. That it was Jake telling that story. There was no way to know, of course.

She had dressed casually, as a young bohemian professor. Too casually, it turned out. The placed seemed to be full of real estate brokers in that brittle business style designed to displease nobody. But Jake stuck out too, with his boots and his cowlicks, and Reiva eventually relaxed into avuncular safety. The table tops were a little too small, made of painted tiles in a trefoil pattern, three laurel crowns around a center rose. Mexican. Anything in those bright ice-cream colors was supposed to be auténtico. Saguaro-rib privacy screens. Blue slat-and-staple chairs and credenzas. Rather a nice window seat by a small courtyard with a patch of grass and a tame bougainvillea growing against the wall opposite, scarlet flowers on honey brick. Now and then a man in blue pinstripes passed through with his valise, sweating a little, closing the tall iron gates fastidiously behind him. Perhaps different men, perhaps not.

Cellphones ruthlessly sequestered, the restaurant whispered and muttered unintelligibly beneath the clatter of tableware. Food began to arrive, and there was a period of chesslike movements as the various plates, bottles, trays, utensils found places on the blue tile. Reiva had ordered a mole, rather more complicated and not so hot as she was used to, but neither so big as to put her to sleep. Jake was having a chicken poblano, which she would have thought would be a poblano chile — the green version of the ripe chile in her own mole, and which her supermarket insisted, thanks to some long-dead food-challenged typist, was a "pablano," which made it sound like some kind of baby food — stuffed with chicken and coated with relleno batter, but which proved instead to be some unrecognizable Asian fusion invention. Jake was not a picky eater, though. He didn't seem to care what it was.

They talked, but Jake's heart was not in the official narrative of the meeting. Yet he didn't seem to have another agenda, for which this blather about research programs and grants and least publishable units would have been only a cover. Jake never had a cover. But at the same time the straight story never seemed to explain him.

Very private man, it was said in the department. Hard to get to know, she'd been advised, probably by people who didn't much want to know him anyway. Superficially accessible, of course, and never a gaffe. Courtly, almost.

The idea was never entertained that Jake was simply not a complicated man, that he was only what he seemed to be, a predictable gentleman, well-trained, socially reliable. With the good taste not to talk about inner profundities.

Presumably it was that zen gaze which he had, his way of seeing through veils and fans. One assumed, as with Nick Charles or Columbo — did Columbo have a first name? or maybe he didn't need one — that he couldn't be that simple if he were going to be that simple.

The Columbo role was intended for Bing Crosby of all people.

Jake was talking about his own early publications, the decline of his sort of intellectual history and his disinterest in the newer sociological kind, his early difficulties learning how to get by in the classroom. The seminar style he now used for encounters of all sorts had evolved, he said, out of laziness and a desire to keep in the background. To let the students do the work. Now that was called active learning, and he was held up as an exemplar of a student-centered method touted to reassure the regents and a legislature suspicious of faculty who would push their responsibilities off onto graduate assistants like Saleem who were supposed not to speak English, or hired-gun instructors paid by the class, or young pups still wet behind the ears.

Such as yourself, he said, and paused to swallow. But really I was just lazy. Or possibly shy. I wanted the kids not to get too beat up over Aristotle and Rousseau and not to be angry with me. I didn't have a research program. I was just interested in stuff.

You published books.

Well yes, after you've been interested in something for a while it begins to come out. To organize itself. You can't keep track of a body of material otherwise. In any detail. It's like that old rhetorical trick with the memory, visualizing a walk through a lot of rooms or something similar. The mind, you know, doesn't remember things. It reconstructs them, dynamically. That's why Gilles and Henry and the others are always blatting about rigor, because it's unnatural. It's a trick, a skill to be learned, which will exorcise the way *artists* do things.

You're thinking of Pissarro maybe, not Vermeer or Dürer surely.

No, no. Have you ever solved a crossword puzzle and then found out your answer was not the one? How did you feel about that?

Who cares? The words fit, didn't they?

Ha! An artist. You are going to have trouble. Rr-rigorous trouble.

Jake's gaze turned aside as he reached for his glass of beer. There was a small smile playing about the corner of his mouth as if he did not take his own remarks quite seriously. That was part of what made him enemies, Reiva supposed. The suspicion that he thought you were a bit simple and needed a simpler version, with fewer and brighter colors, or that he was baiting a trap for fools.

People don't like to admit the truth of stereotypes, he said, eerily guessing her thoughts. Irony is the modernist disease. It makes simple confrontations and uncomplicated emotions seem false, suspicious. You remember how taken we were with Hannah Arendt's notion of the banality of evil, how intuitive that seemed. Oh, of course you don't. Remember. Excuse me.

She laughed, and told him about the parents of some childhood friends, educated people alert to intellectual currents, who had had such books on their shelves, relicts of their own youth. Two copies, sometimes, like married couples now have two or three televisions, or redundant microwaves, from before. It was one of the things that had made her curious about the past. About how we used to be.

And did you read them? Those books.

No... I didn't really care about what Martin Buber or Edmund Wilson had been interested in. But those names, you know, are part of my sense of a milieu. When I run across them now they invoke Kate's mom, her lean beaky face, her way of going at things...

A habitus.

Jake, I thought you said you weren't up on the sociologists.

Here there was an unexpected pause and Jake seemed to go inward for a time. The sounds of the restaurant intruded into the space freed up, became a racket.

Jake's face and shoulders were of that sort animated by the tiniest of expressive movements, and to Reiva he looked tired.

Oh, well, he said at last. I keep up. I have to because of Saleem's dissertation. This business of milieus is basic to his description of factors in the growth and decline of artistic communities, you see. To understand how that works.

Another long, reflective gap in the conversation allowed Reiva to turn aside, contemplate the couple at the next table. Also an aging man and a young woman companion, with a vaguely legal air. No footsie, though. The food had long been cleared away, and the woman leaned forward with expository intensity, her straw-blond hair falling forward off her shoulders and brushing the tabletop. Making a case, prosecuting a case. Not defending, somehow.

He calls it a paradiso artigianati, Jake said — these wellings-up of artistic community. The phrase is a deliberate construction, you know. He means to include all the people, not just Camus and Merleau-Ponty. It means the body of all artisans. Book editors, third violinists, fan painters.

Sensing some confidence in the works, Reiva didn't remark on this.

Saleem, perhaps you don't know, is a third-generation American. His grand-parents weren't Pakistani, of course. I'm not sure where they were from. Secular Delhi intellectuals, I gather. Saleem knows nothing of that part of the world. He calls himself a Pakistani even though Arabic and Islam are a mystery to him. He doesn't even know how the country is governed. He's an expatriate American.

Do you mean exiled?

No. Exile is involuntary.

But he's here. He is, as you say, American.

Spiritually he's left. Departed.

But for where?

Well. That's the question, isn't it? The problem. Where is he to go? If he went to Pakistan they might shoot him. They might shoot him if he stays here. It's the problem we all have, to find some place where you're a part of some community, no matter how small, maybe just one street, like the rue de Hachette that Elliot Paul wrote about. Saleem says it's hard to see now what Paul was talking about, I think he means because of the tourists, but you know Paul says nothing about the Thêâtre des Noctambules right in the middle of the block, these plays by Ionesco going on in the middle of this peasant farce, or tragedy, because that would have intruded a different genre of story... maybe I haven't got that quite right. You'll have to ask Saleem.

About being an expatriate?

Ah, no, that's my idea. I got distracted and wandered off. The paradisos that Saleem is looking into always seem to be full of expatriates, though they don't usually interact with the indigenous intellectuals. Individual exceptions, of course — Mann, de Kooning — did you know that Wodehouse and Simenon lived... Full of expatriates, as I say. One of Saleem's tasks is to explain that, whether there is some connection, some requirement that there be outsiders in order to have a paradiso at all.

And what does he conclude?

Hasn't concluded. Will never conclude, as Tor suspects. Anyway, he's an expatriate. He's got out of here, a place which he dislikes, maybe despises — you'd have to ask him — and gone elsewhere, hasn't he? To Paris in 1951, I think. Much like James Baldwin did.

Baldwin was a gay black man.

Stein was a lesbian white woman, and so was Sylvia Beach but nicer than Stein, and Fitzgerald was a drunk. There are always reasons. You have to have reasons to tear up everything and go live in a foreign place among strangers who talk funny and pinch your butt on the subway. Otherwise you're just a tourist, as Saleem says.

This time Jake's silence conveyed something to her which she had not been aware of before. Alert to. Jake was talking about himself, then?

But what, she wondered afterward, had he meant to say? An oblique, very indirect confidence, the only one she ever had from him, a way of talking about himself without risking too much, but why?

Jake had been ordinarily so detached — well, as she had known him he was detached, perhaps not earlier in his life — that it was difficult to imagine he meant it literally, that he felt lonely, isolated from a community, out of touch, anything of that sort. Perhaps he only meant that he was tired of the effort needed to connect. Tired of samsara, the struggle with the material world and the constant cycle of death and rebirth. When she later read his late writings it was, she noticed, a theme or thread, one introduced in the final articles she thought with a sense of melancholy at the futility of it, the way ideas and schools are cycled in and out of cultures without ever seeming to change anything for better or worse. The apple falls, rots, and comes back as another apple.

It occurred to Reiva that that metaphor would have made more sense locally if it were a grapefruit, but then no one would understand it. Jake had said "apple" because that was the cultural object and a grapefruit is, in this case, just a grapefruit. Which was in turn an instance of the same thing.

Perhaps she could glean from that something positive. Had Jake come to believe it was not possible to make a difference?

From his inability to make good on his obligations to Saleem, perhaps. To get Saleem's dissertation through.

Or just plain decadence

As it happened, a student came to see her just after she left Tor's office and so prevented her from immediately taking stock, assessing the damage, which was probably a good thing. Later on it would seem to be a better outcome than it might have in the first minutes. Later on when her undermind had had time to search out and articulate reasons to excuse her self-destruction. It was early April but already beginning to be hot. The windows of Old Main were open because the air conditioning had other instructions at this season, but at any time the building was inclined to be either blustering or creaky, seldom just right, and she preferred natural air even at three o'clock in the afternoon. By September one becomes very tired of getting none of it.

There was a white oscillating fan on her desk She twisted this on as if hoping to make it cry, and then had to placate it in order to retrieve some unweighted papers from the floor.

This floor was a sort of greenish asphalt tile, shiny but everywhere softly dented by the feet of very many chairs of other professors, instructors, and graduate assistants before her, who had also moved on. Such floors must be in every Old Main in the country. The one in her mother's office had been mopped and waxed at the start of eighty semesters already when she was a baby and had crawled every inch of it. Its smell was distinctive, either the ancient asphalt itself or a formula for wax known only to college janitors, handed down from the early days of the Morrill act along with whatever it was they put on their rags to wipe out drinking fountains. It smelled soft and green, not bright like grass but olives. A quiet smell. Her mother's yellow wooden desk chair squeaked a little as its small casters rolled back and forth. The blades of the oscillating fan turned soundlessly in their black metal cage.

There was a knock, or a tapping, that rattled the frosted glass of the door, which was not quite closed. A shortish person was standing on the other side, one arm raised to the dark wood, the other clutching books to its chest.

Come.

Which proved to be someone wanting to talk and not requiring any voluble politeness from Reiva nor, harder to summon just then, sympathy.

After the student had gone Reiva turned the fan off again and went out, leaving the window open. That night it rained, one of those cloudbursts that fills the underpasses which everyone is warned not to drive into but which someone invariably does and has to be pulled off the roof of their car somewhere downstream, at public expense. Some papers got wet and one departmental file blew out the window but all that was on the computer. The only casualty was an origami camel which fell into a half mug of cold coffee.

During the storm, Reiva watched from the shelter of her patio, a tiny little space big enough for a bistro table and one chair. Water drops as big as marbles struck the roof in a continuous roar louder than the Air Force trainers that sometimes strayed over on scrambled flight paths. Rain dug into the dirt between the patio and the fence, each drop making a crater to be instantly obliterated by the next, a sight perhaps like the surface of some airless acne-pitted world passing through a hail of meteors, the huddled remnants of some destroyed sister.

Then it was over. The pummeling stopped; the sky cleared moodily from the southwest from whence the storm had come, glowing in bruised purples for a moment before sunset.

She went inside. Turned on a ceiling fan, opened a window. Her little shelter, a duplex apartment of only eight hundred square feet which she had rented now for two years, breathed in the suddenly cold air. In a moment it was clean. Sounds of campus traffic arose two blocks away to the south. One of the houses across the street, occupied by a coalition of nursing students, was showing signs of a Friday night party.

She'd had nothing to eat since breakfast. There *was* nothing to eat. Cold pizza, lunch meat, frozen peas, some carrots, beer. She took a carrot, rubbing it like a baseball in lieu of washing it a bit.

A shocking crack, and then the noise of the world came pounding in and ordinary time restarted itself.

Across the street something by Paul Butterfield's band almost as old as she, the blues harmonica screeching and wailing with ancient melancholy.

Four weeks and something until reading day. She lifted up a corner of the flimsy realtor's calendar hanging crookedly over the washing machine beside the patio door. Four weeks until the last paycheck, after having resigned a tenured job it had taken her half a lifetime to get. They would never have made her an associate anyway, of course. Especially not after this.

Her gut bubbled at the thought of four weeks and something. At the thought of students, grade sheets, *Women's History Q.* Burritos and air conditioning and APA style and monthly department meetings. No stomach for all that.

And then what?

No what. That one of Jake's puzzles, something about killing cats. Somebody's dead cat in a box.

She ate the cold pizza, also.

She didn't last four weeks. One of the graduate students taught her last classes and posted her grades, and the short person who hadn't needed any sympathy finished with a very decent 92.

THE RIVER DERWENT

She'd heard the old mission had been restored
recently, put back into place
so to speak, its grubby old age
wiped off like a fogged mirror Jake would say,
and had come to see for herself.

From the front it was no whiter than before.
Unless you are a mission Indian
your approach is coy. Circling
down from a rise some miles away
where the road falls out of the underside of the city,

you see it off to the right, white
in the morning sun. Plaster, of course.
Not a big building, but as noticeable
as an exposed shoulder among brown suits.
Country roads lead around to the face.

There's no mission square. Just a dusty
parking lot, and an arched gate with a small bell
under which you pass. A low wall,
whitewashed. Some Indian girls, children that is,
were selling guidebooks there as usual.

You pay what you like. On a Thursday morning,
October, no cars but hers,
she gave a dollar. From the front
the central bell tower, the white wings,
seemed unchanged. A shop had once been fitted into the dark
    lintels.

Later she found it on the plaza in back
they had made new shop space
more discreet, a museum store truly now.
She sat on a bench in mesquite shade
with bottled water and one of their books.

They. They who had made this place,
the mission Indians who were the people
who owned this place. Whose girls
stood out front with coffee cans
in the dust. They once built it for themselves.

In seventeen fifty something. She drank their water,
warm water under the mesquite and didn't want
to be more precise. In the mercado
a bodega was serving good bean burros in the hot white air
but she didn't want any of that either.

Hers still the only car. A light breeze rattled the tree
overhead. It was their church
after all some foundation's money bought
the research and the skills to rebuild it.
But their girls. Their burros and Guatemalan rugs in the
mercado.

The work was good. She saw it was good,
knowing nothing.

Why then had she come? Past times
worry us, worried to make a shrine
but that someone was here before

polishing and tidying up, putting to rights
some stuff. As Jake would say stuff.
Inside, the intricate decorations had been cleaned,
repainted in the original heavy red and green

garish to the protestant eye. Scary
reliquaries, gaunt carvings painted blood and gold
with big dark eyes. Masses of wavering candle flames
and stiffened lace concealing dwarves in glass
coffins, pulpits and dark crooked lintels grow
from the narrow walls. You feel you could reach right across.

She wasn't much for church architecture.
Didn't know how the parts were — apse, crossing —
was there a rood screen? Or was that Byzantine.
Best to keep such things screened off.
She was a different kind of historian.

She would want to know how they had lived,
what changes the missionaries had made,
why they needed a church
when there was a perfectly good religion already.
She would want to know about dogs

and ball games, and if they also made rugs
for tourists at train stops without a purpose
the way Gray Line tours do. Rugs
using the new aniline dyes, heavy greens and reds
made from coal tar in factories.

Had the friar kept a pariah dog? Territorial jails
were often built by their prisoners too
because there was no prison all ready
to house them. Who's complaining?
She hadn't heard any outcry.

The sort of historian she was
who wants to taste the daily life, maybe
she should go for one of those burros
after all. Beans and chiles
were not the friar's food alone

but had been here all along. She drank the water
which might have gone for Indian beans and squash.
Maybe the friar thought
he was helping to make the adobe for something more
than just another church, already here.

She didn't understand these things, really.
She was that kind of historian. A woman
from somewhere in England, presumably —
or time was, given her name:
Reiva. Or time was.

She herself was only from the place where she was
last. The academic life
takes you everywhere. An itinerant life
like the early printers setting up wherever
there was no press, needing only a few tools to build one

as the friar and the people did whose church it was.
Built this one out of their own adobe,
probably the dogs leaving their paw prints
in it, cried off too late. Now restored
and all the clay of generations since wiped off.

They hadn't neglected a cemetery of course
would leave no one unburied. And a school
which was in the opposite wing. Years
she might have worked to become a teacher,
carrying children from one side to the other.

The River Reiva as the English call it,
always putting the particular last,
is about forty-five miles long.
It comes down from the Howden Moors
in the Pennines between Manchester and Sheffield

where they make good steel, to Derby and Burton
whence the little packets of salts, that is
minerals, that home brewers use
who have only bad water.
Rivers drain a lot of particular geography,

carrying the anxieties of people who have
no calculus and who cannot explain
how one thing by imperceptible degree becomes another.
To bear a river's name as she did bears the name
of a particular passage washing her

from birth to death. The flow, or rather that
infusion, that dispersion which James says
is the meaning of religious experience —
one stands at the confluence, waiting,
and somehow there is always more water coming.

ON THE VIRTUE OF APPARENT SOLIDITY

On the campus where she now teaches stands a memorial bronze casting. Every morning she passes by it on her way to class and in the evening she encounters it again. In the weeks since she arrived here she has viewed the memorial regularly in two lights and several weathers, and from approximately thirty visual impressions and two recent tactile encounters she has distilled a relatively fixed mental image of the solid object. This abstraction lacks, as yet, some of the richness and warmth of the real thing, chiefly because the mental image is more immediately comprehensible than the sculpture, which is so because it (the image) is simpler and hence less ambiguous. But the sculpture is extrinsic and distinctly not portable, whereas her imagination goes with her everywhere, and with speculation and the accretion of ornament the mental image may become richer in time.

It is the founder of this private college, a 19th century educational philosopher, who is here commemorated. The base is a rectangular marble prism about four feet high and of satisfactory proportions, presumably hollow, and suitably inscribed. Atop the pedestal is a three-quarter size representation of The Lector, a middle-aged gentleman sitting erect in a light chair, a boy at his knee; The boy's figure is wholly conventional, but the Lector has been formed with somewhat more vivacity. His narrow face is partly hidden behind an appliqué beard but a faint personality is visible there nevertheless. In the impassive eyes and composed, severe mouth one may detect the oppressive seriousness and singleness of intent of the educational philanthropist and missionary. He was, no doubt, unimaginative, humorless, overbearing, prolix.

What has occupied her thoughts and diverted her mind since she encountered it, however, is not the man himself but the object which he holds out in his right hand, presenting it to the boy's vacant eyes as if he were about to make it disappear. A sphere. A simple, plain, bronze pill. The lack of content of this object is maddening. What the hell *is* this thing which is being proferred for her examination and enlightenment and which the ineptitude of the sculptor prevents her from confronting? This naked metal ball sits lightly between the fingertips of the pedagogue, partaking of all the appearances of reality, yet it lacks essence, a referent. It flickers, an astral substance, and the elegant bronze fingers threaten to close on emptiness.

Long ago minds less fastidious than hers responded to the insistence of this existential void: the locals consider the Lector's sphere to be an apple, which seems to her plausible, if unjustified. The apple, particularly in this context, is a thing rich in imaginative possibilities. But herself the historian must decline. In fact what is being depicted here is a 19th century educational technique known as the Object Method which makes her snicker, for the sculptor could not have chosen less of an object than this featureless bronze pill. It is plainly a failure of Art. Her neediness continues unsatisfied. Without a doubt it is only people like her who are pained: pedagogical types, truth-seekers, meticulous scholars lacking wit. For the others it's an apple and that's the end of it. she herself am the creator of these difficulties. It is she who sees in the sculptor's inability to portray a solid object a criticism of her own character, who sees her own malicious discontent on this man's lips, her incomprehension and boredom in the eyes of the boy. There is neither man nor boy to be found here on the lawn before the entrance to the Department of Education. There is only a monument, a memorial bronze casting. The solid metal rings when she strikes it with her knuckles. The marble base bruises her toes.

« »

The old man went first to the library. Stiff and uncomfortable, he sat down among the works of Ascham, Lord Chesterfield, Newman, his dusty form half imagined, imprisoned as if in a yet unsculpted chunk of marble. Socrates or the young Plato, perhaps, despite the violence to his politics. Something intended for the town square, or to put out in front of the public library as a monument to learning. He had removed his coat and cravat and had rolled his sleeves up to the elbow. In his hand he held a glass of mineral water. Droplets condensed on the outside of the glass and fell, leaving small wet spots on his trousers like holes. He was a distinctive man, tall and gangling, somewhat sepulchral. The reserved and economical manner which he cultivated in public, the air of a magistrate, was, he imagined, proper to a role which suited his predatory appearance; proper to the elongated shape of his skull and the deeply sunken eyes and high cheeks, the beaked nose. But in fact he was badly strung and generally ill-proportioned. His movements, though delicate, were often imprecise. Two joints of the second finger of his right hand were missing. It was easy to imagine that he had lost them by accident, while slicing bread perhaps, or cutting the peel away from an apple in a thin red strip, very sparing of the white flesh underneath. A salt shaker stood on the table beside him and, the apple peeled, he cut small wedges of it, salted them, and carried them to his mouth between his thumb and the blade of the knife.

This knife was a single folding blade not an inch long, the handle inlaid with a piece of mother-of-pearl fastened by two rivets which winked as he held it in the light. A wedge of apple lay on the blade. He had taken a section of core with the rest and at the thin edge of the slice a seed lay on the hard, translucent membrane. He flicked away the seed but then, reconsidering, bent down and retrieved it, examined it, rubbed it between his fingers, laid it carefully on the table among the glasses and bottles.

Salt. He reached for the salt shaker but in so doing upset his glass of mineral water. He tried to catch the glass and the unsliced portion of the apple jumped from his hand and rolled away across the rug, covering itself with lint. The apple seed was lost, too in this accident.

The Apple, he said to himself with a thin smile, was the fruit of the Tree of Experience. He picked up the dirty apple between his thumb and forefinger and contemplated it for a moment. But I am afraid, he intoned, that this is to be a fruitless experience. And with a dry chuckle he picked up his glass from the floor.

His bedroom was plain in the extreme, heated by a small coal fire, and on the bare wood beneath the stove a wedge of blue light flickered. The naked plaster walls were damp to the touch. The old man had very dry skin, porous, like limestone. About the mouth and eyes it was slightly coruscated. The flesh of his cheeks was without tonus. He smelled of oranges.

For a long time he lay staring at the light beneath the stove, at the reflections of a pale flame, remembering a student of his who was killed long ago, struck by a train as he was walking along the tracks at dusk, coming from the store where he had gone for groceries. In his imagination he saw slices of soft white bread flung out in a line along the gravel rail bed, and a bar of soap spat from under the wheel of a boxcar. Crumbled fragments of fat white flesh lay at the foot of a tree a few yards away. Bread, soap, flesh. All indistinguishable.

He had fallen asleep. His mouth hung open and he snored lightly.

« »

During the last years of his life the old man drank prodigious amounts of black, bitter coffee. Like Balzac. Poisonous stuff.

Cups. Small, delicate coffee cups with convoluted gilded handles and handpainted roses; demitasse cups manufactured in 1828 and imported from Vienna after the Civil War, brought to Chicago after his death and from there by train to Minneapolis, carried to Denver in 1910 and to Portland twenty years later, finally to Los Angeles and there sold at auction for fifteen cents and carried back here to begin *la ronde* again.

Coffee. Demitasse and espresso, coffee black, café au lait, with two lumps and cream, with bourbon laces. The physician Rhazes prescribes coffee as a stimulant and a diuretic. The berries are to be dried, he writes, then ground and mixed with a little fat, rolled into pellets, and eaten. Followers of Mohammed consumed these pills during religious ceremonies to keep their attention from wandering. Coffee wine can be made from the skins and green beans. For those who complain of stomach disorders the drug may be decaffeinated. For convenience it may be powdered, concentrated, or freeze-dried —

Quawah. Kaffa. Coffee.

He was very particular about his coffee, grinding it freshly for every pot. He drank a different blend every day and went to great lengths to procure beans which were in every way satisfactory.

There was always a cup of hot coffee before him on the table. As he drank he was aware of the image of his face, a reflection on the surface of the black, steaming liquid. An eye, part of a shaggy brow, the skin of his cheek magnified on the rippled skin of the coffee—

He was seldom without coffee. He was on intimate terms with it and with the white china cup which contained it. His fingers were acquainted with the weight of the cup, the size of the handle, the width of the body. He was familiar with the warmth of the china against his palm. His nail prodded repeatedly a chip on the rim, examining the texture of the exposed ceramic. He tipped the cup in order to look through its translucent walls, and to watch the coffee slide up and down the glazed inside surface. When the coffee was drunk he wiped his little finger through the film of sediment that had been deposited on the bottom and, turning the cup over, watched the black, sandy grounds drip out. The image of the cup haunted him—

On Thanatotaxis

Disturbed this morning by some infuriating regularity in the clock, she was unable to sleep. She lay in bed, alone, staring at the blank walls with disgust and boredom, and in this tender and exposed state the clock imprinted itself on her, impinging its uniform, precise sound on her mind. Under its military aegis she imagined all sorts of horrors. This demon, this troll, this ghoulish excrescence built before her eyes, one click at a time, a vision of destruction. Unaccountable screams in the street. TIME. *Lo, lo, here is a sign signifying anything.* Foul breaths, cosmic gasses. She dropped it. It fell on the floor and broke.

To sleep, perchance to dream. Eye, there's the rub. Mares in the night. Her feet, she thought, were out of control. She held one up in bed and the nails grew and broke off of their own weight. Her hair, too was growing at an irresponsible rate — she feared she would be unable to raise her head from the pillow because of it. And inside her was a lot of raging, stamping machinery, a chaos of pipes and hoses, valves, hissing vents. Her heart worked, pumping blood with a chain of explosions like quarry blasting. The roaring of the wind in her lungs deafened her. Fearfully she palpated the length of her intestines, the skin bottle of her stomach, the dense cluster of her pancreas. She investigated the ductwork, felt the trickle of bile into the duodenum. Liquids oozed through the bog of her liver, dripped from the leaves of her kidneys, puddled up in her cells. And still there came to her the horror of perceptions yet more delicate. She felt the tidal flow of plasma, the evanescent breeze of life itself.

Springing out of bed, she dressed herself as quickly as she could, sitting on chairs with trepidation, unwilling to put her feet firmly on the floor. Within the walls of her wretched two rooms were pipes full of water and sewage, wires alive with electricity. The plaster breathed, the floor rose slightly and fell in somnolent respiration—

The walls were cold to the touch and the white plaster dust came off on her fingers. The heat, she thought, is certainly slow to come on this autumn. And as she stood in the living room staring at the wall the burst of early morning energy seeped away and a familiar torpidity resettled itself in her limbs. Wide awake now, she went to splash some cold water on her face.

Later, as she was making up her eyes, she thought that her skin seemed especially sallow. She would have to get more sun. The flesh of her cheeks was without tonus, dry as plaster, and slightly coruscated about the mouth and eyes. She pulled away her hand and on the tips of her fingers she saw a suspicious white dust.

A is for the Apple that she ate...

ALL THAT IS SOLID MELTS INTO AIR

Title of a novel, too. Who?

Don't know. Reiva Derwent is a historian. She hears these things about the outside world, such as that people write novels, but faintly, here on this campus guarded by the Lector and the promise of the ball of bronze. Well, wood originally, promised on. Got it here somewhere, the actual nump, in the library. From out the boxes of archives the wood talks. But faintly. It is very far away, this place. She has gone very far away. Tiny in the distance.

After those fiascos Reiva Derwent denned herself in Syracuse where she was born, so as to... hmm — there are a lot of nice words for what she wanted then. Reinvent, get in touch with. "Home" is a nice word too. She had always hated the place and found out now after twenty years that she still did. Forever cloudy, biggest small town in America. The Derwents lived (were living still) in their wooden Federal two blocks north of the University. Two or three generations since. Not that she had ever had a choice where to live, either. You go to the best university that you can get into. You take whatever job you are offered. You live hand to mouth and don't get green about the hegemony of the biochemists. You write what you can, in free moments, and publish it where you can; if you manage to get together a book and get your hands on an assistant professorship you go there and start getting ready to die there. You're home free.

The idea of a career, she now discovered, had bored her for years. Whyever had she? Thrown off the tenure track so stay off. She wandered through the cemeteries on the other side of campus. She walked all around Syracuse, sweating, having forgotten the wet air after years of ten percent humidity. Forgot her sunglasses which before she had always snatched up out of habit as she was leaving the house and then left them on some counter. Had to go back. Go back. Go back.

No need for sunglasses here.

Two months of that was enough. There were year-to-year contracts to be had, filling vacancies at places where no one wanted to live. She made phone calls, bought winter clothes. Jeans, a good leather bomber, ski gloves, Something for her feet other than flip-flops

"All that is solid melts into air."

We had heard she was here, pretending to be the real thing, still riding the dharma wheel like a girl barrel racer. Woman, I mean. Past forty. Men don't race barrels anyhow.

She was living in the front half of a railroad house from the 1830s on the Italian bank of the river, which is the rive droit of the place. Houses stood both side of her close enough to touch if the windows weren't painted shut. It had taken six months to find this much, holing up while she waited in one of a row of barns in which the students were penned, also waiting. Second floor back left, near the stairs. Now she had two floors of her own, with a stained glass casement window over a claw-footed tub, and a window which opened and through which a morning glory had found its way inside the wall.

On mornings when the streets weren't ice-glazed she rode a bicycle two miles to campus. Snickersnack went the latch of the heavy door also with its panel of stained glass, for which she had a big key with an ornately encrusted handle in the shape of a heart. "Handle" — that flat piece at the end of the shaft, barrel rather, opposite the... leaf? is it. Doesn't know. A historian she is. Historians don't know anything unremembered, only memories. People write these down and leave them lying around for other people to find kind of like the dimes that come out of your pants pockets in the wash.

Washwoman's wages.

"All that is solid melts into air."

The classroom doors were not as heavy as her own but served anyway to mark out the space, the prisoners' base, where they would talk. A factory course. American history survey for humanities credit, no prerequisites. Twenty-three of them, the room filled with their down-stuffed anoraks, their wet shoes melting snow onto the green linoleum floor under their seats. Ragged makeshift rows of them, a few pathetic outcasts whose chairs had been pushed away toward the walls, at least facing more or less forward. Faces if not bodies turned forward, and the open covers of laptops behind which they would be sending messages and playing at being people.

Reiva had asked about that. In the everyday world, they said, they were not free, not yet real, behind now one door and now another of the long hall of doors, all closed. A long hall of green linoleum spotted with puddles of melting dirty snow and smelling faintly of janitors' rags.

And how was that different? she wondered, and asked no more dangerous questions. The world is a hard place to love, especially in winter.

Thinking back, Reiva guessed that her old mentor Jake was probably faux-wise. It had been a pose which he used to cover up. That would be the cynical view. In any case, his was not a relationship to the phenomenal world from which much could be learned. Or learned by her, anyway. Starbucks was not going to make a fortune on that flavor of coffee.

What she was scraping against was a relationship to the material world. Against having one. She stared out at it from her prisoner's base, not much trying to understand, as if the intensity of her gaze could cross the gap between her and *stuff*. What other word was there for it? And "her" — another nice word which didn't describe what was advertised. What was on offer. Alienated, this state of continuance used to be called. *Not* a nice word. A word with attitude, which put it out that she had been born into an anguished and incomplete condition, pushed from out the warm tapioca into which herness melted and was the only condition truly to be called home. To be at home. Receiving. Thursdays as four o'clock.

Perhaps. Maybe that was about as useful a claim as about the facts of history, that they were pebbles lying around to be picked up, polished, sent off to the gem and mineral show. It's *all* pudding, a polenta which she was tired of stirring. She couldn't concentrate long enough to read any sort of book, even the Harry Potter ones. The only thing she could sit through was a movie. Just to be quiet and become *stuff.*

Which might have made it hard to teach but she found out it didn't. What she said in class was just a comfortable and familiar blather which to the students too was warm and safe. The other half of her mind was available for looking — at them. Other people are as unknowable as stones, but unlike stones, which don't care if you put them into the campfire and then into the soup, people know when you're looking at them. All these children to whom Andrew Jackson was just a rumor, as much a rumor as that powerful sword which it is said can be found in level thirty-two embedded in a stone which nobody has ever seen because nobody is good enough to get higher than level twenty-seven; just as they knew themselves to be only rumors which might be substantiated if she (rumored to be she) would pass them on to the next in the chain of graders, the chain which leads to the outside world which they feared might be as much rumored as level thirty-two — how do they know she is looking at them? How do these kids know, barricaded behind the lids of their laptops, floating in the amniance of thought while they wait to be born as real people, that someone is looking? Are there little particles of curiosity, like orgones, which they can feel passing through them like neutrinos though a billion tons of heavy water, miles underground?

How do trees know you're wanting to prune them and warn the other trees to pull in their sap?

There were twenty-three of them. It was her biggest class of four. Subtly alike in some ways despite their obvious differences. Fifty-six percent women, GPAs distributed with small variance and smaller skew between twoish and threeish, ten ethnicities but all native speakers except two (a Chinese and a French Somalian), all under twenty except the African who'd needed a bit more time. Younger than now typical — how could anyone put themselves through this place? There was nowhere to commute from; there was no air here for urban blood to stay red; there was not a single web-based online degree offered; there was no community college to practice in beforehand. Aside from the college itself there was only one other place to work, a sub shop. These were kids from an earlier time when you went to high school and then to college where you did only the traditional things which were to study, party, and screw. The only odd thing was that here they played hockey instead of football. The hockey mascot was a ball of orange fluff.

Reiva went to hockey games because there was nothing else to do except sit on the floor and meditate. There wasn't even a movie theater. Despite growing up in Syracuse she had no inkling about hockey. She couldn't even see the puck. The puck was an invisible mitogen around which the players coagulated, dispersed, regathered.

Her students were there? Did they see the puck? They saw her. They were everywhere, her students. In the market, buying underwear, in the back half of her house, drinking and screwing and watching the puck on television.

Two of them drew her attention, not because of anything special about them but just because seventy-seven students were too many to see at one time. One was an Italian girl from Queens who was going to be the size of a matriarch someday if she didn't know that now. The other was a multi-racial boy whose papers said was a Barbados from Cortland, of all places. Cortland is the place where all the illustrators of children's books come from who draw red barns and fluffy clouds and cows with two short legs on the hillside. They spend their summers there because they can't afford the Poconos. Cortland does not have reggae kids in dreadlocks, it has journalism students who are interested in international politics and in murderous factional wars in difficult places. Reiva thought this boy Derek would get himself killed pretty quick if he didn't get some street smarts, and where would he do that? Small, fine-boned, and sweet — his raccoon eyes the only clue.

Barbara Scoppone was the girl's name. Black eyes, Neapolitan skin, black hair so thick you could sink your hand in it up to the wrist. A small woman, two or three inches over five feet, with the slimness and muscle of a dancer. For a while yet. You could see by the heaviness of her breasts, the width of her hips, that an hour missed at the gym (what gym?), another beer or a second piece of pizza, and overnight she would become Mama Scoppone. To Reiva, who had no inner Hyde to keep in chains, this was marvelous discipline. If Barbara had had a bigger or faster CPU she could have been a formidable scholar of the hedgehog type, or one of those indomitable trial lawyers who can stare holes in a brick. As it was, after working so hard to stay herself, Barbara was still one of the threeish ones.

Derek Causwell. Black skin so black it looked dusted with flour and reflects no light at all. Not much bigger than Barbara but ethereally light. Where her voice was hard, his was so soft you could hardly hear him, so rarely spoke one never noticed. Likewise quick, but so detached from the business at hand he would never prosper. He needed the stimulus of death. He also needed languages, the ones spoken by the murderous factions he hoped to understand. Perhaps he really was a Burton who could talk to anyone but it seemed unlikely.

Reiva wanted to know them. It was impossible. It was like wanting to know the outcome of global warming or what civilization will succeed the West or what your children will be like when they are as old and tired as you are. They did not want to know her. There were to be no shattering Jamesian insights, no feats of empathy, no intimated clouds of glory. As between herself and such people as Barbara and Derek there were no clues. It was like trying to see into a stone, which if you break it becomes two stones with two secrets inside. The finer you grind it the more secrets you make.

She once saw the two of them together, walking ahead of her on a path through the new-sprung grass toward a grove of pines, the lake visible between their trunks. It was May, still too cold to put off the bloated coats which made Michelin characters of everyone, in various florescent nylon colors.

They were walking slowly, close beside but not entwined. Barbara talked in her intense way and Derek listened in his way. The whole little story comforted the middle-aged professor who followed them on their way down to the water to sit on the boulders and work out who knew what matter was between them in the sharp May wind off the water. She talking her gestural dialect, focused on him, he looking off into that crack between the clouds and the horizon which always promises to open and never does. If it would open, would it reveal the alternate universe beyond where all new people are born real? Or would it open like an eye, a terrible all-seeing world-consuming eye whose gaze no one can endure?

Were they lovers, these to mismatched people yet subtly alike? Lovers of something anyway. In class, behind the door, she asked them to imagine the lives of Americans of the 1830s. Behind the door she imagined the lives of Barbara and Derek. Naked, exposed to each other in that instant of perfection between now and the little death to come. Was that hair, too, thick enough to sink into up to his wrist? Was that third eye open, moist and all-seeing? And he. What images could Reiva invent to describe what she saw of him?

Friday afternoon. The end of the week. Still light, warm enough at last to ride her bicycle home in her shirtsleeves, one tail untidily untucked from her jeans. She stopped by the monument which once marked the entrance to campus when it was a small college for hopeful teachers, teachers epitomized by this bronze statue of the man with the plan. Reiva laid her bicycle on the grass and stepped across the sidewalk to rap on his foot with her knuckle.

Donk.

The school bell was ringing. Donk, donk. But the old boy took no more notice than any metal man would.

Smiling at this joke, smiling first in a long while, Professor Reiva Derwent picked up her bicycle again and headed home, thinking her bidden thoughts, entering her bidden life.

IN THIS PLACE where she lived now people cleft — *cleaved* she might say but that wasn't the right word — to one another as they would not have where there was more of a chance to live in full without a lot of help. So pretty quickly that first year Reiva made acquaintance with a woman about her age (meaning arrested twenty-five) named Simone who taught French. Simone was herself, or had been, French. She was the whole French program. There was also a one-person German program and an oddity who taught Icelandic and Old Norse, or would have, but instead filled in with a couple of religion courses until retirement. The rest of the department taught Spanish, a language locally useful for about two weeks during apple-picking. All these folks lived down the hall from the History Department and it was not more than a few weeks into fall term before Simone showed up in the History adjuncts' bullpen hungrily in search of someone with a bowl of pretzels or chocolate kisses on her desk.

They got on well, as it happened. It helped to be childless, which meant that they could spend a lot of time together without reprisals. The Irish side of town had a number of genuine pubs where one could go and talk over beers, places as dark and quiet in mid-afternoon as at ten at night.

There must be a couple of hundred brands of beer in New York, Simone said, holding her glass up to the feeble yellow light over the taps. It's a wonder they haven't been all bought up.

They have, Simone.

Heretic.

A couple of old men were talking at the bar in low voices, wondrously without a glance for the two women in the booth opposite. There was a Red Sox game on television with the sound off. The dim light was brown with reticence. The table between them was so high Simone might have been nine years old, looking like Kilroy over the edge at a bowl of popcorn she couldn't reach. Outside it was raining, with occasional gusts fueled by wet air off the lake. There were dark wood shutters through which Reiva could see only the gleam of a streetlight reflected off the broken wet pavement.

She got up to fetch two more beers and returned also with another bowl of popcorn. There were half a dozen empty glasses on the table now but they were small ones, eight-ounce glasses which Simone said she hadn't seen in a bar anywhere for years and years.

Have you seen a lot of bars, Simone?

I remember, said Simone gaily, when the men used to salt their beer and there was a jar of peeled hardboiled eggs out on the counter, floating in something that didn't look quite safe. I used to look at those eggs and try to figure out what it was that a detective should be hardboiled. My dad would be in the back playing billiards. I guess the barkeep didn't mind an eight-year old girl. I got soda water in these glasses.

Where was this?

Medicine Hat. Or thereabouts. I never understood why my dad didn't settle in Quebec or somewhere they spoke French and didn't call him Pierre. Pierre is what a person you don't know is called who has ze aksèn fronch. Like Charlie. Chuck.

And this was when, about 1930?

About. I stayed long enough to try the eggs. As you see, they didn't kill me.

Simone, you told me at that age you were eating a croque monsieur in a bistro on your way home from the lycée.

Well I was, but it was the université. I skipped les soixante-huitardes, though. Really I didn't like Paris much. I felt out of place. Canadian. With big feet.

But where were you born?

Simone paused, raised one eyebrow, a gesture which Reiva had studied but never learned.

Lourdes, of course.

Oh. Do you bleed?

For a few years yet, I suppose.

And you had only the orangeade.

How do you know? But alone. Alone, not with those old men. They smelled of cigarettes and garlic and drank bad wine and were never quite shaved and the nuns told us not to do that.

Giggle.

Between them, beside the popcorn among the empty glasses, they laid out a long, contemplative silence.

I suppose the fish fry is closed for the season, Reiva said.

Yes. Rudy's boarded up and gone to Florida.

I'd like some clams — wistfully. A bucket of fried clams.

Fried clams are definitely not good for you. Reiva, you are really on about food.

Food's important.

Why?

Simone! A Frenchwoman. How can you?

Ah, bah.

Well, aside from the fact that you put it in your mouth and that it gets made into you and the social problematics of that, it's maybe the closest you get to crossing the gap with the phenomenal world.

Sounds metaphysical to me.

Simone was married to a philosopher and considered it a stroke of fortune they were both able to have professional jobs. The philosopher was not philosophical about food and didn't care that his wife declined to cook. Their only child was away to school at Brown, just far enough away she said. So as not to make pests of themselves. Simone and the philosopher were on easy terms. There was comfortable sex, they were well off, but in this place they had to spend too much time in each other's company. It was a dangerous situation. Someone like Reiva eased the pressure. The philosopher made jokes and was philosophical but that didn't hide a fragile truth.

Classic Freudian transference, Reiva remarked. It's a wonder you don't get fat.

Well I have some other interests. At least when cucumbers are in season.

Simone's regard, become speculative and skeptical in passing over the tops of her glasses, was not quite so light-hearted as her words. With one finger she slid her glasses up, but they slid right back down.

They had to wait until the next summer for clams. She and Simone shared a bucket in celebration of Simone's fiftieth birthday. At Rudy's shack on the lakeshore west of town they sat on stools at the counter and stuffed themselves with fried clams, passing the bowl of tartar sauce back and forth between them over the crack in the vinyl countertop. Simone was a little morose. She didn't much like turning fifty. And she was wearing a rather unflattering skirt which was too tight and rode up to show a lot of thigh. Simone's legs were not what they had been. Reiva saw her friend's nakedness and fretted.

Simone licked the grease from her fingers. Narrow long fingers which Reiva envied. The wind off the lake, blowing in through the wooden walls, was cold. The wind is always cold. When the fish shack was battened down in wintertime or for a storm the window openings were covered by wooden flaps hinged at the top. In summer these were raised and lowered with a line on a pulley. It was years since the place was painted. At least four layers of garish paint had weathered down to Diebenkorn patches uncovering the gray wood and the whole thing creaked and moaned constantly. The red vinyl on the stools cracked seasonally and the stiff edges were scratchy on bare skin. If the fish had not been so good all this excess of atmosphere would not have sustained the immemorial custom of going there, and the place would have seemed tawdry rather than charming.

Rudy had become an old man. Next year he would not be coming back from Florida. And the shack was not worth even its lumber.

There was still fish and chips on Wednesdays at the wharf but clams were finished. Over.

Simone, what's *forever* mean? How many chapters of the novel do you have to read ahead? Or is it only that the pantry is nicely stocked?

With what?

I dunno. Clams.

Living on the Italian side, Reiva had an excellent little market just around the corner, on the main street, where she shopped when she could. Corvaia's. Sicilian. Two brothers — or maybe three, it was hard to tell when you never saw them together. At Corvaia's she could get real sheep's milk romano so strong it dripped oil on your clothes getting it home, and balls of fresh mozzarella in water. There were fava beans and Spanish oranges and vats of Greek olives and prosciutto and arborio and big Sicilian capers and fiore and, it seemed, all two hundred fifty brands of New York beer. Simone, who lived on the Irish side where there was nothing like this — curiously, no market at all — was making it a habit to stop by Reiva's on Saturday morning for espresso and shopping.

Corvaia's had (had, because it went out of business not long after) a big display window where crates of produce were tipped up. It was tiny, perhaps a hundred feet square, and absolutely crammed. One or another of the Corvaias — brothers, wives, sometimes la nonna (there was only one granny, apparently) keeping an eye on a son of fifteen or so while she knitted something black. Always black — kept shop in a heavy canvas apron in the alcove by the door where the register was and the deli slicer and the vats and rolls of waxed brown paper. The aisles were narrow; the shelves were tall.

Simone said the place was a romance. It's the perfect neighborhood market. I wonder whether there are any left.

There are a lot of old things here which aren't moving, Reiva pointed out, blowing the dust off the shoulders of a tiny bottle of... hm. Crumbling faded labels, crumbling old buildings, crumbly plumbing, morning glories poking through the crumbled walls.

Rudy gone, the last family fishing boat on the lake gone, Simone murmured. Where else can you go down to get fish right off the boat?

Once a week, Simone. And where else do you have to drive for an hour for a bookstore or to buy clothes or go to a movie? An hour if the roads don't ice up. Where else do you slide off and get stuck in a snowdrift and freeze to death for a ball of kitchen twine?

Montana? Well I like this store, anyway.

So do I.

May it live long and prosper. Was that Spock?

No, it... Say, who is that guy?

Someone had come in, making the bell ring. Only a glimpse of someone who vanished down the first aisle. A smallish man in an overcoat too big for him, cinched by a belt — could it have been a rope? — and a lot of straight black hair held on by a stocking hat and small rectangular glasses which flashed in the light.

He looks like Lenin.

Lenin was bald, Simone.

So?

I see him everywhere. Does anyone know who he is?

Some guy, Reiva. Some poor guy with no fingers to his gloves.

Reiva stole down the parallel aisle and peeped around the end but the next aisle was empty. Her shopping basket knocked into a stack of cans which she managed to catch except one. Not dented anyway, she muttered, looking it over. A good thing, because what would she have done with a can of ... hm. This place might be Chinese, she said, for all you can read the labels. Is that Italian?

Of course, Simone said, looking over Reiva's shoulder. It says

—

The unknown Lenin was buying something at the counter, his back to them. The bell tinked; the doorglass rattled; he was gone. Beyond the crates of vegetables, beyond the plate glass window, out in the street passing cars kicked up slush which freezes on the sidewalk in hurtful sawtooth ridges that tear your skin when you slip and fall.

Tomorrow, or the next day, the streets will be dry. The slush will evaporate leaving only the dirt and the gum wrappers. He was like the sun, that man. Glimpsed for a moment in a crack between two clouds, the tail of his coat just disappearing through a doorway or around a corner. You hear him speak, a few words in a voice low and confidential, but you can't understand. Like the sun, never around long enough to give any heat.

Purchases rustling two plastic sacks each, the friends stepped carefully over the icy broken concrete two blocks back to Reiva's flat where Simone's car had been left on the street. Reiva's rusty blue one was parked on the lawn, or what would be the lawn in three or four months, between the sidewalk and the curb in a slot shoveled into the snow just wide enough to get the driver's door open. This was to keep the narrow driveway clear for the people in back, who had the use of a small garage with leaf-hinged doors that folded back over a space about the size of a Model T. The garage was to make up for their having the original kitchen, but Reiva doubted they ate anything back there but hamburgers and frozen pizzas. She herself had a modern gas stove and cupboards, a gas log, and the original bathroom with a colored glass window over the tub, but she would never feel right parking on the lawn. That was a thing done by people she didn't want to know.

Simone came in for more coffee. There was half an apple pie. She warmed her hands on the cup, hunching over it more than usual.

Whatever was wrong with Simone stayed wrong. Spring came and went during a couple of weeks in May just as the term was finished and Reiva was wondering, if she didn't get summer work, how she would be able to live.

At the last minute she got a survey course which no one else wanted because it was one of those which meets all day one day a week and gets in the way of teaching anything else. But as there wasn't anything else, she took it. The difference could be made up with a weekend sales job in a Syracuse department store and by scrimping.

Simone was not teaching at all. There were no French students in summer school. That didn't matter — she had an academic contract which paid a decent nine-month salary and the Philosopher made extra money teaching business ethics and western civ and they were comfortable.

Reiva's Wednesdays were free. At three o'clock in the afternoon the two of them sat in one of the dim unused pubs on the Irish side of the river. All the bars, curiously, were on that side, just as all the groceries were on the other. On both sides there were plenty of places to drink in but they were almost all in the converted front porches of people's homes and mostly not open in the afternoon anyway, and certainly not in the summer.

We had to get rid of a beehive this weekend, said Simone, sipping her beer and following with her eyes the wandering dust motes which appeared and vanished in the striped light according to the logic of a breath too light to be felt by such a gross creature as Simone.

Did you get in the bee men?

What bee men?

Well there's these farms, they sell honey at the farmer's market out on the highway, I thought... well.

No, we did it ourselves. They weren't honeybees anyway. I don't think. The same black and yellow stripes but little. Size of a fly.

They were a problem?

No. Well — there were a lot of them. I suppose we could have been stung, but no, they only went about their business flying back and forth from here to there. We thought they might be carpenter bees or would get into the house. Do carpenter bees live in hives? You wouldn't know where they were so busy going and when we broke open the hive the combs were dry so who knew what they were living on.

Like me, Reiva muttered. No visible means of support.

Hm. Simone passed Reiva a suspicious look, but her eyes soon returned to trailing after the motes and she went on with the story.

We had this garden gnome, she said. Hollow it was, with a drain hole at the bottom. They got in there, were building in there. Gary put a net over his head which we improvised out of one of those bags you wash nylons in and got a rope around the gnome's neck and dragged the thing out to the fence and smashed it.

Out of the pale. Reiva murmered some things about pogroms and enclosures but the stricken, panicky expression this humor produced on her friend cut her off.

I smashed the gnome with a two-by-four, Simone said in an ordinary voice. She drank a little beer, getting foam on her upper lip where she was beginning to show some moustache. Cracked it open with one blow, she said, like in the children's story. We didn't have that story when I was a child. French stories are all about ogres. Nothing but ogres. Gnomes and trolls are German.

Ah.

I expected these bees to come boiling out. There were masses of them clinging to the combs and the broken pottery. The combs were as thick with bees as central Bombay but they acted stunned. Sunday morning we went back to look. A lot of them had fallen off. The rest weren't doing anything so Gary sprayed them with something for roses that is supposed to be toxic to bees. Birds, fish, cats, everything. Why are there such poisons?

The barman was watching television while he idly polished glasses. Just then came a home run and he dropped the glass. Simone started and the sound, her face losing color. Or so Reiva thought — it was hard to tell in the walnut light.

Imagine you're a bee, Simone said when she had recovered herself. These bees. I don't suppose they think of themselves as individual bees, do they? Something a bit creepy about bees, I've always thought. Ants and termites. As if it were Hong Kong or Singapore that's alive, not us.

Protecting the queen, I suppose.

Gary said they wouldn't swarm. As if he knows. So long as... it takes time to make another queen, apparently. One of the drones has to change sex. Or so he said. But that didn't happen. Nothing happened. We busted their hive and Gary sprayed them and the all sat there and died.

Reiva had the good sense to stay quiet now, at the crucial moment.

Imagine you're a bee, Simone said. You're in the hive. Life is going on. Suddenly everything turns upside down and there's a terrific explosion and the light pours in and you're lying in the dirt and it's all destroyed. Smashed, ruined. You die. What in god's name has happened? You die, as stupid as the day you were born. Hatched. Whatever.

On impulse, Reiva reached across the table to cover Simone's hand but Simone pulled back at the touch.

It was me, she said.

The shuffling everydayness of the afternoon had vanished.

Me. With the two-by-four. Crack Smash. Me. The ogre.

After giving thought Simone revised this. Not an ogre, she said. An ogre is just a big ugly powerful stupid ... *person*. Not so dumb as a troll, dumber than Krishna.

The destroyer.

That's him.

Also the creator, Simone.

Bullshit.

« »

After that Reiva went bicycle riding in the countryside on Wednesdays instead. She never did find out what the trouble was any more than she found out what the trouble was with anyone else. Perhaps she was not a person to confide in? Perhaps the troubles were hers instead? Perhaps no matter how much she knew about troubles she never did know anything after all.

She supposed it was something with the husband. Gary, the Philosopher. Something to do with sex. Some faithlessness, jealousy, betrayal — all the purple emotions.

She'd heard it said that most marriages are sexless after five years. That was something Reiva did not care to believe. Sex is like the sandhill in chaos theory when the next grain of sand falls, she guessed — the marriage went flat and took the sex with it and the last grain of sand could be anything. A fight at dinner over who gets the drumstick.

Simone herself had demurred from this view in one of their early barroom discussions, saying that was only a piece of folk wisdom theorized. That was then. Reiva wouldn't have dared ask now.

So if chaos theory provides a calculus of sex, is there also a mathematics of melancholy? Of fear?

Well, yes — there's risk management, but singularly inadequate for problems like not wanting to go to bed for fear of ...

The Philosopher, from what Reiva knew of him, did not seem very purple. Burnt umber, maybe.

All color is hackneyed.

The country roads over which Reiva took her bicycle rides were largely empty of traffic on Wednesday afternoons. She usually followed a circular route which included the farmer's market at the end, leaving only a few miles to ride with a backpack full of fruits, vegetables, and cheeses. At all points of the compass there were crossroads labeled as villages with four or five houses. To the south the land was swampy and there the roads were forced to squirm through wherever there was a ridge of higher ground. It was impossible, really, to get lost. Every road went eventually to the same nowhere. She was easily able to ride twenty-five miles the first time out.

The big trouble was farm dogs. Redneck hounds that made it hard to believe in nature benign and beneficent. Long before she spotted them herself they had sniffed her out, raging out from under shacks and sheds where the stakes and chains lay rusting in the grass. Implacable November dogs, not to be stood against nor threatened. The sort of dogs which will die of bliss with their jaws locked onto your leg, dreaming of bitches in jihad heaven. There was nothing for it but to find another road, turn off or turn around. Behind her the dogs would strut and sneer and piss on some invisible border.

There would be no expatriation to the country of the dogs.

There would be no work visas even for dog work, no green cards for the rest of the pack. The country of the dogs was as unknowable as China in the days of the hunt for the secrets of tea and rhubarb. The speech of dogs will never be deciphered by any Champollions who want to write bibles by Coleman light. From the country of the dogs one turns away, pretending that was the plan all along.

The immanence of trees and water, ponds two inches deep the color of steel variously blue of sheen and dark below as a mirror, thatched over with drowned shrubs and aspen thick as hair. She stopped along the road to look, straddling the crossbar (she had disdained a girl's frame). These swamp roads were only paved paths, unmarked, barely one car wide. What if she were to just walk out into the swamp? Would she ever be seen again? Digested by the Pan of this place, dissolved back into the dao.

She thought of Peter Wier's movie about some girls who wander away from a picnic and vanish, drawn away, leaving the drosser ones to puzzle and fret. That was about sex, too, like everything is. About awakening. Having seen the movie when she was of that age it had stayed in Reiva's mind as a sort of bogey, suffusing any place she couldn't see through.

Pan isn't a nice god. Not safe to know. An elderly pander baiting for children with a wooden ball is nothing to Pan.

A wind had sprung up. The air, never warm, froze her sweaty jerseys. She locked her feet back into the straps and rode away, driving her muscled legs down to move the warm blood, pump up the blood heat from where it had pooled.

Reiva's one class would be done after the first summer session. That would leave her four, possibly five weeks to get over. She thought of going away somewhere cheap. Hiding out in an ashram, maybe, or just yogically vanishing, knowing that when school begins again nothing will have changed.

That year it snowed on September ninth, and Reiva sold her bicycle. Barbara Scoppone will never graduate, she thought, looking over her rosters. The god Pan's dick was shriveled to a blackened stub. She looked for other jobs but there weren't any, or she didn't want them — editing *Bowling News* for an association of trade journals and she would have to live in D.C. Reading proof for minimum wage in one of the most expensive cities in the country. Cashier in the hardware store out at the end of East Bridge street. More junky teaching jobs just like the one she had already.

She began to meet Simone again for lunch. Simone seemed happier now, as if she had digested whatever it was had disagreed with her. Simone herself said that perhaps it wasn't a good idea not to work summers at something, especially here where there was nothing to do but take up a stool in the fish shack and pass on what you ate to the mosquitoes.

Maybe she would translate something. A novel by Claude Ollier who is not well represented in English. She would make some proposals to the specialized press. Whether anything worth her while would sell.

They ate in the student cafeteria in the union, across the mall from the library.

You're looking good, Warshawski.

Yeah, Reiva agreed. Working the speed bag. Living on broccoli. I can't afford to eat anything else until I get paid, anyway. Maybe I should have been storing up fat instead.

This stuff here will do that.

The food in the student cafeteria was not plentiful if you couldn't eat pizza or french fries or meat and mashed potato plates with a side of chartruese-colored peas. Four kinds of packaged salads, two dressings (ranch and italian), or a sub sandwich except the ones with salami and bacon. There was a soggy ersatz enchilada. Reiva missed picante southwestern food. Everything here was under-seasoned.

Well, Simone said philosophically, it doesn't beat that British pizza I had once in Boston. Cheddar cheese on a pizza?

There's pineapple and teriaki sauce.

God. Give me a margarita.

I don't think the students have a license for that, Simone.

No I mean the margarita tart — a crust with mustard and sliced tomatoes.

No mozzarella?

It's the owe-riginal, girl. None of this Neapolitan finger food.

Look, there's that guy again.

Where.

Over there, behind the... never mind.

How many courses have they given you? Simone unwisely wanted to know.

Six?

What? Yike!

And you?

Um, two. The third didn't fill.

There was an embarrassed silence then, full of unvoiced marxist mutterings about the class system and the relations between peasants and aristocrats. Simone would make three times what Reiva did for a third of the work.

Reiva looked around the drafty, echoing commons. Some art had recently been hung up but it didn't change much about the place. She'd rather eat in a grubby scribbled-over place that was important to its citizens else why would they scribble on it. Simone restarted the conversation.

When Gary was a young prof, she said, and all I had was a couple of private lessons — this was during the eighties recession, salaries were going nowhere — we ate liver and onions.

Ick. Whatever for?

It was comfort food for him. His mother had cooked it. *She* liked spam sandwiches.

C-rations.

Gary's father had had to eat that in the army and couldn't stand it. Liver's all right if you don't overcook it. Se we were just getting by, Gary and I, we could only go shopping on payday because when the bills were paid there was nothing left. Liver, you know, is something that doesn't keep. It has to be fresh. So liver and onions was payday food.

Simone stirred her bowl of chile, seeming to remember. The cracker she had dropped into it swelled up and broke into little white fleshy bits. She made them go away.

I hate this work, Reiva said after a long silence. You don't get no respect.

An expression of terrible agony flitted across Simone's face. Don't — She stuttered, recovered herself. Don't fret, it's all going smash anyway.

Hmm.

I learned over the summer that's a vatic noise, Simone remarked. *Hmm.* Us girls use it a lot to reassure each other we're really listening.

Why is it vatic?

Beats me. Means poetic, oracular. Norse word. Origin the frenzy of madness.

Reiva crooked one eyebrow.

You have a regular dialect of hmms, Simone said. Big vocabulary.

Snort. Reiva swept the barny room with her sandwich, sending a piece of ham flying. Simone suppressed a Japanese giggle of embarrassment. This was Serious Stuff.

See these kids, Reiva was saying. You look at these kids, it's like we're in some camp. We spend all day pushed up against the fence hanging off the barbed wire wishing we were free.

Reiva craned her neck. There's Bo and Derek, she said. One day they'll be gone, like leaves, and our skinny wasted bodies will be lying in the mud by that fence.

Simone and Reiva watched for a time the flâneurie going on around their small table.

Simone, is it the same leaf that comes back next year? Or is it a different one?

Are you getting menopausal, girl?

No. Yes. I'm too young for that, Simone.

Well what's happened to your famous aloofity?

It's like a camp, I tell you. We stare through the barbed wire at the sleek, well-fed people and feel our own skinny bodies and we try to imagine what it's like to be out there walking around. We stare, minds empty, tongues hanging. What do you suppose they can be thinking out there?

What did you think about when you were twenty, Reiva?

Sex. Are *you* menopausal?

I don't know. Maybe.

Is that what was wrong? Last summer?

Wrong? Oh...

I wasn't paying attention, was I, Simone?

No.

Simone continued to stir her chile. Slowly the plastic spoon went around and around. She hadn't eaten any of it. The white spoon was stained chile red.

Gary wants to invite some students for Thanksgiving dinner this year.

Someone in particular?

No. Probably. You know the ones who don't go home. The international ones. Orphans. Little match girls.

She tiddlywinked the spoon, which fell onto the floor.

Or so he says.

Oh... I see. It's not that, then?

What is? Not, Simone added as an afterthought.

Are you going to eat that?

TOR

You see, Mr Blake don't dirt.
— Kate

The Chair was angry.

I'll come straight to the point, he said. I'm told you've made a complaint against me to the Graduate School

Yes, Reiva replied. She was equally angry, but herself had a difficulty keeping the brittle edge out of her voice, which grated a little as a consequence.

Dr Tor talked smoothly on. Reiva's gaze wandered the room. Polished nutbrown wood, silver, a few tchotchkes, two nice pottery bowls, a paperweight of petrified wood, a desk fan (silent), an in-tray of solid black plastic which looked as if it had had quite a lot of designery. A window, casement, open, facing north. Demure light even in mid-April, and the faint sounds of student conversations on the mall below, but what they said unknown, obscured by the Chair's voice.

A complaint of discrimination, he said, levelly.

You're not treating Saleem fairly. For Jake's sake, if not another reason.

Dr Greidel. An admonishment. She was not allowed to call him Jake.

I suggested to him, the Chair said — meaning to Jake — that Singh's committee would not approve his work regardless of the deference due to Dr Greidel himself as committee chair, and that this would reflect badly on himself and on the department. Dr Greidel seemed to think there was something there worth the struggle, but convinced no one. That dispute has been set aside.

Buried.

Dr Tor sighed, as benignly as he might.

Laid to rest, shall we say?

No. Not buried while Saleem is left to twist in the wind.

What a banal image. Something wrong with it too, perhaps the hint that if the wind would go down the twisting would stop and the body could hang without offense. That an untwisted victim might recover, go away maybe wiser.

As if it were the wind's fault. And by whom left twisting? Do we do that anymore? Heads rotting on pikes at the gates? Probably somewhere. There's always somewhere. Perhaps she should mention the unquiet ghost of Jake Greidel as well?

The dissertation committee is the Chair's prerogative, as she knew as a victim if not yet senior enough to perpetrate on herself.. The committee's engine is fueled by risk aversion; in Saleem's case the fear of a lawsuit, of some unseemly claim which Saleem might make concerning racial bias. For anyone who knew Saleem, an absurd caution. Tor recognized the absurdity but preferred the expedient offered to entrench himself. To dictate to Jake would not have been seemly. But with Jake out of the way Saleem's prospects could be effectively blocked simply by allowing the succession of the committee's now senior member. With a committee controlled by Professor Lott, Saleem was doomed. He would have to negotiate.

Now here was this monkey-wrench sitting in his office with her complaint in her lap like an old woman on the way to market with a chicken. She was no threat to his power, but his self-esteem was hurt. He did not like to be seen as a tyrant. Seen by himself not least.

He was supposed to have recused himself, apparently. Bah.

For Reiva the question was not what she was owed but rather what she owed to Jake. She felt no particular solidarity with Saleem. They were fellow supplicants, wanting the right to work, she for tenure and he for certification. Jake had defended both of them. He needed to be paid back.

An itchy feeling had been gaining intensity all spring term. It was there as a tadpole already when she turned the knob of Jake's office door, swimming in the effluvia of presentiment.

Lott wanted nothing to do with Saleem's dissertation. He didn't like it, he told her. He thought it could not be rescued, and he couldn't see why the boy should be allowed to defend the indefensible. He was in agreement with the Chair. The integrity of the department would be preserved and they would be rid of Saleem to boot.

To boot, she thought. What does that mean? What role could boots have once played to suggest such a trope?

It was a Saleemish question. It was catching, that way of thought. Maybe that's why they all buried their noses in their hankies as they did.

Professor Lott was a fat man, not quite obese but with that soft white layer under the skin that people in northern climates have who are too much indoors, whose bodies are not busy enough. Most people who move to the desert lose that in a few months. Not so Lott.

On a Friday in March just before spring break, when no one was about except Ariel Trent, she encountered Lott in the office exploring his mailbox. L being further along the row than D but still at the same height, a bit above nose level (Lott was a short man). He peered into the open tube, one extended finger preceding his bifocal eye, lightly touching the dubious papers as if knowing there were no valentines for him.

Reiva intruded a remark. Lott sighed and remarked in turn, the two exchanged some further unspoken and hence not very specific information, and Lott went out with the pile of journals, yellow inter-campus envelopes, flyers, business mail, and stapled student papers which had been in his box. Some of them he stuffed into the pocket of his coat, a dark blue gabardine which that morning he had mated with khaki chinos and a sort of blue tie which had the look of being a comfort to him. His movement toward the door was something between a shuffle and a glide, not quite a sidle, removing himself as modestly and inoffensively as might be.

Reiva turned back to the rank of mail cubbies, encountering Ariel Trent's gaze thereby. Trent's office was the pair to Tor's, occupying the short side of the department's space to Tor's long side. A counter divided the remaining floor into a public vestibule with the mail and a couple of plastic chairs on which to wait, and a staff space behind the counter where Ariel's minions plied their keyboards, re-directed students elsewhere, took phone calls. These were all at lunch and Ariel herself had come out to have a look in the files and mind the counter.

Between them passed a wordless glance of sisterly complicity.

Reiva had no idea what Ariel thought about Jake's suicide, about this subsequent squabble, or indeed about anything at all other than her need, as the Chair's assistant, for discretion.

So what could that have consisted of, that complicity?

TOR'S SONG

We talked about that wretched boy's thesis
which could never be approved of. Jake and I,
one Friday afternoon at the faculty club
where Jake never went, but I suppose
he could have been coddling me out.

Not out of place or conspicuous in those battered boots
and vest of many pockets since we all dress like that
here, sometimes. Jake was never out of place
in his life. Some were only places he hadn't lived in
for years. Now a bit strange, where he walked

quietly, hoping to go unnoticed.
The waiter was discreet (Jim it was,
I've known him for years) who brought our drinks.
A whiskey sour, and Jake's espresso.
The necessary kissing of glass and cup,

a wordless toast. Jake I said listen
you can't go on with this. Your boy
is not going to get by the committee.
He did listen, not as they're saying
now, that I was false to him.

Why would I? She says I disrespect him.
Why would I? That's not how it goes
if you go by the rules
the committee is made up
of people who know about that.

That boy says (I've heard him; I wasn't to)
that it's all monkey talk. Listen
(and he did listen, not what they're saying
now, that I stabbed him) Jake listen,
you're wrong about this. Another coffee?

Your boy, Jake, is all over the board.
But who knows what Jake thought?
Maybe it was just monkey writing to him too.
He was wrong about that.
But Jake was always inscrutable, a bit.

I think, Jake began — I think — chewed his lip,
fished out of his vest pocket a coin to absorb his nerve,
one of those brass dollars you only get at the post office
because they have to use them, don't they?
Judas money, they're saying.

That's stupid. Jake's idea was
— oh I don't know, Jake was not a practical man
sometimes. A fine historian, too fond of pastiche.
Pastiche is not a method. But we got on well.
I asked Jim to bring us more drink.

Jake was explaining the geography of it.
This was some years ago — North Beach he meant,
where Jake was. Degree from Cal, fifty-eight.
Saleem bowed his head over a map of the city.
Here, and here. Jake laid his pencil's point delicately where.

Jack Spicer's papers are at the Bancroft
you see Rexroth's maybe the City Lights.
Jake thought the idea for City Lights came of seeing
Frogé's place in Paris, when Ferlinghetti was there.
Ought to have asked him. Before he was dead, Lawrence

is, and now this boy turned up one day
with an idea about artists' enclaves he'd picked up
somewhere maybe Jane Jacobs,
and someone told him about Jake
had lived there. Known everyone. He hadn't

of course. Only more than some others.
So send the boy. To a conference there,
to the Bancroft, put him on the bookshop theory.
See what he thinks of Spicer, or
Gary Snyder who was that Japhy in Kerouac's book.

Go look at the coffee shop or maybe a nightclub
where Howl was read out.
Not there now, of course, like anything else.
Burroughs the last. Jake laid his pencil down.
There would be more trips. More money for
the Village, Vienna, a summer in Paris,

but nothing would ever be better
than Columbus Avenue in Jake's time.
The cold wind, the smell of fish and bread,
enough for everyone. The People lived
where they could. Weekends anyway

Jake could sit behind the steamed-over window
of that Italian place where everybody went,
Trieste was it. A bistro table with spaghetti, the street.
after coffee, some reading or maybe a party
in a couple of rooms over a Chinese laundry

a girl told him about, too small a place,
too many people, black, smoking —
he never saw the Chinese girl there.
After coffee again, fish, bread, a cold wind
from that island with its little yellow windows —

Alcatraz. One night he stood a long time on some pier
where the prison light streaked the water so black
you lost your eye and thought to stretch out your hand
to touch what you could not. There were people
who'd done things undreamed of.

No nightclub half a mile of this wharf
but still the sound of a saxophone
coming from somewhere. Saxophones sound
tormented. No matter what you play on them
it sounds tormented.

The thing's impossible Jake, I said. Your boy —
why does he want to go on? Or you —
not knowing at the time, of course,
that such a question might mean more
than it appeared to.

Impossible, I said. This digression
on slow movies for instance.
Last Year At Marienbad clipped
into an essay on movies. How does that fit?
I see why he might want to explain beat despair,

of course. But what is explained by a theory of the movie made
afterwards? What do beatniks know about spaghetti westerns? The
boy's astute, Jake said.
    But he explained nothing. inscrutable as always. Why
    did he go and do that? I don't understand.

Astute — as if that explained anything
about how to live. Whys and wherefors
are so much prattle. They poison you,
stop you cutting your losses and moving on,
Jake. Your boy should be not so astute.

We talked about that wretched boy, Reiva
and I. Better at the club, but you can't
go with a woman these days alone.
So between us this desk. A desk bare,
of privilege, with space for that wretched boy,

between us. Without the usual drink, bare
of blue beads even, which the Indians liked so much.
Uncovered by any hospitality her words were plain
enough. Wampum. Propitiation for Jake
and that boy. We'd already spat in public.

Wary me. Weary by now
of the whole thing. Demurely
crossed ankles, waiting
for me to say something hurtful.
Neat in gray wool. Empty hands

neat. She thought there was some link
between Jake and what we did for the boy.
Justice, I said. What's that? A chimera
at best a dangerous marshlight.
Words disguised, softened firstly.

The abyss which confines us to appearances,
Plutarch says, divine justice being slow
as it is, it's hard to know who to blame.
She raised her hand at that but then,
thinking better, let fall.

Best do nothing so? she said.
Biting the words. Hardly that,
but not claiming so much as to be doing
right. Only the best with what can be doing.
Why make pointless sacrifices?

As Jake did, perhaps. But who knows
what was on his mind? He was wrong to do it
nevertheless. Indulgence,
and on the other hand chaos.
Messy, breathless, devotional

chaos. She thought that wrong of course.
Fastidious as always seem who want the scales
driven down by weight, heavy with justice,
but not judicious. A luxury, a whirlwind
of words, delicate and prudish.

Words contemptuous, hateful to repeat,
all face foreclosed. What had she been thinking?
Or afterwards, when Ariel discreetly
pointed out another obligation due. You understand.
Did she then? Ariel certainly heard.

No scholar she said, I was no
scholar. Perhaps that's so. Not one
who can judge. But whoever said
I was? Whoever said —
we wanted only a certain

order. That's all. Left in a rage
probably beside herself, or perhaps
with the certain melancholy of the powerless.
One wants to weep for — oh, for all
those who seek out knowledge.

We all want more blue beads.
The alternative is silence, which is easy
when you live alone. Professor Reiva
— or Reiva I should say, less the prudish don
accused and more in kindness — is alone.

What will she, then? The movies, perhaps
the neighbors are giving a party.
It rained that night, one of our
gully-washers. No portent there.
What god weeps for any of us?

A father in some godforsaken place
— Syracuse I heard, but not that
of Archimedes, who died in battle too.
Rather the mundane place, besieged only by snow.
Could she go there. Not as it was

forty years ago. Leafy hillside, shops
on Euclid Avenue I suppose in every campus town
in the world there is a Euclid Avenue.
Orderly. Prof's kid loose all summer,
those days we didn't worry about that

yet, every empty lot a hideout I suppose
girls have hideouts, don't they?
It rains, every day, the clouds close
so you could open them with your hands,
like pushing aside the packing in a box

that came in the mail from Grandma,
letting the cold water out.
The air smelled of wet leaves and maybe
smoke. Deep in the breath.
Even in August you need a coat sometimes.

Music like soap bubbles from the windows
of student shacks, garages, up back stairs.
The Beach Boys — she'd never seen a beach
in her life, much less known yet
what that all meant. A lot of stones

on the shore of Lake Ontario maybe,
and the water way too cold to swim in.
It was all an affair, they said, of your life
with all these the heroes
and villains. Guinevere, they said

Guinevere, who had green eyes,
like you. Lady, like you.
But you were, I guess, only six
or seven then, too young
to know about that.

Your mother taught Latin, they say. Rope's end
of a time when any language at all was valuable.
Well. In that room the people come and go.
All mines are worked out eventually.
I know about that. The stuff

collects in tailings, lungs, water from clouds,
backs into the ground. He died at a stroke,
they say, spoiling the orange year.
Moved to better-colored digs — green
even in winter. More rain than ever.

And yellow not of sunlight but old oak leaves
fallen, trodden on the wet cement,
making the way to class slippery
with their dead hands. But maybe then
you didn't know about that, green you were.

There's a cemetery next to campus there,
a place for professors' kids to hide.
That's not as common as Euclid I suppose.
The learned and the dead make odd neighbors
you would have thought. But no portent.

No odder than herding the old people
into the desert, letting them die in places swarming
with golf courses like we do here.
The cost of freedom, they said, was buried
when you were a green-eyed girl

and the smell of wet smoke filled the air.
They promised the earth would swallow you,
which is not a promise with much risk,
or even true time was. Lay your body down.
All that is learned will be lost.

It was the boy's idea that Jake be cast
as Grendel. He meant himself of course.
The outsider, lurking there beyond the light,
an imaginary horror to scare us awake
tomorrow morning. Still the goad's role

hurts. The knife's urging draws real blood.
Foucault's visionaries are still madmen
as the boy says — truly, we wouldn't like it
to know that dirty man on the subway who talks
to himself is a painter with kids in school.

Beowulf's the better role. That's me.
Like Ishmael I get to tell the story my way
while that mother's son has breathed out
his soul. I suppose he had one. Why else
would we have wanted him to scourge us?

We forget the dam, the dragon, the broken sword,
the cowards who betray old age, the end
inevitable. That comes afterwards. Fifty years
count for nothing in the algebra of heroes and villains.
Who's this Hrothgar? Naught but Beowulf writ small.

Strutting his bloody drama in a flea circus
the easier to see what it means. Don't look
to Beowulf for exaltation.
You want Grendel for that. We forget
the other meaning of sublime, a gas. The soul

is thought to sublimate at last, pass off as breath
because that makes smart poetry, but bad ends
and bad breath are inevitable
for anyone who enjoys his food.
Tearing out the monster's haunch,

mouth smeared with grease, that was the time
he should have made an end. That was the time
to renounce another dreary fifty years
of pointless wassail and a sword broke
in the guts to show for it. Smart man

that Jake. We broke our bread a few times.
I mean Jake, with his wife, but not often.
It's difficult to seat the single man, coupled
with some dowager or an awful floozy
out of the dustbin. I faced the table alone.

Those times, the hostess was the best woman.
Homely, podgy even. Not aged well. Dour
of mouth. She and Jake had fought for years
there under the swamp's oily skin, a life
we didn't see. Only some viscous bubbles,

the mud sloping away like a shrug,
that's all. Perhaps a hag, as the poem says,
but powerful — Jake's arm was forged
strong enough for fabled swords they say,
once upon a time, rope's end of that time.

She'd played a role in politics I'm told.
Behind the scenes as always, founded
a party or something. Neither of them
public people. Small dinners at home
every week, now only twice a year.

The food simple — peasant fare.
A stew perhaps salmon, potatoes
prepared in country ways, rough red wine,
rough talk — one left that house sated.
I stopped on the step for a grateful yawn,

moonlight strong against my face, less full
than once, not knowing how is had become so.
Life's bounties are spread in strange ways
and taken back with the same indifference
to what we make of them.

So: I must needs play Beowulf so he
can essay Grendel, the victim?
Where once the hero now naught,
only a whining fable of oppression
or an ecological caution: if you choose

to live unwisely near the swamp
you will be eaten by the swamp thing.
How to compare her, neat in gray wool
trousers, neat hands, neat arguments,
to that hag? A neat brittle stick.

They wonder what I do nights. I'm never seen
about, at movies, lectures, shopping.
Thumping down a glass in the mead hall
with the other Geats. Instead I sulk
in my tent, more Achilles than Beowulf.

It's ludicrous. I'll not costume myself so.
That I, a fastidious old man,
should be seen smeared with blood,
found ripping monsters limb from limb.
There are politer ways to rule.

We could do without fabled swords,
without these purple griefs. Without
this crying down of small losses. Without
these testy rebellions and refusals, without
resort to bloody arms at slight excuse.

All reason is slight, a brittle stick
with which to poke the mud, feeling
for monsters. Revenge
must needs have reasons: history
my own, captured for servitude

to what is only ego, Grendel the excuse
for bloodied men to buy grand death.
Monkey behavior.
Leave the poor beast alone.
Would you befriend a bear with torment?

Cure a snake of biting?
We have no need of Grendels,
neither of monkeys, but we have them
anyway. If you will play at war
you must needs to go unburied

outside the gate. And so he sat up
late, rolling an empty glass along its weighted base.
A glass which once held tea, the history of it
still on his tongue, not so faint as the Greeks.
Green tea prevents cancer they say.

No pleasure remains; only death.
There is no power but in death.
There is no ambition but to cheat death.
Let go the glass, which settled fatly
in the barren middle of his desk

where it waited, smugly he thought,
for the next gust of feeling.
He shivered, closed his eyes,
his narrow shadowed face raised
to where the light would be. If it were so.

Prospero then, to his Caliban.
A nicer part for me, with cleaner hands.
And another mother's son for him.
Hie me to the book shelves then to renew
acquaintance with my original.

Powerful place the library. I can see why
someone would like to work here. Someone
who I mean was doing the work of this place.
Not us hedgehogs. The librarian time was
at once weening dangerous, o'erreaching

to hedgehog eye. Prospero: the magus.
Caliban we know. We're sick of Caliban
and his fashionable ramshackle concerns.
Rather he who has wreaked much on this island
but also set the winds about it to protect.

That's an old trope, Circe's eden.
Poor Prospero never invented that.
The inverse of island fever, medieval visions
of a truer world of love and sunshine
somewhere else, out there beyond the scrim,

the storm. That was Jake's territory. Here
rows of young Prosperos learn their craft.
Well, one or two of them anyway.
Friday afternoons for fieldwork, hocus pocus
in bar and gym, jinking practice battles.

I have the place alone, and a stranger too
among these shelves of Donne and Sydney
who am more apt to dig in Hollinger boxes
and ledgers of Phelps and Dodge, looking
for mere copper. Reach me down

a copy. Some old one, tattered, arthritic
not your muscular youth buffed out with notes
and dressed in uniform black, just another
soldier in the set. Something to hand.
Here. A 1938 schoolroom book of plays.

Could be my little brother had I one.
Borne off to anatomize, stately as Buck Mulligan
on a salver, or the Baptist's head
of Moreau, to a table piled with bodies
of earlier experiments still unburied.

When we were young, this brother and I
were kept in the dark with others of the undead.
A word of curious invention, undead. Taking back
what is offered, no sunshine world
out there, just discarded scrimshaw

with a taste for catacombs, we wandered
the passages with our rushlights
held up to peer at what lay in the niches.
Nowadays the sunshine bites the mind
rather than the genitals.

Nowadays light beclouds the senses,
not the blood. The undead, my brother and I
born 1938, our old tombs dug up,
lie Indian-fashion in the air.
No longer moldy and putrid, just dried up.

Once I was master of secrets, dark knowledge
which has crumbled like the dry earth of a corpse
brought under hand again. Now Prospero
studies his formulae another place,
an older building truly dark

his wind made not by gesture of hand
but by intricate machine.
Blows straight, not back on itself.
I see my original was a quondam ruler too,
retired to this place to pout and strut.

We'll overlook this farce about Miranda
and her two monkeys. Doubled all I see,
my sprite with that clod of earth
who fears naught, earth as he is,
to whom we are only noises soon unheard.

Doubled too Prospero and his brother
usurper, lies within my power now
to bury or not. Shall I be generous?
He was. I'm not sure I can.
My powers are only noise and wind.

Making my way out I'm hailed
by old acquaintance, the Dean of this place.
Tiny woman with an elvish face
and powers of her own. Another castaway
with that selfsame hand and eye

to hold you. Bah! I've had enough of Jake
and his boy and this corpse-breath
of memory. I've started to smell
myself. I pass my hand before the glass
to wipe it clean of mist, a gesture

she may interpret as she likes, and pass on.
Out on the brick plaza, blocked now
on its fourth side by that waiting grave,
already hot. The bricks readily give back the sun.
The light stares, struck mute by what it sees to come.

To lunch. My food taken today by need
amid the raucous stinking younglings
which we undertake to civilize. Or did.
Now we hope for less, but
maybe for what we know is done.

A hamburger, I think, with them.
Ketchup and mustard. Onion rings.
But the cafeteria too is Friday quiet.
I sit close by a table of three girls,
an old ghoul absorbing their heat.

I listen to these chattering Mirandas,
eyes by rule and custom kept away,
seeing only the dead meat on my plate
supposed to be food. Or is that too easy
a trope? Bathetic, bitter, unlearned?

We must be subtle. We sneer
at these children and their monkey talk
of clothes and television, sex, their words
crude, vatic, numbered small.
But must we would bite, must we do.

Reiva Derwent doesn't fret for me
but for her own soul, immortal she thinks
but delicate withal, needing the right
as the corpus needs dead meat.
Older than me that way if not wizened

that is, made so by wizards.
There's a reason why I study what is brought out of the earth,
what is brought up from underground by sweat, by dynamite,
by grinding machines powered by money and greed
and the desire to feel hard smooth metal bright under my thumbs.

How the form of life could be passed on
from one creature to the next, magnificent
an idea to make my catholic grandfather cringe
so uncatholic and small yet a trifle
to the next, which we have only glimpsed

out of the corner of our eye,
which is the only way to see these things.
Peek out like an old man at a woman
who is not yet maturely bodied.
Unbodied woman, Reiva Derwent

died years ago, unmourned on her small island,
left to Caliban at last, those noisy spirits fled
to wherever old ideas go. She should know
there is always more wind where that came from.
A hurricane of it.

In June my Trent's son, the bitten one,
by a spider, sickened and died.
As with Jake, I never knew why.
It was summer. We had all gone.
Trent was left to pursue her grief alone.

She's a woman you would have thought
of conventional views. Enter Ariel, invisible,
playing solemn music. But no,
we are men of sin, who destiny
hath made mad. We roar

like mountain lions Shakespeare says
not knowing those silent cats.
Enter Ariel, invisible. Would she not be free?
But no, not wind but tree
her destiny hath made mad.

Are you not afraid? I ask,
to think on earth and dust?
But no. A certain bitterness
of woe and gall damps the air
and hastens the rot.

Free of all that, memory and thought
returns to natural state,
the electric spark passed off to ground.
Unseemly would she rage and cry
purple vows, yet unconsolable.

No freedom when the sin's as deep as that.
Out of that dark well drew calm
forgiveness unsmiling but so broad
some thought it uncanny. So he died,
leaving yet another solitary mourner.

He died at the first of summer
which with us begins a brute season
of general death. No soft airs or gentle
light. One stays indoors, hides from that
truth, our inglenook an air-conditioned sleep.

Ariel went north to heal the bite.
We all have family somewhere north of here.
Imaginary sisters who can put us on ice
until the fever's gone, wash, watch.
Peopling the place to breathlessness.

Just two unchinked rooms, a porch with chairs
from which to overlook the forest.
A stove for heat, to burn the bodies
of the companionable trees. Rare place
now, when even hermits live in villages.

Generations in hand that place, but too rough
to stay long. She was soon back.
And the other one? Does he rub along? He takes it
hard, she said. You get through the sullen years,
look toward a genial, civil time

which doesn't come. Snatched away. He worries me.
Gone back to work. it's true, but Bob's a carpenter.
He'll cut his hand off, she said. He'll get to brood
and not watch what he's doing. He worries me.
I don't think that wound in him will heal.

Just crust over. She sighed and rubbed round
the knuckle of her little finger. Arthritis.
And myself? Would I too go away?
A week, I said. A beach house in Encinitas
rented as I often do, saving more ambitious trips

to go when others don't. I haven't been to Europe
in years. To the Rhine, or even wretched Paris
like that boy and his artists' edens.
My habits fixed one season to the next
as she knows. She has my calendar.

But she not so. She quit. The keeper of my days
took her vacation and vanished. After years
of summers she did not come back. Like Jake
she went, was gone, leaving some girl
not yet bodied out, not to be looked on.

We never knew how it was with Jake, either.
Never knew what emollient had dried up
and caused the wheels to squeak and bump.
They say I was rude over her son,
bitten by one of the Old Ones.

But you don't know what might intrude
on a person's privacy, or trample feelings
unthinkingly. To say nothing might be best
sometimes. Of course it were best
the world be ordered for my convenience.

It's not. We all can't leave the stage
the moment finely judged to be the last
of our powers, but some applause still left.
Someone must be left behind to clap.
One shill, claquer, banging his hands.

The beach house rented long ago
could not be put off. My old skin
takes sun badly now, so I keep away
from it, take a large umbrella on the sand
or just sit on my balcony alone.

There's not much surf here. Not like my childhood
beaches of stubborn rock and spume
spit five times my height above.
I shouldn't say stubborn; they were rocks
after all. Rocks are like that.

And this pacific lake is sublime enough for me
without those histrionics.
Better in fact an anaesthetic —
no I shouldn't say that. Nor sedative.
What do I mean? Jake used to talk

about merging with the great something
or other. There's sand everywhere.
In the pizza, mixed with the tea leaves
in the bottom of the cup, the toothbrush.
My skin's always sticky with salt.

Sometimes you wonder, I suppose
everyone does from time to time,
if maybe you've got it wrong, so wrong
you're as clueless as a rock on the beach
piddled on by the tide, forever.

PART II

HOSTAGES

ROGER

There is nothing too little for so little a creature as man.
— Samuel Johnson

Saleem was sharing a garden apartment on Commonwealth Avenue with a somewhat younger man, a church organist whose day job was to run the library at a school for deaf children. The school's playing fields fronted the other side of the avenue; the buildings stood in a grove of eucalyptus some ways behind that. One never saw the children on the street. If they were to go somewhere it would be in parents' cars or on a schoolbus expedition.

Roger was the man's name. Roger was not himself deaf. Not everyone who worked at the Penfield School was. This, Roger said, was a cause of some friction with the children and their parents, who inclined to identity politics on this point. The truth was there were simply not enough deaf people to go around, or if there were, Penfield didn't pay enough to get them. Roger had had to learn to sign, that was all. It was a condition of employment. Now, when he talked, especially in crowded or noisy places, it was always with a surreptitious movement of his hands. A tic. Like muttering.

Roger's working life was otherwise kept in the background. When he had been especially ill-treated he would tell some unflattering story on the school's Principal, who Saleem gathered was a pompous bully. But then, when things went well, one never heard about the man, who was probably only a bit overweening. His name was King, unfortunately for that hypothesis. Behind his back he went by sobriquet as The Kink, in the nasalized speech of deaf people. The Vice Principal was a dykeish woman referred to in Roger's stories as "Woody." These facts were about the sum of knowledge concerning Roger. He was not content.

The weekend after Saleem was jailed as a terrorist Roger got up a small dinner party to celebrate his release. They were six.

Besides Roger and Saleem there were the Jakobys, Sofka and
her husband James, and Bill. Bill's companion had moved out a
year before, transferred by the government to the Middle East
where his proclivities were a daily threat to his life, so Bill had
brought along a friend whom no one knew, perhaps not even
Bill. Somehow this fellow, a lanky shy man, never got
introduced, so that as the evening went on and it became more
and more awkward to find out what his name was, various
subterfuges had to be adopted and he began to be addressed
mostly in the third person as "B.F." for Bill's Friend, or not
addressed at all.

The Jakobys had a child, an ungendered infant which they
had left with a sitter. Because of this baby, Roger had seen very
little of James in recent months, a friendship already endangered
in any case by marriage. Roger and James secured a corner on
the sofa by the open window where, barricaded by pillows, they
could have a natter about the continuing failure of James's film
scripts to get noticed. Saleem was left to set the table. There was
very little to do, actually. Pour wine. A lasagna was finishing in
the oven, there was a salad waiting to be dressed at table, garlic
bread to be toasted. Soft evening air fragrant with blue gum
breathed in, an odor which would always evoke California for
Saleem since so many of the highway rest stops on the border
are planted with gum trees. Occasionally the clicking of heels
on the sidewalk. Sofka was talking to Bill, leaving the
lugubrious BF to Saleem.

The two men were of a height, BF the pudgier by twenty
pounds or so. His skin had the sheen and color of an unbaked
pie shell. They had made small talk for some minutes when
Saleem noticed BF's empty wine glass — in fact, it seemed
never to have been filled. Saleem found a bottle of red for him.
This loosened tongues and BF, who was mysteriously well-
informed about everyone, asked after Saleem's being clapped
into jail.

Nothing will come of it, I suppose? Quietly forgotten.
Unless you want to sue?

God no. You might as well have some incurable disease. You'd never be done with that.

Mm. BF swirled the wine around his glass, tipped it to one side and the other, gestures reminiscent of Roger's muttering with his hands. Saleem glanced across the room. James was being intense, twisting up a corner of the orange pillow.

You aren't aggrieved? BF asked. His manner was a bit antique, as if he had learned English from a book.

Damned angry, yes, Saleem acknowledged. But I'll soon swallow that. It's their karma.

Mm. Not as if you were wearing a turban or something. A caftan. You don't even look Arabic.

BF made a gesture about his face, perhaps indicating a beard or something else shiekly, difficult to imagine on his Mandarin features. Saleem turned to fetch the lasagna.

Can I help?

Just pop that garlic bread into the broiler, will you, after I get this out?

Saleem glanced again, resentfully, at Roger and concluded he needed to be rescued. Do you want to do the salad? he called, and yes, Roger hastened to do it. They all found chairs, sorting themselves back into couples, with Roger and Saleem at the head and foot. James had contrived to get the corner beside Roger, which put Saleem between Sofka and Bill.

These two were not well matched, Bill being mournful and cynical while Sofka was always bright and full of unwanted advice. That was the way she drove James on, no doubt, but against Bill her coloring looked fluorescent. Naive, narcissistic. Saleem kept the peace.

The conversation at dinner was nothing much. There was an undertext of complaint. At Roger's end James was starting in again to whine about recent movies, while BF ate in silence, taking small fastidious bites between sips of wine, dabbing at his mouth and fingers with the napkin. Everyone was more or less aggrieved by some deprivation or other and tried to work that in like putting english on a bowling ball after you've thrown it.

Still, they were becoming merry. James brought out a bottle of sherry as companion to his earlier house gift, and Roger presented a dessert of cannoli from the Italian pastry shop downtown. There was an exchange of funny stories on the theme of disastrous misunderstanding. But the evening was ruined by someone's turning on the television to find out the weather forecast.

On the news was a story about another hostage in Iraq threatened with beheading by a group of masked bandits. A picture came on, showing the shackled and sweating miscreant kneeling between four men with covered faces wearing bandoliers and carrying automatic rifles. Everyone stared.

My god! Bill screamed. It's Harris!

Bill's chair fell over backward, knocking down a lamp, and Bill himself, feet entangled, smashed onto the table, dragging half its materiel with him to the floor. Thrashing about there among the food and broken glass, trying to get up but knotted into the tablecloth and hindered by the others' useless help, shouting out the name of Harris all the while, Bill was gradually calmed and laid out on the sofa. It didn't help that he had drunk quite a lot of wine. His skin was flushed, bringing out the freckles and making his reddish hair darker.

Harris, it came out after a few days, was a person known to Bill through his meditation group. *Known to* was however regarded as inadequate. Harris had disappeared one day with no explanation. Bill had asked around, but no one was forthcoming. Now it seemed that Harris had been intending to help out with the reconstruction of Iraq somehow, a rather feckless desire since he had no useful skills for the purpose.

In days to come Bill would email friends in various embassies who he knew through his companion, but there was little to be done. The friends were sympathetic in an emoticon way. All were powerless. The bandits wanted some vague, impossible thing, and when it was not forthcoming they made no further demands and poor Harris faded out of memory, neither dead nor still alive.

Bill and BF faded away also. Their ways seldom crossed Roger's and he did not seek after them. James showed up now and then, always without Sofka. He was not adjusting to an infant regimen. At these times Saleem would go out, or to his bedroom.

Tonight James was fulminating about Godfrey Reggio's *Qatsi* trilogy. Surely he can't be claiming, said James querulously, that it's these people at the beginning who've got it right. Lookit. They're half starved, they're carrying these heavy loads of stuff around, they're *barefoot* for god's sake. And why is it that Westernized peoples are always to blame? Why is it that *our* lives are the ones out of balance? Some of us know better, surely. Does living *with the grain* mean this donkey's life?

Well... Roger began mildly.

And there's the visual rhetoric, James insisted, poking Roger in the breastbone. The more critical Reggio is the uglier the images are. It's manipulative.

I thought it was *all* beautiful, myself.

And what exactly is wanted? Is being sought? What would *you* call life in balance, Roger?

This time James was not so quick to pounce, or erupt rather, giving Roger time to think.

Well... I would want it to be slow, with enough time for doing everything the way it should, with attention. I would like it to be regular, not regimented you see, but without the threat of surprises. I mean that I would like to decide for myself what next to do, what counts as important. I would like —

Three wishes, That's all you get.

Startled, Roger acquiesced after a moment. Yes, he said. I suppose others would say differently. Have a different list. A certain amount of agreement would be necessary. Of coming to agree.

Oh, as in *My Dinner With André*, or *In the Heat Of the Night* maybe.

Movies, James.

I only know about movies, wailed James. I only know that our lives are out of balance and that going to live low down to the ground without running water or a decent toilet is not going to fix that. I want to live like the Austrians, who know to put a respectable doorknob on a tool shed. Not this tin gimcrackery we have.

You would have liked William Morris I imagine.

Dammit, who?

Never mind.

Gimcrackery, James spat.

Roger brought home a stray cat. It was a juvenile, a skinny black shorthair with long legs and a limp. It had scratched him pretty badly but was too weak to resist and went rigid under his coat. Already it was eating his guts. When he got home it was so stiff he thought it was dead. Roger laid it on the floor; as soon as it felt the ground again it was gone almost with a pop and hid under the couch. Roger coated his scratches with neosporin and went to make dinner.

They didn't see it for a month. The food and water they left out disappeared in the night, and cat droppings appeared in the corners, sometimes in the cat box where it scratched so vigorously that the bathroom floor was always completely coated in grit. It's digestion permanently ruined by eating garbage, probably noxious, it outgassed a constant rank stink. Saleem mumbled a remark about the methane torch on the landfill. Roger named it Asparagus because of the smell. After a while it was calm enough to box up for the vet to worm and neuter, but it still smelled and it never liked people much. It would let Roger rub its neck but it was wary of Saleem and no one could pick it up. The vet had looked at its crooked leg and guessed that it had been abused.

Asparagus was not an inspiring animal. Messy, cowering, and a little mean, certainly not affectionate, it kept apart. Roger was tempted to put it out. After all, he had done his part to keep down the population of feral cats. He tried hard to incorporate it into some story of courage and persistence (significantly, *dogged* persistence, as he thought of it) but it was no use. The animal's zeit was too black for ihr Da. It was hardly *there* at all.

Every once in a while, though, he would forget to feed it. Then it would look at him from under the couch, following him with its eyes, ears alert, until he put something in the bowl, upon which it would disappear again. Its fear would always be too strong for its neediness. Roger supposed it was fear, and not some anthropomorphic resentment or existential rage. Anthropocultic rather, this attribution of subtle emotions to animals. He supposed they were not subtle. That animals were not. Perhaps he was not subtle. Whenever he felt that way he went out to practice, to play some music transparently reflective of his mood. Transparent to anyone else, anyway. The curate, or whatever he was, was generally the only person in church at those times. Beadle. Roger was under the impression that only Trollope novels had beadles in them.

Considering the amount of time he spent in churches, Roger had absorbed very little in the way of religion.

In the mornings, often before seven o'clock, he went across to the school. The library was supposed to open at eight. Instruction didn't start until nine, but as most of the students were resident there were always a few who wanted something before class. He closed the doors at four thirty. Usually he went home. Sometimes he simply turned his chair around and stared out of the window for an hour. There was nothing to see, really. Just grass. The main building was of brick and had been built in the twenties and the windows were seven feet tall and went down almost to the floor. Sometimes there would be a single figure moving across the lawn, a student talking to himself or a teacher, smoking.

Roger was neither a Chips nor that man in *The Browning Version* whose name he could not remember, neither beloved nor ridiculed. Perhaps, not being deaf, he simply wasn't taken any notice of. Girls and boys would ask him for help with a homework problem, or to find them something to read, but their troubles they took elsewhere. Roger assumed they had troubles. Usually he could help with the homework, though he wasn't absolutely positive that his answers were right. As for reading, Roger always recommended *Barchester Towers* but so far without success.

Saleem was often teaching at night. Being the low man he always got the most inconvenient hours. Most terms he took on six classes. It was the money, he said. What money? He got paid and could barely afford his half of the rent. Roger didn't see a lot of Saleem. They got on well enough, with no squabbling about dirty clothes or food in the refrigerator. Saleem talked in some code which Roger didn't understand and much of the time he paid little attention to Saleem's muttering, like a radio with the volume turned way down. He sometimes wondered how Saleem managed to be intelligible in class but he supposed it was all right since they kept giving Saleem six classes. People have different personalities at work. Probably Saleem was natty and urbane when he was not around Roger.

Roger had a tendency to think that everyone he met had a secret life which was better than the one they seemed to be living.

And so he and Saleem went on from day to day, until one evening when Roger came home from school he could not find Asparagus. He was not under the sofa or in the closets or behind the books. Roger thought that maybe Saleem had absent-mindedly let him out, but when he waited up Saleem said he hadn't been home since breakfast. He didn't seem to notice the panicky sharpness of Roger's voice.

Roger found he couldn't sleep. Most of the night he padded around the apartment signing agitatedly to himself and in the morning when he reluctantly locked up he looked pretty haggard.

That night Asparagus was back on his usual food vigil, always suspicious that Roger would betray him and forget. Or worse. Roger almost cried with relief.

Still, the incident was disturbing. It set Roger to thinking. Probably it was what had happened to that man Harris that lay behind it. He felt out of sorts with everyone. Some festering dissatisfaction. He should move to the desert and become a hermit, Bill remarked. Not fit for society. It wasn't clear whether Bill was referring to Roger or himself.

One afternoon after closing Roger stopped by Woody's office. The Kink's Vice-Principal worked in what had once been a mail room, which she had sought out and refurbished in order to get away from the distractions and politics of administration. Its location also allowed her to bring in students for disciplinary talks without exposing them to public shame, which only hardened the isolation which was the root cause of their behavior.

He tried to explain the concept of life out of balance. Admittedly, it was James's idea and so somewhat fuzzy.

I don't think you mean simply dissatisfaction, Woody remarked after listening for a while. It's not personal, an emotion, though you might experience it in that way.

Woody was short and stumpy, with spiky gray hair and coarse features seamed by deep wrinkles. Mostly poker-faced, she did look as if she were made of wood, but her name was not a sobriquet, only a diminutive. An ability to hide her real opinions served her well as both the school's disciplinarian and its assistant-to.

Roger's eye drifted away to the splotches on the wall. He doubted if Woody had ever had the room repainted. It wasn't exactly squalid, but Roger was often distracted by pictures he saw in the water stains. He supposed that, too, served some purpose of hers.

He essayed a reply. It — life out of balance I mean — seems to have something to do with acting unmindfully, he said. With not respecting, honoring maybe, the stuff you encounter.

Stuff.

Well, people. But also plants and animals, objects... stuff. You remember that thing a while back for drinking wine out of glasses of the right shape, or the way people fuss about tea bowls.

So this is an epicurean thing?

No no, that makes it seem narcissistic.

It's a serious way of life, the epicurean's. Much concerned with right action.

I don't know, Woody. You seem more of a stoic.

She smiled at this, very slightly.

Anyway, it seems so self-righteous, smug, to be blatting about duties to one's fellows or respect for the earth or mystical stuff about... well, however those people talk. You know.

Mm.

There was a long silence. Roger shifted uncomfortably on his chair, feeling like a student with bad grades.

Well, he said. I've got to go feed my cat.

Woody nodded, and Roger slipped out the back way onto the old loading dock.

Saleem was not home, as usual. Now, whenever he didn't return at night Roger began to worry he'd been arrested again. He didn't especially like Saleem, so his concern for the man puzzled him a bit. Roger put crunchies in the cat's bowl and then looked in the refrigerator, but there was nothing he wanted to eat. Experimentally he tried one of the cat crunchies but had to spit it out. Maybe it would be better with milk and banana? For a while he paced the floor, finally settling down with the morning's paper and a bowl of cereal. Saleem had pretty thoroughly scrambled the paper. Roger began an article on new animated movies, the sort that James was always on about, and then couldn't find the continuation. He put the newspaper aside. Washing out his bowl and spoon he fell into an abstraction and stood looking out the window over the sink for a long time while the water ran down the drain.

There was a crackly noise. Asparagus was eating. All the cat's senses quivered. He gulped the food, jerking his head up to throw the hard nuggets to the back of his mouth and swallowing them almost whole. After a few mouthfuls he skittered back under the sofa.

Roger had been holding his breath. Released, he sighed and turned off the faucet.

Saleem was in the kitchen tearing open the mail when he became suddenly quiet.

What.

Roger had his head in the refrigerator, searching for some vegetable for dinner.

It's that lawyer again, Saleem muttered, stupid with incredulity. They want me in court.

Court?

Roger straightened up, a carrot in one hand, still holding open the refrigerator door. His eyes met Saleem's. There was a momentously long silence.

I don't believe it, Roger said. Are they really going to pursue that business?

Saleem's perspective rose slowly to the ceiling, where a bug of some sort was walking.

Flies stick to everything, he said.

Let me see that. Roger held out his free hand. The refrigerator door began to close surreptitiously, but it was too languid to actually embrace the latch.

This isn't from a lawyer, Roger pointed out. It's a summons or something. Bail revoked, it says.

Oh, yes?

You had better call that lawyer yourself, Saleem.

I've forgotten his name.

You had a card, surely. Call the public defender's office who referred you.

Yes, definitely.

Saleem wandered off to his room to look for the card. Roger looked over Saleem's letter with distaste and laid it on the counter. There was a carrot lying there. What — ? Oh yes. Dinner.

Roger didn't follow this stage of Saleem's tribulations very closely because there was trouble at school which drew off his attention. One of the older boys, who had earlier caused a ruckus by pretending to have a bomb, now was discovered to have done some damage in the library. Some computers had been broken — a monitor dropped on the floor, glue squirted into the USB ports — and books thrown around everywhere. Roger's desk had been rifled but since he kept nothing of consequence there it didn't matter except for some unpleasant moments with Kink George III, who had formed the idea that this business was the acting out of some animosity toward Roger. Which suggested that Roger —

       The boy had been looking for something in Roger's desk. Something with which to incriminate him. And what might Roger have done that was incriminatory?

The Kink's squinty regard ambled toward Roger.

Nothing. And in fact, the boy had shied from any violation of Roger's work area aside from looking into his desk, presumably for something to eat or for remarks about his smallboy self. Roger's work area remained a little island of neatness amid the general shambles. Roger refused to make anything of this in the interminable staff meetings which followed. It was simply the boy's reluctance to compound a felony, he insisted. The natural reluctance to attack a teacher, except indirectly.

This remark nudged the discussion to its opposite pole, to interpret the incursion into the library as comfortably inscrutable. Roger shrugged off all of this. It was not up to him, he insisted, to say whether a boy hated him or not. How would Roger know? He had a stake, after all. He was not objective.

Nor was the Kink, who toddled behind all these shifts of mood, formulating new hypotheses as needed. But his Kinkship was a man of power and could not be gainsaid, so Roger had to go for a session of counseling.

Nothing of consequence came out during two pointless hours of self-scrutiny. How could it? Roger thought of that troublesome boy who was no doubt to be subjected to the same humiliation. There would be a lot of dry wringing of hands and nothing would be accomplished except to harden the boy concerning authority. Authority which betrayed him to his parents in order to dun them for the damage. Everyone would be more angry than before and not a whit less mystified.

Saleem waved it all off over dinner. It's obvious, he said. These people are all cretins.

But then, Saleem was preoccupied. And after all, Roger knew almost nothing of the boy's back story or his standing among the other boys.

Jethro Ashburton — for that was his name, though he was universally and logically known to everyone as Bertie — would seem odd in any setting even were he not deaf. He was tall and amazingly ugly. Roger read with interest some research reports which suggested that parents love their ugly children less — and how did they know the child was ugly? Roger wondered, since *ugly* is relative to something. What is the standard, the Greenwich Mean Ugly? Themselves, presumably — well anyway, Bertie *was* ugly; everyone said so. Bertie was not especially bright, either, but with a very retentive memory he got by easily, considering no one else was very much brighter. Roger thought of all the times that Saleem had complained so bitterly about the plight of someone whose mind is quick and who is always being dragged back, victimized by hostile incomprehension. He ordered a reprint copy of Cyril Connolly's *Enemies Of Promise* for the school library. Bertie would not have Saleem's problem; he was rather an idiot savant, but the other boys did not treat him any better for that. Because they could bully him, they did bully him. The little indignities and humiliations added up. Bertie would pop someone and then be hauled in while the bullies were overlooked yet again. It was such a common story, would be banal if it were less consequential. The Kink did not understand any of this and so failed to interpret it to Bertie's parents, who understand even less — how could they not? They had no idea what went on where they couldn't see. Woody and some of the teachers could see. There were some ineffectual attempts at intervention. But all that came of it was that Bertie was locked up with a counselor for some days, his skinny ugly body hunched over, hands clasped between his knees (or maybe he would sit on them?) trying frantically to find the right story that would get him out.

This business about Bertie sapped Roger's sympathy for Saleem, whose plight was Bertie's exactly. Saleem could have used some help himself. But Roger was at this point too mazed to realize the gravity of Saleem's despair. Until afterward, which neglect let Roger in for some dry recriminations of his own.

Somehow the cat seemed implicated in all this. Maybe the ancient Egyptians would have known why.

Good will aside, Roger got nowhere with Bertie because there was no one to talk to about him and so no means of working out a plausible, pragmatic analysis. Roger bumbled along like the other teachers who were spoiling life in the staff room with their complaints and phony empathy.

Roger's colleagues were ludicrously easy even for him to see through and the Bertie business left him with another glop of cynicism to swallow. Here was this man, set up shop in the corner farthest the door: unable to lose weight or quit smoking either, burdened by a lifetime of repeated failure and belittling remarks. Or that woman, one table over, who wanted a promotion she didn't get. The young fellow drinking coffee by himself needed to be kind in order not to take it out on all those who were not kind to him. The deaf old boy with the piggy eyes playing silent bridge at the only table by a window had wanted to be a priest, a minister or something of the sort, and be looked on by everyone — up to, not on — as a wise person who always has the best answers to everything, debarred from sainthood only by his disability.

About half the teachers were deaf. On the school grounds everyone conversed in sign so as not to be rude, the hearing ones glossing their remarks with mumbles, grunts, and disconnected phrases. Only the Kink depended solely on his voice, so that deaf teachers in conference had to work hard to follow along, leaving them little opportunity to strategize, which was of course the point. There was a social gap between the hearing teachers and the deaf ones which had not (yet) precipitated out as a firm class structure, only because general dislike of the Kink served to consolidate them. In the past, Roger was told, there had been some rather fierce episodes. The deaf ones would form the aristocracy, of course; for the present it was more of a crumbling oligarchy. Roger was doomed to the helot's role, being both hearing and the librarian. He wondered whether it were a good thing — good for one's soul, the wannabe minister would say, not productive of good karma or anything — that they were all willing to occupy the common room together only because they disliked it so beyond the pale.

There was something in the *LA Times* about the oldest DNA on earth having been discovered in some people living in the forest in Southeast Asia somewhere. It was claimed that this proved — Roger got his science mostly from the newspaper and so did not follow the reasoning at this point very well — that humans migrated out of Africa only once. A band of perhaps a hundred, sixty-five thousand years ago. Roger tried to imagine a hundred people, small and fragile, people who knew themselves to be the People, maybe the First People, trekking endlessly in search of others like themselves. The elders would stop to confer. Perhaps *over there*. They were Old Ones, the source of all those dim memories we have of having come from somewhere else, of always moving on, belonging nowhere. Leaving languages and epics behind us like bread crumbs to the old woman's oven, like a thread to nothing but a pile of bones. Archaeologists are always discovering bones in caves and trying to work out whether the protein which had once covered them knew anything about art or believed in an afterlife.

A paleontological just-so story, James said with a dogmatical gripe. James was always going on about storytelling, about how phony the stories we tell about ourselves are. *Phony* was a word Roger never heard anymore except from James. Saleem had a cultural theory about this involving debased ideas of engagement, predictably distracting himself from the real problem.

James probably raged about phony stories because he wanted an excuse to drop his profitless scriptwriting schtick, or because he didn't like Sofka's stories about his numerous rejections.

Well of course you get rejected all the time, James said in a relaxed voice which was entirely fake, putting his feet out on Roger's ottoman. You make thousands of pitches to get a few dollars out of one or two ideas and you never get screen credit. Never. Credit costs them too much. This Bertie. You'll never know the real story. Nobody ever knows, because there isn't anything *but* the story. Here's the cops, putting the cuffs on some mousey woman in the parking lot, but you'll never find out why. *She* doesn't know why. The cops don't know why. They're all pitching stories which will never be made into movies. Never. There isn't any why. It's just stories.

Roger had been trying to explain to him about Bertie and about the proliferating hypotheses plaguing the Penfield School. *Stories* was James's take on Bertie's troubles. Bertie needed to tell a better story. He needed a script doctor.

Roger had been surreptitiously asking for sympathy for himself. He would never get any from James. James didn't care. He would only poke Saleem in the chest and say he was telling the wrong story.

So what was the right story?

James shrugged. There isn't any.

STORY TIME. Roger was reading, signing rather, to some younger children who were just learning the language. He'd found an appropriate cautionary tale in an obscure novel about alternate worlds.

When Mr. Ka turned off the time machine, Roger was saying, he found himself a month in the future. The job which Bill had promised him was waiting. So on the next Monday morning, instead of taking the bus to Sandhill Labs as usual, I mean as in the past, Mr. Ka went instead to Microtics Research where he had been taken on as a junior member of the team that was going to build the first heefer.

What's a heefer? one of the children asked.

I don't know, do I? We don't have heefers yet. Now Sandhill Labs also had a heefer project, but they hadn't been able to get over the problem of Loudwine recursion. What Mr. Ka wanted to know (that is, what Bill wanted) was this: had the Microtics people solved the Loudwine problem?

They had.

The answer was very simple, really. It was to hold down the reverberator with a kinkle function until the Loudwine unit had converged on reality. The Sandhill team had just not thought of using kinkle functions, but when Mr. Ka went through the mathematics of it that evening it was perfectly obvious that it would work. He was very excited. The heefer was within his grasp at last.

Mr Roger, sir?

Yes?

Who is Bill?

Well, I've forgotten.

You said Bill was going to get Mr. Ka a job.

Oh. Well, and he did, too, didn't he? You missed that. He's spying on the Microtics people. Remember? Now: although it had taken Mr. Ka no time at all to find out what he had come for, he didn't want to go back just yet. (You remember I told you that Mr. Ka was a time traveler.) If he did, you see, the

Microtics people would realize that he was a spy and they would Take Steps, and things might not work out right. So Mr. Ka went on working at Microtics for another month to keep up appearances. And it was a good thing he did, or he might not have noticed the importance of the reverberator lubricant. He kept this to himself, of course, saying nothing to the Microtics people. Their heefer design would fail without more lubricant. But at last he was ready. That night he went over the heefer plans again. Satisfied, he locked them in the trunk of the time machine, put the machine on autopilot and sent it back two months to the Sandhill laboratory. They would find the plans there and use them to build a working heefer, which Mr. Ka guessed would take them from then until now. The Microtics people, who were being held up by inadequate lubrication, would read in the newspapers tomorrow about the big breakthrough at Sandhill Labs.

Mr Roger, sir?

That same boy again. Girls never ask questions. Roger thought this story would bore girls anyway. Something needed to be done to fix that.

Two months?

Well, Hugh, he'd gone one month ahead and then waited there another month. That makes two.

Hugh fidgeted, obviously unsatisfied but afraid to nag a grown-up. He took a breath and his hands burst into motion.

But where he came from they were living too and they had lived a month while Mr Ka was waiting and so it should be only one. Shouldn't it?

Yes, Hugh, but Mr Ka's trunk would be going back to where he started. So no time at all would pass, don't you see?

Obviously, Hugh didn't see. Standing, stunned, silent — somehow, Roger had said once to Saleem, these kids' silence is more silent than ours. It's unnerving.

Then what happened to the month those other people lived? *That's not fair.* Hugh waved his fists indignantly. Roger scratched his head and pretended to be puzzled. I think it's like a train on a siding, he said. When the other train passes they get to go too, afterward. Hugh sat down, dubious, and Roger resumed the story.

When the time machine had disappeared, Mr. Ka laughed quietly and rubbed his hands together. He was very pleased with himself. Late that evening he went out for a drink, to celebrate

Afterwards, he was run over by a truck.

They'll think I did it because we lost out to Sandhill, Mr. Ka said to himself as he stepped in front of a ten-wheeler. Bill will be in the clear. I hope I remember where I put the key to the trunk.

But he hadn't remembered, of course: it was in his pocket two months in the future. So, back at Sandhill Labs, Mr. Ka was struggling anxiously to pry open the trunk of the time machine. His face was dripping with perspiration thick as snot, which made his eyes sting.

All at once a fierce pain in the back caused him to fall, and at that moment the trunk of the time machine popped open. Mr. Ka got to his knees, his head throbbing, and peered into the gloom at the heap of papers there, covered with his own spidery writing. Formulas, and little drawings of machine parts.

Ugh, he muttered. It feels like I've been run over by a truck.

And he had been, of course.

The children erupted in giggles. Compared to their struggles to get words out of their mouths, the natural laughter was startling and put Roger off his stride. He paused, then chugged on.

As the heefer research was being taken away for study, Mr. Ka looked sadly at the dents and scratches on his time machine. It certainly wasn't new anymore.

And neither was Mr. Ka.

You cheated, another boy complained, by name David. He was upset too. Uneasily Roger twisted the large knuckle of his finger. I think, he said at last... but did not go on. The silence was becoming worrisome. The children were looking cautiously at each other.

I'm sorry, Roger said. I didn't mean to cheat. What did I do wrong?

A rustling arose, which no doubt had its deaf counterpart in some disturbance of the empathy. They weren't used to this. They didn't like winning one — it was unnatural. David was getting some hostile looks, but he stood his ground.

Mr Ka doesn't have to die, he whined.

These kids are getting really good. How do they make it seem to be whining like that? Roger was going to be left behind again, with his clumsy hands. Or maybe it was something else clumsy, some haole insensitivity.

Roger started to reply but he didn't get far.

It's an *alternate* universe, isn't it?

David was near to tears.

What's wrong with Mr Ka going on living? He doesn't have to be dead. He's over there — David seemed to mean outside the library window — and so who cares? You *wasted* him. He's not hurting anyone.

Roger winced.

Is he? Is he?

No, David. But it's too late now, I think. I'll do better next time.

David sacrificed the obvious rejoinder and sat down on his mat with a grumpy plump. The children nodded sagely.

Roger really was sorry. But: it was also a warning to them. Well, he said at large. What shall we do?

Nobody knew, of course.

After Saleem left to teach his seven a.m. film class, Roger stolidly finished his coffee and his newspaper. Then he cleared the breakfast table and set the timer on the dishwasher to run at noon when there would be plenty of hot water from the solar heater. In the living room he found a doll's shoe which Sofka's daughter left behind, which he put into his pocket, and also a stiletto sandal which he dropped into the trash. On the way down to the corner where he would cross the street to the school he dropped two letters off at the mailbox. While he was waiting for the traffic to clear he made a list for himself: milk, laundry, water the herbs on the patio. Besides the herbs, Saleem had bought a dwarf lime, too, which wasn't doing well. For some time Roger had been thinking of putting in a drip irrigation system. On a timer.

After a little thought Roger added a few more items to the list. Some grapes, maybe, if they weren't too expensive. It was an awkward time of year, between the citrus and the melons. His digestion was suffering.

After he'd crossed he realized he'd forgotten to make himself a lunch.

One day some weeks later, as Mr. Ka was boarding the bus for work, he caught sight of a newspaper headline.

HEEFER RESEARCH

AUSTIN (AP) -- A breakthrough in heefer technology was announced here yesterday by officials of Microtics Research. "There will be some scrambling to catch up now," Microtics company spokesmen predicted. Citing the work of a team led by scientist William —

Mr Ka looked frantically about for someone else with a copy of the morning paper. As he pushed toward the back of the bus he tried to work out what could have gone wrong. Had he left behind something incriminating perhaps? Was there something they hadn't told him? Work at Sandhill Labs, he found when he arrived there, was at a complete standstill. Offices were dark, and in the laboratory everyone was at loose ends. More than a year of work was lost. Some people seemed only disappointed; others were angry or depressed. A cup of coffee had been spilled, Mr Ka noticed, on some delicate instruments. One man was working at a microscope in a corner; every so often he would kick the lab table and upset everything, so that he had to start over.

Mr. Ka picked up the telephone, but no one at Microtics was taking any calls. As the day wore on, details of the coup began to come in. But no one seemed to know just how it had been done. Mr. Ka began to wish he had not been run over by a truck, just in case.

The week went by slowly. The lab pulled itself together and got its own machine working. Even with the Microtics machine first, it was better than nothing.

Mr. Ka kept waiting to hear from Bill, who had betrayed him somehow. One morning he woke up with a fearful headache and a very stiff back. And that was all.

Bertie was in the library again. It was the middle of the night. He felt like busting something. It was like waking up and going to the refrigerator in the night except that Bertie didn't eat much. He was never hungry for food.

Last time, Bertie knocked some things onto the floor and pulled a lot of books off the shelf. That was easy, so it wasn't very satisfying. He also peeked into Mr Roger's desk. It smelled of apples. Mr Roger usually had an apple for lunch, which he stored in his desk to eat while he minded the library over the lunch period. The other teachers all had cafeteria duty, but the library was supposed to be open for lunch and the kids who might have minded it were all eating because there was only twenty minutes and you had to eat fast, so Mr Roger did it. So you had to listen to him eating that apple while you were trying to read.

Bertie was a fast reader. He had read all the books in the Penfield library and most of them in the little town library in the square by the train station when he could go there. In the town library he could only see the books in the children's room.

Those were all incredibly boring and even more boring if you read them again. He was, he supposed, angry with Mr Roger for not having more interesting books and had probably pulled them all down last time looking for the other books, the ones that were hidden behind these ones. And then he was just angry. The others made fun of him when he did something stupid and they made fun of him when he did something smart and they made fun of him when he just sat there trying not to do either one. And not even behind his back. At first they had done it behind his back but after a while they found out he wasn't going to sock them so they said stupid and cruel things right to his face and since by that time there didn't seem to be any other way to treat him, when Bertie socked them in the eye it didn't matter anymore, they just went on. Now some of the bigger boys had made a club which only certain people could belong to. The purpose of this club was to catch Bertie alone and pound him back. One boy had an aluminum ring through which he had pushed a thumbtack with the point out so that if he pounded you he would rip something up, your arm or your stomach. Usually they swiped Bertie's glasses so that he couldn't see what to do. So far they hadn't smashed them but only left them somewhere so that he had to feel around for them afterwards. But one of these days that one boy was going to sock him in the eye and he'd be blind, too. As if it wasn't bad enough already.

Bertie hated being deaf. Mr Roger wasn't deaf but he acted deaf. Bertie had an idea you shouldn't do that, pretend there's something wrong with you when there isn't. Bertie thought he would like to sock Mr Roger in the eye, too, but he didn't dare. Maybe he would.

Tonight Bertie had decided to look into Mr Roger's desk more carefully. He pulled out all the drawers and laid them on the floor, making no noise so as not to ruin things right away. He looked in the back and underneath for things which had been hidden, or secret compartments. Then he started to go through what was in the drawers.

He didn't get far. Under some sheets of blank paper was a book he hadn't seen yet. The title was *The Book Of Ka*. He sat down to read, scrunching into the kneehole of the desk so as not to be noticed through the library windows if that guard and his dog came around. Later he thought that was stupid, he should just have taken the book, but at the time it didn't occur to him.

Bertie opened the book in the middle and found the beginning of one of the stories, or whatever they were.

YOU REMEMBER Mr. Ka, the inventor? From the last time, yes. Well, today Mr. Ka was angry with his neighbors. Goat and Cat and Crow, especially Crow, had complained very loudly, and at enormous length, about the furnace which Mr. Ka had built in his back yard. Mr. Ka was using the furnace to smelt metal for the new machine he was building, wonderfully strong and light metal, just the thing. But the furnace belched black smoke, and it stank, and fire leaped from it high into the air and withered the leaves on the trees. And so the neighbors complained, and Mr. Ka was angry with them, especially Crow.

What is his first name? the boy asked.

Paul Crow.

No. Mr. Ka.

Ka. Kaah! Kaah! said Crow, perched on the fence and looking angrily into Mr. Ka's back yard. Ka was peering into the mouth of his smelter, his face red with the heat that gusted from the open door. Inside, the furnace fire roared so that Crow's sharp voice could hardly be heard, and clouds of thick black smoke boiled out of the chimney overhead. Ka was wearing large mittens on his hands, and an apron, and goggles.

What is it now, Crow? he said.

The wind shifted, turning the plume of smoke more in Crow's direction, and Crow hopped down the fence a bit toward the corner. Ka was reaching into the furnace with a long pole, and with it he drew out a little cup of molten metal. The cup glowed hot red. Ka poured the liquid metal into a mold which was waiting on the ground. Then he leaned the pole up against the fence. A black iron pipe snaked across the ground from the fence on the alley to the furnace, where there were two large valves with round handles painted red. Ka turned these valves shut, first one, then the other. The roaring sound became a hiss. There was a bang and then silence, and Crow could hear the crackling of the hot metal beginning to cool. The last black marshmallow of smoke rose into the sky.

Ka took off his mittens and goggles. His face was as black as Crow's and he was smiling with the success of his work, until he remembered about Crow.

What is it now, Crow? You know I need to use this furnace for my work. How can you ask me to stop my work?

What are you making, Ka, that is so important?

I won't tell you. When has an inventor ever told a secret like that?

Crow spread his wings in disgust and flew away. Mr. Ka went into his house and slammed the door. He didn't notice Cat sitting on the corner of the fence by the house.

Cat jumped softly from the fence onto some shelves standing against the wall, and from there onto a wobbly table piled up with tools. This table stood under the kitchen window, which was open. Cat sat quite still there, except for the tip of her tail, which was tapping soundlessly. Her ears stood straight up, turned toward Mr. Ka's open window.

Mr. Ka was walking up and down, from the living room to the kitchen and back again, muttering to himself.

My neighbors want me to stop my work, he was saying, because it annoys them. I wonder if there was ever a time when someone wasn't annoyed about something. Well, I'll give them something to be annoyed about.

Suddenly there was a clatter of tools falling from the table outside.

Mr. Ka froze, his heart pounding. Who's there? he said in a squeaky voice.

There was no answer.

Bah! he said, no longer frightened.

Ka is planning something, Cat said that evening to Crow and Goat. But I don't know what it is. We must be careful. Crow and I will keep watch. Goat, you are the only one of us strong enough. You must be ready.

Baah! said Goat.

A week passed, and nothing was seen of Mr. Ka. His house was dark, and the smelting furnace was cold. Once or twice Cat thought she heard small noises inside, tinkering noises, but that was all.

On Saturday morning Mr. Ka's neighbors were awakened at dawn by a terrific din and when they looked out they found the sky so covered with greasy black smoke that it hid the sun. The air stank of burned meat and rang with the deafening clash of hammers.

Crow flew over at once to see what was going on. There in Mr. Ka's back yard was a huge robot, hard at work forging hot metal. Flames roared from the furnace, leaping high into the air, licking the robot's metal skin. Mr. Ka's tree was on fire. The robot put its bare hand into the furnace and drew out the crucible of molten metal, which it set aside to cool while it returned to forging the metal which it had smelted earlier.

The robot worked without any tools at all. The din of hammers was the noise of the robot's great fists as it pounded flat a gob of white-hot metal. To make wire it drew a bar of metal through its fingers, stretching it out like dough, but with a ghastly screech.

And then, looking up, the robot happened to catch sight of Crow flying high overhead. It seized a stone and hurled it high into the sky, just missing Crow.

Crow flew home and told Cat and Goat what he had seen. Goat was strong, but he was no more than an ant compared to this robot of Mr. Ka's. The three of them decided it would be better to go to the park for the day. So they did, and had a fine picnic.

But when they came home that night they found the robot still at work, and it worked all night and all day Sunday. None of them got any sleep.

I'm going to go visit my uncle, grumbled Goat. Call me on the telephone when things improve here.

I'm going away too, said Cat. This is too much. And she slipped into the bushes and disappeared.

Crow flew up into a tree where he could watch the goings-on at Mr. Ka's from a safe distance. For three more days Ka's robot went on forging bars and rods and wires and sheets of metal amidst the fire and smoke and noise. But finally it was finished, and the day after that Mr. Ka returned home, rested and smiling, with a suitcase covered with stickers from all the places he had been.

Goat and Cat had come home again, too. Goat stood in the alley looking into Mr. Ka's back yard where the fence had been smashed down. Cat sat on his back, and Crow on a half-burned post nearby. The big tree was only a charred skeleton now.

Mr. Ka surveyed the scene with satisfaction, rubbing his hands. Then he went into the house, returning a few moments later dressed for work.

First I shall repair the fence, he announced to his neighbors. Then we will see what to make next.

Mr. Ka began to saw and hammer, putting up the fence again. Cat and Crow and Goat stared in dismay at the huge piles of metal the robot had left. A great many things could be made from that much metal. It would be many months before that much metal was used up: many months of sawing and hammering and drilling.

But somehow Crow and Cat and Goat didn't feel they could complain any more, considering how quiet Mr. Ka's work seemed now. Really it was louder than ever. It just didn't seem so loud. So Mr. Ka's neighbors looked on, grumbling and complaining, but they kept it to themselves. And Mr. Ka whistled a smug little tune as he built himself a new fence, and turned the tree stump into a new table for his tools, and thought about what to do next.

How annoying that his neighbors should still be angry, though now they were polite enough to keep it to themselves. Didn't they know what a fine fellow he was?

I am sure I can convince them, Mr. Ka thought.

Roger's copy of *The Book Of Ka* was getting a little tattered. Desultorily, he looked for another. None to be had. In common with Bertie, he had a sentimental wish that this book be the saving of the boy.

Bertie, Roger supposed, would expect his salvation to come from the book itself, for which he needed his own copy. A copy he would liberate from its unrighteous owner in a daring commando raid resembling *Mission Impossible* à la Jones — or more probably he was too young for those movies and had in mind something from a computer game which Roger could not guess at. Objects have magical powers in those games. As in any consumer society, it is enough to buy the thing — liberate it in some way according to the rules — to wield the power. That was why simply stealing Roger's copy would not do. That copy was the property of a more powerful wizard, certainly, but it was legitimately the wizard's and its powers could not pass to a new owner yet. Of course, there was never in these games any question of long years of study to learn from a master; instead, one studied the game and nabbed the thing from a secret room where it has been lying, waiting like shoes on a store shelf for the buyer dreamed of, yearned to give up everything to with the devotion of a purchased slave.

Roger's sentimental hopes were rather that the book — any book, really — would liberate something already within, some *chi* or Buddha-nature which would come pouring out of the rent like an enormous djinn out of a perfume bottle.

Being one of those with a professional interest, Roger believed that books are healing, a wish entirely unsupported by empirical evidence. Unhappy experience suggests that what is healing, aside from a genetic ability to recover quickly from repeated injury, is the blitheness which makes all wounds superficial. Is a hair-trigger imagination which invents alternate realities faster than they can be ruined. Roger's deep seams of melancholy and pessimism had been formed over the years by the steady drip of blood through this porous contradiction.

He recognized Bertie. Saleem also was a man of this sort, probably, though Saleem had never confided in him enough for Roger to know for sure.

The people of the book.

Chained to their fetish by the Romantic notion that everything truly sacred must be won by blood and suffering, to the books which record victories grasped only in death.

It doesn't help Bertie's growing contempt for social organization that he has to steal his reading. When Roger unlocked the library the next morning and found Bertie asleep under his desk he was gentle with the boy. He agreed to get Bertie some more books if Bertie would stop breaking into school rooms and causing everyone heartache. Bertie accepted this contract, though probably in bad faith.

Upon escaping from the library Bertie made a stealthy way back to his suite. He had learned how to do this without being found out by a choice of route which left him escapes at crucial spots — down a different corridor, into a nook or one of those rooms which were never locked, a double back — together with the deaf person's sixth sense for the nearness of other people. Stairwells he found the most troublesome. His suitemates always cotched him but those boys preferred to keep Bertie's vagrancies among themselves so as to maximize the possibilities for tormenting him.

Bertie stiffened in anticipation as he silently pushed the suite door open by a crack. Being deaf, he could not have heard any creaking or scraping which the door made, but he had satisfied himself by prior experimentation that he could do it. Since his suitemates were also deaf this was an ornament on Bertie's workmanship, but there was always the possibility that some nearby hidden proctor might notice.

This time someone under one of the beds shot out a hand and grabbed Bertie by the ankle. He avoided banging his head on the bedframe and took it on the hip instead. In an instant they had pinned him. The boy now sitting on Bertie's chest stank of piss. Bertie turned his head slightly.

And where have *you* been? pissboy asked. Somehow this one was able to load his gestures with more than the usual contempt. A strange talent. If he hadn't been deaf he might have made an actor. But then if he hadn't been deaf he mightn't have developed the subtlety.

Since two other boys were standing on his hands, Bertie had to say it for his lips to be read.

In the commons. Swipe some food.

Bring us back some?

Bertie shook his head. Ate it, he said. Bertie had never heard his speaking voice, though he knew some could faintly with headphones. He wondered if his own was too crude a noise for a hearing person to identify any of the emotions in it.

Bastard.

Of course he was. There was no point in Bertie's trying to anticipate what reasons would be found to make him more miserable. If he spoiled their fun by guessing right it would only point their viciousness with anger.

He was going to get out of this place. Out into the world. If he was run over crossing the street the first time so what? If Bertie didn't really care about books, he wasn't eager to be educated, either, since he couldn't see what that would offer in the way of advantages. Maybe somewhere else it was done better. Is there somewhere clsc?

If he ran away they would cotch him and throw him in the dungeon. Might prefer the dungeon, if the bread were any good and the water not rotten.

Bertie was too young and inexperienced yet to know what he wanted. That thing might recover him or it might throw him away. It might make him a saint or a murderer, who knows?

Bertie didn't care which, anyway. He might sometime. Not now.

Roger got himself another cat, finally, after he'd done grieving over his betrayal of Asparagus. And maybe a little grieving over Asparagus, too. Would that be what would happen to Bertie? Always hiding under the sofa, coming out only at night to eat, looking at everyone with longing but only able to scratch and hiss when anyone reached out a hand?

That was too easy. Roger chided himself for sentimentality. People are not cats. They're more complicated than that, maybe.

Maybe not.

Roger had thought he might go down to the pound or find a rescue society but decided he didn't want another traumatized cat. He wasn't up to that, or very good at it either. So he bought a kitten from a breeder, one of those kittens which hadn't come out quite right and so couldn't be given papers. A nice, cheap, brand-new kitten. He had dithered over the breed, thinking first he might want a Siamese, but concluding they were too talky and frantic. Maybe one of the Siamese-derived breeds which are less assertive, but those proved too uncommon to be cheap. Persians are phlegmatic enough, he was told, but to Roger they looked to require too much upkeep. He bought a cat book and looked at Manxes and Abyssinians and Kaffir cats, Maine coon cats and Norwegian forest cats, and lots of other interesting animals, but it was the same as with the uncommon variations on a Siamese. In the end he got a plain old domestic shorthair mongrel, black with white boots and a white tip on its tail. A vet went over it and said it was all right so Roger got it neutered and immunized and took it home. He thought, briefly, about naming it Asparagus, but that made him cringe. In the end it became simply Cat.

Sofka

If he would only ask for help,
Sofka was saying.
Remarked the Other:
Probably he doesn't know he's in trouble.
Mmm.

The two women were having their twice-weekly run in the neighborhood park. The Woman Upstairs was watching Baby, as usual.

He goes on about the culture of belief and the culture of evidence. He thinks he's on the side of evidence but he's not. James is a *believer*. James wants to give himself to some system of rules which will explain to him, excuse really, whatever it is he's done. Mindlessly, accidentally done. If anyone is part of the culture of evidence it's Roger. You know Roger.

The deaf man?

He's not deaf. He's just sort of quiet.

But he waves his hands all the time, you know, like deaf people do.

Roger works with deaf children. He's a schoolteacher. It's, like, talking to himself.

Eccentric, said the Other, a little accusingly. What's he saying?

Sofka shrugged. Maybe he's explaining Heidegger?

To himself?

A moué.

They ran on for a while in silence. Sofka was thinking about Heidegger because she was trying to read *Being and Time* on her own and not getting it. Someone had told her that Heidegger spoke to this business of uncertainty, of people having nothing to say to one another, of knowing nothing but their own experience. That person is strong who accepts this, it was said. Who can look into the Abyss.

The trouble was that Baby kept interrupting. She had discovered you can't read Heidegger between times. At least she hoped that's what the problem was.

Sofka's running partner had stepped up the pace, or perhaps Sofka had dropped back while she was thinking about Baby. It squalled so. Shouldn't it be experimenting with baby talk by now? Sofka dreaded finding out that something was wrong. Something miswired.

She pounded down the gravel path, shoes crunching, feeling the separate parts of her bobbling. Vibrating at different rates. Not in shape yet, despite. So slow. Sofka's partner had waited for her to catch up. They continued side by side. Sofka huffed a bit. The Other was trim, tight. Sofka looked, looked away. No bobbling there. The shaped and the shapeless.

It was disgusting, really, to find out how vain she was. Almost moreso than James. And about her mind, too? Why else was she fighting with all these books about enlightenment society and what we can know and the end of secular humanism when she didn't understand half of it? It was, she thought, because she was afraid of Baby. Afraid of being eaten up. Saleem had told her that what she was trying to learn was All Over, meaning she supposed out of fashion. But she read it anyway, like a thirsty person who will drink anything liquid.

Piss, even.

Was that vanity? Of a sort — *schadenfreude.* Another new word, very fashionable. Vanity in the Ecclesiastical sense.

Not that she thought Montaigne or Habermas was...

Well. She wasn't in a position to say, was she?

Saleem got sort of panicky when she tried to talk to him about this, as if he didn't want to hear it, but who was she supposed to...

You're awfully quiet this morning, the Other one said.

Sorry. I was thinking... um, about...

The baby?

Sofka had worried aloud betimes about neurological errors. That Baby would be stupid. Was stupid.

No. About James.

And what about James, then?

He's gone to Santa Monica to run with one of those film industry people he's always sucking up to. It makes me angry. It's pretentious of him.

I thought that was how you made your way in films, by sucking.

The Other woman was a magazine editor and ought to know about that.

No, Sofka said. Because he's pretending. He doesn't have a clue. He's not good at it.

At sucking?

Heh — Sofka laughed for the first time in days. No, she said. I mean he watches all these old movies. He likes movies. He likes knowing stuff — who was in them. It's *trivia*. He doesn't *know* anything. He can't explain to you the reasons. In fact, he gets angry and starts sneering about stupid intellectuals who have no understanding of craft. Like he does, you're to suppose. Understands craft, whatever that is to him. I don't think it ever occurred to him that if you put one thing after another, this bit or that bit, shots, you have to have a plan. He wants it to be done by instinct. You just *know*, he says. That's what he means, I suppose, by *craft*. Revealed truth. Do you get it?

No, the Other admitted.

All he knows how to do really is fuck, Sofka said after a time.

You like to fuck, said the Other. I'm pointing that out.

Doesn't everyone?

Nooooh...

Hmm. Well what do they do instead then?

Do for themselves, I suppose. What about priests and hermits and like that?

I thought they thought it was...

Sinful?

James would like being a priest, I bet. Except for that sin business. He would be really serious about it, really grim about not screwing up, not following all the rules. Maybe he would beat himself, do you think? With sticks, you know, with thorns on them, if he screwed up?

Maybe.

The Other woman really didn't know much about James. She had talked to him only at parties. Probably they had done it once or twice. James liked bobbles, but he liked the other kind better, Sofka knew.

Sofka hoped sometimes that James would get some terrible sexual disease. Ebola. That was just spite, of course. Which was another thing she had been surprised to learn about herself, that she was spiteful. Sometimes she felt that wasn't really a good thing, knowing about yourself so much. Who said that you should?

Saleem would know.

They all orbited around Saleem, though no one seemed to be aware of this but Sofka. They thought Saleem wasn't in the picture. But he was. They all took their moods, their attitudes and obsessions, from Saleem who wouldn't talk about it.

Because he was Not There. He had expatriated himself somewhere.

Sofka wondered sometimes how that could be, how Saleem could have such influence when he was Not There. Was that what charisma was? Or was it just that he was so much older than they? Was it some kind of effluvia, like bad breath that they all smelled unconsciously? Charisma pheromones.

Saleem was Not There like a black hole is, around which they all orbited.

Sofka was of the opinion that Saleem was lonesome and then made himself be alone so as to explain to himself why he was so lonely. Another person who thought he was part of the culture of evidence but wasn't really.

Then there was that terrorist business which he couldn't seem to get over, when after nine-one-one he was arrested because he looked Muslim. Couldn't get past that. But if he'd got past then he would have one less reason to be lonesome. One more reason to return from the land of the lonely. From Heideggerland.

Well, he *was* Muslim. A third-generation Pakistani Muslim from Fresno from when Pakistanis were invented by Hindus and exiled there.

The Other woman had grown impatient with Sofka's long ruminations and run on ahead again. Sofka stopped at a bench to rest. The bobbly parts were beginning to ache. She tried to fluff up her wet hair that was plastered unappetizingly to her knobbled skull.

Knobby from thinking so much.

Maybe she should wear a hat to cover that up. A cap with a bill longer than a dick, that said I ♥ Heidegger on it.

Bad idea. People would think she was a Nazi.

A NUNNERY OR SOMETHING,
Sofka offered.

Hmm, said Roger, as he did to everything.

These enclosed places, he went on after some slow thought. Everything about Roger was slow. Cautious.

Enclosed places where you go to get away from this and that, only it comes in with you. Like the cat. There are no peaceful places anywhere in the world.

They don't give you a taste, though, do they? Beforehand, to see if you like it. Like ice cream. With a tiny spoon.

That's what a novitiate is for.

Oh, but it's years, a novitiate. You can't tell a vocation by looking, like short and tall or bad skin. And what would I do with Baby?

There are retreats.

Yes.

Oh, she admitted finally. I'm just wanting to duck out, that's all.

Sofka had arranged her Saturday morning run so as to stop at Roger's on the inbound track. Roger was the only one she could talk to now. He had put two chairs out onto the cement forecourt where there was still a bit of shade, and made some iced tea.

Roger was chewing on his lip. After a bit he got up and went inside. In a few minutes the distinctive high voice of a child could be heard through the open window. A song, which seemed to mean something which Sofka could not quite make out.

What's that? she asked. Roger came to the patio window.

The Pie Jesu from Fauré's Requiem.

What's she saying?

He. No idea. It's Latin.

A boy?

Yes. You know, before the voice breaks. At eleven or twelve, thereabouts.

They listened to the music a few moments, and the piece was done. Roger put away the recording and came back outside to his chair with another pitcher of tea. He flopped down, put out his legs.

So they're like pears, Sofka remarked, her voice a little sharp. These boys. One day green and crunchy, next day soft, the core starting to rot. There's just a few hours when they're ripe. After that into the garbage.

Well I wouldn't say they were being exploited.

Hmp. The factory is going to use up a lot of raw material to turn out any amount of something with such a short life.

Roger sighed and gestured in a way as if wiping a mirror. What I was going say was, um...

Sorry.

I wanted to point out something that might help. It's a requiem. There's two kinds of requia. The kind that's all awe and terror, like Britten's — it hits you with this bass drum to start, *wam*! and paces away, the drum slower, softer, and then these ominous two notes, sort of growly, dah-duh, dah-duh — you're meant to think of the futility, the waste, the senselessness of life.

Oh, for sure, Sofka muttered.

Then, Roger went on, there's the kind that is supposed to console you. You're meant to think of... well, things being at peace, at rest, like that.

What was it called, what we heard just now?

Pie Jesu. As in pious. Holy. The point is, it's sentimental. There's this tyke in a surplice and these wonderful pure notes are coming out and it's all so beautiful it makes you weep. Whereas if some burly bass with a five o'clock shadow had stood up to sing, to comment on the way of the world, you'd feel differently. Different.

But don't people want to feel better?

Fauré is a shuck, Sofka. A placebo.

Sofka pondered this, pulling on her lip. I don't know, Roger, she said tentatively. You're dying of cancer, you want some morphine. Those horrible places that won't give you any, like you might get addicted. You're *dying*, for god's sake.

She leaned forward in her chair, seeming in the grip of some new-found idea.

When I was pregnant I was, like, totally loopy. Like I was on something. Well I suppose I was, these hormones. Sometimes I wondered whether that was to make you forget how much it was going to hurt to get this thing out of such a little hole, you just sweat thinking about it, but that's not what I mean. You don't think you might die, but really, why would anyone have wanted to get pregnant in times when you might be there screaming and thrashing around for days and then you die from the pain, or you get purple, I mean puerperal fever and then you also die, there's a lot of heavy chemistry you need to forget that. Where was I?

Loopy.

Oh yes. Well I mean, the whole time I felt like everything was connected to everything else. It was this mystical thing, I'd put out my hand — Sofka held her hand out toward Roger palm

down, fingers spread — and there would be like radio, I imagined I could just touch, through the air, everything there is. I —
me — didn't stop at my fingers, or anywhere else. I was happy
all the time. Someone would be reading, on the train or somewhere, and they would laugh at something in the book, and I
knew that was because of something that happened thousands of
years ago, in Africa maybe. Or would hand me something at
work, a pencil or a box, and all the people, us, the Spaniards, the
Indians, would be standing around filling up all the space, overlapping sort of, and the pencil was part of everyone like a blood
cell moving around or something. I was mad, I guess. Crazy. No
one seemed to notice. And then Baby got out and it all stopped.

Sofka looked at her hand, sadly.

Post-partum depression, isn't it?

I suppose. We're getting to be way post though. Baby and
me have been partum quite a while.

Mm. More tea?

No. I gotta go. I'm starting to stiffen up.

She didn't get up, however, but continued to study her hand
as if it were something she'd found along the road, purpose unknown.

I feel like there's a switch somewhere, she said quietly.
Which would turn all that on again if I knew where the switch
was.

Roger did not remark on this, and after a time Sofka really
did get up to go. After a few deep knee bends and some touching her toes she was gone. Roger poured himself another glass
of tea.

The run home was not refreshing and a long shower didn't
help much. Sofka fluffed up her hair with her fingers, put on her
jeans and sweater, and barefooted upstairs to collect Baby.

These clothes were, in fact, just about the only ones she
owned. Since Baby she hadn't wanted any. Hadn't wanted those
gaudier costumes or disguises; preferred instead the habilment
of the penitent. Maybe she was playing at humility and impov-

erishment but soon enough she would pass though that looking-glass. On the other hand she could fill the apartment with *stuff* — furniture, pots and pans, gizmos — those *immeubles* as she thought the French said — immovable covering for the naked-ness of inward space. The French include *stuff* among the *meubles* but they're wrong. It was James's stuff. It belonged to his integument. James's scruff.

Upstairs Woman handed over Baby kicking its feet in the air and sucking furiously on its thumb but thankfully quiet. It was an embarrassment to both of them when Baby squalled at this moment. A judgment. One or the other of them was not wanted.

I won't be needing you after today, Sofka said to Upstairs when Baby was sitting on her hip. Upstairs raised one eyebrow but did not remark on this.

I'll pay you for the week as soon as I have a hand free for the piggy bank.

Where go?

Sofka had never figured out what Upstairs's native language was. Something without pronouns, unless that was just her way of not seeming to pry. She understood well enough what was said.

Mm. San Francisco, maybe Portland. It's probably my only chance to afford living there. Later on I'll be too rich.

The eyebrow declined a fraction.

An *imperceptible* fraction Sofka might have said. Why do people say that when they can't perceive it? By their own testimony. How do they *know*, then? Idiots.

Him?

Stays.

Baby?

Goes. I suppose. Him wouldn't know what to do with it.

Tch. You go advice?

No. That's not what it's about. Anyway, what does some smarmy ex-minister have to say when he won't tell you bad stuff about yourself? Too upsetting, won't heal that way. Foo.

These guys don't know what's going on and can't find out. It's a secret.

The confession?

Zo. Upstairs is Catholic? Or does she smell it on Sofka?

I don't know why people rat on themselves, Sofka grumbled. And in public yet.

Rat?

You've heard — you can't help but hear— everyone's troubles in Borders or Starbuck's I suppose? It might as well be a Russian study group they're so loud.

Upstairs started back. *Imperceptibly.* Zo. Another clue. Ukranian? Chechnian?

There was some air kissing and then Upstairs closed her door forever. Sofka padded back down to her own.

And anyway, what else is there about yourself but things you don't want to know? These people always want to be happy. To feel good. You have to invent the good stuff. Pull it out of the air.

Loopy, these people. Always wanting to *fix* things. Things aren't broken, damn your eyes. Unless you fuck it up yourself of course, trying to fix it.

Baby was already asleep. Nap time. Upstairs must run it ragged. Did run.

Sofka was going, what she said. Now. This afternoon.

She stood beside the crib looking mixedly at the source of all the trouble. When she and James were children themselves, before Baby that is, they were idiots and everything was OK. Nothing busted. You had to love it, that's required, but it *was* Baby's fault. Baby put a stop to a lot of things which otherwise might have gone on a long time

Love. Because. Fault. What *are* these things? More imperceptibles.

Him will have a small success, she foresaw, now that he can go back to the old way. Some uncredited script revision for which they won't pay him properly because he's not in the union. Zo — being exploited for something is better than being exploited for nothing. Really he does belong with those people. God knows he's stupid enough. Too bad he's missing so many other basic skills like how to dress, how to schmooze, how to lie. Not fibs: lies. Him is just bright enough not to know how to tell real stories, which is why he'll only get the uncredited revision.

She will be punished, of course, for not believing in him.

Belief!

And what will the punishment be? God knows. From now, all misfortunes will be because of that meanness, for not being able to give Him any encouragement. From now, there will be a reason for everything, and it will be because she done Him wrong.

When Sofka is gone she will leave no trace. Gone from here, yes; also gone-gone. She clings to all the living, even Him, but she is already among the dead. In her grave, Sofka foresaw, she will truly be a part of everything. Not this miserable *dasein* Heidegger talks about.

If there really are such things as love and because they're too complicated for her to understand. Too subtle. Evanescent, perhaps — bosons that can't survive more than a wee fraction of a second from the big Bang. Was that what they're called — bosons? Like someone who drives a ship. Pilots a ship. The boson's pipe.

Does Baby understand this? She was, Sofka foresaw, going to have to take lessons from Baby.

JAMES

James and Sofka were having a pointless Sunday morning fight. The proximate cause was Baby. James had wanted to go out for coffee and the paper, perhaps to sit in a café somewhere with a brioche. Split one of those two pound muffins with Sofka. But Sofka was feeding. Sofka was working. Something. Whatever.

The problem with Baby, to James's mind, was the banality it brought into their lives. James thought *his* was banal; Sofka thought — well, he didn't know.

James had had these plans for breaking into film, for being a raffish bohemian artist, plans which he had carefully watered and kept under lights for years while he made this ludicrous bourgeois round of getting and spending. Of accumulating *stuff*. Too much stuff. Furniture, dishes, rugs, babies. And with the stuff came all the stuffy rules. The proprieties, the things it was not safe to do. Slup hot coffee. Point. Say that word.

He was not dealing well with this. It was the end of hanging out in some pub talking about Habermas and those postmodern movies that double back on themselves, erasing their own plots. Erasing that plot and substituting this stupid one out of *The Sound Of Music* or these endless tricked-out *Bambi* scripts from Pixar as if singing and dancing and whizbang animation were the summa of all a poor forked animal can hope for.

James was dimly aware that his unhappiness and impatience were so common as to be themselves banal but before he come to that foggy barrier his creative and explanatory resources had run out.

Sofka, unambitious pragmatic soul, thought the trouble was sex. Not enough, too scheduled, too timid. Because of the baby, of course. There could be no ruinous primal scenes.

Not that there ever had been sex of any ruinous sort. She had had an idea, unfortunately to dim to see clearly, that the concept of a honeymoon was to try out every kind of fucking they could think of to find out what was fun, not so fun, icky, or scary so as to get that clear from the beginning.

How many kinds of fucking could James have thought of anyway. She herself could come up with only as many as there are spins on a quark.

Maybe, she speculated, that from the foothills of ambition, sex is just a pebble on the plain below. Living in the cities of the plain herself, she couldn't say. Lacked the perspective. But to disappear into the Misty Mountains in search of some Shangri-La of success and fulfillment was a cockeyed sort of thing to do, wasn't it? Only dead people come back from Shangri-La.

So they squabbled, unthinkingly, as a duty, as a married couple with a first baby ought to, are expected to by those same people who decide that this year half the crop of new humans shall be named Faith.

Sofka worked as a warehouse dispatcher, leaving Baby with a minder. James was a loan officer in a bank. Both James and Sofka moved stuff around, she said to people at parties. He moved money, she moved boxcars. James thought that was funny at first, but not anymore. For one thing, he didn't really move money. Other, more important people did that. He *stirred* money, like Baby sticking its finger into the mashed peas.

On this Sunday morning James was ranting about something. It didn't matter to Sofka what. She wasn't going to dignify a rant. She was sitting on a stool at what passed for a breakfast bar but was really just the other side of the kitchen counter and not room enough to spread a newspaper out on if there were a newspaper. News gave James the rants, so she read the paper at work, and listened to the radio.

Needing to look somewhere else, she gazed through the sliding glass door at their tiny back yard: a cement deck with astroturf, ivy ground cover, a block wall close enough to touch. A pomegranate belonging to the neighbors on one side, and a jacaranda on the other, shaded this little nook for most of the year and it would have been a pleasant space to grill, read, open the mail, play solitaire if anyone had time for those things.

Formerly they had eaten out, or had frozen dinners or pizzas if they were too tired to go out. Someone was going to have to learn how to cook. Mostly the mail went unopened; everything important was on automatic bill pay. Money flowed through their bank account like water in an underground river, unnoticed. The mail was all junk. It piled up in a drift by the carport door until one of them cracked and threw it away. Things got into the pile that shouldn't. James threw away a credit card. Sofka threw away letters from her sister. More squabbling.

Sofka wanted to lie down, or play with Baby, anything but listen to James. It was futile. He would follow her around the house until he was hoarse and burned out, and upset Baby, which the hollered until *it* was hoarse and exhausted. James thought you could solve problems by talking about them, but you can't.

She got off her stool and spread out her toes on the cool tile, padded around to the other side of the counter to wash some dishes. To be doing something.

I'm listening, she said, but she wasn't.

Outdoors there was a haze, heralding a change of season. Sunless and cold, she wrapped her bathrobe more tightly. Knobby toes. She disliked her toes.

James ran down finally, sinking into Pinter-like silence as he stared sadly at the screen of his laptop. He did some desultory typing.

Here's what Saleem was saying last week. Defining "slow" as a critical term. Unfairly used — he's always on about fairness, fairness — used as a term of opprobrium — what?

Dumping on it, Sofka said.

Oh.

James read for a while, muttering as he scrolled down the page, then burst out "A common element in these movies is the presence of an inscrutable Other, an epistemological back hole which absorbs meaning and gives none back." Can't he give that a rest? *Epistemological.* Who wants to read that on Sunday morning with your pajamas on?

You've never worn pajamas in your life, Sofka pointed out. Not even underwear.

Get thee to a nunnery, b…

Having managed not to say it, James was momentarily wordless.

"Continued next week." Who reads this rubbish?

James pondered morosely this word *continued,* and banged down the lid of his computer.

I'm going out for a bagel, he said.

Sofka drank her tea and stared at her toes. She did suppose that once, in some inarticulate way — is it possible to have inarticulate thoughts? — she had thought that people with nothing in common could not be in love. That it was really lust and you would get over it. They hadn't gotten over it. She hadn't. Mysterious. Who knew what James thought. Doubtful. James didn't like mysteries. Except the whodunit kind which aren't mysterious, really.

Maybe nobody has anything in common. Were they ever going to quit squabbling and move on? On. Where was that? Some kind of promised land full of wise old people where you can go when you've gotten over it. Whatever *it* is. Squabbling. There are no wise old people.

A pomegranate was hanging over the wall, only a little pecked by birds. Sofka stepped into the ivy to pick it. Bad idea. Crawley bitey things, cat poop. But she returned with the prize. A lumpy thing, not very round or ripe. Big hole with a bug in it, some thriped-looking toothpick-shaped thing.

Was that what they were called? Thripeds? Thrips?

She had never known James to actually eat a bagel. *Bagel* was just a word, a formula like a kid's rhyme. Step on a crack. Meaningless. Probably he was having a run. He was vain about that, about his appearance, which neither running nor bagels would change. His appearance nor his vanity either,

She peered into the hole in the pomegranate. Poor seeds, packed so tight into their leather-covered world. Why would Persephone eat that?

Sofka tossed the pomegranate into the ivy and went inside. It was time to feed Baby.

Monday afternoon. James was on the street, which he rarely was on a weekday. It was a pointless errand, inherited from someone who was ill, but it was going to take him close enough to Sofka's office for him to drop in, which was still more rare. Bad idea, James. And sure enough, when he got off the bus there was BF#1 with a baby in a backpack.

It was a hot day, with a chemical haze that sapped James's energy. BF#1 hadn't seen James get off the bus, and by the time James had oriented himself the other man was out of hailing distance. James felt too enervated to catch up, so he followed along behind hoping the man didn't turn around and wonder what James was doing, behaving like those people you know from somewhere else who won't speak to you if you run into them in the grocery store.

BF#1 seemed to be going in the same direction as James had intended. It was not a district very pleasant to walk in, consisting of big windowless buildings in pastel colors dressed up on the street side with iceplant and ivy, with human access through a vestibule stuck onto one corner like a booger. All the vestibules had the same tile floor, the same letters blocked out in aluminum to spell some incomprehensible acronym that was the company's name, and behind the same beige counter the same brightly colored receptionist standing with empty hands lying on the counter top, looking out seemingly at the surface of Mars. James recalled the recurring episode of the Xerox men in *The President's Analyst* and chided himself for an unoriginal image.

That baby looked familiar. And the baby seemed to think James was familiar too. Riding facing backward, it reached out one hand for James, now only twenty feet away.

It was his baby. He, James. What was BF#1 doing with James's baby? He didn't even know who BF#1 was. The only time he'd seen the man was at Roger's condo the night Harris was kidnapped by the Iraqis.

It looked as if Baby were going to holler. Perhaps cause BF#1 to turn around and spot James following him.

Horrified, James dropped back and ducked into a parking lot, keeping Baby in sight. The next warehouse on, the blue one with rose trim, was Sofka's. There was a café in that building which served this part of the warehouse district with breakfast egg and toast, and ersatz Italian soup made of cardboard. BF#1 went in. James contrived to look in the front window without being seen.

Sofka was there. She was drinking dreadful coffee. They exchanged pecks. He shrugged off Baby's harness and passed it over. Sofka propped Baby on the chair beside her like a bag of groceries. BF#1 sat down opposite.

What on earth was going on? What was Sofka going to do with Baby at work? Put it on the floor and feed it Coke and chips? Why wasn't it at the minder's?

It began to look as if BF#1 were a pseudonym, and his real name was SF#1. Or #2 or #3.

BF was eating a sub. Rubber slabs of ham and cappicola stuck out of it all around, and bits of lettuce and chili dropped onto the paper plate. He put the sandwich down, wiped greasy fingers on a tiny paper napkin, and took Sofka's hand. Reached across the table and covered it with his own. Their hands were copulating there on the plastic table in front of everyone.

Well, actually the café was empty this time of the afternoon. Even the barrista or whoever had disappeared after sliding the sub onto the table. But that didn't make what they were doing *private*.

Sub. James once, when a boy, called them grinders.

The sun fell full and heavy on James where he stood and he backed up a little to get some shade from a small tree, but from there he couldn't see. Glare blocked the window. He wiped his forehead with the sleeve of his shirt, ran his fingers through his hair, wiped his cheek.

This was so stupid. So sordid and common.

Angry, James turned away and consulted a scrap of paper from his shirt pocket, the address of the property he had been sent to look at. Something being foreclosed. Was it occupied? Had it been trashed? They hadn't given him the lockbox key because the other man had it, home in bed with the flu or something.

Leprosy probably. Why wasn't there a second key? Why had James come so far out of his way on a hot day? The neighborhood stank of barrio food, and the empty house looked a little beat up but not wrecked. He took a few Polaroids.

Only when he was back on the bus, the air-conditioned bus, did he begin to recover from being stunned. Anger, humiliation, and unhappiness jostled for attention.

Sunday morning. James and Sofka were fighting as usual, though of course not about the real thing. James had made some remark about "what is owing to me" and Sofka, aggrieved, had laughed at him. It had been a bitter laugh, he could tell.

Baby was asleep. They had made cups of tea and were sitting on the terrace in those molded plastic chairs you find in Home Depot in stacks of — well, in tall stacks for a few dollars. Sofka was barefoot. The wings of her robe had fallen open on either side of her crossed legs. Heavy with milk. Curly black hair all over, uncombed. James gritted his teeth.

I want to be in love, he said. It would be nice to be in love.

They talked in low voices so as not to wake Baby, so as not to be a laughingstock for the neighbors, to practice civility.

And what's my role in the relationship, James? To be in love with you, I think. You arrange things so you are at the center. "Owing to you." What nonsense.

He made a feeble defense which was knocked down at once.

You think you are grown up, James, because you are tolerant. Think yourself tolerant. Magnanimous. You are still in love, after all, in spite of everything. That is grown up of you.

She sipped her tea. James goggled.

Tolerance, she remarked half to herself, becomes self-centered once it is named.

Who on earth have you been talking to?

Saleem.

Oh. Of course.

Well for God's sake, he won't let anyone help, James was saying. Saleem seems to think it's not fair if you have help, as if it were a game of golf or something. A test. Not to cheat.

Grace abounding to sinners, the other mused. Works and days.

Fuck that. Let's move on.

They had paused at a shady bench to watch the surf, but they were sweaty from running and had quickly become cold,

Speaking of which, said the other one, what is wrong with your friend Bill? He's been impossible to talk to since this Harris was murdered.

Yes, well. I suppose you've touched on it.

How do you mean?

Harris. And anyway, Bill's own hands are hardly clean. Perhaps it's guilt. He betrayed Roger about the cat. He refused to acknowledge knowing that fellow my wife was seeing. Is seeing. He knows the fellow well enough. What did he have to hide? Perhaps he put the man up to it somehow. Let them use his place. While he was away in Singapore or London or wherever those people are who he consults for.

A silence fell, smothering a possible outburst. They moved off, but pace was slow. James had stiffened up at the break. They stopped again at a spot in the sun to stretch.

It seems to me, said the other man astutely, that there is an elephant in the room.

Eh?

A small earthquake passed underneath, hardly felt. A lurch, a shudder. They glanced at each other to see whether it had been noticed.

The ocean heaved itself onto the sand, forever tired and homeless, to rest a moment before getting up again.

After a time the other man moved off, leaving James sitting alone holding his toes and seeming to look at the horizon. James needed to go every so often, like Melville's storyteller, down to the shore, but he never seemed to profit by it. He never got farther than the beach. Sofka suggested they go to the islands some weekend, but they didn't. James wondered what it might be like to live on a small island. By himself. Whether he would get claustrophobic. There weren't many opportunities to try that question.

He twisted around to see where the other fellow had gone.

Ridiculous to call him a fellow. He was not. Fellowship was unknown to him. No club would ever have him as a member. He was the Tim Robbins character in Altman's *The Player*. And James was the schmuck Robbins killed.

Monday to Friday at the bank, Saturdays for running. It didn't seem to do any good to repeat that mantra about how many poets have worked in banks, customs houses and so forth. The task of the Player, why he could get away with murder, was to see, but also to accept, that there can be no fellowship in this game. This business.

James would never be a script writer. He was wildly unsuited to the work. After some years this felt realization was coming to be articulated. And Sofka, bless her, had never said a word against his foolish aspiration. She had just gone and had a baby and made it impossible to aspire to anything. James berated himself for being so stupid, and his own muttering merged with the ocean's into one cosmic mutter. James would never make his way forward with brains because he hadn't any; he knew that of himself — knew without words. He hadn't any words, either.

Some other way was required.

Saleem wasn't short on brains or words, though he had sort of clammed up of late, since being in jail. Pulled off the street as a terrorist, in those first panicky days.

Saleem would talk of a Way. It was something out of Eastern religion. Saleem seemed to know a lot about such things. At least, before he was consumed by this new indignity. Now, if there was a Way, he kept it to himself. James would have to work it out on his own.

Lost Horizon. Ronald Coleman. Robert Riskin got the screenplay credit. *Mr Deeds, It Happened One Night, The Strange Love Of Martha Ivers.* Some good stuff, considering the opportunities for silliness in Hilton's book, that Shangri-La business, immortality and so on.

James would never have stood the competition. Always having your stuff messed with, never having your own voice, other people taking credit for nothing, endless treatments and pitches but nothing *done*. Bunch of narcissists.

He didn't agree with what Saleem said in his newspaper columns about film anyway. Movies, dammit, for one thing. Not film — movies.

Saleem claimed that you could work out what a movie was about by analysis. What it was *really* about. Saleem wasn't interested in plots and what ordinary people — quotidian was the word —suppose movies are about. He'd actually written this in one of his reviews and was told not to do it again. That *Cahiers* stuff doesn't sell papers.

It doesn't sell *Cahiers*, either.

James objected to the notion that movies mean anything. Feelings, not ideas, were what they are about. Movies do things to your insides. You come out different than you went in. Like *Soylent Green*, he thought sardonically. He was fond of little jokes like this.

Well, different for a while, anyway. Very few movies had a permanent effect on James. *The Pawnbroker*, maybe.

He saw that in an art house at a time when he would skip school to go to the movies. Like that Walker Percy person. Like everybody, actually

There aren't any art houses now. They were dying already before the DVD came along. It had been hard to see old movies then, to find out what had been done already. What you got from old movies was precious, rare. Now old movies are everywhere, and every dickhead knows about *Grand Hotel*.

He sprang up and turned back the way he had come, not wanting to get into a rage. It wasn't good for him. It was not helpful.

The wind off the ocean was picking up. How does that go? The sun heats the land and the land air rises and sucks the cold air off the sea in underneath. Then at night it goes the other way.

Lotta hot air.

James turned into the wind. Always into the wind.

Idiot.

The wind blew his hair back and brought tears to his eyes and the sun rising over the low skyline of Santa Monica burned the back of his neck. The man he had been jogging with was long gone, along with the script idea James had been working out.

Maybe, James thought, he ought to learn to play golf. How long does it take to be good enough? Maybe it would help at work, too — get him to know some people outside his office. No one in his office golfed. They were all either women or else too fat to put one foot in front of another much less swing a golf club.

Losers.

He was blocking the path. A little person blazing along with her ponytail streaming out behind knocked into him, spun off, and ran on cursing. James moved off the path.

This running business was only an excuse to go down to the beach anyway. James was long past the time when he could claim to be working on his tan or trying to pick up babes. That was the way it would be with golf, too. He never told himself the real reason for anything. About life being out of balance and what-all else. Probably you can't get good at golf by using it to pick up babes.

If Saleem were to get off thinking and go with his feelings he would be a terrorist for real. Like that Harris. Sticks and stones, that's what words are worth. Saleem tries to beat you up with words, with ideas. Whereas movies — oh, well, James thought, that was only back to the same thing again. Ranting.

Saleem was becoming an obsession.

He wondered what relationship Bill and that Harris could have had. Bill had clearly been upset, yet in the café that morning when they were all speculating on what it might be like to have your head cut off and what your head might think about that afterwards, Bill had been cold but not offended. And if they'd been lovers how come that Harris could go live half way around the world and Bill not say a thing to prevent it? What kind of lovers were that?

Was Harris his first name or his last? Did anybody know? Besides Bill.

A terrorist, now, is more than someone who mugs people and leaves them dead on the ground. A terrorist does do that, it's true, but not for the fun of it.

Well, maybe it is fun, but that's not the point. The point is to erase a few infidels, for there to be fewer infidels, and to scare the others, the unerased ones, into thinking they ought to stop doing whatever it is that infidels do, and in the bargain you get to go to heaven. That's why terrorists always rape the women. To pollute them. Not that women go to heaven anyway, polluted or not, but it gets to the men who can't stop it or get revenge, plus it takes away their women. Without women you get crazy. Crazy people don't go to heaven.

How was it to rape someone? James boggled. Like screwing a sandbag, wouldn't it? What was there in that? If you were really angry why would it help to go and rip somebody's clothes off and see them try to hide behind their hands? It was another of those things not worth thinking about.

You have to get into it another way.

The Way of rape. Maybe it wouldn't be a good idea to ask Saleem about that.

James wondered what he would do if he were bound and naked and threatened with having his head chopped off. Would he wet himself? Or would he smile and be beatific and sit up a little straighter? Would his head be pleased with itself?

Christ. They always wanted you to plead for your life, didn't they? Would he plead?

Of course he would. He liked not being dead. If that's what he was — not dead.

He had reached a spot where there were stairs down to the beach. James went down and walked toward the shoreline, getting sand in his shoes. The tide was going out. He sat down on the wet sand and folded up his legs and rested his hands on his knees with his thumb and forefinger making a circle and tried to see across the Pacific to where the people of the Way live to see if that would do any good.

The East. Saleem hadn't liked *Crouching Tiger*. He'd written that it was dishonest and lacked the quotidian. Of course, Saleem didn't like any action movies. He said it was the same as *The Incredibles*, though of course when he wrote that about *Crouching Tiger* there weren't any Incredibles yet.

Saleem hadn't liked *The Incredibles* either. He said the robot had been betrayed, taught reason and desire only for the purpose of glorifying its creator, and turned out to die. Saleem thought no one had noticed this. His review had been really angry, as if he'd had a personal interest.

Robots. Sympathy for robots.

Christ. What next?

Sympathy for terrorists, of course.

How were you supposed to save a robot who was bent on killing you and smashing everything? And what would salvation mean to a robot anyway? It's a *robot.* for Christ's sake.

Is a robot going to plead with you — you being Incredible, not some wanker like James — to have mercy? And you're supposed to believe that this robot has accepted grace while at the same time it's smashing everything up?

James's butt was wet and cold and he was sounding to himself like Archie Bunker.

What else did Carroll O'Connor do that was good? Nothing. *In the Heat Of the Night.* No, that was Rod Steiger, like in *The Pawnbroker. The Music of Chance.* No, that was Charles Durning. The rest of them were dogs.

The back of his sweats was soaking. Who would believe he was sweating there? Not in some sports drink commercial where the sweat pours off you everywhere, not just there. That's what you got in you. Sweat.

It was maybe a mile to his car. Anyway it was starting to get hot. James picked up the pace a little.

What does it mean to be saved? he wondered. He and Sofka weren't any better off for having forgiven each other. Or he had forgiven her anyway. James wasn't certain what Sofka thought. About anything, actually.

Are there movies where someone is saved?

Blade Runner. Dekker and the girl escape to the wilderness. Who is actually a robot — what do you know. Of course, all the other robots get wiped because they're not human enough. That one played by Rutger Hauer, was he saved in the end? James had forgotten that sim's name despite Saleem's always using him as an example. And what else did Hauer do? German movies, but not speaking German James couldn't know whether they were any good.

Hauer's line about death being a waste he made up on the set, James heard. That was good.

Is that how you're saved, you get the girl? Because you get the girl, or do you have to be saved first? Neither one of these was exactly the story between him and Sofka. In fact, James didn't see much of Sofka now. Somehow they had come to live separate lives. What does Sofka do in her life? James wondered. Besides feed the baby. And change diapers. And presumably have a nice wank now and then..

Like James.

How long was it since they'd fucked? Two weeks?

Christ.

But he'd been trying to think of other movies where someone was saved and forgiven, or maybe the other way round.

How about that Japanese monk in *The Burmese Harp*? Who gets a mission to bury all the people they killed in the war and won't go back to Japan with the others? They think he's nuts. James supposed that was how it usually was with saved people. He remembered a scene at the end where the monk is standing far off and looking back, with his white robes, in a hieratic pose. What did it mean his looking back? Probably it meant nothing. It's natural to look back. People do that.

James was having a hard time coming up with any good examples. How about Edward G Robinson's character in *Soylent Green.* Was he saved?

Robinson was completely deaf when he made that movie. There had been some complicated business about telling him when to speak his lines. However did he know how to deliver them, to interact with the others?

Maybe Roger would know.

James reached his car, winkled his keys out of the little zipped pocket in his sweats, and opened the door.

Already hot in the sun. Little raisins. Roll down the windows. Let in air.

Good idea, letting in some air.

What about Bill Murray in *Lost In Translation*? he thought as he drove off, taking a last look at the ocean, making the upholstery wet with seawater.

Inevitably, James got into a shouting match with Saleem. The provocation, or pretext, was Saleem's weekly column in the local alternative newspaper, the *Voice*. Saleem was defending a movie, *Last Year At Marienbad,* which James couldn't abide, the penultimate intellectual's movie.

I think you mean "ultimate," Saleem remarked quietly.

Eh?

*Pen*ultimate means second to last.

Fuck that. This movie is like thirty years old.

Forty-one. *West Side Story* came out that year. *The Hustler.* *Judgment At Nuremburg.*

Exactly. People liked those movies. They still do. They're on cable. People talk about them. Who the hell remembers *Last Year At Marianburg?*

I do. It tests the possibilities of the grammar of film.

Grammar? Horse's ass. It's *boring.*

You seem to know it too. And your parents were maybe in kindergarten. It's part of your film culture, a critical reference point, The type specimen of a certain meme. You acknowledge this just be knowing about it. Whether it bores you is irrelevant.

And *you* — James was losing control. Saleem's superior tone infuriated him. *You* probably sneaked out of school in Peshawar to see it.

Saleem paused. His eyelids drooped slightly. I'm forty-one, he said after a moment. The same age as the movie. I saw it in college, in a pocket theater in San Francisco a block from the beach at the end of the streetcar line. There's a Korean grocery store there now, I think. There aren't any more of those theaters. Anyone can watch it on DVD whenever they want.

What do you mean, irrelevant? Why do you watch movies? Is this some kind of penance, a hair shirt, watching only movies you don't like?

Well, James, I didn't say I don't like it. But that's of no concern. I want to understand how it works.

Why it's boring?

If you say so.

Christ, you idiot, it's obvious. Only people like you can't see that.

People like me —

Roger intervened at this point, strongarming James into the kitchen for a beer and leaving Saleem to fume harmlessly. His self-control was, after all, only marginally better than James's.

Well, Roger said in a conciliatory voice after stuffing James's head into the refrigerator, I never heard of that movie until I met Saleem. I suppose most people haven't.

James came up red-faced and spluttering, a beer in each hand, knocking himself in the eye on a corner of the open freezer door above. At once, Roger was all over him with cold rags and sympathy, smothering an outburst of incoherent cursing.

Get offa me, you damned — ! but he managed to swallow the rest.

Saddened, Roger left a now contrite James to sit at the kitchen table and returned to the living room, where Saleem was quietly chewing his lip. The sound of a beer can opened rapped the silence, and then quickly a second one, a sound like a brush sliding over the head of a snare drum and then a soft hit to the rim.

You're not surprised, I hope, Roger said, You're both provocative, intransigent...

Am I?

Yes, I think so. You should try, Saleem, to be more — um — *beatific.*

A gargling noise, either a snigger or a choking spasm, was all Saleem could manage. He got to his feet. Passing through the doorway of his room he ducked, a habitual precaution, though it wasn't necessary here. The door closed slowly behind him. The latch snicked reluctantly into the hole cut for it and no more was heard.

BILL

They had all gathered for breakfast at a café in Long Beach, an undistinguished place in its food, ambience, and neighborhood which had unaccountably acquired a terrific cachet among some people and, being rather a small place, was correspondingly hard to get into, which only increased its desirability. There was always a line.

It was after ten when they were seated finally and now brunchtime. Some wanted eggs, some wanted croissants, some wanted sandwiches. A muddle.

The talk at the table was all about Harris, who they heard had been beheaded as promised. This news came to them through Bill's partner, who was attached to an embassy there or something, whose embassy wasn't known, or perhaps to a private contractor, and who, Bill said, had been trying to do something to prevent it. In this he had not been successful. A videotape of the grisly thing had been broadcast somewhere as usual, thankfully not on the evening news, and in fact the Western media seemed to have lost interest, which was why Bill and the others hadn't found out about it out until now.

None of them knew — had known — Harris, other than Bill. What could he have done to get himself kidnapped?

Nothing, I imagine, said Bill absently, stirring his scrambled eggs with a fork. Standing about in the wrong place. If there are any right ones.

A couple of women at a nearby table had overheard, jammed in as they were practically shoulder to shoulder. God, said one. What unpleasant luck.

Hmp, snorted the other. If you go to bars at two ay hem you're likely to get pounded. Same thing.

This exchange had a ritual air, as if it were a long-standing difference needing to be renewed now and then.

Those at Bill's table were horrified by Harris's death. By its mode.

I imagine, James said, something like a kung fu movie where the emperor takes a famously sharp sword and zing! at one blow, and the head tumbles off and rolls under a table. James giggled uneasily.

These ruffians, Roger countered, probably don't have a sharp sword. Sawed it off with a pocket knife, I'd bet. Probably rusty.

Jesus, Roger.

Well, he replied, acting aggrieved to cover up his agitation, what about these executioners one reads about who would take three of four blows with an axe to do the job? I wonder what that would be like.

Well, Saleem remarked clinically, if you get whacked in the back of the neck with something heavy — an iron pipe, a penny falling from a tall building — if you're not killed you're unconscious.

As James would have it, said Roger, does the brain go on working for a couple of minutes, staring at the emperor upside down from under the table? Thinking what thoughts do you suppose? Ugh. Haven't we always looked for a more humane way of judicial murder? That was what Guillotine had in mind.

I don't suppose terrorists think much about humanity, Saleem murmured, but in the din of the crowded café only the nearest woman at the next table heard him.

What? said the other, the one with a preference for luck, who hadn't heard.

A look passed between them, a quick assessment, melancholy or cynical.

Through all this Bill was mostly silent, continuing to toy with his fork. Saleem, too, had said little, which Roger took note of, remarking to himself that Saleem's own experience of terrorism might make him uncharacteristically quiet. No more of those manic outbursts which once had so marked him. No more of the compulsion to annotate, gloss, footnote.

Nobody else wanted to mention Saleem's run-in, either. He was probably still sore. Might provoke something uncomfortable.

Sofka's feelings also were unknown. She unwrapped her croissant quietly, putting a thin coat of strawberry jam on each rag of pastry, down to its heart of nothing. She and James were now at serious odds. Sofka had more or less invited herself to what was in some fashion Bill's party.

Whoever, remarked Roger, sitting between her and James so as not to risk the proprieties — Whoever thought of filling a croissant with chocolate or cream cheese? That's a blintz, isn't it? They even look like blintzes.

What's a blintz?

It's a crêpe, said Bill quietly. Well, a blini. As Roger says, with cream cheese.

Somehow this factoid stopped all conversation. It was definitive. No one knew how to hook onto it. After a time, when everyone began to be restless and it looked as if brunch might be over even while there was coffee to drink, Bill rescued them from his own bungle.

I don't know, he murmured when everyone else had practically to shout to be heard, as if perhaps he didn't want to be heard but somehow was anyway — I don't know... he came to a stop. The engine had conked out. Then a cough and a sputter, and it was notable how well Bill's soft voice was audible.

I don't know whether it's worthwhile speculating what a severed head might think. Like vegetable people: suppose there's a mind in there imprisoned in its brain. What an awful idea. Perhaps we go mad for self-protection? Rabbits, they say, go numb from shock when the dog bites it. Convenient to think so. I don't suppose anyone cares enough about rabbits to verify that.

Or kill a lot of rabbit, Sofka said, carefully picking up bits of croissant with a dampened fingertip.

You could bite 'em yourself, James added, leaning forward a bit to speak around Roger. Snap snap — rrrr. Give you an insight into the real thing.

Don't Japanese swordmakers test the blade by cutting the heads off straw men?

I did some trout fishing once, Saleem remarked now, as if he found this new topic more congenial. Convenient fish, trout. They die practically as you take them out of the water. All that fight in them, pouf! A brittle fish, trout.

My grandpa took me fishing one time we went to see him, James added. Caught a pike. On the chain all day, and when we brought it home it was still flapping and bucking. Grandpa said I had to clean it myself, so I got it into the fish house and tried hitting it with a hammer so as to make it lie still. Couldn't even get in a good whack it jumped around so. Tried a two-by-four. Must have hit it a hundred times. Pulverized, and it's still wiggling. I didn't know what to do. Grandpa just shook his head and cleaned it himself, but I think he threw it away afterward, when I wasn't to know I'd spoiled it.

So how did your grandfather do it? Saleem asked?

Speared it with a fish knife and just cut it open, Sofka said, to everyone's surprise.

While it was still thrashing?

Why not? If you want to eat pike. Is vivisection worse than having your head beat to mush?

I remember a show on television, Roger said. He waited a fraction of a second before starting the story in case someone else was going to talk. I don't know what it was about, what the TV show was about, but there was this woman in it who raised rabbits for food. Tough woman. While they were interviewing her she took this live rabbit and did something to it with her hands — killed it — and she hung it up on a tree branch by the hind legs. Then she took a knife and made a cut and pulled the fur off it like a sock and never missed a beat in what she was saying. I have no idea what she was saying. This dead rabbit was hanging there, not bleeding even, sort of glistening. Raw. The rabbit lady. Probably something about poor people, she was saying. I can't imagine.

We don't know anything about other people, Saleem said. The world outside is a black hole which sucks up meaning and gives nothing back.

Bill objected to this. Come on, Saleem — you're still sitting on a chair even if your butt doesn't hurt.

Saleem shrugged, as if he'd wrestled with this elementary stuff long ago. A slight lift of the shoulders not disdainful but rather a little sad to have found all this out it. Knowledge he might have preferred not to have, and not all that profound, either. Trite, even.

It's trivial, he said.

Chairs exist, Bill growled. because you sit in them. Just because you don't fall on your ass on the floor when you try to sit on it doesn't mean we agree on what the thing is, or what to call it. Even a stone-ager from chairless New Guinea can see you can sit on the thing even if he never thought of that and may wonder why you'd want to. If you don't think so then how are you going to live a rational life?

Knowledge creates the phenomenon it pretends to describe, Saleem remarked. What's a life?

James, at least, was nonplussed. He turned to Bill. Is this, he inquired suspiciously, something to do with computer programming? With what you do?

Maybe. I never know what my stuff does except superficially, until after it does it. If I did it wouldn't be interesting. If you understand something then you haven't thought it through. I impose myself on the world, not the other way around.

James turned on Saleem. Well, do you suppose that the head under the table creates the executioner's sword, then? Death concentrates the mind, they say.

Bill winced, glared at James. His jaw worked slightly. This was about as much as Bill would show his feelings. If he had a secret life they would never know about it, or what Harris had done there, any more than they knew why he owned so few chairs. Two or three, all valuable, like old masters, not to sit in.

What do you suppose this Harris can have been doing to get himself so in the way? James went on, unable to let go. It was eating on him some way.

Christ, James! Sofka bleated in protest.

Now what?

Why do you think it's always the victim's fault? Sofka was really angry. Who is responsible here? Is it all right that these people are loose in the world so long as *your* head isn't lost? She was beginning to screech. The two women at the next table stared. Do you *care* who's guilty so long as it's not you?

Everyone is guilty, Roger said in the midst of the silence which followed this imbroglio. Guilty of everything.

But pretty soon the chatter in the restaurant started up again. When people realized there was to be no dramatic scene, no descending curse, no spectacle, they recovered the thin thread of their own concerns.

James, however, clearly felt humiliated. He pushed back violently from the table and pounded out, knocking over water glasses and barging through the queue. After breakfast when the others had gone their ways, everyone wondering what fate now awaited James. Sofka went off in Saleem's old junker, now running only about half the time. Bill and Roger headed up the walk together, making for Bill's car where he had parked it on a side street.

Saleem, said Roger after a time, his hands clasped meditatively behind his back, thinks it was me who denounced him.

And was it?

Roger looked away, one eyebrow raised, refusing any confrontation.

No, he said simply. We had a row. Perhaps he'll move out and stick me with the whole rent.

Short, are you?

No, not short.

But Roger's hands silently revealed the lie, if Bill had known how to read them. Roger didn't like to talk about money in front of Bill, who probably didn't know anything about iron spoons.

The school pays enough to get by, he said. I could always find another organ gig I suppose. But what got into him?

So Saleem supposes that you tattled, or that someone did? He doesn't like it that this thing fell out of the sky like frozen shit from an airplane and happened to hit *him*.

Aw — why pick me?

You're available. Lots of people are available.

They had reached Bill's car. Bill unlocked the door.

So he said, musing. Saleem is more committed to rational explanation than he lets on. Something of a poseur?

No.

Bill gazed into Roger's eyes, smiling faintly.

Ride?

No, Roger said again, a little frustrated by Bill's lack of sympathy, and walked away in the other direction, downhill toward the harbor.

In a few days James recovered some equanimity and it wasn't long before he again brought out his life-out-of-balance hobbyhorse.

He, Roger, and Bill were occupying a table in a downscale wine bar one stop along the Metrorail from Roger's apartment. They had been talking for some time, twirling empty glasses between their fingers and staring at the table top, aware of the waiters who were trying to shoo them out to make room for some better tippers.

The Rotonde this is not, Bill said, passing around a plate of blintzes, which he had discovered on the menu, moving the chessboard of glasses, espresso cups and soiled plates to make room, all of them in the clumsy grip of a sugar and caffeine buzz.

Sofka showed up partway through the evening. For a while the waiters were more enterprising, but soon returned to their old ways.

There was still no consensus on what it meant for life to be out of balance. Whether a time of ideological violence was unbalanced, for example, or whether that was just the usual thing and if this imbalance were extraordinary why then take notice for help was on the way whereas if it were the usual thing, imbalance, then not to fret because another state devoutly to be wished would never appear anyway.

Roger suspected that James did not want a definition of balance, because if there were one it would contribute to disproving the original thesis.

So. Bill was taking the role of socratic moderator. The world is like a top, wobbling and wandering drunkenly across the floor, but still spinning nevertheless.

James grasped this knife by its blade.

Where does this idea come from (James was whining a bit, like a car with a loose fanbelt) that you can whack and cut your way into heaven? That it doesn't matter if you kill these other people if you yourself are saved?

Sofka eyed James rancorously. What did he think it meant to be *saved*? Two virgins instead of one? The word unspoken was sand in her mouth.

Now it was Bill who was coming unglued. Marty Harris, he growled, was never interested in virgins. Nor in being *saved* — nearly spitting on James out of contempt for this word. Sofka, who might have felt vindicated, looked worried for James.

Saleem says, said Roger, inserting himself between the combatants to give Bill time to relocate his urbanity — Saleem says there are two cultures. One is the culture of evidence, the other is a culture of belief. Believers trust only what is oracular. Experience, the empirical evidence of the senses, is discounted.

No fucking, Sofka muttered. Done that.

And so the couple's byplay went on beneath the conversation. Roger was put off and forgot what he wanted to say. His fingers drummed on the table.

Belief is given to you, Bill said, taking up the thread with authority. It descends on you without asking permission. Everything else is a fraud.

I thought you were a hard rationalist, Bill. Economics explains all.

Those were Marty's views, Bill said. His voice was quiet once more, but his eyes were laying a torch to James's tinder.

It goes to show, James said with a total lack of caution. Sofka winced.

What does that mean, exactly? *Goes to show.* Show what? That all our assumptions are always wrong? Goes. Goes how? Something about cattle being led into the show ring?

Roger made a noise but was cut off by the sound of breaking glass. Bill had crushed a wineglass in his hand.

And which are you, James? Declare yourself.

I suppose I would fall with the believers, James said slowly, beginning to see where he had put his foot.

Really.

Your hand, Bill —

Yes? And your meaning is?

There was no way to reply to this, and the evening was broken up in a few minutes, to the relief of the staff, who were a little free with elbows and scowls as the late disputants abandoned the field.

James and Sofka went their own way, walking toward a bus which would take them eventually home. They said little, just a word from Sofka. After a couple of blocks James reached for Sofka's hand, which she instinctively jerked back. Then, reconsidering, she offered a finger and they walked on, drawing a little closer together. The baby-minder would be waiting. Impatiently as minders do. Baby would have been fed with a bottle of Sofka's milk which she had saved for the purpose and would have fallen asleep, believing all will be well for all time, as babies do, clutching its minder's ring finger.

Eventually the cat had to be euthanized. It barfed up whatever it was fed, staining the rugs and making booby-traps to step in, or deposited incredibly foul-smelling liquid turds, though since it could no longer keep anything down it was a puzzle where the poop could be coming from. Roger took it once to a vet who wouldn't come to any conclusions without exploratory surgery which Roger couldn't afford, so he brought the cat back home again. It grew weaker, finally ate nothing at all, which at least put a stop to the booby-traps. It only lay on its side under the sofa, it's eyes growing bigger and bigger, until Roger could stand it no longer and took it back to the vet to be cremated.

Almost paralyzed with dread and anxiety, he asked Saleem to come along. Saleem was willing to carry Asparagus out to the car in a shoebox, it was now so unresisting, but he would not open the box to look. Since Saleem was driving Roger ended up with the box anyway and could not help but look. It was a mistake. A sour expression not exactly a smile flickered over Saleem's face. It was clear to Roger that he would have to bear this trial alone.

He did not bear it. At the veterinarian's it was Saleem who had to explain what they wanted. The request was received in mortuary calm, and Roger handed over the box. A woman in scrubs appeared to bear it away, through a door marked *laboratory one*. The door eased shut, whisking and tsking, and Asparagus the cat, whose life had been nothing but suffering and fear, was no more.

It was that easy. All that was needed was grit and money. Roger had neither.

Saleem noticed how Roger's mouth was working and how his hands were giving advice on what to do. No existential discussions, he said. They aren't good for you. His fingers brushed Roger's wrist.

So after a small hesitation, Roger's hands went into his pockets. He pushed them deep, causing his shoulders to droop.

Despite what may have been Saleem's intent, whether to make peace or out of unforced sympathy, this experience did not improve relations between the two roommates. Never rancorous, still there were now two bottles of catsup in the refrigerator (his and his), and two washings up, and other demarcations sprang up like autumn flowers in the cooling air.

And Roger now had more reason than ever to speculate on Saleem's secret life. Saleem, he knew, thought that people were too complex to see whole, and oneself most of all. All one knows is a mask, a small set of characteristic behaviors assembled to form something like a mnemonic. Everyone expurgates his acquaintances in his own way, so that one passes from one occasion to the next as a sort of dress dummy or store window mannequin, each costume to suit the buyer's desires. The rake acquires respectability upon entering the lady dowager's salon, and sets it aside on leaving like an empty wineglass left among the others on the sideboard for the butler to take away.

Saleem tended to images of this sort, taken from old novels and movies. It was his view that when someone criticizes a novelist for not inventing 'realistic' characters they are asking that people in books be made to resemble those we encounter daily, and thus ought to be less realistic rather than more. A *real* person is unimaginable. The human-shaped object known as Roger, or Bill, Saleem or anyone else 'really' consists of nothing but masks, onionately inside one another, and if they all could be peeled away one would be left with nothing but a damp spot left by tears.

The difficulty Roger was having in getting over the fate of Asparagus was thus one which would not have afflicted Saleem. Whatever was wrong with Saleem it could have nothing to do with empathy.

The trouble was Harris. Analogies simply leaped out of that thought like djinns out of a whirlwind, rushing to strangle him. Roger found himself vis-à-vis his dead cat in the position of those deathbound hadjis to whom Harris had been only a convenient blob of protoplasm. Proto, not actual plasm. Conscientiously examining himself for what he supposed were the marks of terrorist thinking, Roger could not completely absolve himself of the secret link between his purity and his convenience.

What is the worth of cats? Is it all right, as some do, to go around all year squashing bugs and then on the day of festival offer up conciliatory blessings to them? Really, can one be absolved of inadvertance? To say nothing of — well at least he wasn't gloating about it, or passing around videotapes.

Absolution, he thought with disgust. Something James would be preoccupied by. Plainly put, the cat had trusted him and he had betrayed it. Perhaps that was what James meant by life out of balance.

Roger would still run across Bill now and then, for they moved on similar paths and it was only due to Bill's increasing hermeticism that they didn't meet more often. When they did, at least for a while the subject of Harris was a natural opportunity for social remarks. Roger was somewhat obtuse about this, not noticing Bill's reluctance to chat. Harris evidently belonged to some other persona of Bill's. Talking about Harris to others would confuse the masks, leading Bill to put on the wrong one, with whatever consequences. Perhaps the Harris persona was a spy, or was connected to a squalid past or some seedy doings, or —

The shock of seeing Harris on television, kneeling, clothed only in sweat and blood, revealed when the bag was jerked off his head, seeming thus to pop up like a leering jack-in-the-box

In a few seconds all their lives were changed.

Casting about for some small talk, Roger mentioned that he had had to euthanize his cat.

But Roger! Bill said. I would have paid for that surgery. Why didn't you ask?

Roger gaped. This was blatantly untrue. Bill had known the situation perfectly well.

Afterwards, looking for excuses, he guessed that Bill was lashing out in response to his own demons, to the other things he had not paid for, just as by crushing the wine glass he revealed that he had punished James as a substitute for himself.

Saleem would have hooted down Roger's narcissistic psychoanalysis.

Roger wondered if he ought to be referring these matters to Saleem.

After that Roger went out of his way to avoid Bill. He found some new acquaintances in other places. He began to think he could do better with a roommate less neurotic and obsessed than the one he had, but if he began to look for somewhere else to live he'd end up in Redlands or some other impossible place. So he stayed put.

No one quite understood what Bill did for a living. He had an important degree from Cal Tech and a job which enabled him to live well even on a fraction of his income. Supposedly a fraction. He drove a decent car of an inconspicuous sand color and had a condo in a gated neighborhood in Long Beach which, it was reported, was very sparsely furnished, though there was some nice art, mostly drawings, photographs, or prints in small editions of twenty or so, but never with ostentatious low numbers. Whether this was all to his own taste or that of his absent friend no one knew. In fact, no one in Bill's present circle had ever met the friend, or even knew his name.

Whatever it was that Bill did, it had something to do with computer programming, and to do with something very fundamental. He worked for himself as a consultant, one of those people who has no need of advertisement because he is one of a very few who understand that thing, whatever it was, and the business came to him by word of mouth. He had done something important once upon a time, and after that had had no need of further creation, but perhaps he was not so lazy as that. No one knew.

It was through Roger, who circulated in a neighboring but moneyless milieu, that Saleem, the Jakobys, and others of that heterogeneous group had come to know Bill. Before that, before his companion went away, was whisked away by his embassy, Bill had lived even more quietly: just the two of them. And the work.

Nowadays it was mostly the work.

He'd been out a few times, but he found he'd grown tentative, and disliked the need for protection which he had become unused to, having only a single partner. After that he kept even more to himself and lost touch. Friends from the old life called, but his phone was often not turned on.

So he was a little nonplussed when James showed up unannounced, ringing the intercom at the gate late one morning and asking to be let in. He was on foot. He had taken the bus. Which meant at least an hour.

Took the day off, James said as he came up the walk to where Bill stood holding open the door. Supposed to be sick. Suppose I am, actually.

He said nothing about being on a bank errand to evaluate some property.

Bill wore frayed jeans and a Lakers t-shirt with a hole in it. He was barefoot. James, who at other times would be found wearing a coat and tie, was dressed similarly except for the athletic shoes and under a seersucker blazer, an Angels t-shirt without the hole.

Do you remember that fellow you brought along to the party at Roger's last weekend? said James after a few formalities. It was too early for a drink, so Bill had given him a Perrier. There were some grapes that looked not quite fresh in a bowl on the glass coffee table.

No, Bill said.

Ah.

There was a long pause. How amusing it would be to simply go away now, leaving this cryptic exchange behind to smog up the rest of the day.

He came with you, James said, determined to keep any note of accusation out of his voice.

Did he?

It was only two days ago, Bill.

James described the man BF#1. We all thought he was with you, he insisted.

Oh. Well, he was, I suppose. But I don't know him.

What?

We met. I was going to Roger's, he came along. Albert or Alvin or somebody.

Oh Christ, James muttered disgustedly.

What's the problem, then?

James turned rather red, blinked rapidly, changed the subject, returned again obsessively.

This Alfie, Bill. Where can I find him?

No idea.

You met somewhere. Where was it?

James was becoming brusque despite himself, intentions peeping out from behind his feather fan, and Bill, always the more alert, shied away. He named a club, not the right one. James should stay out of such places anyway.

They went on chatting, James nervously eating moldy grapes, looking for a polite exit. As if, business finished, he wanted to stroke their relationship but was only building up static. Bill's attention wandered off, but he was good at seeming. Better than James ever.

Bill's impression of James after two encounters was that he was ignorant and narcissistic. Slow of brain. All these people from Roger's other life, outside the school and the church organ, seemed — well — quite unlike Roger himself, so that... It might have made Bill curious, but it didn't. That woman Sofka, James's wife — supposed wife — was marginally more alert. Women usually are, in Bill's experience: a trait developed by anyone who spends time as a courtier. James and Sofka did not seem to Bill well matched. Not a couple, just two people. How did that work? It seemed to work or at least to continue. No one was doing the heavy lifting.

So Sofka had apparently taken up with this Alfie, screwing up a delicate situation. Had taken, maybe long before. Who's to know? A bad time for her secrets to be given an airing. Given the anxiety of husbands at a crux of loyalty and paternity. Paternity accepted, paternity questioned. Make him out to be a chump, an ugly fat chump at that. She could dump the baggage on him and skip town, or she could wake herself up with an Alfie or two.

Bill clucked his tongue at these reflection, causing James to pause. It was, after all, just the same with Bill's own relationships. That Mariwiki person after all had only wanted to go to the party so as to give Sofka a squeeze. So why should he dump on those two for being weak? Bill was tired of being lonesome. It was such a focusing condition, you think only of yourself, of what you deserve. You pine and fulminate alternately. You —

Tch.

This noise brought James to a halt entirely. Something was going on under the ground. He made some polite remarks and fled. Bill stood in the doorway watching James struggle with the security exit, break free, vanish into the woods. Groves of proxy houses doing duty for woods. The sky was its usual pale blue shading to white, a streak of brown on the horizon if he could see the horizon, hidden by these expensive shacks.

Bill closed the door quietly and went back to minding his own business.

Bill's Friend No. 1, whose name was Hideoki Marouishi, turned out to be a freelance designer whom Bill employed now and then. Or someone whom Bill employed.

Hideoki's impressive memory for the small facts about other people, some of them facts it was a puzzle how he came to know, was a talent which had served him well in business. In his personal life people were more cautious about his unnerving omniscience. It turned out to be no more than an idiot savant's trick, however. A very retentive memory for detail, gossip, and casual remarks, plus an unusual sensitivity and a medium's skill at drawing inferences from tone of voice, movement of eye and lip, all combined to produce the effect. He didn't work at it or practice. An unconscious process working like a sausage machine brought him knowledge from somewhere. Perhaps he manufactured some of it himself: the cereal which binds and bulks out the meat. Plus all those things which people are willing to believe about themselves and so make facts of them in the end.

Hideoki seemed, however, when one knew more about him than Henry the Mathematical Horse, a refutation of Saleem's beliefs about the knowability of other people. And so he drew Saleem's suspicion, his paranoia, finally his wrath. It was because Hideoki seemed to know so many secrets that Saleem became convinced finally that it was he, Hideoki, who had denounced him.

Two things worked against this idea. First, Saleem had no such secrets. Second, his run-in with the police had happened before he ever met this Japanese clairvoyant. But in the way of paranoid minds always, Saleem was able to explain these things away. Even, Roger surmised, to invent secrets to be found out and used against him

This would have been a melancholy commentary on human relations and on the probable fate of nice people (if there are any) except that to Hideoki, Saleem's descent on him was as arbitrary and purposeless as a dust spout, which is why people suppose there's a djinn inside. How could one explain it otherwise? It was as inexplicable, undeserved, as the arrest of Saleem which had started it all.

Hideoki did not like being an arbitrary victim. Unlike Saleem, he knew the cause of his anger, the locus of arbitrariness.

Saleem had the guidance (only the guidance, Hideoki would have said) of the fervent. Whereas Hideoki's actions were motivated diffferently. When Saleem appeared to him suddenly, as unwanted as the visit of a saint, ranting away about what he, Hideoki, was supposed to do, poking him with that rapid and precise Pakistani English not quite comprehensible to a Japanese, talking as loudly and dangerously as an Uzi in the ghetto of cubicles where Hideoki worked writing mindless code at any hour of the day or night, it was obvious to anyone what the problem was. The situation was perfectly evident. Hideoki was backed into a corner of his cubicle; Saleem stood two inches away stabbing him repeatedly with a finger, and everyone had come out of their burrows staring like meerkats. The Marouishi was being assaulted by a madman. Undoubtedly an affair gone bad. Cherchez la femme.

Hideoki's prescience, which leaped over facts to certainties, had misled him with an erroneous idea of Saleem's origins, so that what he assumed to be Pakistani was only that Fresno accent. The dark skin of Saleem's face might have been enraged with blood too dark for Hideoki to see. The two men were Mutt and Jeff in appearance, causing Hidekoi to seem to cower no matter how militantly he stood. Their eyes wrestled. Saleem was thin, almost gaunt now, a Daumier poor man, while Hideoki's baby fat made him look like a miniature tycoon. And Saleem had the advantage of twenty years of struggle.

This gaunt, heavily strung man, Hideoki saw with all the force of Holmes's recognition of the retired sergeant of the marines, before Saleem had let the door to the bullpen recoil behind him, was here to avenge himself on a Japanese web designer who knew too much. But it came only to words after all. Accusations, threats, promises: the stinging of a bee.

Hideoke

What was that all about? the man in the next box asked when Saleem had blown away in his own windstorm. No idea, Hideoki muttered, and sat down peremptorily to his coding, ignoring the whispers and snickers.

In the days after this embarrassment, Hideoki asked around and very soon had become as knowledgeable about Saleem as he had been thought to be from the beginning. The deeper rationale of Saleem's actions eluded him, but that was always the case. His talent for empathy was useless when it came to entirely interior turmoil. He was used to waiting to see what would transpire. Perhaps in this case he could not afford to wait?

And so, intimidated and obscurely frightened, Hideoki Marouishi began to talk indiscreetly about kidnappings, narrow escapes, threats and warnings, a madman who was going to decapitate him.

Hideoki's best contact among Saleem's acquaintances, he thought, would be Sofka Jakoby. He went to the warehouse where she worked, but she wasn't as approachable as he had expected. So when Sofka went home that night, while stripping off the jeans and oversize sweater which were her habitual working dress, she attacked James for actually doing what Hideoki had insinuated she might like to do herself. James's undignified spluttering caused her to rethink, and next day when James took it out on the other loan officers, even the tellers, so that the branch manager was obliged to have a word, Sofka decided to leave a discreet message.

Hideoki was now reliant on a quality he didn't have: judgment. He appealed to Bill.

Bill was even more terrifying than Saleem, in that he appeared to be enjoying himself. He actually owned a sword for one thing, which he whirled about Hideoki's ears, mocking him for supposing that a feckless film critic and wannabe intellectual was a threat.

Afterwards Hideoki, now completely at a loss, sought out Sofka at work, hoping for advice. If Hideoki himself had to work regular hours he would not have been able to pester other people at work and perhaps none of this would have happened, or less of it anyway. He tracked her out onto the shipping floor among the lift trucks and stacks of pallets and towering shelves of shrouded waiting objects where she conducted her business as if it were a symphony orchestra. She was standing in the hangar-sized doorway. Outside on the rail dock a car was being unloaded and Sofka was taking inventory with an RFD sensor and a small computer in a holster. Framed by the big overhead doors now raised, a slim silhouette in tight jeans and a billowing white sweater which hung down almost to her knees like a cape, Sofka Jakoby was as unready to deal with Hideoki as he had been with Bill.

No one knew what he said to her because Sofka wasn't telling. There was a brief exchange that ended when she socked him in the eye. Hideoki clapped his hand over the injury, turned and stumped out of the building. Sofka stood awhile on the dock in thought, shrugged, and went back to work.

Hideoki went to apologize to Bill, belatedly realizing that he had damaged a business relationship along with a few other things. Bill may have accepted the apology but it was hard to be sure, since he received Hideoki naked, and with an enormous erection. Although this made it hard for Hideoki to concentrate, he spoke the piece he had prepared, albeit not very artistically.

To be needy is not wise, he thought as he closed Bill's door as softly and unobtrusively as he could.

The unmistakable groan of completion touched his ear.

So I can credit myself for something anyway. Hideoki smiled weakly.

And so Hideoki Marouishi ended up doing to Saleem almost by inadvertance just what Saleem had falsely accused him of. He denounced him.

«

Bill was having a dream. He had been having it for several days before the wretched Hideoki reappeared.

He was intending to hit someone with an axe. A man. Kill him. Drive the heavy axe down through his shoulder, splitting open... there didn't seem to be any reason for it. Bill had an axe, he had found himself with an axe, and in front of him stood, with his back turned, a person on whom to use it. The horror was that unlike an ordinary dream where he would wake up at this point, Bill did actually hit him, did actually swing the axe from beside his leg in a circular arc overhead and down onto that man's shoulder, missing the head. Bill could feel in his dream the effort, the muscles working in his back, arms and shoulders, grunting with the effort, straining to swing the heavy axe with as much force as there was in his square, compact body. He saw the axe bite. In his dream he saw, he felt in his hands, the blade crack through the man's clavicle, angling though the breastbone and the softer stuff. Lungs. Bill had hit him on the right side. Not the heart, though there was blood enough. Lungs as fibrous and soft and a pillow of mold on something in the pantry. Not white mold — black, gray, poisonous looking. The blood exploded over him. It slapped him warmly on the face. In his dream he felt it.

Now he woke, only now. Violently awake, hitting his head on the nightstand. He must have been lying half off the bed, and then that dream —

Screamed. The first time, anyway. More of a howl. He was shouting inarticulately. Then he broke down. He covered his eyes with his hands, moaning and rocking back and forth. Oh, oh, oh...

Oh god, he croaked. What kind of person has a dream like that?

Whatever he was, whether or not deserving, the dream did not go away. The next night, just as horrible. Exactly the same dream down to the slap of blood, exactly the same horror, though he didn't bang into the nightstand this time.

After the third time Bill was afraid to go to sleep. He sat up on the couch wrapped in a blanket to be sure there would be no third time. But there was. And what if he had managed to stay awake all night eventually and then fall asleep on the bus and wake up screaming in the midst of all those people and try to strangle the woman with the string bag sitting next to him?

That dream seemed to want something from Bill. It behaved like a beggar in the street. Baksheesh! Baksheesh! it cried, pulling insistently on the leg of his trousers.

To put a stop to it he went down to the Federal courthouse to see some justice done. There was a security check, which spooked him, but he carried nothing more dangerous than a cell phone and a PDA. The phone was to be turned off, and the guard, a rather slight woman, gave him hard looks until it was done. Perhaps the fumbling made her suspicious.

Inside, the lobby was full of hard men in uniforms, mostly police, and individuals, sometimes pairs, of people in civilian clothes, some hard, some not. Undercover somethings, Bill surmised. Women tighter wound than the men. They stood out mostly because they were surrounded by lawyers, resembling diplomats or political toadies, distinctive in a way Bill could not quite identify. Their crispness, perhaps. Business dress, unflattering suits and dark skirts, the ubiquitous valise. This ground of navy and black was shot through with veins of more brightly dressed women, a great many of them hispanic, some carrying more papers but most just making their way across the lobby from one office to another. Within each small office was a processing desk or counter, though there were hardly any people there who looked as if they might be trying to get processed.

But Bill was reassured by the solemnity on display, the grimness. At one time not so much earlier he might have found these people pompous, ludicrously theatrical. That was before. Now he was in need.

The courtrooms were all on the upper floors. Here the hallways were empty, punctuated at long intervals by recessed double doors of dark wood, rather taller than in a house, as if to accommodate stage scenery or —

Bill couldn't think of anything else tall.

He had hoped, somewhat less than realistically he found out now, for a parade of grisly murders, Bordens and Daumers, perhaps a freeway gunman unleashed by road rage, a rapist or an angry woman who strangled her husband. For that he had come to the wrong court. He and not taken jurisdiction into account, but simply headed for that court which was at the top of the pile. Here there was nothing on offer in any of the rooms as identical as those in a movie theater, except that there seemed to be hundreds of them, except the equivalent of shoplifting and drunkenness carried on across state lines. There were incomprehensible frauds and droning breaches of this and that going on wherever he cracked a door, all as identical as the movies in the mall except much quieter. The prim paper signs posted to the left of each entrance, which identified the litigants, were as uninformative as the squiggled menu tacked up outside an Iranian restaurant.

Next day Bill went to the State court. There it was the same security barrier, but he had left the phone and the PDA home this time. And in the lobby it was the same darkly clothed men and women, with grim mouths, and the same bright seams of ore running through the black rocks. Upstairs the courtrooms were identical to the Federal ones, and the droning performances going on inside were more or less the same, too. But in the Municipal court, if he went *there*, it would be sordid drunks and pitiful petty thieves trying incompetently to defend themselves in a parade of self-delusion and ignorance.

Bill opened one silent leaf of the door to Los Angeles v Mulvaney. Men, speaking in low unhurried voices. Professional voices, with neither boredom nor angst in those unaccented words, nor malice, nor fear. Bill opened the door further, just far enough to slip unobtrusively in, and took a seat, the only spectator.

Mulvaney, so far as Bill could piece it out, had molested someone. Whether adult or child was not clear, or not yet clear to Bill. Mulvaney sat with one lawyer at a rather long table, the two of them looking forlorn. The prosecution too was just one person, a woman who had only begun the cross-examination of someone who Bill deduced was Mulvaney's business partner. The questions were all about bank accounts, as if this were a fraud case. The prosecutor was working him with deliberate circumspection, pausing every minute or so to turn back and consult this or that page of a stapled brief which was the only thing lying on her table. She always licked her thumb before flicking though the pages. Then, having found what she sought, she squared the file up and turned again to the witness.

Do you say that — ? she began.

I'm wasting my time here, Bill said to himself, and he half rose in his seat, but then sat back down. There was some fascination in the very monotony of the voices, the slow pace, the quiet room suffused by a barely audible air-conditioned hum. Perhaps he had wanted not so much to see justice done — he was not so naive as to have mixed up legal justice with the other kind, after all — as to reassure himself that...

A small man in the audience jerked to his feet, took a gun from the pocket of his sport coat, and shot Mulvaney in the back of the head. Blood spattered on the lawyer beside him, on the white papers...

There was no small man. Who in any case would have been bagged by those other, hard, men at the gate. Would not have been let in with his plastic gun which was made only just good enough to fire that one shot. Or because a bullet was spotted mixed with the keys and change which he spilled into the orange plastic bowl. Really an awful orange color, reminiscent of Melamine plates set out on the gray Formica top, chipped Formica there where it met the chromed edge of the kitchen table, an orange plate on which were lying two fried eggs not quite centered, beside a little pool of the grease in which they had been fried to lacy-edged solidity. Melamine, Formica — stuff which was dull and chipped already when it was bought just after the war, and in the twenty-five years since nothing had changed. Fourteen thousand three hundred eggs fried in an iron skillet the sides of which were by now caked with a thick, seamed and cracked black crust of burnt grease, rough and glistening. Even the metal spatula had survived, though its Bakelite handle — was that what it was made out of? Bakelite? like in old electrical switches and inside radios? — was kept on by a pad of strapping tape wound round the tang. The kitchen was only large enough to hold the table, with chairs on three sides and a passage between it and the stove so that all she had to do was twist round, that orange plate in her hand —

There was a window. Outside the window was a tree which they called a May tree because that was when it flowered, sprouting small five-petaled white blossoms about the size of a thumbnail. Never any fruit or seeds. Only flowers. It was an easy tree to climb because the first branches were only a few feet above and there were many horizontal ones above that up to a height of about twenty feet where there was a good place to sit all day and look over people's fences at empty lawns and abandoned dog bowls.

He ate his eggs with a fork and looked out of the window. The plating had begun to come off the fork.

There was no small man. Only these quiet voices questioning the circumstances of an attempt to sell a Mexican girl to a booking agent to be used to satisfy some people attending a convention... eh? Was that it? Or was it that Mulvaney's partner, the rather jowly man now being slowly questioned by the prosecution, had conspired with Mulvaney to keep quiet about someone's daughter? Not a little girl, it seemed, but a teenager, something of a slut in fact, who it was claimed by Mulvaney had vamped him until he couldn't help himself. How was he to know she would die after only three times? Why did she want it so bad if she couldn't have it?

And now it seemed that the partner had paid Mulvaney to get in on it. Paid out of the petty cash for god's sake, which was why there was all this talking about fraudulent books.

No, it was worse than that. Some other people had paid, too. Had lined up to pay, to get into the back room of the — Who were these people? Importers of something or other. And there was a small man after all. The fat man in the blue suit identified him as one of the customers. No, not that. Customers for whatever it was they were in the business of importing. Furniture or something. Had the girl been smuggled in then for the purpose inside a load of tables? Those rough Mexican tables made out of pine, with bright paint rubbed over them, burnt and scratched so as to look like authentic peasant-made stuff. Bought from the peasants for some pesos and a girl, sold for five hundred dollars. Six, seven.

The prosecutor was becoming exasperated at these entanglements and digressions. The case was growing magically in her hands and it was plain she needed more than the single brief. There was a pause while she rooted through a valise which had been on the floor under the table, leaning against the leg beside her chair. Nothing. Request for a recess. Consultation below the judge's dais. A short recess, your honor. Office across the street. Apologies for being so unprepared, but one can see that. Yes, granted. The jury is excused until after lunch.

A general rustling. The bailiff requests them all to rise, and in the briefest of moments the room is empty, Mulvaney and all.

Bill kept his place in the gallery. In the well of the court nothing had been left behind, nothing forgotten, not a paper clip or one of those little circles of paper left over after preparing a sheet for the binder. No wad of gum stuck under the desk.

How many courtrooms in this building? Was it like the fourteen thousand eggs, this river of malefactors who have done everything wrong that can be imagined? One could convict them all. It would be like the eggs, all eaten, nothing left over, nothing changed, still the same frying pan and green linoleum.

After breakfast an orange bus. Maybe that was the problem with the Melamine, that it was schoolbus-colored. He hated school. Everything moved so slowly. Simple primitive ideas which no one understood, perhaps even the teacher, except him. He got it before all the words had even been said. He could always see where things were going, and then he had to wait for everyone else. It was painfully boring. Even in college. He looked out of the window a lot. Once someone's escaped pet crow landed on the sill and looked into the classroom. The bird walked back and forth, pecked the glass one time, said something derogatory and took off.

He had been one of the bullies in that school. There was no other way, he thought, to make use of the place. After classes he beat up the big slow ones and waylaid the little quick ones, mostly younger than he was, and twisted their fingers and stole their money and proposed unnatural things which would make them cry and keep quiet about it. Still, some sanctimonious people said they would keep him out of the honor society if he didn't stop it. He had thought about that. It was his first confrontation between craven cynicism and crazy jihad. The cynicism seemed altogether more sensible. He was not going to make his way by swiping dimes and giving little boys tears.

After a time that early violence melted away. He remembered it sometimes with a wince. Such behavior was stupid, certainly, but he was not so stupid as to fail to understand the emotional logic of it. And petty of course, which was more puzzling if not less justifiable. Pettiness suggested a want of self-understanding, an undervaluation of oneself, a lack of appreciation of the possibilities. And then, after a time, he did begin to feel his behavior had been a little sleazy, like the small man who didn't seem to know what was right, who acted only out of momentary lust and its equally momentary reward and forgot about the debt of karma that was growing in him like the fat on his belly, either one of which would kill him in the end.

But now what about this bad dream?

Bill breathed his last and got to his feet. One leg had gone to sleep. He stamped impatiently to wake it. He saw it was nearly twelve.

The building's cafeteria, which he thought would be a bleak place in a sub-basement or a tunnel, was in fact a sunny room with a pleasant courtyard view. The food on offer was plain and not very healthy, but he was able to get together a tray with a spicy tomato soup, a small salad, and a soy burger. No fruit, which all looked sorry and days old. This tray he took to a table in the center of the room — the window seats were all occupied — but from where he could still see the courtyard and where there was no one sitting nearby.

The fork had not been well washed. He got another.

Munching on the burger, Bill was able to reflect on his dream with some calmness. Was it really accusatory? Perhaps he ought to regard it as a portent of something. What is the cause of violence? Is it only fried eggs?

Bill knew himself to be still a violent man. Others didn't know. They thought him competitive, or rude, or cold. And what were these things but flowers of violence?

No fruit. Just flowers.

This Saleem was a ninny. He had read too much Kafka or Cotton Mather or that variety of Buddhism — hin or mah, Bill could never remember — which Mishima had had to confront in his reincarnation novels. Saleem's thought in general was too religious for safety, was Bill's opinion.

Bill recognized Saleem as kindred, another of those blighted souls who can look but not see, reach but not hold, dream but not wake. But he was a ninny just the same. He hadn't gone down to the lower levels to wrest for himself weapons of power; he hadn't sat in the snow for years before the closed gate; he had done nothing but fume and cry.

Harris had been that way. That's what comes of wanting to do good rather than wanting to be of use.

Bill wished his former companion had been able to do more for Harris. Though of course he realized that a diplomat's reach is limited and a small man's is nearly footling. Harris's was too great a punishment for a feckless man only wanting to be a good person.

It's stupid to feel regret over something you have no say about. That's not the correct emotion. Or rather, not the correct name for it, which is — hmm.

Bill bit down on something hard in his burger. He worked it out with his tongue and spit it into his hand. It was a round piece of metal like a BB. What on earth? It's a *soy* burger. You don't shoot anything to make soy meat.

At least it wasn't a finger like that case some years ago.

Eventually the dream went away on its own, melted away like a dead plantar's wart into wherever it came from leaving only smooth skin and a spot a little tender for a time.

SALEEM

*In heaven we'll all sit around talking about the good old days,
when we were dead.*
      — Samuel Beckett

Inevitably, James ended by beating up Sofka. She took Baby and a rucksack with a few clothes — she only had a few — and her copy of Heidegger. The rest of the sack contained things for Baby. And that was how it would be for years: two pairs of jeans, Heidegger, and mostly Baby.

Word filtered back after a few months through Bill's incomparable grapevine that she was living in San Francisco. Hand to mouth, uneasily dependent on lovers and — better — some women friends, but getting by. Roger was curious, but lacked an excuse to go north and pry into her affairs. Not to speak of the deaf, who were more difficult than Baby because you couldn't just put them in a sack and make off.

He supposed he would be prying. Taking himself as an example, himself being the only person he knew much about (excepting Bertie, now), it would have seemed so. Roger was aware that other people were flattered by attention rather than made uneasy, suspicious, as he was. He was aware that other people often grew warmer as they were allowed to talk about themselves. Why else would Sofka have sought him out during her earlier troubles, than that Roger was a practiced listener. A professional listener, actually. He said little, and always finished with the words *te absolvo, requiescat in pace.*

Roger was aware of these things, but distantly: by report, by observation (which was a kind of report — one was never safe in reasoning from appearances). And since himself thought otherwise, he was never eager to open negotiations. He could never for his life ask a personal question.

And so the fate of Sofka remained a mystery.

Which made Roger's subsequent relations with his housemate Saleem a surprise to him.

He was not sure how it happened, only that after many weeks of frosty silence, Saleem asked — wondered aloud, almost accidentally — while he was fixing dinner for himself one night (the two of them had never cooked for each other) —

Do you think it's important to wash under the label?

Eh? Roger blurted out.

These labels they stick on everything. Fruits, vegetables. Are you supposed to wash under the label?

Roger laughed quietly. Best so, he said, trying not to smile too much.

Saleem turned to him, leaning in his apron against the sink, a paring knife in one hand and a peach in the other.

Of course, he said. You're the cautious one.

There was more warmth in Saleem's voice than Roger ever knew. At best he had been harsh of speech always, never more so than recently.

This little exchange was, it proved, an earthquake. It broke up the dam across the straits and let the Atlantic into the mediterranean basin. In no time it had become a sea, and they had become ancient mariners feeling their way along the coast, gathering courage to strike out into open water.

Over the dinner table that night, and afterwards wine, Roger told Saleem what he knew of Sofka and James.

Saleem made a sour face. So, he said. James is still with us?

Roger thought not. James had gone to ground somewhere, outside of work a full-time pariah on the society of writers of filmscripts, with nothing left over for his old circle of friends.

Friends, Saleem muttered, somehow making the word an expletive, bitter as a decorative orange.

Roger made some polite excuses for James.

Pariah, said Saleem, and after a long pause repeated the word. Pariah.

Yes.

As I am.

Oh, now…

As a Turk, you see. An outsider for everyone but the Turks, for whom I'm an Armenian. I'm Everyone's Other.

Then, after a thoughtful pause — Is that word *pariah* applied to anything but dogs?

Well, I've never heard of a pariah cat, if that's what you mean, Saleem.

No. Only dogs have that relationship to us. There are no wild dogs, no more than there are ex-Catholics. Or ex-Jews. Even the most abject of black slaves was never that. So long as there are freedmen there can be no pariahs.

I'm thinking of Frederick Rolfe, Roger said. A pariah on the Catholics.

Baron Corvo, yes. *Hadrian VII.*

Startled by this unfamiliar complicity with his taste for obscure novels, Roger was struck dumb. But as he – quickly now -- grew to know more of Saleem he discovered the man to be the most omnivorous he had known, as obese of mind as he was stick-thin of body.

I don't see how you can call yourself a pariah, Saleem.

Oh. Well, perhaps less so now than I was as a student of intellectual history.

But you are still – aren't you? – a student of, um…

No, said Saleem. Rather more matter-of-fact and less barking than was usual with that word *no* in his mouth.

And for the rest of the evening Saleem recapitulated for Roger his sorry former life as a Pakistani child of lapsed Muslims, a graduate student, and much else.

And then there was Jake's suicide.

And you have no idea? Roger asked.

Yes, an idea. Without foundation, of course. Impossible to verify. An idea somewhat presumptuous as regards myself and so best left quiet.

That was all he said about that.

The next evening followed another conversation, this time about what had happened between James and Sofka. Roger did not want to ask himself what was behind this new talkiness of

Saleem's, Why should he? Did there have to be a behind or underneath to everything?

It's not hard to understand, Roger said, if you consider that chimpanzee behavior is not yet an atavism. With us. What I know is that James lost it one night with Baby's crying. He went and thwacked it. Perhaps he might have started to shake the thing if Sofka hadn't stopped him. Shaking, you know, is fatal to babies. As I'm guessing, out of remorse for having beaten his child he turned to beating Sofka instead, to make up for it.

Plausibly Jamesian.

She certainly was in bad shape when I saw her. Black eyes, cuts all over her face, clumps of hair torn out —

Huh, Saleem mused. Hard even to get a grip on hair as short as hers.

But worst where you can't see. I think he may have damaged something inside. I don't know what happens to breasts when you pound on them, but lower down you can really spoil things.

It was about sex, of course, at bottom. Vulvular.

I suppose so. He was going for that, it's obvious. She was bleeding, but managed to protect herself by curling up. She was too strong for him to pry open, from working on the shipping dock.

How do you know this, Roger?

I went to the hospital. Um... She put me down as an emergency contact, actually.

Saleem's regard fell on an abashed Roger, and he was speculatively silent a long while.

Press charges?

No, Roger said. As soon as they let her go she was gone. And James isn't the sort to pursue her. He's too narcissistic. Would never think another person was worth pursuit. Stalking. Not James.

Well, Saleem said quietly. I know something of the unwisdom of involving yourself with the law. Now I do.

Some years had passed since Saleem's doctoral pariahood. He was teaching on a year-to-year contract in a community college in this unnamed and possibly unnameable southern California town and writing on film for the local paper. Saleem's part of California is an onion, with the round bulb at the bottom and the narrow flower stalk of it being the Central Valley shooting up to Fresno and Sacramento where Saleem was born. Or it is like the bottom of a flask where the chemical residues coat the glass with iridescent purples and gloomier silvers. Saleem's parents were also native to Fresno, he said. It could as well have been Idaho. They had been lumpish people native to wherever they were and not inclined to expatriate themselves across the street. His grandparents skedaddled to California during the Partition, for safety.

I never felt safe in Fresno, he said. People want to sneer at Fresno. If, being of a different urban tradition, they know of these places at all. Being of a different relation to their hinterlands. Here, everywhere is hinterland.

Then Saleem was jailed overnight as a terrorist. It was a ludicrous mistake. At least, he speculated, I wasn't shot and killed by some ignoramus who can't tell a Sikh from a Persian.

The college was sore about his missing class and it's possible neither the college nor Saleem's students felt entirely easy about his innocence after that. One couldn't accuse him outright, of course. That is, accuse in a fleshly way. Saleem wasted a lot of time turning over blogs like so many stones with bugs under them. At least he was wise enough to keep silent about what he found. Although with Saleem it's not perhaps correct to call that wisdom. He tended to absorb hurts. Probably learned, he said, from his grandparents, a form of the same lesson in caution his parents also learned from them.

Roger worked it out from Saleem's age of 42 that his parents had been children of eight or ten years at the time, and his grandparents in their early thirties. The whole lot of them emigrated, to California and to Fresno. Saleem's father was dead now. The clan were all from Bombay -- or as it was called then, but not by them.

So what happened was that Saleem was arrested as a terrorist. Two men in police uniforms stopped him in the college parking lot one night after class. After a cursory identification he was handcuffed and stuffed into the caged back seat of their car, and tossed into the pokey.

No one went to see Saleem in jail. The police station was a rather cozy one-story building of red brick with an entrance resembling a fifties bungalow. A narrow portico, a pair of white French doors. Stuck in the lawn outside was a discreet sign, dark red letters on dark gray, to the effect *here be cops*. Inside there was a waiting area with low square tables and a coffee pot, and a somewhat incongruous stand-up counter behind which an officer sat on a tall stool looking at a computer screen.

But only Saleem passed through this movie set to the other side. He had been, as he said to Roger over breakfast, not quite awake. It was not the lassitude which always followed an evening class, often compounded past ten o'clock by students with two jobs who had only this hour before bed in which to pour a little oil on their anxieties. Saleem was stunned — cognitive dissonance was what he said to Roger. The ends of his nerves buzzed and popped like tinfoil in a microwave oven.

I was walked past that, Saleem said, into a less cozy part, a short hallway with two holding cells. Both were empty. I was told to "wait here" and the gate was closed, clanging shut with rather excessive theater, I thought. After that I was quite alone. They had taken my wristwatch, my wallet, and my keys, but left me my belt and shoelaces — apparently I wasn't a suicide threat. Or not threatening to them, anyway. One less Muslim bomb-thrower.

They key which now I should have been feeling through my pocket to find as I walked up the sidewalk between the double row of garden apartments, past my elderly neighbors' flowering jade plants and potted philodendrons, not a rusty bicycle or an old towel to be seen on the drying rack beside two old metal chairs on the other side of the small gate. Some dimly colored underpants which I believe were yours, Roger, clinging stiffly to the bar.

Instead, I was here in this windowless cell in a suburban office, lurking incongruously behind the façade like a pornographer's secret studio.

I wondered, briefly, whether I were not entitled to some conversation about all this. What had happened to my rights, my telephone call, my official succor? I could, I suppose, have hollered and rattled, but perhaps that was the excuse they hoped for.

Pretty soon a new officer appeared with a homeless man, who was put into my cage, and then a more sharply dressed, ratlike person who went into the other lockup by himself. Neither of these new captives protested, either. But I could not unburden my tongue before the bell-like gates rang.

My new cagemate stank pretty badly, but otherwise did not intrude himself. In fact, he was catatonic. During the course of the night two more men were brought — marched — in, and stuffed also into my cell while the little man across the hall remained by himself, sitting without demur but looking across alertly at our crowd.

These new captives were less pleasant, two muscled pachucos in sleeveless jerseys, with shaved and tattooed heads and gold earrings like stanchion rings. They were loud and restless. One, named Diego it appeared, started in on the homeless drunk but this was not much fun. The old boy was too torpid to react. It was like playing with a dormouse, and the bald cat soon fixed on me instead. But I had learned something now and played dead, and eventually Diego and his compadre began a feinting round of kick-boxing.

Time passed more slowly now. Then a new more ominous threat, a Black or perhaps Indian man who brought the rodent across the hall to his feet, all nose and ears, was stuffed in with me and the others, now five of them in a cell intended for two, and still the rodent across the hall, all nose and ears, remained alone.

He was a big man. With a glance, the swaggering pachucos crushed down their swagger just enough to keep from losing face and went on with their banter in a low voice, taking up one of the two benches. I waited stilly on the other. The old man lay on the floor as he was used to do.

The time which had been tired and slow before now came to a complete stop. Only one word was spoken, to which I did not reply. The tension and the smell, and the lack of food, were turning my stomach.

A crazy-making time followed. The new man neither asked for my seat nor sat down himself. Then the jailer appeared and, opening the cage gate, pronounced the name *Singh*. "Singe," he said, without the least mockery, and nodded toward the door at the other end of the hall. This proved to lead to a conference room, empty, but soon enough entered from the opposite door by yet another policeman and a tired stubby man in a tan suit and a spotted blue tie.

Mister Singh, he said correctly, pulling out his own chair. You are suspected of being a terrorist, whatever that is. I have not found out your plans – the lawyer's little smile conveyed the truth of this remark – but it isn't bad enough to deny bail. You are not going to be held here.

A what?

A terrorist. I'll arrange for your release after we've talked.

Bail? I don't have money for bail.

Of course not. Nobody does, here. I'll settle the bond tonight.

Bond? What have I done?

Yes. Well – Mister K, that is the question, is it not? You are guilty, but of what? Who knows? Were to perform your feat on Saturday, they say.

The little fellow in the toast-colored suit tiredly wiped a lock of hair away from his eyes and brought some papers out of his valise. These, it seemed, were to be signed. I drove my stiffened fingers over the paper, nearly blind and deaf, completely ignorant of what I had signed.

Can I go now?

Yes, when I've arranged things.

The lawyer went out and I was sent back.

Meanwhile the two teenagers, the drunk, and the pickpocket had been taken away, but I was not put into the now-empty cell.

The new man had not moved from his place. Diffidently, I sat on one of the empty benches. Time passed.

So the drama now was resolved to just two people: myself and the Indian. Obviously Indian, now that I had the courage to look at him. He had straight black hair gathered in a thick ponytail, a wide square face with high cheekbones, dark brown skin almost black with sun and dirt, a nose a bit askew and a healing cut on his lip. Two fingers of one hand were twisted with arthritis. Mountain boots, pressed jeans, a new chambray shirt. Some kind of necklace, which I worked out to be a med-alert tag.

This man exuded menace like a third hand. It glistened on him like sweat.

And I had to pee. I saw that I would wet myself. I would get down on my knees, press my forehead to the sticky east-facing concrete, and piss in my pants. This man would squeeze it out of me without a twitch. His third eye would fall on me and I would do it, as required.

The lawyer did not come back. During the night this other man's voice crawled out of the dark, speaking words like invisible moths which brushed against my skin. Mysterious words in an incomprehensible tongue.

Whee-yew! the guard said when he brought us breakfast, wrinkling his nose like old Wishbone. The Indian laughed, guttural and hard, and from that moment my eyes closed forever and I was a blind man.

The bail bond was posted. I was released before noon. The lawyer wanted to make a scene over the flouting of something or other which I did not care to understand. What I wanted was clean underwear and dry pants and toast that was not made of burnt cotton gauze.

So I was turned out onto the street.

My lawyer — one says, but mine in no sense — was a down-at-heels man from the public defender's office, an old-time idealist from the Spanish civil war at least, He offered a ride in a dubious Cuban-looking mixed-breed car which I declined. I wanted to walk, to feel the air on my face. Though my legs were so chafed, and I was so dehydrated, that I had to sit down wherever I could, thinking that if I stumbled I might be rearrested as a drunk.

You were at the school. None of the neighbors seemed to be home either, or else they had heard the tale and hid themselves behind the curtains, whispering. I turned the key with shaky fingers and slipped inside. The narrowest crack between the door and the jamb was covered up quickly, furtively, leaving heat buzz outside.

How am I to pay that bond? Thousands of dollars. I don't have thousands of dollars. I'm a poor teacher, living from paycheck to paycheck. I buy groceries twice a month, cut off the moldy crusts sometimes. Thousands of dollars? Ridiculous.

Roger tried to put an end to this fretting but Saleem brushed off his attempts to commiserate.

Yes, he said. I'm threatened. But that's not the real source of this malaise of powerlessness and frustration, That comes from inside.

Roger waited nervously. No one other than Bertie had taken such a risk with him before. No one had ever confided in him so much as a lost dime. Afterwards, Roger gained a dim awareness of the extent of Saleem's hurt, his hidden desperation, that he should have said these things to Roger, of all people.

Saleem's self-analysis was characteristically wonky. According to current thinking in neuropsychology, he said, the channels between your sense-organs and your brain don't have anywhere near the bandwidth needed to convey what is going on in the outside world. Your brain gets about ten percent. The other ninety percent is tossed.

Which ten percent?

I don't know. I don't think it matters. It's like those executive summaries for government officials. If it can't be said in fifteen words it doesn't exist. Go to the National Archives or one of the presidential libraries and look at the mass of paper which layer upon layer of redactors has reduced to fifteen words. Since no one has the whole picture the relation of the end product to the incoming data stream is totally unpredictable.

And?

What that means is all your memories, all that incredibly detailed awareness you have of the beauty of the world and its sounds, smells, the feel of it, is not *out there*. It's the creation of your own mind, using a small amount of sense data and a large fund of experience, guesses, tested and untested hypotheses, whatever seems plausible.

So Bishop Berkeley was right, eh?

It seems so.

Roger said: So the deranged person, for example, is deranged because he is bad at constructing plausible worlds out of this very thin sensual information, for whatever reason.

Mm.

And I suppose, Roger went on, that explains why your awareness becomes richer as you get older. You build up a fund of details which can be used to fill in the blanks.

Saleem was beginning to tap on the table with his index finger as his argument was building up.

So what, he said, is the difference between artists and ordinary people? It's that they get better faster at this game, and are always ahead of the rest of us. That mysterious familiarity which invests some paintings, for example. It's not that you were there before, it's that you aren't there *yet*. It's a hint, a hallucination of what it's like to see with older eyes, hear with better ears. Why is it that the only person to season the food in a traditional Indian house is the oldest woman? That's why. When we taste it we know it's right, but she's the only one who *really* knows. Without that old woman our tongues would be dumb, our noses stuffed.

Well, Roger said. It fits our experience of art, I suppose. Intuitively.

Now then. Tap tap. What about *tap tap tap* the poor person *tap tap* who has the artist's eye, the musician's ear *tap tap* but can't make the thing – the painting, the song -- which would give that experience to others?

I thought artists were taught to be authentic and paint, or whatever, to please themselves?

This remark caused Saleem to stop tapping with annoyance. He peered narrowly across the table at Roger.

Have you ever, he said, spent any time in a country where you don't speak the language?

No.

What about among the deaf?

Roger was non-plussed, but Saleem could not wait.

It's incredibly frustrating, he said. Have you ever had one of those dreams of speaking in tongues? Suddenly you break out in perfect, eloquent Italian and everyone is enchanted by the beauty and profundity of what you are saying.

Well, Saleem, I don't know as I know anything beautiful or profound. Unless someone points it out.

Saleem sighed. His eyes turned far away.

You're locked up in yourself. You're a marathoner who has lost a leg, a painter who can't paint, a writer with writer's block. You're blind, deaf, and dumb. Overnight in the jail is nothing to that. Everything you most value is locked up inside. Release from this torment is at your finger's ends if you could only stretch a bit more, make a little more effort to save yourself from suffocating in quicksand.

It was long past midnight. They had been talking for hours. The dishes were not done, the wine was all drunk, the coffee cold. Roger stood up to make more. Saleem jumped up too and began to walk agitatedly around the room.

You can do nothing for yourself, he bleated. The artist saves himself, and ordinary people don't wander into the quicksand at all. You are at the mercy of others. It's up to them whether you live or die. This contempt — for your person, but also for your way of mind, your poor weak ideas, the banality of your thought and the crudity of your expression — only serves to affirm what you had already concluded: that you are a worthless, contemptible, and ridiculous human being.

Roger looked up from measuring the coffee but Saleem's face was turned.

What defense, then? What *bail bond?* There are Kafkaish philosophies claiming that *no one* serves a purpose, that we *all* stand on the edge of the Nietzschean abyss save a tiny few, mere two or three in each generation. What good is a philosophy of two or three saved?

That Jamesian obsession, Roger thought. Which might explain some of the instinctive antipathy between those two.

Or, Saleem went on headlong now, there is the zen strategy of repudiating the self and the phenomenal world both. But to actually do so is a talent, and like any other it is rare. We all have buddha-nature but only the buddha can do anything with it.

That's harsh, Saleem.

Of course it is. Hopeless, in fact. In my scholarly days I was writing a thesis on what I called the *paradiso artegianato* — the company of all artists — which appears in artist communities now and then. Paris 1830, 1870; Vienna 1900; New York 1920, San Francisco 1950. What I wanted to do was to explain the conditions necessary for the paradiso to precipitate out of the ordinary life of art. A Jane Jacobs sort of explanation. But also to elucidate, to bring out into the light, the bohemian legend which underlays it, gives it its modern resonance.

And did you?

I might have. I wasn't given a chance.

The coffee was beginning to bubble. Saleem was at the window staring out into the night. Everyone else was in bed, and their little alley of old folks was dark.

I have these nightmares, Saleem said. His voice was quiet, matter-of-fact, but also speculative, with a touch of wonder.

I hear you up in the night sometimes, Roger said.

Nightmares of jealousy and betrayal. Of being cut off from life. I'm afraid to go to sleep sometimes.

The coffepot came to rest. A light wind was blowing, the only sound, a precursor to the Santa Ana that was always coming.

It's not a fear of death, Saleem said. It's an unreadiness to die, not the same thing.

After a time Saleem wandered off to his room and Roger, yawning and amazed, went too, forgetting to turn off the coffee. In the morning it was gone. Saleem had drunk it all during the night.

Days passed. The problem of the bail sank to the gunwales and then was sunk by a new obsession, the question of who had denounced Saleem to the police.

The very word *denounce* seemed counterfeit, imported. Roger was incredulous at first, then annoyed. He began to avoid Saleem by staying late at Penfield, until Saleem had gone off to teach the evening's film class. On Monday, when Saleem got up early to write his weekly column of movie reviews, Roger at first tried getting out of bed even earlier and having breakfast at Starbucks, but this arms race did not get far. After a few weeks Saleem's paranoia stopped begging in the streets and moved into a shelter, acquiring a habitation and a name. This was a joke belonging to Saleem's other self, that bubbling mud geyser which had almost ceased now to erupt.

First it was James, who could not be got at, somewhere among his ever more obscure brands of beer and running-mates.

Then it was Bill. Bill was not amused. He began to think of Saleem as a crank.

And so, under pressure of these and other events and recriminations, the small group of friends was now balkanized.

Saleem next began to ask around school, suspecting first one of his colleagues, then another, then his students. Such behavior did not endear him to anybody. Hints came to him like voices in his head. He wouldn't get any classes in the fall. The Chair was angry. It was all frustratingly familiar.

As before — as it was after his dissertation adviser killed himself — whyever had he done that? Saleem, who clung so tightly to whatever he could reach, thought he would never understand what Jake did. Which also left him, Saleem, bereft, defenseless. As before, it was not the paranoia which caused the pain but the other way around. He knew himself contaminated.

Overripe, moldy, now broken open by that denunciation and left to rot.

Someone at the newspaper, perhaps. For one trifling column of reviews which paid hardly anything and which no one else wanted to do? His opinions about movies meant nothing and it was hard to imagine, ordinary prejudice aside, why anyone there cared whether he was a terrorist or a reincarnated rabbit. They had never seen him. His copy went in by e-mail and was published under a pseudonym.

An injudicious word, then. Something which from another person would not be noticed, but from a Turk or a Bedouin, an Afghan, carried hidden significance. Who exactly is this fellow Singh? Wherever he comes from, he will have friends there, family, abettors of all sorts. Singh, they said, is the proverbial loose bit of yarn on the knitted sweater.

There was one man in the warren of cubbyholes which the college provided to those instructors who were paid by the course, a makeshift office warranted by his status, without even enough privacy for a student consultation. Plenty of sources for denunciation there. And there was one man, who worked on the other side of the wall, kept similar hours, had opportunity to overhear, to misinterpret. If it were not actually worse and Saleem was being deliberately spied upon. At the time of his denunciation, Saleem had gotten to that part of his syllabus which was concerned with noir, evil doings, and espionage. He looked through his gradebook for students who had come to see him that week. With whom he might have exchanged remarks seeming dubious to the man over the wall.

This man was an unsympathetic sort who did nothing to discourage Saleem's suspicions. Hasselblad was his name. Taught history. Or was it Spanish. Saleem was having a squint at Hasselblad's course schedule posted, or rather pinned, to the wall alongside the opening to his cubby when a scratchy tenor voice behind him said, with some outrage:

What do *you* want?

Hasselblad himself. A short, tightly-packed man. Like a sausage. Translucent skin under which one could see the lumps of meat.

Hasselblad, Saleem said with a gulp of air, maybe you know why I was arrested by the police in the night a few weeks ago.

What for?

Making a bomb. Thinking about making a bomb.

Hasselblad sniggered. Mad bombers never know why, do they?

Trumped up, Saleem replied angrily.

Naturally. Naturally.

Someone had denounced me to the authorities.

What? Rubbish. Whyever for? Who cares about *you*?

As a black man. A sympathizer.

You're not black. You're a Persian.

The English say black. A wog.

That slang has been out of date for years, the historian responded in quite a different, classroom voice.

The sort of person, said Saleem, impatient as always with details — the sort of person likely to be dangerous.

You? Hah. Now get out, will you? I've got hours.

You've been listening to what I say to my students.

Hassleblad goggled, going more white than ever. He pushed past Saleem, banged down an ancient brown leather valise on his very tidy, in fact empty, desk, and threw himself into his chair. It was an old-fashioned valise with an accordion bottom and a corroded clasp, a wedge-shaped thing stuffed with papers which were marked with thick red lines and blotches. An apple and a banana spilled out. These Hasselblad put away in a drawer, along with something else from the valise which looked like a pair of underpants.

Get out, Singh, he said. Somehow Hasselblad's soft fat and see-through skin made his words more menacing.

Saleem, in the grip of blossoming rage, was insensitive to this. The man's voice was too piping ever to growl. Whine, possibly snarl. But Saleem heard only boredom and fatigue and disregard for himself.

Hassleblad swiveled around, turning his back to Saleem. He pulled out one of the lower desk drawers and put his feet in it for an ottoman. There was a large pimple on his neck just above the collar of his green polo, which was dusted with black hairs as if he had just had it cut. The hairs tickled his neck, which he had rubbed red.

Saleem turned away finally, a melancholy shame for what he had wanted to do darkening his face, replacing the anger.

After that confrontation a susurrus of amused remarks began to follow him about. Some students — not his own — said rude things to his face and his email began to collect more seriously offensive accusations. Saleem began to skip his office hours. No one was coming for help, anyway.

The day came when flattened tires and various defilements began. His nom de guerre as a film critic was Henry Hyde, a witticism which no one seemed to understand, and so for the time being that part of his life remained untouched by vandals.

Roger had stopped speaking to him after Saleem had stupidly included him in the plot against him. That was painful. But that did make it easier to meet his Monday deadline. After the column had gone out it had been Saleem's habit to treat himself to a pastry at a shop nearby, and then if the weather was good, to go for a walk.

He who had once been so voluble and full of unfocussed enthusiasm for everything was now almost silent, speaking only in the classroom, but with so many hesitations that no one listened any longer. He wrote more slowly, the ideas refusing to come out. He walked more slowly, his long legs still taking their stride but so methodically, deliberately placing his feet in accordance with some unknown requirement. Increasingly rare bursts of hilarity, far from being reminders of his old self, seemed mad, hysterical

But then, when had he had any real friends since childhood? Never. There was no one he confided in other than — once — Roger. No one who could be counted on, who would not betray such a small unworthy person as himself. His way had been to cover that up under a burnoose of words, but the tugging wind had flown away with that garment.

He had always been a little giddy. But the decision to go back to school, to seek a PhD, had released some clockwork inside him which then began to whirl, driving both an exhilarating energy and a relentless, exhausting force which pushed and dragged him along willy nilly. Predictably, someone soon stuck a finger in the works. Now he was wandering the streets of some Los Angeles suburb with an uneaten cruller in his hand.

His shriveled self began to fill up again, like one of those balloons even now being inflated, queuing to present arms in that morning's parade. He walked all the way home, a four hour distance, and arrived at his door at dawn. Roger was already asleep in his own room, one bare leg sticking out from under the covers and his head underneath a pillow.

And Saleem was truthfully in agony, like a man with dysentery perhaps, in the grip of painful and uncontrollable convulsions, trying to purge himself of what was killing him. It was baroque, fantastic. He had always relied on intellectual work to keep these demons down, on unrelenting thought. His mind was like a pump which could not be allowed to run dry or it would destroy itself. The benefit had always been an amazing if somewhat unfocused productivity, but now…

On a now (again, now) rare evening when they sat down to their individual dinners together at the dining room table Saleem blurted out what Roger later supposed was the buried central truth, that he had never known unconditional love.

It was an odd, antique – shocking thing to say. The sort of thing which in Roger's experience one never said, even in books, or only very old books. Not, indeed, thought. It was vaguely embarrassing. Saleem might as well have begun to describe his masturbation fantasies. Another of those things that everyone has but… Roger supposed that everyone had. But were not supposed to look at.

Saleem glossed what he had said to mean community. That he had never had the benefit of that.

By now Roger had heard enough of Saleem's past to guess what he might mean. The traditional sources of community – that is, unconditional love – such as religion and family, were unknown to him. Everywhere he went he was an outsider. He had hoped – it was a piece of romance – for there to be an academic community...

Jake.

I don't know whether Jake understood me, Saleem said. He seemed to. I'm sure he thought it was important to understand, but more important that it not matter.

And then he went and killed himself.

He had put some trust after that in Reiva Derwent, who after all had made some sacrifice for him. Rather a large one, actually. She wished him well, but. There was always a but.

Saleem had begun to wonder whether his was not the human condition, and to think that everything which we hominids do is first of all to defuse this bleak loneliness. To deny it.

The poet and his poetry are one thing, he said. You cannot respect the one without respecting the other. If you have unconditional love for art then you must have so for the artist. Disrespect the artist and you disrespect the art. It is the thing which keeps us human.

Roger felt himself blushing. The heat rose from his belly and washed over him in dizzy waves. He made no other reply.

And so it came to pass that one evening soon after there was a tremendous crash and Roger rushed into Saleem's room to find that he had swept everything off his desk and was smashing his laptop with the kitchen hammer.

What's wrong? What's wrong? Roger was shouting in a panic.

Saleem lifted his head, eyes blind with self-pity.

I can't do this, he said, his voice shockingly calm. It's too much for a rag and bone man. I'm tired. Really, really tired. Tired to death.

A prophetic remark, as it happened. Positively Delphic.

Roger helped to clean up the mess, saying nothing.

《〉》

No one was surprised when Saleem tried to smash his car into a tree. What they didn't know at first was that when he missed the tree he ran over some people and killed them.

The dead people were a middle-aged woman and two boys who were having a picnic. The tree Saleem had picked for the purpose of killing himself was an old oak likely to withstand the crash without much damage. It was very like Saleem, said the people who knew him, to take such solicitude for the tree and not give a thought to anything else, for the tree stood at the edge of a city park crowded with people on a late spring Saturday afternoon. Of course, Saleem expected to manage things better, not to bungle it so as to miss the tree entirely, but still he should have seen...

But then, people who want to kill themselves are sometimes not very lucid, Roger supposed. He didn't know, not having thought of it himself or known anyone who had, until now.

It was because of the curb. Saleem's car jumped the curb at an angle and the steering wheel was wrenched out of his hands. After that he had no role in events to follow. Just behind and to one side of the tree, placed to take advantage of the ample shade, was one of the brick barbecues which stood here and there in the park. This was a substantial three-sided structure waist high, with the barbecue grate set into the middle side above a square opening in which to put charcoal. It was rather a large firepit since at one time, fifty years before, it was thought people might want to have a wood fire in it, but wood was now out of the question. The city might condone fireplaces, reluctantly, but certainly was not going to contribute to its own dirt.

The woman who survived had been grilling hot dogs here, protected by the bricks. Saleem's car had only glanced off the barbecue; if it had been merely a hibachi mounted on a post he probably would have run over her instead of the others.

The victims were the survivor's older sister and her own two boys, six and ten years old the city daily reported. They were sitting on a blanket on the grass nearby. Perhaps they might have rolled to one side or something of that sort if they had seen the car coming, but they were only a few feet from the tree and a few more from the street and Saleem had been going above sixty miles an hour. They knew nothing. A rusty blue thunderbolt had flattened them in a blink. Their mother, a greasy spatula in her hand and wearing a pink gingham apron to keep from spattering on her shorts, watched stupefied as Saleem's jalopy continued on down the hill, not comprehending yet the disaster.

The car skidded down the grassy hill sideways, engine still shrieking, cutting two black scars down to the public swimming pool where it smashed through the wire fence, slid across the wide concrete deck, and plunged into the pool. By luck no one in the pool was hurt. A diver still on the board had seen the whole thing and some people wading in the shallow end were swamped but the pool was otherwise empty. It was early in the season. The water was too cold.

Two quick-thinking men who had been working on their tans while their children paddled about rescued the stunned driver, otherwise he would have drowned. Would not have preferred to — that was too slow; suffocation left the mind too clear, too much able to struggle and fight despite all that had been decided — but still he would rather have drowned than survive, which is what he did. It was obvious to them all that Saleem had not reserved his options, counting on someone to give him surcease if only he could get their attention. After all, that was not his ordinary experience.

Knowing that did nothing for Saleem's despair when he woke up in a hospital bed. He had broken both legs and his hip, they said, as well having a concussion. One lung was collapsed and his pancreas had very nearly been speared by the steering wheel lock that had been loose in the footwell, but he had lived. No one thought it a good idea to ask if he were pleased, including Roger, who came to see him the next day. By that time Saleem had been told about the dead people. The police had been there earlier in the morning. He was charged with vehicular homicide, and would be taken into custody as soon as he could be moved.

Not manslaughter, Saleem said when he had explained this to Roger. Murder. They think I did it on purpose. He turned his head away in despair, his voice so roughened by fear, frustration, and regret that Roger could hardly understand him. Roger tried to take his hand but he pulled it away, wincing at the pain of such sudden movement.

What a nebbish, he said, and Roger had to silently concur.

After a time Saleem spoke up again. Do you know anything about those people?

No.

Nor I. A woman and her sister, they told me.

Two boys.

They said it was girls.

No — but Roger did not bother trying to clarify matters. It wasn't worth it. He studied the hospital furnishing while he waited for Saleem to take up the thread. There was an IV drip hanging from a hook on the other side of the bed; it bent over Saleem somewhat like Homer Simpson's evil boss, gloating. He hadn't merited a window, though because he was a criminal he was spared a roommate. A uniformed policeman was posted outside the door. Sort of posted — he was sitting on a plastic chair that was too small for him, reading a news weekly through large glasses. There were shelves piled with sheets and blankets, other shelves of equipment and supplies in sterile plastic, a television not on and a telephone not working. The telephone number of the room was printed on a sign above the phone. Inside the bedside table was the inevitable Bible and a pencil which had been gnawed to a rough point. Saleem's room was only a kitted out closet.

Is there supposed to be a Bible here? Roger wondered, just to be saying something. I thought that would be illegal. It's a public hospital.

The chaplain was in, Saleem observed distantly. I told him I didn't want anything and he skittled out again. Thought he might put up a little fight. Looked like he wanted to. Maybe my imagination.

Probably. If one were the intruding sort, you'd find somewhere else to ply.

Another interminable pause. There seemed to be nothing to remark on. Saleem took air noisily into his good lung.

Dead, he said.

Roger waited for the follow-on, which came after several moments.

I have trouble understanding that. What it is. Being not dead, myself. Yet. One can't *be* dead, actually. There's no *dasein* of deadness. You just are. I think. I don't understand that. Perhaps one isn't supposed to.

Was it you who told Sofka to read Heidegger?

Yes.

I think that did some harm.

How can it be harmful to learn new things? Stupid people... uninformed people are not better off.

You haven't profited much by erudition, Roger said with unforseen cruelty. He thought of apologizing, but didn't.

Actually, no, Saleem admitted with an almost amused calmness. It was a small life, wasn't it? Too small to be evil, even.

Startled, Roger did not reply and the moment was over.

Dead, Saleem said again, the single syllable like a thump on a drum.

Roger stared at the blank television, waiting.

What do you know about those people I killed? Saleem asked.

Not much. A woman, fifty-something, worked in a store of some kind. Her niece and nephew, school age.

Well off?

Hardly. Middle class, working class maybe. No man in the picture. Father excused himself years ago. Well, six years. I think he died of cancer after a while.

You know an awful lot. I just heard about it last night. Saleem seemed to be a little irritated at being scooped.

From the school, Roger said apologetically. I've been to school.

On Sunday?

Yes, well... I was bored. One of the boys has been giving trouble, I thought I'd check up. The live-in teachers always find out everything. They get it wrong much of the time, of course.

I thought... they told me it was a mother.

No, no. The mother's alive. It was her sister you killed.

Christ.

Saleem was looking at a spot on the ceiling.

Is that a bug?

No. A corner of the ceiling tile is broken off.

I suppose she'll want my head, Saleem remarked distantly. I've got nothing else.

In fact, the living woman did prove to the something of a nemesis. In interviews she said she would see him gassed. In pictures and on the evening news her face looked puffy and bruised. It was probably from weeping, but Roger had gotten to the point where his first thought was make-up.

It did seem to be all right to run over a middle-aged unmarried woman, to judge by the press. And by his own feelings, Roger admitted. Can one be sheepish and cynical at once? No, it was about the boys. One does not want children to be run over before they found out important things that it was too soon for them to learn. Found out that matters of importance are not sometimes disposed of fairly, for instance. One does not want to think about dead boys who never found out anything.

Really, *was* it too soon? We didn't think up the notion that children need to be protected from ordinary life until recently. Before that the kids seemed to get on all right. Dickens notwithstanding, it was the grown-ups who weren't doing so hot. Juliette was fourteen, wasn't she? Twelve? Romeo younger than Sal Mineo, who after all could drive a car.

Of course, Pip and Oliver saw the evidence around them every day. They didn't come on it all of a sudden, like a rape in church or something. Like a snake in Ireland.

And of course when the boys' mother found out that Saleem had been free on bail as a terrorist there was no containing her. So that was the end of Saleem.

At least the children were spared knowing that ludicrous business with the potato salad.

No one went to see Saleem in jail. Or they presumed he was in jail. No one knew where that was — jail. In Bakersfield or out in the desert. Who would have gone to see him? There was no one close. Saleem had not been the sort of man to have friends. No one could share his obsessions, his manic interests, remain upright in that tidal alternation of exaltation and despair, rectitude and remorse. There was no one who knew him. So he lay in jail, forgotten.

Is that what one does in jail — lay? Rather more in dungeons. Terrible stories are told of the fate of certain kinds of prisoners in jail. Presumably Saleem was one of those kinds. But no one went to see if it were so. It is necessary to imagine the continuation, the next thing. It is necessary to commit a fallacy, to project into the future what the past has intended, like the gross intrusion of one of those sequels which tries to find out if they did live happily ever after, after all. Whether marrying everyone off has restored the life of matte tan pudding as advertised and they are now all going on from day to day without event. So goes life in jail, they say, one thing following another.

And now Saleem is dead, silent as a stone, vanished in memory. He is like a person with some degenerative neurological disease, a person who we imagine to be thinking and noticing and feeling all the while but who has no way of telling us about it. He can't so much as twitch an eyelid to show that he is still in there. Is he screaming soundlessly to get out? Is he lost — we say truly lost, as a person blundering alone through a pathless forest — lost in thought? Who knows?

Saleem has been beheaded. He himself is not yet among the stones, but that is only a temporary condition.

THE ICONOCLAST

Likewise we imagine Gregory Hawkins, or Dawking — whatever his name is; it doesn't matter — is Out There lying in wait. There are thousands of him — for Hasselblad has been busy — waiting to pop out like those targets used for police practice, flat but dangerous.

What is he doing, this Gregory person, to amuse himself, to remain vigilant, while he waits? Is he doing the *Times* crossword, the Saturday one, always the hardest? Is it always Saturday where he is, in his hole? Is he rereading his favorite passages in his bible of choice? Kierkegaard's *Either Or* perhaps, or if that's too wishy-washy some koranic book like Pound's *Cantos* or even a *Mumonkan*, seeking passage through a gateless gate. Because he is going nowhere, this Gregory Whosis, because he is supposed to be *waiting*, not gadding about. How can he scare anyone when he's not in his hole?

Maybe he'll get leg cramps and jump up at the wrong moment and spoil it all.

Not hardly.

Gregory had been taking Professor Singh's film course. The professor disappeared at mid-term; the gossip went everywhere like the flu; Gregory intuited a vacant room somewhere. Better than here and there on the floor. He could get a month or two out of it without paying.

Roger proved to be a chump. A sort of hobbit, but unfortunately with a hobbit's dislike of dwarves and for that matter anything unbidden, and Roger saw no more of him.

Gregory was supposed to be studying something. In reality, though he was a regular in class and was seen everywhere, he had never registered. That would have cost something. Nobody cared if he sat in so long as he didn't speak up or make work for the instructor by writing a paper or taking a test which would need to be graded. That he would have to put his name on.

And he was too proud to get by subterfuge what was his anyway. His name really was Gregory, family name Hawking, but he hadn't belonged to any family since high school.

Gregory's tenure in the community college was abetted by the school's practice of using mostly instructors purchased to teach by the course rather than fulltime faculty. This meant a continuous supply of new teachers who didn't know who he was and he could sit through the same course over and over, always anonymous. That guy again, the regulars said, encountering him in the hall or the cafeteria. But no one bothered to find out where he belonged. Somewhere.

After failing to secure Roger's spare bedroom, Gregory expected to go on as he always had. It was getting to be summer. Summer offerings tended to be long on beach reading, pottery (which was out of the question; ceramics classes meant using up resources, inviting scrutiny), investment tips and such like. Boring; also useless.

Gregory's idea of what was useful was that it be not boring. He had an idea it ought also to conform to some beliefs of his but he didn't know what those were. And that the number of his future options would be increased thereby, or anyway not reduced. There always had to be at least an escape option.

Life, he said, is a creosote bush. It spreads. All creosote bushes are connected to each other by the roots. It's all one bush, incredibly old, old as sin. You had to keep moving, following the creosote roots. You had to spread.

Then he made the mistake of going by Saleem's old cubicle to get a squint at who the new man was who would be teaching film and fell into the clutches of Saleem's neighbor Hasselblad.

Hasselblad taught history, was regular faculty, and Gregory had sat in on one too many of his courses. Hasselblad had taken offense. His services were being exploited. *He* was being exploited. He was a senior man and had never been able to afford not to teach in the summer and he resented freeloaders. He had said to several colleagues that he intended to put a stop to whatever it was this Hawkins person was up to.

Gregory had never allowed himself to become the archetypal dirty bohemian, unwashed and unshaved and stinking. He could not even be "clean but patched" — he needed to pass, to be taken for granted. He did not use drugs; he was a vegan in fact and practiced a fastidious purity in all respects. He was a neat man in chinos and walking shoes and a whole if wrinkled cotton shirt or polo in some common color. His only trademarks were a big straw hat that mostly hung across his back from a string around his neck, and reading glasses on a lanyard. Hat, string, and lanyard had been filched from craft fairs years before.

Hasselblad took Gregory firmly by the elbow in an unbreakable grip and steered him into the office, or what passed for such. It did not take long for the two men to come to an agreement.

Enough is known of the conversion experience, and not least from the converted themselves, who are always eager to blab about it, to make it obvious why Gregory was such an easy mark. Credit is due to Hasselblad's astuteness in recognizing ripe meat. He himself took no further part, as he knew enough not to foul his own nest.

Nothing arduous was asked of Gregory, which in any case he would not have had the commando skills to carry out. Merely to go into the desert and knock down some watering stations set up to keep illegal immigrants from dying of thirst. The biggest concern in this was to keep Gregory himself from dying of thirst or sunstroke, but he had good advice.

After a while, though, he began to feel that something more was required. People found a sniper's rifle for him with a monstrous scope through which he could see an ant at a hundred yards. The challenge was to hit it. Gregory began to practice, and was surprised and pleased to find he was quite good. He had the required steadiness and calm attention to detail.

It wasn't necessary for him to hit anything, really. Merely to reveal the presence of someone Out There. Nevertheless, he did manage it twice, neither fatal.

Then one evening he came face to face with his opponent. This man had crept up on Gregory's post with plenty of cunning and Gregory knew nothing of his presence until some dirt was kicked over the back of his neck where he lay on his stomach, at watch in the wrong direction.

A Mexican. Very dark, with a Pancho Villa peasant's look about him, though without the bandoliers. He did have a side arm and a sombrero, though. But then Gregory also had a sombrero. It was necessary.

This man was a coyote. He made his money by arranging to get people across the border. After that he had no interest in them. What the hell was he doing here? What did he care?

The two of them sat down cross-legged on the ground. No word had yet been exchanged. Gregory's rifle lay across his lap.

Ah, said Gregory to himself, now we will have a profound discussion about life and death. It is necessary.

Nothing of the sort. Word had filtered back that someone was taking pot shots at people crossing the desert here. Bad for business. The coyote was willing to come to terms, if in bad faith. Gregory was no desert rat; rifle or no, he would lose any confrontation with this hardened operator from whom he would have been willing to take lessons if one could truck with such persons.

Thwarted, he returned to campus in the fall from this summer adventure and picked up his former habits. He had not stopped his shooting at Mexicans but other vantages had proved not so rich in targets. So he came back, and it wasn't long before Hasselblad found an opportunity to talk. Gregory was sitting at a small table in a corner of the cafeteria, behind a pile of books, his backpack and rice-picker's straw hat tucked under his chair and his reading glasses upon his nose. Professor Hasselblad took the empty chair opposite. Gregory jumped up to shake his mentor's hand, but this upset his coffee cup and there was a moment of clumsy confusion.

Gregory was embarrassed. These new opportunities to which Hasselblad had introduced him had taken away his old self-possession and left him less sure of himself than he had been since he was a fat thirteen-year-old.

It was just as well that Gregory's unthinking gesture was forestalled. Hasselblad would not have consented to take his hand. The two men did not this time come to so easy an agreement.

Gregory's self-image had drifted rather far from the truth over the summer, coming to be something like The Man With No Name, and he was angry with himself for falling short in his craft. But Hasselblad knew how to play on this concern. The real issue was threats to purity. Gregory's vegan diet, once simply a concern about poisoning himself, had become over the summer something like a warrior's regimen. Gregory had come to see that it was not enough to purify himself. He must also do something to reduce the load of pollutants which were killing others as well. It was not difficult for Hasselblad to associate this notion of pollutants in Gregory's mind with people who do not live a principled life, who live without values and take their cues from the fashion of the moment. They are impure, these people. Themselves pollutants. We require instead a rule of absolute virtue, the rule of pure, enlightened men. He suggested that Gregory study Plato. It was all there — the foolishness of chasing after false merit and chimerical imagination, the need for strength, censorship, punishment, and the reestablishment of a system of right relations between the classes of men and women.

The summer's experiences had prepared the food. Gregory was ready to receive it.

Not that Hasselblad himself thought in these terms, though some of the enthusiasm he conveyed to Gregory was his own. In casual conversations spread over several weeks, in the cafeteria or on shaded benches around the commons, in the library, Hasselblad sidled closer to his true purpose. The methods were expedient, but the purpose was not. Hasselblad was enough of a historian to know the inevitability of his vision, to know that each reiteration of the cycle, each turn of the great wheel brings the world ever closer to its final congruence.

And so it happened that Gregory was seen no more on campus. Everyone supposed, when they supposed anything, that he had graduated, and that was so.

It was not some weeks before Gregory was provided with a demonstration of what he was to do. Someone obviously with the same instructions, but from another cell and unknown to Gregory, tried to assassinate the mayor of a town to the north, one of those beach communities full of young slackers, queers, and liberal groupies. The mayor was a figurehead — the place was too anarchic to be *governed* — had not been strong enough.

The result drew more bugs than a corpse. For two days there was nothing else. Gregory got himself a cheap second television so that he could watch more than one channel at a time and looked greedily at the wall of televisions in Circuit City all stupidly tuned to the same game show.

But when the weekend was over the event proved to be another *Dog Day Afternoon*. The mayor was let go, filthy and sweating but beamish with happiness, while the nebbishy hostage-taker was himself taken away in chains, his face hidden.

Gregory's apartment — through his new connections he could now afford such a place — was stuffed with pizza boxes. Gregory threw himself in disappointment on the unmade bed and stared at the ceiling where there was a black spot, a bit of the popcorn coming down, which always drew his eye. What had gone wrong? Had it only been a failure of nerve? Or had there been procedural mistakes, or a lack of craftsmanship?

In one of the possibly hundreds of courses he had sat through, or almost through, Gregory had learned about a concept on which he afterwards based his own performance standard. He'd forgotten what the professor intended by talking about this but he remembered the words. There were two sorts of craftsmanship, that of risk and that of certainty. Risk is characteristic of artistic processes and discovery and tolerates small imperfections as being the mark of the maker. Certainty aspires to perfection and seeks the precision and control provided by industrial processes. Before encountering this distinction Gregory would have proudly thought himself to be of the camp of risk. But that inarticulate allegiance was false. He was in fact of the other sect. His conversations with Hasselblad proved that was so, provided him with a history — a narrative he might have said but of course did not — which explained the inevitable outcome of this struggle, and gave him a vocabulary in which to explain himself. He might have said that Hasselblad had outed him — but of course he did not.

So Gregory went up north a few days after the culmination of events there to see and learn from what went wrong. What had been lacking.

After asking around in some bars and other places he knew to be safe — not much safety here but one can always count on *some* help — Gregory began to draw some conclusions.

Firstly, the assassin had made a mistake by involving himself. By doing that he had destroyed his future usefulness and turned the situation into one that could be resolved only by giving up or by suicide bomber. If he had been capable of killing himself he would have done so at once and not tried to weasel out. He *had* brought a lot of media attention but only for the proverbial fifteen minutes. He had changed nothing. He had created a dead end.

The method must be that of the *Jackal* or *The Manchurian Candidate* or for that matter Oswald or the (once) anonymous killings of abortion doctors. The mistake there was to keep doing it, like those snipers in Virginia. The right way was once, or at long irregular intervals like Kazinski before he blabbed about it in order to preach some stupid ideology. To get credit. Ego, that's what it was.

Another of Gregory's many courses had been about spies. What undid the Secret Agent and the Man In the Cold was not working alone. They had to have links. Loose links sink ships. Sip shinks, that should be. Whatever. Ties that bind. Yellow ribbons.

There were a few other points. These were not, Gregory suspected, profound observations. One shouldn't claim such a thing for oneself anyway. It's tacky. Gregory was not and did not want to be profound. Profundity was what crippled the intellectuals.

As Gregory explored the town, more and more he wanted to put his ideas to the test. He had kept the rifle acquired for his earlier adventure because he was told he might need it. Here (unlike there) it could be used only the one time, but someone could tell him what to do with it. He might learn something. If so, it would be worth the cost.

Gregory found some rising ground in a park. The top of this little hill, which was probably made of garbage, had a fringe of bushes which would make it possible to withdraw afterward and not be seen. An long distance away in the park (impossibly long, so they would look first nearer by, giving him more time) was an exposed sidewalk which attracted a lot of lunchtime foot traffic, bicycles, children on skateboards, and other beneficial confusion. A public drinking fountain just there forced a bend in the path, making a bottleneck.

He lay on the grass for a couple of hours studying the situation through the rifle scope and considering the options. The day was bright and sunny, windless, dry — optimum conditions. Making up his mind, he unpacked the gun from its canvas bag, assembled it, and loaded it with one bullet. That's all he would have time to deliver. It didn't matter who he took out. Not to complicate things with a moving target he waited until someone stopped for a drink at the fountain. As good fortune would have it, an Asian woman. Her head exploded like one of those apples he used to put cherry bombs in. He wasn't interested in seeing more. It was too far away to hear what was going on. Sliding back off the top of the rise, he packed up the gun and in half an hour he was on the road south. He had left a few marks around town of course. You always do. Gregory was confident they were un-interpretable.

So that was put right. People here would think it was not over. There was a gang of them and that knucklehead in the mayor's office had not been alone. Pointing the correct lessons from this was someone else's job.

It might be possible, Gregory mused as the rickety little blue sedan headed home, muffler blatting, that the mayor's assassin had had something else in mind entirely. Perhaps he was not with them at all, in truth, but had only wanted to make a case for artichoke prices or depressed whales. No matter. The fellow had been hijacked.

This car was too distinctive. It would have to go.

Hasselblad was pleased with himself, too. He saw himself as the Johnny Appleseed of the resistance and the ground had been sown with the possibility of another fine tree.

Some words need to be said about the woman killed in the park. Being squeamish about the details, we will avoid any unnecessary realism and move on to something of what followed.

This woman was merely a passer-by. There were other passers-by in the park, some of them close enough to be splashed with blood and other things, some more distantly horrified. Some people seeing it on television maybe had bad dreams while others closer by shrugged it off, and somewhere there might have been a person with just the right neurosis to take the news as a kick in the pants and go flying over the coping, off the cliff and onto the rocks. There are eight million stories in the naked city and way too many forking paths to calculate a destination. Whose story gets told?

Does it matter?

If it doesn't, should we just keep quiet about the whole thing?

That doesn't sound right. Rather like not taking your blood pressure medicine and hoping to go off with a heart attack in your sleep. Why do people do pointless things? An ancient question. Perhaps among the people with some connection to what happened to the woman in the park there is one erudite enough to explicate the history of this tradition and the various solutions to its conundrum.

Such entertainment would help to pass the time while we are waiting for our medicine to kick in. Most people would not be amused, however, and prefer to go about their business instead, pursuing an analog strategy to the less approximate but more troublesome analytical one.

Being squeamish about unchecked emotions, something inherited from a repressed childhood — but there you are, is it worth the effort to resist? — we will avoid the stories of close relatives and anyone who might threaten to be *amok,* as they say on Typee. We will instead point out a fellow sitting on the grass getting some sun, pinching his arm now and then to check on whether he might be too burnt, a folder of papers beside him on the lawn weighted down with a small rock. Of the accidental onlookers he alone, through some precognitive talent for ballistics computations, was able to see where the shot must have come from while everyone else was still stupefied by the woman's grotesque fate. He twisted round his head at once to look toward that improbably distant hillock and thought he saw some movement in the bushes, quickly stilled. When the police arrived he suggested they look up on the hill, which they did after a time, thinking it only a dubious hypothesis. There were marks on the grass there, crushed and bent blades, as if made during a noontime shagging.

During this investigation the fellow's paperweight had been accidentally kicked away and some of his papers were blowing down the sidewalk to the water fountain where the headless woman's body still lay. He went to retrieve them.

It was a beautiful day, sunny and crisp with early signs of autumn. The long eucalyptus leaves moved like hair in the breeze and the trees which lined the park just here were smelling as powerfully as pheromones, a pungent, slightly sweet odor as fragile as smoke. The hollering and chaos which surrounded the fountain was to him ghostly, translucent and inarticulate. He was able to retrieve all his papers but one which had got far enough to be trampled into wet fragments. Papers in hand, he stood at the margin of the crowd looking on, not one of those straining to see the grisly remains but watching, Weegee-like, the people themselves.

An astrophysicist inferring the presence of unseen planets through the behavior of suns flaming in a gravity well, a

sociologist trying to understand crowd behavior using the
formulations of economics, a historian who sees something like a
lynching which he only knows from books, an engineer trying to
improve the performance of an orifice intended for a plasma laser
that could burn a hole through the moon, all would recognize the
curiosity of this man. He walks away now with a few ragged
papers in one hand, taking deep breaths of the scented air. One can
see he is thinking. What?

Everyone is familiar with the phenomenon of six degrees of
separation, or the probability that of twenty-five people in a room
two will have the same birthday. Things like this abet the
performances of mediums and palm-readers by reducing the
alternatives to just a few. It is often said that there are only half a
dozen stories, or three, or two, to which all the world's apparent
variety can be reduced. Not often just one, though. *Don Quixote*.
Whichever divine narrative one favors. *The Maltese Falcon*.
Restricting oneself to the hermeneutics of a single story requires an
Oriental ability to find a world in a grain of sand, or else suffocate
in our own tapioca tao.

With only bad memories of textureless, slightly gluey foods,
we search desperately for some sort of freudian transference.
Caught between a horror of the arbitrary and the threat of the
ghastly, inexplicable particular, we find there is nowhere to look.

The man with the folder of papers, which are covered with
spidery marks suggestive of profound insights, gathers his things
from the place where he had been sitting and walks away. He has
had enough sun. Behind him, the blades of grass are beginning to
stand upright again. Portentousness has returned to the scene like
one's hearing, temporarily dulled by the explosion of a roadside
bomb.

MUSICKE

But then, Woody was saying, Roger is not a psychological animal. For me, significance is in the motives of others. In conflict, opposition. Roger is not like that.

Things.

Matter. Intransigent, inertial stuff. He'd have something of a flair for data processing, wouldn't you think? Files, records, and so forth. Thousands of bins and boxes.

No, I don't think it's a contradiction. Organizing power of the intellect. The stuff is pretty stubborn, after all. I don't know why. Perhaps because it never seems to go away. It could never be got off his desk.

Music, I think. He plays the organ, doesn't he? At some church?

Well no, I wouldn't have thought so either. But how would one get an organ otherwise? A really large one, I mean. These electronic things with the drums and the cymbals. It wouldn't compare, would it?

Something of an experience, I suppose, yes. To make that much noise. It must make one quite giddy, mustn't it? Very German.

Like that, yes. A minor god. Hair flying, wind and rain called up with a flick of his baton, a storm of brass and so forth.

Liszt, I suppose. No, I was too young. My parents took me to hear Lenz one Christmas, though.

Well, the man who brought in that idea was a Frenchman. Berlioz.

No, it was because of his determination to improve the standard of musicianship. Fidelity to the composer's intentions, and so forth. Not what one commonly thinks of as a product of Romanticism. Typically French.

Because he likes all the buttons and knobs.

It must give one quite a feeling of competence, mustn't it? And there are the pedals as well.

Four manuals, I suppose. It's been years since I've seen a really big one.

Yes, I would like to hear him. Oh, ages. He must be quite decent to have been kept on as long as that.

You know, I haven't any idea at all. He never talks about it. Not a Methodist, I suppose, or any of the reforming sort either; I can't imagine them having anything ornate enough to suit.

No, mine were Presbyterian. Grim Scotch childhood.

Upstate. Syracuse.

God, no. The most uncatholic personality you could imagine. I would think Episcopalian, or an old high Lutheran.

I'll find out, shall I? Perhaps next weekend, or the weekend after. I haven't been in a church in I don't know how long.

The telephone rang then, and Woody made her escape while the Kink was talking to his secretary. She had long favored this type of exit for its superior tact. It was informal, and thus egalitarian. Forced the matter, not allowing oneself to be dismissed. It also encouraged the pleasant idea that they were all extremely busy, having numberless anterooms filled with suitors and retainers from whom one was only too glad to escape for a moment of intelligent conversation with each other.

Woody glided through the administrative reception area and passed out into the hallway. Her own office was a cubby next to the mail room, which she had managed to salvage from the old days because it kept her out of office politics. Insofar as a taste for old clothes could keep an Assistant Director out.

The Kink's idle suggestion had appealed to Woody's sentimental, antiquarian inclinations. She made inquiries. Several Sundays later she was there at eight o'clock in a back pew of the St. Francis downtown, waiting for the early service to begin, thinking of Walter Scott. Episcopalians her traditional enemies. How long since she first read that book! 'Tis four hundred thirty-five years since. She had worn a discreet black dress to church, which proved a good enough guess. No hat. She hated hats.

It occurred to her afterwards that she could have looked in the hymnal for some idea of the order of service. She supposed Episcopalians called them hymnals. As it was, she had no idea what was to happen next. The organ loft was overhead, so that the organist was not visible to the congregation whispering quietly below. She could not in any case imagine Roger striding forward, probably in great robes, to take his seat before a crowd of penitents, hushed in expectation. His legs were too short to be striding forward.

The valves opened, a thrum Woody felt mostly in her stomach, and with an inrushing of air as the great machine drew breath to begin. There was a small silence of attention.

Dah da daaaaaa, da, dada daaah. Dah da daaaaaa, dah dah dah daaaah.

But that was not it at all. Well of course, one couldn't play such dramatic, angular music every Sunday. As in ancient Syracuse, always cake for breakfast, and two meats for lunch. Musical equivalent of. How did they live through that, those Saxon mothers' sons?

And it wasn't really suited to him either, was it, that bombast?

Are you religious, Roger?

Woody cleared a space on her desk for Roger's teacup, fussing with papers and saucer to excuse her lowered gaze, to make the question more casual.

I mean, all that time spent in church?

Oh, yes.

The pause that followed was so long that Woody was forced by politeness to look up.

I never thought about it, he said.

You surprise me.

She had thought his religion would be mental. Orderly, insured. The alternative is muscular, isn't it?

I believe that's the word, yes.

Is it possible to be religious without thinking about it? An aesthetic, right-brain religion?

Possibly. The only sort of religion, perhaps. That one might take seriously. It's the burden of zen teaching, I believe. But there is no zen organ.

Ah, no.

I went to hear you play, Roger.

Did you. When?

The twenty-fifth, I think. Last month.

Ah, he replied after a moment's reflection, and smiled. The Couperin. A favorite of mine. Did you like it?

Indeed.

So that was what it was. She could never understand how people were able to talk that way, of the Mozart, the Couperin. There must have been as many Couperins as Louies. Le Grand, Le Fat, Le Bald, Le Nephew. Au tombeau de Couperin, pleasant memories of that. Such a wonderful time in the auditorium at the Met, with her father. Carrados. The old man, of course, not the son. That was getting to be a long time ago. Longer than that in cultural time. Eccentric, backwater heritage she'd always been proud of.

Could it have been Carrados? Was that the sort of thing he would have played?

Chacone en re, Roger said. The registration buzzy, the notes in a dense swarm. No pedal, no attack, but simply beginning, sliding down from the fifth to the tonic as if continuing a conversation broken off a moment before. How typical of him.

He did play well.

His first teacher had been the usual one, remembered with distaste but no great fear. Some ability was found in five-year-old Roger, however, and a more expensive, imposing teacher was soon obtained. Poor Mrs. Ribier, always abandoned by anyone with talent, anyone really teachable. She'd lacked imagination, he supposed. He preferred to suppose. She hadn't noticed. It was years since he'd thought of Mrs. Ribier, but now he was getting to be of an age when his mother was sending him newspaper obituaries. The parents of his childhood friends, and other people such as Mrs. Ribier who had become so small and distant. One grieves, he supposed, mostly for oneself, for being so undeniably little. Roger was not inclined to think himself ambitious, but then he must be, mustn't he? To sink his emotional life into the organ? Suppose he had been a tuba player? How unassuming tuba players are, with their magnificent instrument, its great range and singing power, so little heard or known. By comparison, Roger had hardly a double life at all. He hadn't thought about it.

There were, he supposed, a great many things that he didn't think of which puzzled other people unmercifully. Woody had wanted to know was he religious. Was that like being musical? But he didn't know whether he was musical, either. He played well, it was said. Ex cathedra, though he could play lightly too, when it was appropriate. Still, he was without that great passion that he associated with musicality, not Romanticism of the Bruckner sort but rather of Beethoven's last two piano sonatas, or the Goldberg variations. Roger, however, was always competent. Always just, or just so. He doubted if he were musical.

Perhaps he had once wanted to be? A forlorn hope, poignant as a tiny coffin?

Why was Woody coming to hear him play now, after ten years? Wanting to know if he were musical?

He decided to make a test, and set himself to master the first Hindemith organ sonata, a not exactly alien work, but one he had always thought outside his emotional range, music inclined to brooding, only just speculative, with the sternness of a priest who will wink at a nervous altar boy. As he had done all his life, he practiced on Saturdays from about mid-morning until dinner time, now devoting an hour or so to the Hindemith before the cleaning woman and then the Rector began to bustle about with their preparations.

Massig schnell, the first movement admonished him, and Lebhaft. Sehr langsam. Phantasie, frei; Ruhig bewegt. Over and over he played it, more intensely after the demands of Christmas and Easter were over, and by May he felt able to bewegen the music enough to risk an outing.

It was a piece too long to fit anywhere within the liturgy. He would not consider breaking it up, and so played it before the service in place of the usual short prelude, beginning while the pews groaned not, with only a scattering of early worshippers. No one, he thought, noticed. For lunch he treated himself to a Napoleon.

But not entirely unnoticed. The next Saturday, before her usual time, the cleaning woman climbed the steps into the organ loft as Roger was laying out his music.

She said nothing, only sat for an hour listening. Then she returned to her duties below.

Her name was Martha, and Roger knew nothing else about her. She had been the cleaning woman for at least as long as he had been the church organist. He supposed she had been listening to him at Saturday practice all that time, while she worked. Below.

Well if he were not going to be able to practice undisturbed he would have to put aside thoughts of learning any more unusual music

It was now summer. The loft was warm even at ten o'clock. The cleaning woman wore a light shift to work. Martha was of a nondescript middle age, presentable and sufficiently unlike his idea of a charwoman to be suspected of dark secrets, of being someone of another class working out some penance. Roger was not sure he believed in dark secrets.

He wondered if she was paid for the work.

It seemed unfair to object to her presence. But he did object, nonetheless, as much as if she had been the soul of Paganini come for him. He did not want an audience. On Sundays he did not mind the congregation; it was hidden beneath him. Over the railing of the loft he could see only the Rector. They had grown old together, the Rector and he, without ever having gone down, either one of them, into the pit. Roger doubted whether they had ever spoken. To him, the susurrus of prayers and gossip and restless feet was nothing more than the heightened panting of his organ. The appearance of the cleaning woman in the loft surprised him no less than applause would have, and seemed quite as indecorous.

I hope you have enjoyed my playing, he said, hoping to suggest that the enjoyment was now at an end.

The cleaning woman nodded, a little bob of the head of the sort that Oriental people give when they don't understand.

You know, he said the next Saturday as he was opening his music, I learned to play at a quite advanced age. It was a great effort, but music has been an immense solace to me.

The cleaning woman nodded again. Roger on the organ bench turned somewhat toward her.

I was twenty-two when my thirteen brothers and sisters were murdered. Even now it is difficult for me to speak of it. That was when I turned to God.

Again the little bob of the head. Satisfied with what he had learned, Roger set up the Vivaldi which he had planned for Sunday. He needed only to run through it to refresh his memory.

Deaf. Probably the music tickled her somehow, by making the floor quiver. Washed her with a great, silent surf. Something of that sort.

Two more weeks passed. Roger was beginning to think about the second Hindemith sonata when the Rector, who had been pottering about in the chancel plainly waiting for Roger to finish, waylaid him at the bottom of the loft stairs.

Good morning, said Father Ortega as casually as a little boy who is planning to ask his teacher for a kiss.

Roger nodded, a slow and very slight inclination, so that it might seem as if he were stretching out a cramp in his neck.

I wanted to tell you, the Rector went on, how much I liked your playing of the offertory last month. I don't think we've heard that one before?

Perhaps not. I don't recall.

Yes, yes. I don't recall myself, sometimes. I've had to begin a little file, you know, because of that. To keep from preaching too often on the same subject, you see.

Ah.

I might be thought a bit harping otherwise?

Yes.

But I imagine that you must be contemptuous of any little file which I might make. You know, it has been quite a few years since I have been to the university. There have been astonishing changes, I suppose. Probably I wouldn't know my way about, would I?

There have been some superficial changes, Roger allowed.

Bosh. Quite intimidating, I'm sure. It's difficult for me to imagine why we should need so many books. But then, who am I? As ignorant as the caliph Omar, no doubt.

Roger smiled faintly.

Señora Roba tells me you have led quite a life.

Who in hell is Señora Roba?

Something of a swashbuckler, to hear her. No doubt she exaggerates. You know how she is.

Yes, replied Roger, blinking. Somewhat exaggerated.

Ha, ha. Well, I only wanted to let you know how much your music enhances the worship of God. We are fortunate to have someone as able as you among us.

An awkward little pause. Belated pleasure.

Whatever it was, the Rector could not bring himself to say it.

Roger nodded, a bit more vigorously, and Father Ortega went on his way back up the aisle, through the chancel, and into his office. Only when the office door had shut did Roger lower the half dozen books of music he had been clutching across his chest.

Yess indeed, for the high spirits of a moment one pays for a lifetime. If you're going to carry on that way, dearie, you ought to get your tubes tied, don't you think?

By now it was mid-summer. Señora Roba in her shift looked distinctly frumpy, rather like a chocolate bar which he had put in his pocket. Probably she smelled.

She began to sing.

Roger stopped playing in amazement. Martha Roba was humming loudly, swaying a bit in her chair, until she realized that the music had ceased and she, too, ceased, returning slowly to her attitude of patient attention with her head tipped slightly to one side. The next week she was a little bolder, and the next, at last wailing, keening an old song of abandonment, of Ulysses never unbound, of the last archaeopteryx high on a pinnacle of red sandstone beneath a bloody sun, black wings spread wide, giving voice to a thin piercing cry that rose higher and higher—

He stopped playing. The shrieking went on.

He waited, hands in his lap, for it to stop. Slowly the cleaning woman's voice faded to a distant nasal hum, then a vague tuneless whine that he seemed to hear long after, like those inaudible notes a pianist plays at the end of the concert.

Roger gathered up his music and retreated down the stairs and into the brassy August glare of full summer. The heat fell over him like boiling oil dumped from the battlements. He wiped the burning sweat from his eyes. The woman would have to be removed. If she were not removed he would not play. He would speak to the Rector.

The Rector, however, was reluctant. He seemed disappointed, as if he had expected to hear a memorable tale, not this precipitate demand that he fire the cleaning woman. Who was only a volunteer, after all.

But at last he promised to say a word or two. At the earliest opportunity. Not too obviously, of course. Tactfully suggest.

Roger was relieved that no ultimatum had been necessary. Before now he had never thought of quitting, and when he did think of it, it was with an unhappiness at least as great as Señora Roba's.

But the Rector bungled it. Next Saturday the cleaning woman was still there, silent and a bit grim about the mouth. Roger laid out his music. He listened to the organ fill itself, take breath. He set up the stops and linkages. He waited. Señora Roba waited. Then he turned everything off again. The blower sighed and mumbled and Roger went home.

That Sunday he played the service cold. There were rough patches in the introit.

The next weekend was the same, and the introit was more rugged.

Señora Roba, he said, turning on the organ bench to face her. The cloth of his trousers hissed on the polished wood. Martha. Get out.

There was a long moment filled only with the placid breathing of the organ.

The charwoman lowered her eyes at last, to her hands lying palm upward in her lap. Then she picked up her bag of rags and bottles and went down the stairs from the loft. A bit later the vestibule door closed, reverberating through the empty building the way it always did no matter how carefully it was pulled to.

My God, he thought, looking over the balcony rail into the darkness of the nave.

So I asked him, Woody was saying, that was it?

Well, no. He'll make some long explanation about public and private religion. The great importance of the former, yes.

No, not at all. Presbyterian, yes. Grim Scotchmen.

Syracuse.

Well, you know, I think he would be rather afraid to. He's quite committed to a belief in the organizing power of the intellect. No taste for that sort of thing at all.

Then the telephone rang, just as usual, as Woody had always counted on, and she slipped tactfully out of the Director's office with the usual excuse.

The Director's secretary was certainly a capable woman, to know so exactly when to call.

For half an hour afterward, Woody sat in her office by the mailroom, her feet up on the desk. Since there were no windows, she stared at a blank section of the wall just beside the door where the dirty green paint gave the impression of vague swirling clouds.

She thought about the beginning of the world.

There was a time, some years ago now, when she was quite jealous of university students, of these children just on the point of deciding their lives, these eighteen-year-olds who had not yet decided anything and had not yet come to be mostly what they were not.

III

REFUGEES

THE BANSHEE

SIMONE SAID: Gary wants to invite some students for Thanksgiving dinner this year.

She stirred her chile. Slowly the plastic spoon went around and around. She hadn't eaten any of it. The white spoon was stained chile red.

Someone in particular? Reiva inquired cautiously.

No. Probably. You know the ones who don't go home. The international ones. Orphans. Little match girls.

She tiddlywinked the spoon, which fell onto the floor.

Or so he says.

Oh... I see. It's not that, then?

Some time passed. They both looked at the spoon on the floor.

What is?

There's this Scoppone woman, Simone admitted.

Philosopher?

No. I don't know — art student.

So what is it then? Reiva asked with deliberate ellipsis.

Nothing. She has this Jamaican boy. Man. Derek of Unknown Intentions, academic and otherwise. Speaks eight hundred languages.

Gary is, I take it, the Rocky Raccoon of this story?

No. Gary would prefer to find Gideon's Bible without being shot up first. You'll come to dinner?

On Thanksgiving Reiva helped to make dinner. It was the first time, she was startled to realize, that she had been in Simone's home. Reiva had brought along someone from the bullpen, Lindsey, who she had been spending a little time with and who it turned out was good with knives so Lindsey got those jobs. Simone made a pie. Reiva washed green beans and dishes and tidied up after everyone else. There was cranberry relish already in the refrigerator. The sweet potatoes were to have been baked in the oven along with the turkey but Gary had bought an extra-large bird which didn't quite fit. Lindsey sectioned it by taking out a triangle of ribs on each side, which made it kind of squatty but then it did fit. So the sweet potatoes would go in the microwave. There was the usual discussion about whether they might be yams but Gary had a book and they weren't, they were potatoes. Lindsey said she didn't much like microwaved potatoes because the chewey outer layer gets tough so Simone buttered them and wrapped them in tinfoil but then there was this big casserole of beans that had to go in so the potatoes were evicted again.

Steam 'em, Lindsey said. The beans, I mean.

How many are coming? Reiva inquired.

I don't know, said Gary. He was eating a bowl of cereal and milk. Not all the students will show up, of course.

Gary rested one hip against the counter and stood with his ankles crossed and reminded Reiva of a mop leaning there. Mets sweatshirt, new jeans, dark shoes, dark socks.

The Foswells from the art department are coming. Some people of Simone's.

Where's the beer cooler? Simone hollered from the top of the stairs where she had gone to change into something fresher.

In the garage, Simone.

Christ, it'll freeze solid.

Feet coming down. Some hopping to get a shoe on. The door. The tiny gunshot of a beer can opening.

Events moved on. The Foswells, George and Marge, arrived early on bringing a not quite ostentatious bottle of white wine. Reiva and Lindsey were introduced and a Dum-Dee joke was passed around because they looked so much alike, which gave the Tweedles a pleasant feeling of complicity. Drinks were set up and a map to the cooler was tacked up. Students knocked diffidently on the mud porch door after walking all around the house and finding no other way in. There were tall young men studying engineering or business who spoke with Indian accents too quickly to follow, others the same but a built a little thicker who were from one of the Stans and spoke too slowly to follow. Barbara Scoppone and Derek, decorously a little farther apart than they wanted to be. Two other couples connected somehow to the Foswells, central

Europeans who looked as if they had been coupled for the occasion. One of these couples proved to be a little frosty and somehow ended up sitting apart, but the other pair dug into the drinks and peanuts and wandered through all the rooms together talking to everyone. The one, Marta, was a printmaker, maybe Czech or something farther south, with courtly manners and a charming accent. Glazer or Glotzer or something Reiva was mysteriously too shy to ask her to repeat. The other was a German boy quite a few years younger, clearly the escort haled up for the occasion. Marta was someone in Marge Foswell's school. Reiva had a brief attack of lewdness somewhat like a caffeine hit, provoked by all this coupling, and sought out the knot of Indian engineers.

The meal went well. There was an air of sozzled merriment which eased the isolation of the two men who weren't drinking and were probably Muslims, which explained the nuts and vegetables stuffing Simone had made to replace the other one of sausage and apples.

Conversation was becoming general, the neighborhoods and villages which had prevailed during dinner coalescing into a larger seminar over dessert and coffee. Typically for the occasion, soteriological topics dominated. The Muslims were questioned about Koranic views of purity, to which Marta, who proved to be Jewish, was able to add something learnedly rabbinical.

The question distilled from all the less articulate cross-table arguing was what does it mean to be thankful if there is no transcendental agency to which (whom?) the arrangement of circumstances can be attributed? An attempt was made to quiz the Indians about reincarnation but they were Christians and completely ignorant of Hindu doctrine. It was all very high-spirited and ecumenical and self-congratulating.

Meanwhile, Reiva reflected, Out There, the natives were celebrating over their own pie and coffee. What do you suppose they were talking about? Homey things. Well, they were at home after all.

Safe at home. Chatauquan New York had been rife with utopians dreaming of perfect communities though possibly not over pie and coffee among the remains of dead galliforms.

But Marge, whose field Reiva had thought was *art* history tutted that. Several others joined the tutting and it turned out even the Stanians knew quite a lot about 19th century New York.

The dream of the perfect community always descends eventually into some form of totalitarianism, was the consensus. This was too debunked for Reiva's taste, but even Lindsey was being clear-eyed after all the bottles of wine. In order to remain perfect the community must purge itself of wrongdoers, as one of the Indians put it, and finally of those who are just different. He looked up and down the table with a significant twist to his lips.

It's like sorting apples, the earthier Marge said. You want to toss out the little ones, and when those are gone some others which didn't seem little before, and so on.

Enforcing conformity to the rules offers a way for the strong to grab the capital of the weak, rejoined the Indian engineer.

And then the social capital of the weak, the mantle of righteousness, said one of his fellows.

And then the weak themselves, Marta finished, to general uneasy laughter.

Monkeys have their police, too, George Foswell remarked.

Eh?

George explained. A few high-status members of the troupe, who can do this without fear of reprisal, will act to keep down aggression, principally by getting in between two monkeys who are getting a little out of hand. These can be males or females, and the monkey police appear to be quite disinterested. But if they are removed from the troupe there is less grooming and playing and there get to be cliques and the social network breaks down. What the police do is take out some of the risk in socializing.

Marge laughed. George of the jungle, she said. It was a big round laugh which drew then all in.

So, Marta's escort asked when the merriment had died down, the monkey police are manufacturing trust?

It would seem so.

Disbelief was general, this not being the experience of most of them with the police.

Yes but you see, George broke in, that's why it's essential that it be disinterested.

The concept of a disinterested police was soundly rejected. George seemed a bit put out.

It seems to me, George, said Marge, that a utopia would encourage hypocrisy as a life strategy. One learns to dissemble competitiveness in order to disarm resistance and fear. One makes a pretense of egalitarianism to buy time to gather strength for a coup, justifying all this in the name of peace and harmony. What on earth prevents the monkeys from doing the same?

No idea, replied George complacently.

Simone interjected a more lugubrious tone. Maybe monkeys are more authentic than we are. she said. Her voice struck Reiva as hollow. We say we can have material comfort without sacrificing — oh, spiritual depth call it. But we have neither.

Depth. It was Lindsey's turn now. De profundis. Suppose "profundity" is only another hypocritical illusion? How can there be anything profound when you are living one moment to the next? When it's one thing after another?

You can pretend, Simone shot back. The same way you pretend you're a person and that things have happened — to you, to other "people" — the same way you choose what to do next. For no reason. Because.

Interesting word, *because*, Gary put in. Means "for cause" and we use it to mean the opposite. What, I wonder, he wondered professionally, is the cognitive function which creates the working sense of what is profound?

Memory creates history, Lindsey said.

Thought-police create the hive, was Marta's gloss on that. Create it so transparently it's as hard to see as a quantum cat.

By mechanism you mean, said George, a bit of brain wiring I suppose. Is there a spiritual gizmo that has survival value?

Probably somewhere in the hindbrain.

Huh. What do you suppose lizards believe in, then? What lizard religion is like.

Especially, Reiva said, those ones in the desert that reproduce by parthenogenesis and are all of them female.

This remark seemed to hit some sore point. Everyone fell silent and twitched nervously on their bottoms the way academics do when a Republican speaks up. Had there perhaps been some bedtime arguments here over whether men were of any use? Drones, whose survival value was only as a stock of potential queens?

Indeed she remembered Simone saying once she couldn't see why we needed so *many* of them, fer chrissake. If we gassed the extras think what that would do for environmental problems.

Reiva had broken up the table. People began to stretch, to circulate around with more of the sweet things on offer, to talk in corners and on sofas.

After a while Gary herded them all out for a walk in the biting end of a winter day. He passed out scarves and they walked down to the jetty on the left bank but it was too cold to stay. Across the river the yacht berthings were empty, a rope hanging from a stanchion into the water. The students began to wander away in pairs or single men making their excuses, their thanks. The flattened turkey had been a success. By the time the walking party reached the bridge they were eight: Simone and Gary, Reiva and Lindsey, the Foswells, Derek, and Barbara Scoppone. Derek was going to be Gary's project for the year, it seemed. He had got out of his old apartment and moved in with Barbara, which had driven out Barbara's previous roomie because the landlady had complained and anyway she couldn't study with all that going on and flounced out.

Reiva kept an eye on Gary, suspicious of his good will.

Under the bridge it was a little warmer. The wind flowed with the water here, colliding with the much colder wind off the lake farther long, out in the open. There was a small protected place to stand, not really big enough for eight. Gary said they should have brought wood to build a campfire on the pebbly shelf here, and

George Foswell said a 55 gallon drum might be more apropos which left the impression that he thought they were all playing at something. The wind from the south smelled of chocolate.

Um, Gary? Why are we standing out here in the cold?

I'm not cold.

That flummoxed everyone. The little group pushed back defensively farther into the niche, leaving Gary the closest to the river. The knife-colored water, seeming thick as paint, oozed over the egg-sized rocks along its banks.

This is a cold place, Gary said. There was a smidgen of irritated incomprehension in his tone which he quickly brushed away like spilled salt. I mean, here we are, who wants to be always indoors just because it's cold? Is that *authentic?*

All eyes on Derek, the Antillean, who shyly waved away this attention. They all pulled their heads deeper into their collars in silent refutation.

Look. It's beautiful.

That was a bit much. Even Simone, who presumably knew something of the Philosopher's quirks, was annoyed.

Gary, she said with asperity, we're hiding under a bridge, the place is deserted, it's covered with litter and tin cans and unmentionables, everything is a joyless gray —

Yes, and just over there — he pointed to a tiny spot of color downstream opposite, in the dockyard — over there is a popcorn machine.

It was only a red and yellow speck which Reiva could barely see, but when Gary told them what it was she could recognize it as that pushcart with bicycle wheels the Kiwanis used in the 4th of July parade and a couple of other times during the summer. She wanted it to be forlorn, but it refused. It would not be ludicrous either. It was just a welcome speck of color in a colorless industrial landscape. But as the scene organized itself around Gary's discovery, around that focus, it did take on a sort of dignity. Her attitudes fell off it like rimes of dirty ice in a little thaw, uncovering the thing itself. There it was, replete.

Gary was itchy to make it beautiful, but it wasn't. Nor was it bleak. Nor dignified or anything else, including replete, Reiva thought with some embarrassment. All that was just more of talking to herself inside her head.

Gary, however, was building up steam. He was about to explode the boiler with enthusiasm.

I mean — his gestures were getting larger — here we are. We're *here*, aren't we? Why is this a worse place or an uglier place than — I mean, do I want to spend my time indoors eating industrial turkey when I'm dying of prostate cancer and I could be out here?

What?

Simone's eyes were as round and white as Orphan Annie's and her face, once red with wind and cold, had gone bloodless.

What? What did I say?

Gary and Simone glared at each other. Then, after far too long a still moment, Simone turned and stomped off, stepping down hard in all the puddles to make the slush squirt.

Winter passed, after all. Came a second summer, or rather a promise of one. Simone and Reiva had both posted their grades. The term was done. Again the empty pub, the walnut light, the soundless Sox on television above the bar.

They had not seen much of each other since the afternoon under the bridge.

We don't *do* anything, Simone was saying. She twirled an empty glass on its heavy bottom. We talk. We look around. We talk some more, about our epic journey round the Great Rock. Standing on top of the Great Rock you can see for inches.

That's a song. John Denver? I don't remember.

Of course you don't remember. You were five years old.

Sounds right.

The silences between were getting longer. The beer glass came to rest. Simone got up and walked out.

Huh, Reiva remarked to no one.

‹◊›

Simon I am. I've taken Her name, leaving her nothing.

She shall be known henceforth as Die Leere, or the Empty One.

What's in a name, anyway? Difficult question, that; not for amateurs. Der Venticle would have an opinion, of course. It's something to do with identity, but what is there to identify? I, there's the rub.

Presumptuous woman, Reiva. The Little Wind, I shall call her.

What's at stake here? This matter of identity: the mystery of the solid, palpable object. The real thing. You see it, my boy? A wooden ball. You know my methods — tell me what you make of it. And so you learn to *enpalpulate* your makings.

In this place we train workers for the knowledge mines, delving for that ore which is the food of speculators. Many will die under the Eaters' lash. Many will be asphyxiated by infodust. Many will fall to their deaths or be crushed. Those still living emerge naked from under the ground, a long procession of exhausted miners trudging one by one to be hosed down, scrubbed senseless lest they take away some speck for the morrow, any bright thought belonging to the Eaters.

Ourselves, we live on apples, a kind of ambrosia. All apple trees are cloned from the original of their kind, that Other tree of whereabouts now forgotten.

Coffee is not a food. Those of us who live on coffee are doomed. We are deluded by caffeine's false promises. Coffee negotiates in bad faith.

George Foswell says I'm becoming a little mad with this disease. Perhaps.

Die Leere's big sister died of cancer a few years ago. I was too cowardly then to sit with her. Die Leere says that at the end her sister's brains leaked from her eyes.

I think I'm going to cut off my dick. A smooth join then, my borrowed woman's third eye sewn shut.

A Slide Show

Here you see the country of my fathers, my forefathers, four fathers, foreskinned men of no… prescience. From the wreck of that time only this t-shirt has survived. All we have of the past, of lives live, is these artifacts around which we spodge the wet clay of yet another golem.

I shall tell them, George, to preserve my diseased balls in oil. They were never any good to me. Die Leere can stuff them in her quim for solace.

Yes, I know where the prostate is. It's where the milk of human kindness comes from, which is why it's inseparable from the rest of that apparatus.

Yes yes, I know the waste piss goes the other way through the same sewer. I, wank, am Death, the creator and destroyer of worlds. Thicker than brothers, piss and milk. I've been reading a book about extinction. It's a hollow feeling, the author says, to think of this world without humanity: vast tracts of beauty without our eyes to behold. I get a hollow feeling myself beholden to my own eyes. Those who have crossed, the author says, with direct eyes to death's other kingdom, remember us — if at all — not as lost violent souls, but only as the hollow men, the stuffed men. I read a lot of books like that now.

This business about identity, about where I'm coming from, is I think a pennant in the wind. Which moves, the pennant or the wind? That old fascist Socrates did us a bad turn when he nixed the answer to that. What I should do with all these books, George, what I should do is what Mumon advises concerning the sutras. Tear them up. If you meet the Buddha, kill him. We could do with a little less veneration these days.

We lived here a while, after where we lived before. *Here*, though, is a vague sort of idea. We used to send postcards home, remember, when people of my class didn't travel, when you traveled by flivver, before the motel was invented. Some soul proud of what he has accomplished sends a picture postcard back on which he has printed in irregular capitals **WE ARE HERE** with an arrow pointing to one window in the row. But those times are gone. Now you guess where here is.

Here was where we went out at eight o'clock on Christmas Eve and bought a tree. I think we put cookies on it. Cat got 'em. You can't do stuff like that now. You couldn't find a busted pumpkin in an alley on Hallowe'en if you were world champion ragpicker. By then they've all got candles in 'em. By then all pumpkin souls are on fire. They won't last the night. It's an actuaries' world now, George.

The shop on the corner used to be a hardware store. I worked there one year putting myself through college. Across the street was a laundry where they shot a scene of *Escape From Alcatraz*. Or maybe it was a delicatessen. There was no streetcar on the left-hand side by then. You'd have to look at the movie. A Chinese laundry with a streetcar going by which Clint Eastwood gets on to get away from that picture. We had *our* laundry done at a real no-tickee no-shirtee place up the block where you see that red building with the white awning. But I think it was really a delicatessen.

What this is, George, is a fork in the road. You have a choice to make. Which road goes where you're going? Which streetcar are you going to get on — left or right? Maybe it doesn't matter. They're both going where Clint Eastwood went, anyway.

Now we have to talk about religion, George. Unctions. Yes I know, the picture's a little fuzzy. That's how these things are.

Missions like this are all over southern California, though as I remember, this one was a repro. A fake, as we say, from about 1920. Now you are expecting me to go on about identity again and what it could possibly mean to be fake, like we used to do with our high school biology teacher who could always be got to waste classroom time with war stories. I'm not sure it was time wasted, though.

You won't deflect me that way anyhow. I won't be looking for death in church, George. It's too easy.

Anyway, recent events have made it harder to push a materialist hypothesis. People don't want to hear that. They want this squabbling and bickering among the spiritual tribes stopped — I think the hive is getting ready to swarm. There's always this unrest before a division. Remind me to ask Der Venticle about the Hundred Years War. Yes, I know it's not her period but trust me. She's a fox. She knows a little about everything.

She and Die Leere were pretty thick for a while, at first. But Die Leere is not a thick person. She is *ausgeleere* — dispersed, tenuous, subtle, filamentous, transparent. Not a materialist. Sensitive to immanence rather, to aether. No, that's with an *a*, George. It's the stuff the world was full of before we materialists substituted dark matter. But yes, I imagine she would be sensitive to the stuff without an *a*, also. She is not one for drugs. No peyote cults, no hashish visions, no bhang bangs. There's no significance to it; it's like being allergic to scallops or peanuts. A peanut unction is not likely to save any souls, I think.

That was one of the things we never could agree on. Die Leere always said I'd frustrated her spiritual needs. George, do you have spiritual needs? I'm not sure what she wanted me to do, like maybe go out to the store for something to put on them, kind of like that itchy feeling you get when you're pregnant. I gather, George, that you've never been pregnant. It's called a couvade syndrome, where the two of you go through the same experience, one of those creepy things that make you wonder where the boundaries are. I suppose it's such phenomena give rise to the notion of a soul.

I wonder if a soul can be allergic to peanuts.

I think this is one of those tests they give a child to find out something or other, to get you to make up a story about what do you see here in order to learn whether the right side of your brain is talking to the left or something.

Der Venticle was fretting about what was I up to with that boy, Scoppone's shadow. Die Leere was telling me this in bed which is not a good place to be saying such things but it was really her who was worried, I'd bet. You hear women talking to each other about the damnedest things, right there at the next table about whether her husband might be a pederast or something. You can't take an interest, people think you're up to something. Does Marge spring these things on you in bed?

No, I thought not.

Our old cat is on its last legs. Why do we say that, as if it once had other legs, as if the stock of legs were used up. If there extra legs maybe I could get one myself to replace this diseased third one? It's an old cat. I'm going to have a hard time putting it down. You wonder what goes through its mind at such times.

Listen to me. As if I should live so long as to — put it down, pick it up; such language. I'll be saying *passed on* next. Dead, George. Dead. I'm going to be dead, maybe two, three months. The mothers weep and groan — what does it profit them to hear that the child they have buried has become an angel? What good is an angel? Is it like a pet fish that lays on your chest all night, purring and giving you bad dreams?

Die Leere wasn't very happy my keeping this secret, was she? I just couldn't — *empty* myself. I don't know how bulimics manage that. If you were a hunger artist starving yourself to death maybe — maybe you could see the point then. Maybe if I were in the habit of barfing up my sins in the walnut toilet...

She found that cat under a mail sack, you know, discarded on the loading dock of administrative services. Would have froze if she hadn't stuck it inside her parka. How it lasted that long. Some student tossed it out with the dorm trash at the end of the semester. What I want to know is, if Die Leere can pick up a stray cat why aren't we sitting here worrying about it? What she might have in mind. Whereas if I pick up a stray boy. There's an asymmetry here, George. A lack of balance.

Well you know, I didn't take that boy on thinking I was going to die in the middle of it. Scoppone will pick him up, though. She's tough. Tough as ice cream.

I was going to say cannoli if it weren't for that hackneyed idea of being soft in the middle. *I'm* soft in the middle. Not enough exercise. What's the point?

You know those cartoons where one hand draws another one and then erases itself, and so on? That's how we get on, George. One thing after another. We live in the moment, like a frame of a movie, and there's always a next frame until there isn't. It's the puzzle of the flag in the wind again, whether the flag is moving or the wind. It's the mind moves. The past is in the past. It doesn't go there from the present. We create it out of this crap lying around, artifacts. Think about that word, George. The facts of art. The art of memory, eh?

Die Leere is tough too, tough as air. We're the wind and the flag, we two. In the winter the wind comes off the lake and if the street's icy it'll blow you along like on skates until it blows your feet out from under and upends you like Harold Lloyd.

You go with it. It's a riff, George. A riff.

I found these pictures in Die Leere's stuff. Snooping around in her stuff. I didn't know her at that age, of course. We met in college, in German. She always hated German. Hard to learn and easy to know, she says. French is the other way around. In German a neologism is constructed, built — like a building, out of blocks of stone mortared together. It's an erector set. You can make anything out of it. In French no new word is new. All French words are like shirts made out of old rags. The cloth is soft, comfortable. You can see everything it used to be — a coat worn by the man who trims the grapevines over the winter, a pair of pants that used to belong to the Duc de Guermantes, a blouson worn by some montagnard — see the blood stains? — underwear, a uniform...

I never did learn enough German to read Heidegger. Not really read. I was never a phenomenologist anyway, despite what it seems like.

She didn't learn that much, either. After the first term she went for Italian instead, but we'd already done all the homework by then.

Columbia. And we end up in this hole. No wonder she's angry.

Cute little beggar, wasn't she?

I personally think the message here is banal. Suppose we turn these pictures around. Switch them, left for right. Doesn't help. It's only making your guests sit through the slides of your trip to Lapland backwards. That was why you gave them all that wine at dinner, wasn't it? So's they would?

Would you like to do it all over again, George? Not with what you know now, which is always the blandishment offered, but sozzled? Wordsworth was three sheets to the wind, I think, with his intimations of old glories.

Now suppose instead of switching them you put them on the side of a bus. Two busses, an hour apart. What message then? A message from outer space, maybe. Dits and dahs, one dit a century. I don't think you could spot one dit in all that noise. They say if there were intelligent life in the universe we'd have heard from them by now. They also speculate whether the universe is alive, that there are an infinite number of universes where lives go on by different rules. Maybe all the intelligent life is over there. In the big city, at the party you didn't get invited to, the girl you didn't marry.

You wonder if the universe may be getting fat and old and is needing to be put down. What do you suppose it's thinking? Does a universe understand itself as a separate being? Different from the other universes? With a life? Probably it doesn't remember where it came from or how it got here, just as we don't remember being born either.

Did you know that maybe half a child's brain cells have to die off before it can organize itself? Be self-conscious? What are all those superfluous nerves for? A primordial plasma of unrealized possibilities? Maybe that's why we always have this vague feeling that something's going on. Under the ground. Somewhere. It's the sound of all those other lives, partying it up.

Do you suppose a universe knows when it's the end, when the fingers and toes are starting to get cold and that stuff you stuck in me is starting to work and you wonder why. I was your friend. Why did you betray me?

We don't go to parties anymore.

I don't know what to say about this. Maybe it got screwed up in the camera.

This is from backpacking in the Adirondacks. Someone I knew had this cabin where he said we could sleep over. I don't know what it means to *have* a cabin — it looked to us as if it were the trees that had the place. The idea was to go fishing or something. I can't imagine Die Leere wanting to catch a fish. The place was full of mice. We put our sleeping bags down and before we could shut our eyes these mice were all over, getting into the bags, into our pockets and under our pajamas. Little bitty things about the size of a finch. They had long bony fingers, minute vampire fingers that could hold onto a seed or a crumb and turn it around like a watch-maker with a balance.

Cute, but we wouldn't have gotten a minute's sleep, so we had to pick up and move to a clearing outside.

There was another time, camping in Maine. The no-see-ums were just awful. It was an ordinary campground village. Black night, no moon. About an hour after dark we heard this woman's voice rising like lamentation, in this perfect New Jersey accent — You didn't tell me about the bugs, Morris.

Morris, I'm being eaten alive.

Do something, you jerk. Where's the spray?

That's it. Pack the car. Throw all this stuff in the car. We're going home. And you can go to your brother's wedding by yourself.

There's this peculiar relationship to the phenomenal world, George. We talk of *having* a house. Like it belongs to us somehow. As if by noticing it, however we do that, we're taking out a deed like we do with a foxy woman on the street. *Having a wife.* I wonder if the mice and the no-see-ums know about this? One day, maybe two, three years old, you notice yourself for the first time, and from that moment you're supposed to have a life.

We don't go camping anymore.

We don't do anything much anymore. We wait.

WHATEVER HAPPENED TO PEACHY CARNAHAN?

SIMONE

Gary Richter's death (or Simon's death, to use his own mortal, and moribund, taxonomy) in August was resigned and quiet. The Empty One carried on through the fall term, but she was walking on quaking ground as we later learned. Around midterm she had started an affair with Gary's erstwhile protégé Derek, and by New Year's the two of them had decamped to Paris. Or so we heard. Anyhow, she vanished from this place. In the middle of a blizzard.

Her behavior had been growing offensive. In a small town used to student ways it was nevertheless annoying to come across her in an alley or a nook with her hand down the front of some boy's pants. That the boy may have been black was noticed, of course, but here the tribal animosities run on different lines, and in any case little is to be expected of college people other than to keep quiet. The attrition in Le Vide's already thin French classes was soon noted, as students passed the word among themselves that Professor Richter was not a safe option. A rumor went around with the final exams that she had been found masturbating in a storage closet. That wasn't true, of course.

Anyway, she and Derek turned up in Paris about Easter time. Formerly known as Derek. Simone had by then taken to calling him John John. The name on his passport had turned out to be Fairleigh, family name Stipe. This had been way too mannered; he exchanged it for one he liked better, which precedent authorized Simone to exchange it yet again for one to *her* taste. A baby name was not much of an improvement over Fairleigh, especially with the connotation of *Her Little Client*.

In the History Department Reiva Derwent was pointed out as one who had had a similar breakdown, but she hotly refused to speculate on older friend's case. Former older friend. It was not clear to us whether the heat was directed at the purported association or the presumed likeness of their cases, but Ms. Reiva was too

prickly to be worth our sorting that out. So Simone bore her ago-
nies alone.

One wonders whether she had not been lonely for a long time.
How long had Gary kept his secret?

We ourselves know little of Paris, having at that time only visited for a week or so, and might have thought it more likely that
she would turn to the west instead, to that house she inherited from
Gary, in the picture the one with the high gabled roof — no, that's
a church.

It was an imaginary house, but then so was Paris imaginary.
Die Leere was thus our advance, scouting the imaginary for the
main body of troops in the rear.

Or perhaps, considering the sobriquet conferred on her by the
dead man, our vessel.

The place was as foreign to her as to us, she discovered, though
she spoke the language well enough and had been born in Chartres,
practically under the cathedral. Henry Adams probably walked
over her family's graves. She did not take John John to Chartres.
They found an apartment in the 19th arrondissement among the Africans and Arabs with whom John John was more comfortable.

And it was cheap. Relatively cheap. John John's French was
sub-par, nor were his other languages as advertised. He spoke Barbados English. He couldn't have worked if he wanted to, which he
did not. He had expected to be kept. When he found he would not
be, he took himself off, probably to Rome, afterwards English-
speaking Malta where he could pick up a little Italian on the side.
We heard that he turned up in Vienna under the name Giovanni
Stirpa, decamped again to the Greek islands, thence into Turkey,
perhaps in search of Byron's blue mosque.

Probably Simone had exploited him to make a new identity of
her own — younger, more bohemian, more innocent. She found
work with Monsieur Otto, an importer who had been getting by
with his own rickety English and even more rickety receptionist
and thought she was worth enough to be a little negligent about her
documents. So Le Vide found it expedient that Simone Richter
vanish and Marguerite Vonleere take her place.

She had never felt like a person anyway. Standing now on the platform of the Pyrénées Métro stop at eight-thirty in the morning she pondered her fellow anthropoids. A sorting device had sifted out the rather more well-dressed office workers from those on the street above — women in leather coats and fashionable shoes, men in blazers and wrapped in scarves. Up there it had been a gray day, with a biting damp; here a dry warm wind pushed by the trains lifted hair and ruffled hems. To Marguerite the men looked all a little rackety. Perhaps it was their narrow, fine-boned faces and the suggestion of their having shaved in a hurry. The women were mostly coarser, with dark hair cut round their ears. Marguerite had let hers grow out, and had discreetly lightened it to the color of maple wood. She wore it loose. Strands blew across her eyes and stuck to her lips; she brushed them away. Men waiting looked resolutely into the tunnel mouth or at their *Figaro*, for the sake of their unease with blond hair and pouty lips and thick white sweaters. Next train two minutes, they read on the overhead crawler. Marguerite smiled privately.

Le Vide had begun to *compléter, se remplir*. She had begun to form an idea of what sort of being she was. Whether other people were *trés solide,* as full of themselves as they appeared to be, she didn't know — she thought it unlikely they were, and would discover this if they gave it any attention, which for that reason they were unlikely to do. Marguerite was sufficiently humble to suppose that her ideas were in general circulation, else how would she have come by them? But as with legends, always said to be of someone else.

Marguerite made a cursory survey of men's shoes, not so well-polished as those going to *La Défense*, and trousers. Two in jeans nicely pressed. Some showing the effect of morning coffee and some, she hoped, the presence of herself.

A train glided into the station. The mouths of the cars drew back. Although the train wasn't full, Marguerite saw there were no good seats and chose to stand near the door.

Her idea (which the Philosopher hadn't thought much of) was that there is no such thing as a self. At any rate, when she looked, she didn't see one, and had come to regard selves as an illusion created when one regards one's own being without noticing the mirror. Individuals, to her thinking, exist only as parts of some larger social, genetic continuum, a continuum in which one is embedded, indefinitely extended into an infinity of persons, no more able to see the whole thing than a dot can see a line.

Marguerite's persona she thought of as a clump of... well, she didn't have a word for those... *impersonations*, tangles in the brain. They seemed to behave like transistors in a network, amplifying energy by passing it around. A karma network. One of the family of characters in a novel, a mixture bound together by the story the way a soup is bound by those little frozen balls of flour and butter dropped into the *mélange* of karma being manufactured by the toing and froing and hat-raising of all that of the knot of beings. Every knot in the network in every network in the universe in every universe in an infinity of universes buzzed with the karma produced within it, all of it created out of the mitochondria-like shadow beings thought to be persons.

Perhaps not only persons? We — she really ought to refer to herself in the plural — wonder if cats and trees have shadows. What would happen if a forest decided to swarm like a hive of bees? Could a cat divide itself into two cats? That reminds us of the old experiments of putting flies and old rags in a bottle to find out where new flies come from. The mistake was putting them in the bottle. We contemplate the network of energy paths around us — the Métro car, the backside of the 1re arrondissement, Paris — and consider further explorations to other worlds in formation, explorations which will only generate more karma to power the synapses of the galaxy. We have intimations. Marguerite supposed this to be the source of what the Philosopher had wanted to call spirituality, that thing which he always said she had frustrated. Perhaps it was. Though she didn't see why it was assumed to be frustrated. "Frustrated spirituality" seemed to be a bound phrase, a diptych like Alphonse and Gaston, or "unrequited love." Is there anything which is unrequited *other* than love?

An unrequited plumber is one who doesn't show up, like the one who the concierge was supposed to have obtained for the toilet.

The train slowed for her stop. And up on the street the sun was supposed to have burst through and scattered the clouds, but it hadn't. Marguerite walked briskly the blocks from the Métro to the courtyard of her building.

Bon jour, she said brightly to the ragged man who was always sheltering in the passage. Up the stairs on the left, one floor above the passport photographer on the rez de chausée and overlooking a linden so ragged it must have been on stage with the original Pozzo. Another bon jour for the receptionist who had either just quit or hadn't been hired yet.

Bon jour Monsieur Otto!

Bang. The glass panel in the door rattled ominously but had never yet fallen out.

Bon jour, Marguerite… et comme ça commence de nouveau…

On weekends she explored the bookshops of the Left Bank as she was expected to do, tried on clothes, sat in cafés when she could get a table by the window. It was too cold now to sit out on the street, and most places had pulled in their umbrellas and iron bistro furniture. She spoke French. A sort of French. She had no street language, no words but Academy words for the things of contemporary life. She suppose she sounded like Racine or (hopefully) Bouvard.

In the new year Marguerite began to be troubled by depression. At first she thought it was only a delayed — very long delayed — reaction to bereavement. It did have some of that quality. There was the unfocused sense of loss. There were the flashes of anger at having been cheated in some obscure way. She had often been melancholy but now the dominant feeling was one which she only knew how to describe as an ache. She supposed it resembled homesickness only that was an emotion she had not much experience with, never having felt much at home anywhere. All her life up to college and meeting the man who would be Philosopher was blurred.

She was finding it difficult at times to keep up appearances. Otto found her a doctor to prescribe her an anti-depressant but that only made her loopy and after a month she stopped taking it.

Certain places and scenes made trouble for her. A particular kind of blue sky with a wind rattling leaves along the pavement. The ladder of bridges on the Seine. The inside of the Gare du Nord. It was inexplicable. Walking over the Pont Marie toward the Quai d'Anjou she clutched her companion's arm with both hands, leaning her head on his shoulder to hide her reluctance to look. Or if she were alone, the dark water of the river, the narrow street with its low parapet and the yellow-brown stone of the buildings ranged in that sinuous curve along the edge of the island, the bare branches to which only a few crisp golden leaves still clung — something about the scene seemed to dig into her chest and squeeze things — her heart, her stomach — she wanted to weep with frustration and also, strangely, fear that she might fall into the Seine. And be instantly poisoned. Or so it seemed; her eyes were dry all the same.

In hunting around for ways of explaining this awful combination of sudden joy and despair she hit upon a somewhat Dickensian vision of a mother whose grief over a dead baby suffuses everything, whose longing is always just out of reach, unsatisfied … It was a bathetic image, and helpful for just that reason. On some weekends she dragged reluctant men to the Louvre and sought out all the treacliest genre paintings. One said, at least, that he preferred the Musée Gustave Moreau; most preferred something else entirely. Le soccer. Or they went to the Orsay where the paintings repelled her, mocked her feelings, reduced them to no more than a spent stocking held up between two fastidious fingers. She felt herself becoming hysterical, in danger of making a scene, and went out to wait on the street. Her companion took a curiously long time to follow.

At Easter there was a program of Gregorian chant at Notre Dame. She expected trouble there, but came away with no more than numb toes from the cold stone floors.

The first indication that something more than depression was wrong with her came at the Louvre. She had gone by herself because, poking among the art books in a store a few doors along the boulevard from the Café de Flore she had come across an illustration of a Pietà by Bartolommeo. The image of Magdalene had given her a strange knot in the stomach. To her disappointment, the picture credit said the painting was in the Pitti in Florence. So the next weekend she went to the Louvre to see if she could find another one and ended up with a Delacroix oil sketch.

The knot had been given an extra twist. What was going on in the picture was as through a window to a room which she was not permitted to enter. She knew very well this was nothing but the existential angst of a bit of shrapnel moments after the big bang, the separation trauma of birth, any number of analyses which did nothing to make it easier to breathe. Marguerite supposed she had been set up for this particular painting by her Catholic childhood and her present circumstances but that didn't explain the panicky despair which had flooded her eyes. It could have been anything. It just happened to be this particular painting.

The finished work, she learned, was in the Eglise du Saint-Denys on the rue de Turenne not far from the Place de la Bastille. On Sunday she again abandoned the tall man in the blue yukata to the European Cup and *comme tu voudras*. Coming out of the Métro at the Bastille there was a moment's gleam of pleasure as she looked up the Boulevard Richard Lenoir. This was where Inspector Maigret lived. The brief tumble was like that peek at the sun just at the horizon between the clouds and the water that was all the light she had ever had in that place where she had once been a professor.

She had been careful to avoid mass. There were people about, mostly old. The smell of these churches was an ancestral memory for Marguerite, covered up by the more recent (recent! a quarter of a century) smells of wooden American churches, dusty cushions, and basement suppers. Fried chicken and potato salad.

Here was the clue. But she could not decipher it. A priest found her standing in an alcove, hands over her eyes, snot dripping onto her scarf.

The priest was a youngish man, with the same narrow face and blue cheeks which she thought, an insight ludicrously mixed with her inexplicable grief, must be the birthright of every Parisian. Why do they all look like Truffaut? Do they do it on purpose? And all the while she continued to weep, unable to stop.

It was fortunate for Marguerite this happened in a church where there was a chance of being noticed by someone other than a gendarme, who thought it his duty to intervene. After a bit she began to calm down and finally ended by hiccupping and sniveling. Père Inconnue even had a handkerchief.

May I help? he murmured.

No, she said, but was perversely nodding yes.

Unfazed, the priest made what was probably a habitual gesture — hands folded at his chest, one index finger raised to his lips, looking over the tops of his glasses — and waited.

In vain. The hiccupping subsided.

I'm sorry, Marguerite said, accidentally in English and corrected herself. I don't know what... happened. Perhaps I'm ill. I hope you don't catch it.

Do you want to call a doctor? Or perhaps to rest somewhere?

No, no — and this time her head obeyed and made the right sign. Just... can you sit with me a moment? Until I'm not so wobbly.

Certainly.

But she saw that there was a watch beneath the sleeve of his vestment. Cassock. No, that's what a monk wears. Gown, like a don.

Her thoughts were becoming less scattered. As soon as she could, Marguerite rose to her feet, made her thanks, and stepped away. Her leather heels clicked forthrightly on the stones and she made an extra effort to be tall and walk straight.

Outside, the sun really *was* shining. The spring air was milder than it had been in some days. Marguerite hesitated when she reached the Boulevard Beaumarchais but decided not to go and consult Inspector Maigret after all. But she would walk home. Perhaps a bus if she tired of walking. She felt to see if there were any coins in her belt pocket.

This was no time to go back underground.

However, matters became rapidly worse. She began to have anxiety attacks. She couldn't decide whether to go left or right. Disasters loomed whichever way she turned and she would freeze in a panic until the danger lessened. Seemed to lessen. What if this happened to her in the middle of a busy street? She began to fear the Métro. She was not afraid of a wreck or of getting lost in the tunnels. It was the stairs. It was becoming harder and harder to make herself go in, no matter how many people were pushing by or reaching around her for their morning copy of the free tabloid which provided headlines and a listing of the week's events. Marguerite was sometimes late for work now.

And after work she was finding it difficult to be alone. The man in the blue yukata didn't like that, though he was still too polite (cautious?) to say so. Nor did he like the frenzied sex she was demanding, which was not really sex at all but a demented effort to swallow the ocean. He was not especially eager to be swallowed. If he were out, Marguerite after half an hour or so had to go out too. She walked, sat here and there, tried to behave naturally and not whisper to herself. Deep under all this was a sort of wonder at what she was becoming — an educated, cosmopolitan, mature woman who found herself, for no reason that she could see, sliding helplessly into a pit of madness. She had a rather vague idea that it was time to find out what was wrong but the idea remained vague. She was already beyond that sort of planning. It was all one now whether the trouble was chemical or possession by devils.

One Friday night when it was especially bad, after waking up alone, walking for an hour around and around the walls of her apartment which, as if she were a silversmith, she could make bigger by gradually stretching it out — at the moment when she realized what she had been doing, at that moment Marguerite discovered that after all this time in Paris she had no friends. There was no one she could ask to sit with her.

There was the concierge.

Marguerite crept downstairs. Madame Jules's light was on. Timidly, more frightened that she could remember, Marguerite knocked on the door, at first so lightly she herself couldn't hear it.

Madame Jules came at once. She had no trouble seeing what was wrong. Interrupting Marguerite's apologies, she took her arm and drew her inside.

Tonight you are on your own?

Yes.

Sit. How about a Calvados?

Yes, please. Very much. I mean thank you very much. A little glass, please.

Marguerite had never been inside Madame Jules's flat. She of course was the only resident of the ground floor and so had the only outdoor space. The evening was mild. A pair of doors stood open, beyond which Marguerite could see a bit of brick paving and a kitchen garden. A cat started to come indoors but, seeing a stranger, it hesitated and thought better. A small, square gray cat just like its flatmate.

Marguerite knew there was a Monsieur Jules. She had seen him at dinner sometimes when the concierge's door stood a bit open. A balding man with a napkin tucked into his collar, eating soup.

Probably Monsieur was now asleep. The light was dim and yellow. Madame had been reading under a lamp; a paperback was splayed face down on the arm of her chair. A Maigret novel.

You are surprised that I already know what your trouble is? Said Madame Jules when she brought the two small glasses of amber brandy. She waved away Marguerite's still unformed question. It is the business of a concierge to know everything, is it not? It is a sign of craftsmanship in my trade. How could I call myself a concierge without this deep knowledge of human nature?

Her eyes twinkled with good humor, and laughter crinkled the skin around them, but this was a sham. Marguerite sensed the alarm and wariness in this small, square person. A woman not much over a meter and a half tall wearing a gray jumper over a thick black sweater and on her feet some felt shoes which were neither slippers nor clogs. Madame Jules could hardly be ten years older than Marguerite but her salty hair, weathered face, the consciously constructed manner of a *femme de terroir* set the two women far apart.

Well, I will not ask you to tell me just yet, said Madame Jules, lowering herself into her thickly padded chair. She raised her glass. Santé, she said, took a sip, and set the glass down under the reading lamp. In the dim room, in this pool of light, the tumbler of brandy gleamed like a magical eye from which Marguerite could not look away.

Madame Jules delicately opened Marguerite's casket of needs, getting her to talk about work, America, the ex-philosopher as if she did not know all these things already, things she had found out when she agreed to let Marguerite and John John rent the top-floor apartment in the first place.

And you, Madame? Marguerite ventured a question uncertainly.

From Marseille, said Madame Jules firmly. But I was a soixante-huitarde, and after that I did not want to go back. So I stayed in Paris. The Sorbonne did not seem important anymore. There are many thousands of students in the Sorbonne, Madame Vonleere, who want nothing there but a place to go one or two afternoons a week. I had fallen in love with Jules, and as he had come into an inheritance — a sweep of her hand indicated the floors of apartments above — we decided to take advantage.

Ah! So you own this place, Madame Jules?

My husband does.

Would it not have been better to take the rents and to live in a more fashionable arrondissement? And yet, you are comfortable.

Oh, indeed. That is what matters. A warm room and a bowl of onion soup, hein?

I suppose so. Have you children, Madame Jules?

But of course. One is clawing his way up in the government — his department has sent him to Lyons for the present. In another ten years they will let him stay wherever he is senior enough to go. He would like to go to Brest, of all places. I think they will send him to Besançon instead.

But you would never see him then.

Oh, yes. These people have to return to Paris every month for some confabulation. But of course he could not stay here, he must go to where the government is.

Madame Jules indicated the direction with her nose.

In Besançon he could marry, have children. By then I will be a crone — with the fingers of both hands she drew her nose and chin together to indicate the necessary beak and sharp chin of a crone's mask — and one long black hair just here, eh? A proper granny. She laughed merrily and took a second sip of brandy, then returned the glass carefully to its place.

And the other, Madame?

Oh, petit Jules is an officer in the merchant marine. It is why his brother wants to be posted to Brest. Have you wanted children, Marguerite?

Le Vide noted this shift to a more informal address, without which the question would have seemed impertinent. But had she not come down here for just such confidences? Not to now shrink from them.

No. When one is a professor of an unfashionable subject it is difficult to get taken on anywhere permanent. We did not have much money until recently. I think we were poor, actually, though it is not the thing for university professors to be poor. And by the time matters had improved it was too late. I suppose I wanted children once. When I was a girl. I don't regret it. The world is not a good place for children.

Ah, you think so?

Well, I — yes. I do.

Madame Jules's smile was a little sardonic. She forswore the chance to play the countrywoman's card, the wisdom of onion soup, and merely nodded to acknowledge Marguerite's opinion.

You are not enjoying your little time in Paris, then? Madame said after a moment's silence. Marguerite noted the assumption that her life in France would not be permanent. She squirmed on her chair and almost tried to cover her unease with a gulp of brandy.

Oh, it's nothing to do with Paris, Madame Jules.

Is it not? That's good to hear, because I am a Parisian. But you were born in France, Marguerite. I can hear it in your speech if I did not know it already. Are you now an American, then? A New Yorker?

Oh, no. We — I have lived too many places in the United States to belong to any of them. I liked southern California best, but I couldn't say I was a Los Angelino. People think Americans are mobile, but they aren't. I had a friend —

Marguerite paused. This friend was long dead of cancer. It had never before seemed to Marguerite that he was dead but only someone Marguerite used to know.

I had a friend. She would have been your age, Madame, she said, feeling an obscure need to change genders. She grew up in Oxnard. In the early sixties she was a surfer bunny, when that culture was at its height. There was an enormous difference between her California and mine. Americans are marked forever by their origins just like anyone else.

And yet you are not French, either.

No.

You are not a great many things, Marguerite. As your concierge I can say this. Do you not think that this is your trouble?

Oh... Marguerite took a long breath. There are a great many things I have desperately wanted; things to have, to be. It is fitting that I should not have them until it is too late and the old need has been hollowed out. There would be nothing from that cup which I could drink with pleasure any more.

She swallowed some Calvados, not thinking until later this might be construed a criticism.

Madame Jules's cat hopped into her lap and curled up with its nose under one paw. After a bit it began to purr, but one eye remained brightly open in perfect imitation of its mistress.

Perhaps that is everyone's experience, Marguerite went on. Perhaps it is a rule of life that what you want will not be given you. Isn't that why they put candy in the checkout aisle in supermarkets? To learn to endure taunting? But I would not like to think that this... this loneliness is only because I did not sit on the Spanish Steps or fight with Byron at Missolonghi.

Byron died of a fever, said Madame Jules curtly.

Yes. There has to be something more to it than this longing for the impossible.

It is a miswiring in the brain, I think. The left side does not talk to the right or something.

Hmpf.

You are mystical, Marguerite. Like an old Buddhist, you should go to the mountains. Paris is not in the mountains.

Marguerite looked at her feet for a very long time. She had come down in jeans, barefoot. Her toes were twisted and cramped. She had ugly feet. She had always thought so. Long feet. Don't they say that women with long feet are crammed with lust?

She stood up, thanking Madame Jules for the brandy and the sympathy and, saying firmly that she was all right now, went quietly back upstairs, looking all the way at the feet which were supposed to have taken her to the mountains.

After the confrontation with the Magdalene Marguerite began to buy books she couldn't afford in order to be able to study the pictures in them.

There was one by Hopper which was an uncanny realization of her mood. But what was depicted here — despair or lassitude? She
—

Uncanny was the wrong word. Feelings of dread certainly, that she would become the woman in the picture. Or worse, that she already was... But there was no strangeness, nothing eerie or supernatural here. Marguerite did not suppose that she was the only other woman who was or had been in the condition. The plight is common, surely. What is eerie or supernatural about encountering another sufferer. No, it was the *exactness,* the thoroughness with which Hopper surrounded, enfolded her, leaving no excuse or refuge, intending to suffocate her with one of those pillows...

Marguerite's mind wandered off, as it was increasingly prone to do, leaving her staring at the painting for she didn't know how long, half an hour? while she rummaged for the right word. She knew there was one; all those she found had something wrong with them. It was necessary to find the word before the page could be turned...

When this first happened she was embarrassed for herself, especially as she had been eating in a prix fixe and the waiter was wanting to bring the next course. Eating alone, fortunately. The more it happened the less she noticed it. Her life went on from moment to moment without her knowing that some moments were longer than others. People jostled into her when she blocked the path. The obsession grew like a goiter...

One Sunday afternoon Marguerite cajoled a man she was with into bed. Or for him, back into bed, since she had never gotten out. The sheets were full of croissant crumbs. It was that ache again, that now quite unbearable melancholy that must be pushed down, cruelly rejected and pushed out to die on the Spanish Steps. There was a little anger mixed with it now. Marguerite was often angry. Quite black with it sometimes, in fact.

He would not come. He had exhausted himself. She hadn't. She never did now.

He was standing beside the bed on one foot, the free foot propped gracefully on his knee. She reached out and gripped his handle at the root. He slapped her hand, not losing even his balance.

Why not?

I don't like the smell, he said; then more firmly — I don't like how you smell.

Are you squeamish now?

What?

Marguerite had to explain *dégouté*.

No. It is not to my taste. Let go, Marguerite.

Defiantly she pulled back her hand and thrust two fingers into her swollen — What? It's no longer acceptable to call it a *wound*, but that's what it was. A Thomas, a monster of unbelief — but no, that was not his name — it was — or did she mean *disbelief*?

The man scowled and turned away.

She could tell he was dressing by the sound, that he was going out, but just as the door opened the spasm took her and she couldn't speak to say goodbye. Then he was gone and her gasps and cries turned to a wretched yowling that went on much longer than any useless orgasm ever had.

Then Monsieur Otto sacked her. The problem was that she had begun to hear voices and would break off a telephone negotiation to talk to them. She became silent, intent, unavailable. This rarely produced positive results with clients. Fortunately these conversations were mostly in her head, but Monsieur Otto thought sometimes he could hear Marguerite whispering, as if she were talking to a potted plant or a chair. It was a bit ludicrous, and definitely bad for business.

What it amounted to was that the part of her that been the manager of her obsessions had moved out, rented a place of its own, and started talking back to her. What had been an internal, private quest had become a public wrangle. She was beset by a buttonholer who took her lapel, or elbow, and insisted on telling its tale. *It.* She could not see her nemesis very well — felt its presence, a vague odor of smoke or something, a disturbance of the air —

Sacked, she had no other way to pay for herself. The energy and confidence of the previous autumn were gone. She managed to hang on for a few more weeks with some sordid favors that the Otto didn't really want and when he began to fear blackmail that was the end.

Money ran out quickly after that. There was an experiment with bread and water which after two days convinced Marguerite it was hopeless. She had a word with Madame Jules. That evening, carrying out of the wreckage only a small bag and a sack purse stuffed with underwear, she boarded a flight to New York using a credit card which now would probably never be paid for.

The same card got her some cash and a rental car at JFK. Fortunately, her driver's license had not expired. Jetlagged and hungry, just barely presentable enough to convince the rental agent of her good intentions, she wobbled out onto the Van Wyck Expressway and headed north, getting as far as Yonkers before having to find a place to sleep in the car.

Yonkers. With the white awning and the yellow streetcar and the forest of poles.

But it was dark now. She didn't see any of that.

Very early some sixth sense still operable woke her with the information that the police were patrolling the street. She moved on. It was four o'clock, hours before sunrise. By following the access road she found the next expressway entrance, where there was a cafeteria. She ate two eggs, which threatened to come back up until paved over with extra dry toast.

At Albany she intersected the Thruway west to Utica, Oneida, and Syracuse, three hours. Now it was noon. She had not really slept in three days. She could not present herself anywhere in this condition.

The desk clerk at the Super-8 was extremely wary. Jetlag, she mumbled. Her signature was very shaky.

Luggage lost.

This was becoming plausible. The clerk, a weedy young man with weightless brown hair, remarked on declining standards of service. These days.

Escaped only with my underwear, she went on, holding up the canvas sack.

All dirty.

The sack was dirty too. Imprinted on it was a faded butterfly and some French words partly rubbed off.

The weedy young man recoiled. This disheveled old woman, her hair a mare's nest, with huge purple eyes and sunken cheeks, was scrabbling with one hand on the desk top as if she were picking at a sore and saying far too much about her personal affairs. He quickly found a key and steered her around the corner between the ice machine and the sodas to the stairs.

Third on the left, he called out and retreated back into the reception area and the comforting smells of burnt coffee and stale danish.

When she woke the next afternoon, Simone found herself lying crosswise on the still-made bed, still in her jeans and sweater, suffocating in crusted sweat. After a shower and a change of clothes, the only others she had, and something like a meal at a Denny's on the other side of the parking lot, she turned in her room key to the same pale-haired long-nosed man who was at the desk before.

No luggage yet? he asked, still cool.

I'm going to call, she replied, signing the bill a second time with some black marks which meant nothing. The key to the rental car was in her pocket. She drove off, leaving even her underwear behind this time.

It was close to four o'clock when Simone pushed open the door to the ex-philosopher's law firm. No one was about. With temporarily recovered step she crossed the teal blue carpet and sat down to wait.

On the wall of the reception area opposite was a framed print.

A woman at a writing desk, in a room of her own, in an enclosed place, behind hedges; tall casement windows standing open, filling the room with light and air and the smell of flowers and grass.

A retreat. A haven possibly, antique seafaring metaphor notwithstanding. Also a cincture which the woman sitting there, her face not to be seen, absorbed in... Not a writing desk. Perhaps a small piano. And what might that gizmo be which hung on the wall between the windows? A letter rack? A calendar?

A cincture to enclose, hold together, assemble, collect all those woman's parts which might be otherwise dispersed: thoughts, resources, scattered like panicked soldiers routed from battle, fleeing every which way, some to safety and some foolishly to capture or death on the enemy's lines —

Someone was talking to her. Had been talking and talking...

Oh! May I help you?

A girl who seemed no older than sixteen who had, sometime in the past far gone, emerged from a door hard by.

I'd like to see Mr. Ambler, Simone requested in a quiet voice. He probated my husband's estate. I've just returned from two years in France — do you think I could see him for a few minutes without an appointment? I've been out of touch. Simone hesitated, but managed to speak her old name and magically, Simone rose up within her and took calm control.

I'll see, said the receptionist, and returned through the door she had once come out of.

Mr. Ambler would see her. He was an anonymous-looking man, not elderly yet old, with a square clean face as smooth as an automobile headlight. He wore a blue pinstripe, white shirt and matching tie, and had not even allowed himself a pocket handkerchief.

What might I help you with? he said in a clear tenor voice, sitting down again as soon as Simone was herself seated.

There followed an exchange of polite lies, and also some false assurances from Simone about her annuity.

Mr. Ambler, she said then, opening her business, the business that had been on her mind since she fled Paris. I would like to know something about the property my husband was supposed to have given me. There was a house, I believe, in a town near Denver, that had been in his family.

I beg your pardon?

He mentioned it once to me.

Denver.

Mr. Ambler reached for a file which had been extracted from the file room for him.

Why would your husband have come into such a property? the lawyer inquired.

It was in the family.

Oh yes, you said so.

Silence then. It took only a few moments from Mr. Abler to turn over the papers in his file. Simone looked over his shoulder, out the window at nothing but gray clouds. It was beginning to rain.

Well, Simone, said the lawyer, it's not among the property declared in the will and it wasn't probated.

Simone sensed she was beginning to stutter. To be enfolded by shadows. To become thin as smoke.

Of course, I don't know anything about his background. It's not as if I were an old family retainer. Mr. Ambler laughed shortly through his nose and tried to smile. He did not ingratiate himself. Behind Simone there was some noise going on, as if a heavy piece of furniture were being pushed into the room.

I believe he did tell me he was born in Greeley, I think it was. I take it you did not discuss the will with him.

N-no. I was… I didn't know he had m-made a w-w-will until af— until after —

Ah. I see.

We met in c-college. I — unh… I never —

And that was the end of Mr. Ambler. Simone woke up in a hospital bed. Her legs were encased in some heavy pads which expanded at intervals, vibrating so as to make her toes ache. When she tried to roll over she found that one arm, fitted with a saline drip, was strapped down.

Someone was there, just out of sight. She tried to turn her head but a hot pain shot up through her neck and she squeezed her eyes shut against it.

The person waiting was Marge Foswell. When Simone began to stir Marge pushed out of a beat-up tan vinyl chair where she had been reading and came nearer the bed.

What's happened? Simone whispered. Her mouth was dry as leather.

Well, Simone, we're not quite sure. You were in Dick Ambler's office and apparently you began throwing things about, screaming about something or other. He got some help and they brought you here. You're pretty strong for an old lady, my dear. Even malnourished as you are. It took a couple of orderlies to get a sedative into you. Or so I'm told.

How did you get here?

Oh ho! You've been gone a while, my dear. No one knew who you were. There was a receipt in your pocket which suggested you were a Marguerite Vonleere but when they looked into your rental car the paperwork in the glove compartment you had a different name. Dick Ambler finally came along and sorted it out, and called me.

When?

Yesterday afternoon. I stopped by after breakfast to see how you were.

Oh, I... Did you, that is — thank you, Marge.

Yes, my dear. You've been in Paris all this time, I understand.

I was — it was in Paris, yes.

Marge sighed very deeply. I haven't been there in too many years now. George once, when he was young, had a copyist's license to paint in the Louvre, you know. I was researching my dissertation. Too, too romantic.

She patted Simone's free, bare arm. My dear, she said quickly, dispelling the brief moment, I was to ask you. The doctor here wants to know whether you have been depressed lately.

Simone nodded, wincing a little.

Very depressed? For a long time?

Yes.

Have you thought of killing yourself?

No! That is... I wouldn't have minded if I... why are you asking me this, Marge?

Well, my dear, the doctor asked me to find out. He seems to think — well, I don't know what he thinks, do I? Dick says that while they were trying to get you sedated and you were struggling, you were crying a lot of things they didn't understand and then later, I suppose after the drug had worn off a bit, George says you were sitting up, rocking back and forth with your head between your knees and crying out *Why is it taking so long? Why is it taking so long?* It seemed autistic to him, but George is a painter. That's why you were strapped down, so as not to tear your IV out again.

Oh. And the doctor thinks, he thinks, um...

Well, my dear, you were in pretty bad shape. It looked as if you hadn't had a bath in a week and had been starving yourself for longer than that, and there were some welts and marks on your wrists and other places that looked as if you'd tried to commit suicide.

What? I — Marge, what? I don't remember...

Yes, dear. Don't struggle, you'll pull the thing out again. That's hurts, I know.

But I never did those things! Of course I hadn't eaten, you know how it is on airplanes these days, but I stopped in a motel and got cleaned up I thought. I had only the one set of clothes. My luggage —

Yes, dear, they're trying to find your luggage now. Air France says —

M-Marge, M-M-Marge...

Yes, dear. Let go, please.

Simone fell back onto the pillows and stared at the dingy yellow ceiling.

Is Reiva Derwent there? she asked quietly.

Who? Oh, that woman in the History Department you were friendly with. Let me see. One of the adjuncts, wasn't she? I believe she took herself off a year or so ago. Don't know where to. Perhaps the department would know. Is it important?

No. No, not important.

Marge Foswell kept up the conversation a while longer with amiable remarks and slipped away when the resident came in. On the way out of the hospital she stopped to say a few words at the nurses' station.

What was it, she wondered, that was taking so long?

MARGE

Marge Foswell was a big, ugly woman. To herself, in the mirror every morning, she resembled a certain *New Yorker* cartoon of a society matron, somewhat trapezoidal from all points of view, with the big end up of course, and another, smaller trapezoid on top with a very minimally indicated nose and mouth and no eyes at all. She had always looked like that. But she was past being angry with herself for it.

People always, from the first, had called her Marge. Margaret was another person entirely, fated never to be awakened. George, poor fool, had kissed the wrong sleeper. But Marge had been a tolerable success as an art historian, with one respected book on the Fauves to her credit, and George's work was hung in good small museums in the Northeast. Approaching retirement, Marge was content.

Because of her profession, Marge mistrusted appearances. It was not that anything is hidden or secret in the world — that would be as absurd as trying to see what was behind a picture canvas. But to Marge the ear is not so duplicitous as the eye. Nose and tongue are as unformed as a sumi-e drawing still in the brush, and the fingers inhabit an alternate world. The ear is mature, intelligent, and yet innocent in its eagerness to engage with life. It is the least naïve of the senses, and yet the least worldly. The trained eye is cynical in a way unknown to the other senses.

These reflections occupied her mind as she prepared for church. Marge did not use cosmetics, merely a bit of eyeliner to keep from looking so wall-eyed. Quickly done with the mirror, she put on a tan linen jacket to which she affixed a small pin one of George's students made years and years ago, and went down to where George waited with the car keys, as usual not fully attentive to the business at hand.

This was a division of labor which they struck on early in their marriage. The roles may have been conventional, and were out of date even then, but that had never been of consequence. It was no different than couples who choose to play Catherine and Heathcliff, or Lambert Strether and whoever it was. Madame de Vionnet. But they were not a couple, were they — more like a bolo, a rope with a weight at each end. Like so many relationships. She thought of Simone.

Undone Simone.

The morning was thick and muggy. That was the point of the choice of linen, which always looks exhausted no matter what, so little is expected of it.

The old cat which had been Gary and Simone's was lying re-proachfully by the door. She hated to be left alone and had been dreading this moment since she woke up. Marge reached down to rub it behind the ears, which did nothing to palliate an abandon-ment likely to be permanent. In an hour, though, Marge would af-ter all return, the ordeal would be over, and the cat which had been fasting would return to her food bowl with an air of relieved satis-faction. One is marked for life by one's origins. Marge herself was inclined to a tolerable determinism, and the cat, it seemed, never quite forgave these little daily traumas, but stored them up some-where as an accumulating proof of the world's indifference. Who knew how old this cat was. She had been old for years and years already. For all Marge knew she might be a spirit cat, and immor-tal.

The Methodist church where the Foswells and some others conducted their Sunday networking was a small but handsome brick bungalow within walking distance. Therefore they walked, summer and winter, and when cold weather made this uncomforta-ble they stayed home. Marge was a sensible woman and wore flat heels for this reason. Being older she was usually quite carefully dressed, everything she wore a compromise between sense and sensibility. The shoes, for example, had a narrow gold accent over the instep. It had been a relief when social practice found other ways of differentiating a group and left off ascribing so much sig-nificance to clothes.

There had been a rackety time, of course, for her as for every-one, when she wore unflattering gladrags which announced her allegiance to this and that. It would be hard now, for anyone know-ing only the present Marge, to imagine that she could have been those people. The present Marge, homely and matronly, every-one's flat-heeled aunt, well-meaning if not always welcome in her intercessions, must surely have been born that way else however could she have become as she was?

Their way took them up a moderate hill along which mostly undivided three story homes sat well back on rising ground. These places on the high ground were getting a little too expensive to heat but their owners preferred to allow some inconspicuous dilapidation and other hidden economies rather than cut them up into flats. Their powdery blues and pinks went well with a fastidious lawn, anyway.

The church was just over the hill, protected from the lake but not out of sight of the river. Here they were far enough from the mouth for the banks to be bordered with sumac and some large trees and the broad sweep of it, which was after all enough to float some pretty large yachts making their way to the Inland Waterway, made a rather picturesque sight a hundred feet below. If only the sun had been out.

There were only distant exchanges with other parishioners before the service; serious traffic would be saved for afterwards like the ceremonial drinking after a wake.

Marge herself had never been to a wake. Where she had come from wake-practicing Catholics had been non-existent and here such nuisancy dawdling had now gone out of fashion.

On this particular Sunday the minister chose to preach on the topic "We Stand In the Light." What nonsense, Marge thought. We stand in the dark.

The minister's view of things was like that paltry little bourgeois Bonnard, whose concern was all for the comforts laid out on the breakfast table, whose windows existed only to provide the necessary morning light. What was beyond the scrim did not concern him. Marge's best work had been done on Matisse, his antithesis. One does not see through Matisse. *His* windows admit only voracious flowers.

This minister had another insipid suite of remarks which he would trot out at graveside. Apparently his intent was to make the grieved less melancholy and to lighten a circumstance which he had already done his part to make lugubrious. "The Great Escape" was his title for this set piece. A month ago, at her mother's funeral in Philadelphia, Marge had been non-plussed to hear that minister make exactly the same speech as this one. Do they buy these things in a shop? The minister's words had occluded Marge's sense of the occasion a bit.

Her mother had been demented for almost ten years. When Marge and her sister first put her into residential care the old woman, then late into her seventies, had made things difficult for a time. She had been in a flaming, inarticulate rage, actually, for months and months. One would have thought she hadn't the energy for it, and in fact it was that after a time she didn't have enough brains to be angry that put a stop to tearing off her clothes and shouting and attacking the other residents. It was a good thing the family had had enough money to afford a place where these things were overlooked.

A matter of fact attitude toward dementia also disposed the staff to some frank discussions with Marge at the end of her bimonthly visits. She and her sister had agreed to alternate months, though it wasn't clear why they bothered since Muggsy didn't seem to know she was being visited. Marge would query the staff as to what they thought was going on inside her mother's head. Always lurking in Marge's thoughts was the uncanny suspicion that Muggsy — the former Muggsy? — was still a more or less lucid being with no means of communication, or only woeful means she was still too enraged to want to use. That the actual dementia had come only after some years, her mind's protection from itself, a relief from pain.

George, sensualist that he was, had tried to debunk the brain in a bottle notion. And really, it is hardly credible there could be a personality without a body in which to house it. But the notion persists, akin to vampires and trolls and other bugbears.

Really, it was incredible how ordinary, unassuming people without another thought in their heads are wont to ask these everyday questions which a generation ago were the business only of pundits and fabulists. Marge looked surreptitiously about her at the congregation, mostly the same people who were here every Sunday. Placid cud-chewing beasts in various pastel shades decorated with picador's feathers.

Both Marge and George had always understood the wisdom of humbly plugging along. It was not a question of being dull to be safe but an economic calculation of the best return on investment.

Burning your candle at both ends was all right, but hollering and throwing the crockery was a waste of resources as well as a sign of unjustified self-importance. Better to write something like *Howl* and put the anger to work. George, of course, was too ethereal to howl about anything.

After the recessional and some ritual hoo-hah with their quite ineffectual spiritual shepherd some of the people of the college were standing to one side, just on the lawn, recognizable as being not so tweedy. As this group today included the Provost, George wandered over to join it and Marge, with occult trepidation, followed.

And indeed, it wasn't long before Gary Richter's death had intruded into the general gossip through the agency of a remark by the Provost on the difficulty he was having finding a replacement.

You would think, said the man with an owlish frown, that jobs for philosophers would not go begging, given their other opportunities.

The Provost was a biologist and his valuation of cultural capital was determined by conventional economic wisdom.

And now Mrs. Richter has gone too, he grumbled. There's always a trailing spouse in the package, it seems.

Oh, someone said on hearing this news. Where to? Does this mean we won't offer a French sequence now?

No one knows, replied a colleague from Simone's department. That is, no one knows where she's gone. She turned in a letter the first of June and disappeared.

A morose individual, said the elderly chair of English. General agreement.

Marge kept her opinions to herself, and when George entered on the business which was on his mind the conversation turned elsewhere. Some people wandered off, including the doddery individual from the English department.

Yes, Marge knew, Simone *was* morose, and subject to fits of giddiness and anger. When Gary was alive she kept all that under a manhole cover and all that intruded into public life was some steam. This was, Marge suspected, a difficult endeavor and ought not to have been a source of censure.

Marge's connection to the Richters, or to Gary rather, was thicker than probably even Simone had known. In this small town there were very, very few people with whom one could carry on a personal conversation. Few to choose from to begin with, fewer who were trustworthy, fewer yet sympathetic, and the probability of discovering this person at all practically nil because it would be so unwise to say the things that would reveal yourself. So when by chance Marge discovered, now some years ago, that she and Gary had similar origins, and a reminiscent exploration revealed other qualities, it was hard to prevent some confidences being traded along with the rest. A habitual reliance had followed, and when Gary was buried Marge had had the peculiar feeling that something of hers had been safely put away out of sight. On the other hand, that thing of hers she was now without, and she was not about to exhume the matter, as Rossetti did to recover the manuscript of his *Poems*, impulsively buried with his wife's presumably tear-stained corpse.

George having unloaded whatever was on his mind, he took Marge's arm and steered the both of them away and onto the path home. While everyone had been occupied with transcendental matters the sun had continued to boil the sauce which was trapped under cover of clouds and by the time the two of them were back indoors Marge was thoroughly stinking. Resolutely ignoring George's financial misgivings, she turned on the window cooler in the bedroom while she changed out of her church things.

For quite some time Marge, a big ugly jovial and old woman, sat in her underwear on the side of the bed, stockings crumpled in one hand, thinking.

Muggsy had been a difficult parent. In her youth Muggsy had wanted to paint, but bad counseling and parricidal opposition had prevented her from taking advantage of the opportunities which Philadelphia offered to become an artist. Instead, she married an engineer who had hydrological and hydraulic opportunities with some dam projects in the West, got de-materialized in an accident,

and left Muggsy with two girls and no money, marooned. She ended up in Cheyenne where Marge grew up in a household mongered
in class pretension, ad hoc rules, and passive-aggressive sadism.
No one, least of all Marge, was to crawl under the furniture or ask
what little Claude de Villiers of uncertain sex was looking at.

Nothing. It was outside the frame. It didn't exist.

More than her sister, Marge had been willing to make allow-
ances for Muggsy. The consequence for Marge had been lifelong
depression. Marge had learned to minimize this. The constant vigi-
lance was implicated in the choice of the Fauves for her dissertation and, a decade later, her book. She avoided dark music such as
Britten's *Sinfonia da Requiem* and anything, such as certain of
Beethoven's late piano sonatas, which had come to be associated
with gloom and Last Things. She chose her movies very cautiously
and eschewed indulgence, which was invariably followed by a
dangerous letdown. Countless such strategies had kept the problem
out of sight — her own madwoman in the attic. Marge did not
know how any honesty about her condition might be received now,
if she had dared to risk an exposure, but she knew perfectly well
that in her earlier years she might as well have had leprosy.

Marge's sister went to the University of Wyoming; Marge to
Brown. Muggsy stayed in Cheyenne in what she bitterly referred to
as her House On the Hill, Cheyenne itself being on a laser-flat nine
thousand foot high plateau. For years Muggsy had tried to blackmail the girls with the prospect of inheriting this worthless house
until finally she gave up and moved back to Philadelphia, at which
point she began to refer to it as her House in the Country.
Muggsy's last years of sanity had not been any happier than any of
her others.

All Marge's life this *Westward Home* had served as the icon
for everything in her life which Marge knew to be toxic. When, in
Marge's twenties, the rock band Blood, Sweat and Tears produced
a song entitled "House In the Country" accompanied by manic
laughter, it was so magically apt as to have become code, or short-
hand, for all of Life Before George. In the song there was a person,
one Glotzer, who was told before an impending riff to "hit it."

Who Glotzer was, what was his mysterious purpose, was never ex-plained. It was now her pet name for George. Not his official en-dearment; not one he even knew about. Glotzer was the hobbitish slightly contemptible house-dweller who could have been the counterweight to Muggsy, but wasn't.

During her rackety period Marge had been impatient with George. She had had some rackety affairs, and while she was writ-ing her book and could use an extended stay in the south of France as an excuse, she had been positively reckless. This was to cover her nausea at the life they had been leading.

Glotzer was oblivious to it all. He, a painter, hadn't a drop of bohemian blood in his veins, no more than Muggsy had had. The sine qua non of life for George was a cup of tea and a *nature mort* on the easel.

Marge, big and ugly as she was, though not yet old, had had several *misalliances* while she was in inner exile but nothing to shock an Esther Hawdon as a Lady Dedlock. In fact, Marge had reflected with some rue afterwards, even her insurgency had been quite in the spirit of Muggsy's *Little House*. Her memory of that time was bound up with Bonnard's picture, though neither she nor he (any of them) had been that presentable. But now Marge saw there was a quotidian regime to the painting that she had willfully overlooked.

This knowledge did her now permanent depression no good at all.

Gary Richter had had a sympathetic ear for these things which Marge could not say to George, or even to her sister. Gary had had an inclination to take in strays, his last one being that Derek child who Simone ran away with, that Barbara Scoppone had had the good sense to dump.

Marge had, she thought, gained some security and resilience with age. Perhaps Muggsy's death would counterbalance this other one. She would come through.

Marge held up one bare white foot. A foot as ugly as the rest of her — twisted and cramped by a lifetime of accommodation.

She wiggled her toes, spread them to embrace the world, and smiled faintly.

Thanks to some mysterious aura, Marge Foswell had never any difficulty with men. Or women, for that matter, who never thought it worth their while to be envious. She had been hustled by women a few times, of no particular type, toward whom Marge had always been kindly but firm. As for the others, all she could think was that there were a lot of men in the world who were deluded as to their best interests. That, or faulty libidinal wiring.

Marge herself was not wired entirely correctly. Somewhere there was a disconnected feedback loop which allowed every emotional breeze to grow into a pounding electrical storm, abetted by a capacitor or two of the wrong spec which stored up too much feeling and then delivered it all with a ruinous jolt at exactly the wrong moment. She supposed there were better metaphors in the DSM IV but she had never looked for them. What she knew was that something read in the newspaper could strand her on the shoreline of an infinite ocean of melancholy loss and longing, or that some agony would shake her senseless, a craving so desperate that she would eat sand and algae foam.

All this had ever been, of course, from her girlhood a particular problem where sex was concerned. Marge had wrecked the car several times, metaphorically speaking, and was fortunate, she knew, that she wasn't crippled or dead. Metaphorically speaking. Marge thought in metaphors, whatever was at hand when it was necessary to explain something to herself – except that she avoided imagery from the arts. She thought perhaps because George was a painter, or that the facts of art history were sacrosanct, or perhaps worn and dulled by her pedestrian everyday use of them – George said (affectionately) that she had a ragbag mind. She did, but it was a big bag. Made of patched, dirty canvas and full of anecdotes which had stood her well in the kind of teaching and writing she did.

So it happened that Marge understood well enough that part of what had gone wrong with Simone. She knew that crazy-making moment when a new relationship takes your head off, as she thought of it, like the effect of certain drugs, and she knew how the rush itself becomes the thing sought, and the relationship that might follow will be discarded as something like a hangover. More dog hair. But Marge also understood that sexual adventure could be used like alcohol to push down or forget some other, usually existential problem. Simone's particular case remained obscure, but Marge had been able to guess at enough to ease her through the last days. To know that Simone had not been the 19th century victim of hysteria and syphilitic excess, as some who'heard the story appeared to think.

Somewhere, at this very moment, Simone was perhaps also sitting on the edge of her bed, perhaps naked, perhaps running the hem of her housecoat between her fingers, perhaps examining her stockings for runs. There were never any runs because she never wore them, but perhaps if she looked more carefully... Her suitemate, a cranky old white-haired woman with a bald spot and a wonky arm, said Simone was expecting to find contraband sewn into her housecoat but that was silly. She rubbed hems and seams to threads just as she might have done with a nubbly blanket as an infant. It calmed her mind, and gave her a tiny thrill like an affectionate touch or a bite of chocolate.

As for nakedness, that was imaginary. No matter how she itched, or how polluted she was by the things her body demanded, she was not going to be sent off to the little room where they kept the men who were compulsive masturbators.

In that regard it would have been a good thing if both of Madame O'Connor's arms were crippled. Madame was unaware of how little Simone slept. Of how quietly she could lie, taking scarcely any breath, waiting.

That winter Marge made up her mind to retire. There was no special animus, and she intended to go on with her lifetime's study of the Fauves. It was just time to go. For some months she had been semi-aware that she was re-imagining herself as a retired person, and the day when she first met this person was the first day when it occurred to Marge that she *would* retire. She told George. That phlegmatic painter said merely "Ah" and looked momentarily inward. She never knew what George was thinking. Really thinking. Perhaps nothing, if a thought must be born out of words. In all her years of teaching art history Marge had never made up her mind whether paintings were thoughts. Ideas certainly not. Nor quite how one gets from a thought to a painting, and back again. George was no help. George never went anywhere. Even when he went somewhere he didn't.

Then there was a bad spot, a few days when the prospect of free choice blew up into an unfettered exhilaration that she hadn't felt in forty years and provoked in her some eidetic memories of times when she stood, or rather lay, on the edge of a precipice she was going to throw herself off. Pretty sure she would. She looked over the edge, saw the thin silver line of the distant river turn a bluish venous color, and felt herself melt, go liquid, awake among the rocks bruised and satisfied. But then the memory faded, the storm in her brain blew over, and she was left wet and cold, and was cut open with regret as much as if she had been struck in half by a Japanese blade, four hundred years old and still of supernatural sharpness.

The pain was very great. She cried from it for two days, nose and eyes running as from a bad cold which she told George was what she had but he didn't believe it. She could tell by the way his eyes turned cloudy and he gave a special inflection to that "Ah" which he said in response to almost anything.

At the same time she felt like an old fool, which didn't help at all.

What did she want? The first night she clung desperately to George; nothing came of that, of course. She didn't have enough skin.

Next morning she looked into the mirror and cringed. She felt cheated, robbed of her life, just as she had felt when she was eight years old and realized she would never be pretty but when she was so young she had not yet been actually robbed and so had not yet encountered that emptiness which made her stomach rise.

This was the center of the tornado. Marge had felt it coming on. What tormented her was an old chance for love not taken, broken off like interrupted coitus. This was sentimental nonsense, a cliché invented in order to explain the melancholy and nostalgia she was determined to undergo.

That she knew somewhere inside that her moods created their own reasons didn't do a thing to alleviate the pain. She felt like she had swallowed a hot stone.

It was, fortunately, not a teaching day. She put on an anorak, two pairs of jeans and some LL Bean boots and went down to the lake. The wind was blowing as usual, so hard she could hardly keep her balance against it, along the length of the lake, coming from the Canadian plains. All the round rocks which covered the lakeshore were encased in ice, a layer an inch thick and clear, shimmering in the scudding light like a pomegranate seed around the tiny brown speck at the center. The driftwood was also wrapped in ice drawn out by the wind into horizontal icicles and tattered rags.

She could not face the wind, even covered. The mist on the water caused the horizon to evaporate within a few yards. Here, all her senses were null. She had been taken into the world's womb – as it really is, not as imagined in pictures and poems, mostly by men.

Some other person than Marge might have started cursing God at this point, conveniently in a place where no one could overhear, even God. Marge only stood for a while with her back to the wind, hunched, arms crossed and hands tucked into her armpits. Then she walked back to her car and drove away.

Away from the lake the roads were dry and the air merely wintry. In fact, compared with her childhood in Laramie, the weather in upstate New York was mild. Every few weeks the snow melted away, except the inevitable lake-effect storm which sometimes reached the second-story windows before it stopped. Most years the trees did not bud out until mid-May, but that too was familiar.

The smell of bread in the oven came to her, unbidden but so thick and real her stomach groaned, begging, just as the fetid, fishy smell of sex calls up a longing for the remembered touch.

Bread, however, could be had.

On the west side of the river, on a county road going south through Minetto and Granby and Lysander, was a watermill which sold sacks of locally ground wheat, rye, and other grains. Until she came here, Marge had never had freshly ground flour and had not, in fact, thought it would make a difference. She had gotten out of the habit of going there in season despite that, just as she seldom went to the farmers' markets at many of the country crossroads. So she turned the car south. It was ten o'clock in the morning of this second of most peculiar days.

Low ridges of frozen dirty snow lined the narrow asphalt road, but farther off the snow lay clean and white beneath skinny naked saplings. A valedictory, elegiac feeling was materializing in the warm car like the fug of young bodies packed in after a football game. Marge was on the bottom. A thickly mufflered and swaddled girl was sitting crossways on Marge's lap, pressed backward by a boy who was trying to squirm his way beneath the wet loden, himself flattened by another, bigger boy drunkenly kissing Marge on the forehead...

To her horror, Marge found herself driving on the wrong side of the road. A car coming the other way, already keening and wailing its lament, caused Marge to jerk the wheel sudden right, missed by a bare inch and almost careening into the opposite ditch. The frozen ridge on the shoulder saved her. She struck it at a shallow angle. The car pitched up but stayed on its feet, crawling and stumbling away from the scene is a rusty daze.

Marge was in a sweat. Her eyes stung. The next car came. She drifted helplessly left, fighting the magnetism of the center line. Again she missed, the breath knocked out of her by a blow to the stomach. No, the blow was farther down.

And a third time. A scream escaped her, as agonized and exultant as an orgasm. She was now shivering so as to be unable to control the car, which was moving slowly enough that it could be brought to rest half off the road. Marge broke into wrenching sobs. She gulped and gasped with the effort to breathe through her howling cries.

Ah! *Ah, ah. AH!* ee aah… she wailed, an inarticulate parody of George and a protest at the pain.

But the storm passed off. It had been the worst she'd known since her teens. Drained, she began to wonder how she would recover enough to get home.

She turned back onto the road. Her driving was slow and shaky but the road was empty of any new temptations. In town, her reactions slowed, she skidded through a stop sign but again, without further challenge. Across the river, up the hill past the church, missing the mailbox. She turned the key. The engine grumbled and bucked but finally consented.

In the fresh silence she heard the wind off the lake picking up, bringing with it some fat flakes and the smell of old ice.

Inside, through the front bay, she could see George priming a canvas. The yellow light fell over the top of his head like frosting. George liked to do this in the living room. He said the harsh light of the chandelier helped him to see uneven patches in the gesso. Of course he always dripped gesso on the floor. Which he did clean up. More or less.

In her by now ample life, most of it spent with this quiet and kindly man, Marge had been through several cycles of explanation for her particular incubus, parasite, perversion. At times it was an existential angst which tormented her; at other times it was a spiritual crisis; yet again it was an unresolved neurosis. Still, she had acknowledged now some years the spectacle of having accomplished nothing but get old. She was an old woman with bad hips and patches of raddled skin, beaky nose and sunken cheeks and a bald spot like Lady O'Connell's. O'Connor's. She had joined no cults; she had examined to no end the history of some adolescent rough handling which nowadays she would call rape; she had interrogated her occasional periods of promiscuity and outrage and learned nothing. The problem was, she was now sure, purely organic. In earlier times she might have been a seer or a shaman – or a witch. She might have been revered as a wise but dangerous old woman. These days she taught her classes, wrote and studied, and tried to ignore the whole business.

Marge took an inventory of her feelings. There was nothing she could not manage, and her appearance could be ascribed to the weather. She closed the car door behind her. Inside, George looked up from his work. Marge strode forward, keys in her gloved hand, as big and homely as always, and George smiled in welcome.

BARBARA

Barbara Scoppone graduated in the spring without the least idea of what she wanted to do next. She was unencumbered with Derek, anyway. His defection had not been any sort of trauma. Derek had had aspirations of a sort, but in bad faith — he had too much wanted to be inconspicuous. She thought he was sneaky. He had a saboteur's mind.

Four years of college — five, actually — had soured her adolescent enthusiasm a bit. Barbara was a smart woman and she now found the world a little slow. And being slow, obtuse. Being obtuse, inclined to bad behavior.

So the question was what to do now. What does a hundred fifty credits in pre-law make possible? What opportunities, and did she want them?

She did not. The idea of sitting for the law school exam turned her stomach. Once it had seemed that lawyering would be the means of... well, various earnest longfaced things. More likely a practice would be a cynical accommodation, likely to breed a creeping rot.

Young Ms. Scoppone, twenty-two, assesses herself and her chances. Traditionally this is done naked, before a mirror, but Ms Scoppone has spent too many hours that way already, in twenty-two years, and prefers to take the number seven train and walk around in Central Park instead. An inventory of physical condition is positive. She has a good figure but already running to fat and no more than five years to trade on it. Scoppone sits on a grassy knoll and watches the runners, notes the tight bodies and the whipping ponytails. The smell of sweat coats the breeze. Intellectual advantages are fewer. On the right, the Met; on the left, the university. But Scoppone knows herself to be lazy — why else settle for a generic B.S. from a nowhere place? She is hard to get up in the morning.

Young Ms. Scoppone takes the number four train down to Washington Square. She looks for a decent chess game to kibbitz, sits on a bench on the west side, in the afternoon shade, and watches the mixed crowd of suits, whacked out underfed men, and rackety hip-hop kids circulate around the closed track. Her inventory of social skills is encouraging: she has networking skills and a taste for many acquaintances and few friends. People talk to her on the bus, tell her stories, even ask advice which she is too sharp to give them. She has no off-putting bad habits, and though she has bohemian tastes she isn't likely to embarrass any useful people with them accidentally. She is in control.

A light dinner, another train across the river to Brooklyn Heights where she can sit at a sidewalk table with an espresso and look at the Chrysler and its friends, window-speckled and black in the mellow evening light, or downtown toward the old fish market and the stock exchange. It is a good place to consider economic prospects. These are less satisfactory. She has some money but her employability is low and she has a settled distaste for offices and anything which pays by the hour. Her loyalty is likely to be poor and after a few years of that her resumé will be hard to explain. On the other hand there is that five-year window of her looks which she is not averse to trade on.

The next day she makes her way out to Fire Island beach and sits for a long time with the ocean sucking her toes and refusing to succumb to cosmic thinking. She requires a cosmopolitan place. She has no further tolerance for cold and darkness. She wants good food and late nights and decent sex, not too frantic or frequent and not always on top.

A week into June she borrows some money from her parents and takes a flight to Key West. She finds a share in a cottage on

Catherine Street and part-time jobs in a law clinic and a counseling center and one night a week volunteering on a suicide help line. She buys a new wardrobe of straw hats, loose shirts, white shorts and sandals, and a bicycle, and tacks a note to her doorframe to remember the water bottle, the sunscreen, and the chapstick.

It was a good choice. She is content.

But things go wrong. Her bicycle is stolen. She buys another. That is stolen. She walks or takes the circular tourist tram. A woman propositions her in a bar and turns abusive when turned down. She is followed home early one morning but nothing comes of it and the potential stalker doesn't reappear. Her flatmate welshes on the rent. The refrigerator dies and a lot of bad-smelling food has to be thrown out. She is robbed on the street for drug money and gets two black eyes. She picks up an interesting straight guy but he won't use a condom so she has to squelch home and take a shower. Someone on the suicide help line actually does commit suicide and for a week she is too strung out to work. The lawyers understand but the counseling center is short-handed and the social worker has a hissy fit. Despite her repugnance for the work she takes a job waiting on tables to replace the counseling center income. The customers grope her and she only lasts a week. There is a lean period after that, but the counseling center eventually takes her back. Right away there is an OD in the office. 911 is a little slow and the medics are not too sympathetic but at least the guy doesn't die right on the floor. She tells the woman at the opposite desk about her suicide. That seems to help. An old lady turns up at the law clinic and makes a pest of herself for a week and Scoppone loses her objectivity. One of the lawyers has to take Scoppone out. It seems this old woman turns up periodically and has managed to annoy everyone, which seems to be her purpose, so it's all right but it isn't.

You seem a little tense, the lawyer says. There is a lawyer joke on his t-shirt which no one gets except him.

Scoppone tells him what has happened since that girl died on the telephone. She wonders whether this lawyer would use a condom. It turns out that like almost everyone else he is gay so he probably does but then it doesn't matter.

She gets a summer cold and then another one. It rains every afternoon. She forgets the sunblock and gets a terrible burn, mostly on her ass and can't sit down which everyone but her thinks is hilarious. She gets her white shorts bloody and has to throw them out. At least she figures out what to do before she gets heatstroke and dies. She picks up that same guy but he's hopeless. He's not going to get old, anyway, she thinks.

By the time winter comes on Barbara Scoppone is taking stock. It has been a tough start, she has to admit. She is inclined to resent this and to feel singled out. But on balance it's still worth it. At Christmas her parents fly down and actually have a good time. They stay in a hotel because there is no place for them in the cottage. Her mother says they would have slept on the floor like they once did which is a confidence Barbara has not heard before. They visit the Hemingway house while Barbara is at work and at night they eat pizza and grouper and her father goes along to the suicide phone and looks grave. At the airport there is a three-way hug and Barbara is so elated she considers walking home. After New Year's her mother writes to say they are proud of what she is doing.

The second summer she takes stock again. If she were not living here in Key West which she really likes but in some awful gray place it would have been a pretty bad year, but it was not. She wonders why there are so many gray places and for the first time begins to reflect on the country she lives in and is glad she doesn't live in it.

There is a cautionary tale her father once told her. It is one of those five-year-old's memories that are mysteriously brighter and more intricate than anything acquired since. She heard it around the time the family was preparing to move to Flushing, deeper into the city, for her father's law practice. Uneasy, she has crawled into bed with them and pushed her way in between her parents and pulled the covers over her head.

Once upon a time, her father says, there was ... He yawned. A woman. Let's make it about a woman, all right?

All right, tiny Barbara says, her voice muffled by the bed covers.

Once upon a time there was a woman whose name was Josephine.

Is it Josephine that works for the phone company?

It could be, Squib. Let's say it is. So you've already met Josephone?

Pheen!

Well then. In that case, let's call her Barbara. Barbara worked for the telephone company. She was a security code. She carried messages back and forth, and reported on the condition of the wires and switches, and helped to make important decisions. She got to do a lot of traveling (on company business, you see) and wherever she went she carried a lot of numbers in her bag. A great many numbers — too many to say in bed, in the dark. Ten to the jigundus gigundus. And when she came back, if any one of those numbers was a bit dusty or dog-eared, or missing, or anything at all, then Barbara knew that something was wrong and she would sit down immediately, without even a cup of coffee, and figure out what it was and what to do about it.

That was Barbara's job.

She loved it.

She wanted it never to end.

Well one day Barbara was sent away, far away to a place where there were no telephone wires. She had never been to such a place before. But Barbara, you see, was very good at keeping secrets. This was a place where there were a lot of secrets because there was a war going on. The secrets were getting away. Barbara was supposed to fix that.

In this place it was hot and crowded and sweaty and there were not enough bathrooms. Before, she had lived in a big airy house and traveled alone, in the fastest airplanes, everywhere in the world. She had even been to the Moon, and to Mars. Now she lived in a stuffy hovel and traveled on foot or in old trains with poor farmers and chickens and only as far as the mountains and back.

This was Barbara's job.

She hated it.

She wanted it to end immediately. Right now.

She missed her old friends, of course. They never wrote her one letter. Barbara told herself this was because they never wrote to anyone. Then she thought it was because of the secrets, and their letters were not being let through. Finally she knew her old friends weren't really, and had forgotten her.

Days and days. No letters. No picture post cards. Not even a smoke signal.

Then the hurricane comes and for a while Key West is gray like everywhere else. The old residents say this happens all the time, it's like shoveling snow in Minnesota, and they get out the plywood from last time. There is a run on the grocery stores but everyone stands in line politely exchanging pleasantries about what each other thinks it is important to have in the pantry. One man has a shopping cart full of baked beans. Fresh fruit is not very popular.

For several days they watch the hurricane build up in the Atlantic to the east. Perhaps it will turn north and mess up the Outer Banks instead which is not very gracious. Still, these things never go to Brazil, do they?

However, the storm wants to get into the Gulf and after a few days it's obvious they are going to batten down.

Not long after that the wind starts to pick up and then the raindrops are hitting the house like bullets and then the electricity goes out. They have candles and a Sterno stove; the candles won't stay lit in the draft but they rig a shelter and manage to heat up a couple of packaged dinners. Barbara wants to go up to her room for some different clothes but everyone says this is a bad idea and she ought to stay away from the windows because you never know what might come crashing through. A chair, a dog, a length of pipe.

At the height of the storm, while the eye of it is passing to the south, Barbara gets claustrophobic. She has to go out. This is not a good idea either, her new flatmate tells her, but Barbara is getting tired of being cooped up with this person who has nothing intelligent to say and she goes out anyway.

The wind tears at her and the rain hurts. Still, it isn't much worse than a winter storm off the lake in that other place. If she can get along William Street without being killed by a piece of debris or squashed by an uprooted tree she will be able to see out into the Gulf and this she very much wants to do. She doesn't give any more thought to how she is going to get back than Honoria Dedlock did. It crosses her mind that this is not a very intelligent attitude but just now prudence does not seem to be the virtue called for.

At the bottom of William Street the beach is occupied by resorts to she goes right on South Street which turns her into the face of the wind. Her nylon squall jacket balloons out like a Krispy Kreme. Although it isn't that cold her bare legs are numb. She has to keep her eyes on her feet because she can't face up to the wind which means she can't see where she is going. Palm fronds blow by silently because her ears are now full of water. The fronds' fans slice at her clothes and skin and the other, heavy, end might break her leg. Several times she loses her footing and stumbles, once into a picket fence which she knocks flat, piercing the fat of her hand on a nail. But she pushes on and eventually reaches a place where she can see a length of coast.

There is too much water in the air to see any distance. The ordinarily placid Gulf is raging, tearing at the land, at the string of islands which pierce its side.

This was what she wanted to see. To see the angry waves coming in, the sea livid and heaving, the wind breaking down trees and smashing up beachfront geegaws, sky and water swirling, indistinguishable, like some amniotic smoothie.

Now it is obvious, just for a moment glimpsed through the rack during a momentary lull, what is the truth of this life she is living. She is going to be scraped away by these mindless — no, not mindless, but uncaring, which from her limited point of view amounts to the same thing. She is a little person who if storms and fires and plagues are struggling among themselves for mastery, is too little to see what is going on. She is not in the way of these forces. She is part of them, one of the grains of sand which is being used to wear away all the solid things of the world.

But she stands on a planet which is itself one of the solid things and will itself be scraped clean in time to drift, again a lifeless rock, toward its frozen nemesis. By then it will have been dark — way past gray — for untold eons, all the suns burned out, all their homeless photons dead.

The wheel continues to turn. In some other universe of an infinity of universes, like a flea surveying untold riches of opportunity, she will be reborn.

Scrape the earth clean, damn you! she shouts at the destroying army of waves which claws at the battlements. It's what we deserve, damn you! Go ahead! But I'll be the last to go.

In the coming years, if they are years which will come to her, she will be a little embarrassed at this rather gothic outburst. But she is young, is Ms. Scoppone. Already she has wounds, and scars, but she is right to struggle. She can see through the wall of rain with her third eye what might be done and she is right to damn anything which might get in her way. She is not here to be happy but to live. She will not live, of course. When one first imagines home one thereby invents homelessness. It is inevitable that she will be driven into the street in some foreign place, unable even to ask for help in this language made up of varied groans and incomprehensible scribbles, to die in a cardboard box, covered in rags, cold and alone, old and ugly, too feeble to wipe herself.

Go ahead, damn you! she shouts, enraged, into the all-scouring wind. It's what we deserve! But I'm staying. I'll be the last to go.

Of course nobody hears her.

One time, in the mountains of that awful place to which her father had sent her, Barbara found an old radio. It was so old she didn't recognize it at first. Just some wires taped to a board and a

signal key. She tried sending some messages but there was no reply.

At that time there was a routine to her life: their enemies would
find them in the mountains and the planes would come with bombs
and Barbara and her new friends would have to move. After a couple of weeks their enemies would find them again. This went on
and on. Every time, Barbara would walk all night through the forest carrying a heavy load of supplies, always including the useless
old radio. At dawn it would begin to rain. Cold water would drip
from the big leaves of unfamiliar trees. The red earth would be
slippery underfoot. Barbara began to miss the city below, in the
plain, and the slow trains and the chickens and the heat.

Then the planes began to come at night. They dropped their
bombs in the dark. When the sun came up the camp was gone, just
red dirt ploughed up by the bombs and shattered tree stumps and
shreds of tent cloth and dead people on which the cold rain began
to fall.

Barbara let her pack of belongings fall into the mud. She sat
down on a splintered crate and covered her face.

Five-year-old Barbara poked her head out from under the quilt.
Her mother was knitting and listening to the story and her father
was staring dreamily at the ceiling.

He said: Barbara pulled her radio out from under a sodden wad
of blue fabric which were all her shirts. She dried the wires and
reconnected the battery. It seemed to work. She laid out an antenna
wire in the clearing made by the bombs and tried the signal key.

Help, she tapped out.

Help me. Please come. I'm tired of this. I don't want any more.
Find me.

Over and over, with dirty numb fingers, Barbara tapped out this
message. Somewhere, she hoped, it was being converted into numbers, more numbers than you could ever say in the dark.

But there was no reply. There couldn't be, because the receiver
was broken. There was no way to tell whether anyone was listening, whether there would be any help.

It quit raining. The air hissed as drops fell from leaf to frond. Barbara slept at the edge of the park, under a bush, wrapped in a strip of green nylon. When she woke it was afternoon. The sun had come out, lighting the tops of the palm trees a soft gold.

She stood up. Slowly, for her muscles were stiff from sleeping on the wet ground. She hauled her wet bag onto her shoulder and trudged back into town in search of her new friends.

GEORGE

George Foswell had always advocated living small but when Marge told him she wanted to go back to France he assented without argument even though he had a feeling they wouldn't be returning.

It was supposed to be for three months. Given the housing shortage they had no trouble making a lease to a new professor and her husband. With two infants the place would have to be child-proofed. Marge put away the more valuable things and the renters agreed to do the rest.

The department was somewhat annoyed to learn they were losing a third of their faculty on short notice but the retirement paperwork did go through in time. With two pensions, George's Social Security, and the investments they had been making from years of unthinking frugality — what was there to spend the money on? — they were well enough off to go on being frugal pretty much anywhere. The biggest tangle was health coverage and medications, for which there were still unresolved uncertainties (George was tickled by this notion and spent some time pondering the nature of a *resolved* uncertainty) and some bureaucratic shuffling on the first of September; Marge waved her hands, tapped the brim of her hat, and said they were going anyway. She took a fat notebook of telephone numbers of people to complain to, gathered hers and George's passports and tickets, freighted some belongings and extra luggage, found friends to drive them to Syracuse, and pushed the keys through the mail slot.

Marge had found an apartment rental in Paris. They were staying only two weeks in the city; the question still unresolved was where to go that was less expensive. For George I was a question rather of comfort. Paris was too busy, the trendy restored farmhouse in the Loire was not busy enough – he'd spent two decades in that village he had just left and had no interest in moving to another. Marge suggested Occitania where there would be, George said, far too many writers of tour guides, travel books, and memoirs taking up space.

They were sitting together on a bench in a little square not far from the quai, on the Left Bank near the Cluny museum. Despite being a *Fauviste* Marge knew a great deal about the objects there and had given George a number of lessons. George had no taste for medieval art. To him it looked all alike, like the roomsful of portraits of 19th century men in black to be found in every regional American museum. It was not the medieval hermeneutics which sought, but that it was Marge telling the stories.

A long time passed in silence between them. George listened to the gulls squabbling, and the traffic. At the back of the unnamed *Place*, behind them, was an English-language bookshop, with occasional customers coming and going, so that George heard more than he liked of a language which he was finding an annoyance. His shaky French was set back by hearing things he understood, just at the time when he was making sense of the subjunctive, or trying to remember the word for postage stamps.

Timbres, he said aloud.

Que?

Ne pas des estampes.

Ah oui. On n'obtient les *gravures* là.

George pondered the Préfecture, a large, square, and for Paris feautreless, building across the river.

Quoi de Rennes? he said.

Ah, bien sûr.

Rennes seemed a good place to start looking. Mysterious networks of privilege and mutual assistance turned up an unprepossessing eight hundred square meters, a train was booked, permits were signed, the TGV moved quietly and almost imperceptibly out of the Gare de Montparnasse and into the suburbs. For some reason everything was beginning over again.

Marge was reading a detective novel, *Monsieur Malaussène*. George studied a map of Brittany. From Rennes they could visit Quimper, and Brest, St. Malo, Mont St-Michel — they had seen Mont St-Michel's British twin off the coast of Cornwall years ago. Scylla and Charybdis guarding the North Sea, but he no Jason. What was there in Rennes? A university — a polytechnic really, with nothing much of interest for the two of them. The cathedral of course, where all the kings were crowned, or was that Rheims?

George stared out of the window at green embankments alternating with housing blocks and then warehouses and wrecking yards and then fields of young vegetables.

Marge had done all the research. George gave his attention to a map of the old city center and its medieval tangle of streets. Eighteenth century, the guidebook said.

This is crazy, George thought. I haven't the faintest idea where we're going. I never was outside Paris until before. I don't even remember the language. I've forgotten what a *croque monsieur* is. Happen to me soon enough.

He turned to a picture of the flat they had leased, or sort of leased, on the strength of Marge's voodoo arrangements. It certainly was charming. On a curving street with an old house half-timbered in red at the mouth, then a row of three-storied buildings, white with blue windows and boxes of geraniums perched on the railings of miniscule balconies, garrets above and shops on the *rez de chaussée*, then a short one like a child trying to get a glimpse of the parade, then more of the others. The picture was too small to see what was being sold in the shops. There would be a *boulangerie* surely, where he could go in the morning in his slippers for a baguette and two fresh croissants. People on the street were wearing leather coats and fleece things with hoods.

George looked away from the window and turned toward Marge. He had never minded being married to a strong woman, and he himself was no milquetoast, but this was something new. A bit scary, actually.

Marge, he knew, thought herself to be ugly. This was a reason to instead be… *strong* wasn't quite the word, though that was what people said. Nor autocratic. What used to be termed *character*, he supposed. George himself thought her handsome. That's the scrim that comes down at the end of a long marriage.

He loved Marge. His painter's eye ran down the long slope of her nose with the slightest of doglegs where her glasses always came to rest. Her lips were full and of a natural color shading to rust which she did nothing to cover, wonderfully. Flat cheeks and high bones, skin still soft and unmarked and of a doe color picked up by her lips and eyes. Over the years she had tried many hairstyles. Anything at all long looked absurdly feminine. When they were first married and her hair was much, much thicker, as thick as raw wool, she had coiled it on top of her head but that fashion could not survive the Vietnam years. Various bobs and pageboys had failed and even a rather intriguing spiky thing. In the end she had settled on something partway between Gertrude Stein and Alice Toklas and George had approved, especially now it had gone a bit gray.

Her voice was as the rest of her, a rich alto full of viscous overtones. She could make herself well heard but had never yet shouted at anyone. In fact, George still found it difficult to tell when she was angry. He relied instead on the eyes, on a slight tension he found there, to know when something was not worth the candle.

Left in the dark, he supposed that meant. George enjoyed working out the original metaphor behind these worn-out figures of speech.

The train was going around a long curve, pressing Marge a little against his shoulder. He smiled, very faintly, a smile as hard to see as Marge's anger, what she called his Buddhist monk's smile.

He did have some inkling of what France might be for her. She thought he didn't know about all that. And he didn't, in an artifactual, narrative way. She was as secret as the womb but he knew anyway. He had pondered the thing and found out what meant more to him and did it, like a brush stroke, a decided streak of white in exactly the right place, first time. What he did not know was why she had come back and whether she regretted that. Some years went by. George concluded it was all right. And now this. It was worrisome.

The leased flat proved to be about as comfortable as quaint places usually are. There was indeed a *bouangerie* within slippering distance. They rented a car and made some trips afield. But there was no room to paint or write. George became tired of only sketching and Marge was taking an interest in some regional artists nobody had heard of elsewhere. Their simple suppers began to be stretched out with extra glasses of wine and cups of espresso and stale brioche. Before long Marge began to look around for a congenial neighborhood and cheaper arrangements which could be more counted on.

One day when Marge was out marketing George was rummaging through a box looking for a photograph he wanted to copy and ran across some pictures of where they used to live, a place which they would undoubtedly never see again. He pondered them much as he had pondered Marge's infidelity years before.

About 1980, he supposed, to judge by the car. That had belonged to… someone in language and literature, he thought, moved on long ago. Never could have afforded such a house even then. Impossible to heat; astronomical bills. They always froze. Looks fantastical now, George thought. Fairytale house. He did not remember it so. Moldy basement, dark rooms, bad plumbing, worse wiring. That Mt Vernonish thing on top would have been a better solarium. That round veranda to the right had been a good place to sit for a couple of months a year but nothing to the row house stoops in Philadelphia that Marge had grown up with. Before her mother hied off to Laramie, of all places.

Sort of stuck behind this picture was one George couldn't recall. It seemed to be a parade, probably Fourth of July. There were no parades at other times, if that's what it was.

Who on earth were these people? He didn't recognize any of them. Students. Too young to be anything else. Townies? Maybe about 1970. With some discomfort George realized he himself would have been only thirty.

This picture unsettled him a good deal more than the other had. Perhaps it was because there were people in it. He would have thought a photo of home — even an old photo — would have been more nostalgic than this one of strangers, their lives unknown, their fates inexplicable. He could not imagine something as far as this from 800 square meters in Rennes and the life he was living now. What on earth had possessed him?

To what? Leave, not leave, go there? Go here? Not go here?

How many of these people now were gone? Gone to ashes he meant.

Thinking of Marge's depression which was another thing he was not supposed to know about — things were as bad as a Victorian novel for keeping mum — he came to wonder about what had happened to Simone Richter that summer. Perhaps Simone's crash had been like a death experience for Marge, jarring loose old resolves.

Marge had had a bad patch after she decided to retire, he knew. That was the conventional wisdom anyway, that retirement sometimes brings on an existential crisis. He could not imagine Marge having an existential crisis. The bad patch was something to do with Simone which the exposure to change had jogged loose from where it had been hiding.

Perhaps Marge and Simone were each only aspects of another, vastly more depressed being. Very gnostic idea, that.

The end of Simone was not good to think on. She could have been a holy fool, have gone to the mountains, if she didn't keep waking up. A fool's life is a torture, able to see but not have — hold, knowing that when you are at last able to fall asleep they will come and turn on the light, that light means pain.

Do people think it justifies doing to same thing to mice, and pigs.

Am I not thine ass upon which thou hast ridden all my days?

Simone's husband Gary, the philosopher, once explained the concept of authenticity to George. Our values and goals are given up by our situation, Gary said. Usually we just absorb this identity uncritically. The authentic person takes responsibility for who he is, for his life. But because it is hard to be always critical and deliberate, unreflective action prevails and inauthenticity creeps back in. You can't guarantee authenticity by your own effort. Salvation is given you.

Or not, George had observed.

Or not, yes.

Whose ideas are these?

Heidegger. *Being and Time.*

Should I read that book?

I think that would be a bad idea, Gary said, and George had a notion that anyway, the concept had fallen into disuse. This feeling he traced to Andy Warhol – George understood notions mostly in terms of what he himself knew about, which in his case was modern art. That Warhol's art could be *authentic* was absurd. George had known this as a young painter in 1960 when he encountered it for the first time, that it would no longer be possible to paint as he had been taught, to make stand-alone images distinguished somehow as *art*, authentic art, as opposed to everything else.

But he had gone and done it anyway.

George shook his head to clear it, and smiled, and went back to work on his drawing, which would be a painting when he found space to paint it.

RESURRECTION

John John turned up eventually in Vienna, now calling himself
Giovanni Stirpa, a Maltese, — which we knew was not the case
but as we did not know what the case was we kept quiet. Vienna is
not our town — no place is. We are not townspeople who know
everything that happened to the Karamazovs and the Webbses, the
residents of Paterson or Athens. But the story, always already finished, nevertheless goes on. Immortal, we begin again as best we
can.

We thought by that time he might have become a spy or a
smuggler, a character somewhat like Dimitrios in Eric Ambler's
novel that quite a good movie was made of in which Dimitrios
starts out dead. We never could understand why the coffin of Ambler's title becomes a mask in the movie — it should be masks,
anyway; many identities — the first of which is that of a dead man
in need of a coffin. And of course it is irresistible, that is, we can't
resist seeing ourselves in the role of Peter Lorre as the outsider
who continuously rediscovers Dimitrios the fig-packer, trailing
him across Europe, unmasking his guises, and who almost gets
himself sucked in, the voyeur entangled in the object of his gaze.

And it was just this — not wanting to be implicated, a Bartle-
by-like desire to not desire anything — which was John John's, or
Giovanni as we are now supposed to call him — which was his
most prominent characteristic. This being so, Gepetto might have
been more appropriate.

Anyway, such a role for Stirpa would stray into Graham
Greene territory except that Greene's people are conflicted but
straightforward — honestly confused as it were — and are unwilling outsiders. The which is supposed to reveal something about the
human race. These people long for faith and membership. Incom-
patible desires. Whereas Gepetto here was quite the opposite. Uncomplicated, secretive, wanting if anything to get farther outside,
his way faithless and crooked. One thinks of Lowry's Consul were
this not to be setting a peasant hovel beside Chichen Itsa.

But now our feelings are sticking out. We apologize.

Still, it was because Stirpa did not care — in this case care how things turned out, that what happened turned out as it did. Perhaps we should not speak of *because* and *turned out*. These are story-telling conventions, and ancient ones at that, traditional figures of speech that imply what is not true. All we know is that one thing followed another when it might be only that one thing did do that; or that anything at all turned out. We get tired of supposing these things. Our attention wanders; someone dies and puts a stop to that when we are not looking, and now something is following some-thing else some where we don't know about.

This Giovanni Stirpa (you see we are reconciling ourselves to the facts as they are for the time being) had no credentials in Vien-na. He was merely a young black man who spoke bad Italian as might be of a Maltese more used to Arabic or Coptic. He knew no one. He had money enough, we did not know how, but lived fru-gally. Frugality was in keeping with his obviously ascetic tastes. His manner was delicate, scrupulously fastidious, as that of a craftsman with some careful work in hand or a politician not to be distracted by any sensual excess. He represented no one but him-self, he said, but there were shadowy figures slipping like so many Harry Limes through the deserted streets at his back. We did not know where he lived. Perhaps in some undistinguished suburb in this city where every corner has its place in a fine-meshed net of status, or one of those medieval relics without toilet and running water and so inexplicably in demand by the powerful.

Every day he appeared at one or another of the famous coffee houses, now no centers of culture as a century ago but still useful as meeting places, more ample and anonymous than those bistros where Maigret spends so much of his time drinking wine, watch-ing…

Sooner or later Stirpa would be found in conversation with one or two men, never more than two, always men, a little seedy, older men of the sort who still wear overcoats and homburg hats. Gio-vanni never himself stopped at any table or greeted anyone. He was simply there, sitting with a glass of tea and his hands lying flat on the table on either side of his glass, waiting. And they always came to him, these men in hats, as if my appointment.

By appointment to do what? We did not know.

And so it went on, and then it didn't go on, and he was seen no more.

Some weeks later two of these men, one of them not well shaven and the other with very dark eyes, met in the Café Sperl. To the left of the bar was a long passage which ran looked out on the Gumpendorfer Strasse with two rows of tables, one along the windows and one opposite, against the wall. These two men, who came in together, chose the table at the far end, away from the window, on which they laid their hats. One pulled out a chair and sat down heavily on it; the other, still wearing his overcoat, went to the bar and returned with two Schlagobers and a small plate with two small torten. The seated man looked sourly at this plate — white, heavy china without any dressing at all, not even a paper doily.

No strudel, the unshaven man said, putting down the plate.

Too late, said the other. He had taken off his coat and hung it on a peg by the table. The unshaven man sat down still buttoned up. They both turned their chairs toward the window to look out at the gray day, now well advanced, and the slush in the street. Neither spoke.

About Herr Stirpa, the dark-eyed man said finally, and said no more, as if in a Pinter play. Some time passed.

I understand Herr Stirpa is in Greece, the unshaven man said. He picked up his cup, sniffed the whipped cream, and then set the cup down again, carefully, without drinking.

He intends to return?

I think not.

More time passed. The second man pulled his coat closer around himself.

Did you have anything from him, Hänsel? said the first.

No. Nothing. And yourself, Rumpel?

No.

Well then. That's an end to it, said Hänsel.

Apparently.

After some morose rumination Hänsel took up his hat and went out, leaving both his coffee and the pastries untouched. Rumpel pulled the coffee to his side of the table, pondered a bit, and drank both of them. He wiped a bit of whipped cream from his upper lip and smiled, a bit privately, sitting on as the twilight deepened outside, his large hands lying flat on the table on either side of the two empty cups. A residue of coffee and milk of an unappetizing brown color adhered to the inside of each. Rumpel tipped one cup toward himself, looked into the bottom of it a moment, and returned his hand to its place on the table. Laughter and the clicking of pool balls sounded faintly, coming from the large area on the other side of the bar. Rumpel began to nibble at one torte. By the time it was full dark both of them were gone. He rubbed a finger across the saucer where a white linen napkin, perhaps with a narrow border of blue, should have been.

Another man came in, better dressed than the one who had gone out, and moved briskly toward Rumpel's table, nodding toward der Kellner as he passed. The two shook hands.

Gruss Gott, he said.

Gruss Gott, Deutwert, said Rumpel, not so lugubrious as he had been.

You have been here a while, Deutwert observed indicating the empty plate and cups. Am I late?

No. You are quite on time. Hänsel has just left.

Excuse me. I'll go and get myself something.

Deutwert returned with an espresso and a Topfenkuchen and a folded copy of *Die Presse* under his arm. All this was placed on the table. Deutwert hung his own coat on the peg and sat down. He wore no hat.

No strudel, he said.

No.

Deutwert's suit was of dark blue worsted with a fine stripe. His coat bore a faux-sable collar, probably rabbit, and an interesting leather yoke which was not quite Austrian in style.

Our friend Herr Stirpa is in Athens, said Deutwert imperturbably, sipping his espresso.

So I understand.

He intends to go on from there to Cyprus and thence to Istanbul, perhaps by way of one or two of the islands. From there I do not know.

What does he want?

Deutwert laughed quietly, a discreet snort. Why, nothing at all, he said expansively. You have heard him say it many times. He is a Bartleby, that one, though I don't think he will starve. He doesn't care what he eats.

So I noticed, said Rumpel, reflectively wiping the forlorn saucer again with one finger.

Perhaps he is seeking wisdom, eh? When he gets as far as India he will put on a saddhu's loincloth and vanish into the mountains. Perhaps he will turn up in the old tales of the patriarchs.

I think not. Rumpel's mood had soured. He's gone off without.

Yes, I don't doubt that. A regular Skimpole.

Who?

Ah. Perhaps I should have said Grüne Heinrich.Rumpel and Deutwert passed half an hour in agreeable conversation. The Deutwert rose, made his goodbyes, and departed with his coat over his arm.   But outside, shrugging on the overcoat, he appeared decidedly less complacent. A grave expression came into his lips and eyes. Combing his fingers through his blond hair he started off up Lehar Gasse and the U-bahn station at Karlsplatz.

This Giovanni Stirpa, this Gepetto, had done Deutwert an inconvenience. It was he who had found Stirpa and had vetted the man's claim to have some influence with those who were holding Korn a prisoner. Now it seemed that Signor Gepetto had been one of those who will say whatever is expedient, and had dinged

Deutwert's credibility for not having found that out. In this business credibility is one's working capital.

Bah. They might all have been Masons or characters in *The Princess Casamassima* or mere bomb-throwers, with these ludicrous noms de guerre and dusty Balkan furtiveness. Here in Vienna it was hard to remember that elsewhere real lives were being sold at below cost. Herr Korn, the immediate object of all this rootie-tootie, was somewhere being twisted by agents of somewhere else. Gepetto had claimed to know this. Or rather, to know who controlled these people's resources.

Well it was too late now. Probably there was not much left of Korn, whoever he was. No one close to Deutwert knew his identity, of course. Deutwert had been asked to do a job and had muffed it, and now those whom Korn gave away would disappear unobtrusively and be twisted in their turn, their mangled and blackened bodies returned like so many snooked Lazaruses to the street corners and bedrooms from which they were taken.

Deutwert's heel clicked on the steps of the U-bahn entrance. Down below it was pleasantly warm, softly lit, quite sedate on this quiet evening. He took the train around to the Schottenring stop, made his way among the brightly lit shops, and eventually got a bus that would take him to the west side of the Augarten. Hänsel's flat was in that neighborhood, with a view of the flakturm.

Hänsel's son was also among the disappeared. Unless there had been a gross breach of protocol somewhere he was not this Korn for whom they had been searching, but what did that matter? To Hänsel and Käthe it was all the same. To save Korn would have been a step toward saving them all. Gepetto's notion of salvation had been somewhat more narrow.

There was, in fact, an ugly scene over that at a supper at the Reichmann's, in that scuffed and nibbled-at flat in a dark little street over a clock shop which was always closed. Gepetto showed up there about eleven o'clock on instructions which Deutwert had even then begun to fear would be ignored or forgotten. But here he was, a lean floury-black man with big soft eyes, dressed in a ski sweater and jeans. The others had mostly eaten but Käthe put out some more wurst and beer, dark bread, olives. The table, bare of cloth, was littered with scraps, the napkins were mustard-stained; the empty steins were clouded by foam.

Inconclusive remarks were passed around by the half-dozen people there, of whom Käthe was the only woman. Herr Stirpa took a swallow of beer but left the bread and olives untouched. The wurst he wrapped in a napkin and put into the wallet which he carried on a lanyard around his neck.

About Korn — said Rumpel impetuously.

Rumpel was a sleek man but now running to fat. He had a narrow Slavic face, that of the never aging boy , with straight black hair parted in the middle. The young Kafka perhaps. Bit in appearance only.

Yes? was all Stirpa would venture.

You can help us?

There others at work, I suppose. What do you want me for?

Oh… Rumpel glanced at Deutwert across the table. We were told you had influence. Suitable influence.

Hah! They are not your Austrian bureaucrats, these people. They are ideologues.

Rumpel persisted. They need money, he said. Everyone always needs money.

Hmm … Stirpa seemed dubious on that point.

Ideologues, bah! Hänsel interrupted impatiently. Chaos, murder — politics as usual.

Stirpa crossed his rather long legs and smiled to himself, goading Hänsel by his languid behavior.

You see nothing wrong with a politics of destruction? Hänsel retorted, sharp and angry.

Oh, it is not politics, Herr … Hänsel. Stirpa was amused by this comical name. If it were, you could count on them to be practical about the matter.

Meaning a ransom.

Well, yes. But the faith is implicated here. One does not buy off God. Or be seen to do so.

Oh that's — rubbish, he was about to say, forgetting himself for a moment. That's nonsense. What sort of religion offers salvation by blood? Herr Korn's blood!

Blood and soil, eh? returned Stirpa with an impish and troublemaking tone.

Dammit, I mean cutting off people's arms and legs. Sticking needles in their eyes. Pulling off their —

Hänsel was brought up short by a gasp from Käthe, recalling her own torment.

Crucifying them? Was Stirpa's arch comment on this, but Hänsel said nothing now. Stirpa turned to Käthe.

Your little Solomon is dead, he said brutally, twisting a new yelp from the woman before she could stop herself. How would it be otherwise? Stirpa went on. You need to find some detachment, before you drive him — indicating Hänsel with a sideways and dismissive jerk of his head — to do something foolish. Let me tell you...

Stirpa leaned forward, forearms on his knees, and ran the fingers of one hand across the palm of the other. It was a discursive gesture which might mean that a bit of simple wisdom was now to be offered. It might mean that he was merely brushing off some dust, but the gesture strongly reminded Deutwert of bribery. Of geld passing as dust, returning to dust, created anew from dust.

The child in the womb, Stirpa said, must learn to differentiate itself. The first step in learning — wisdom — requires the infant to discover itself as an object, a being distinct from others. Not the cat, not the bowl of oatmeal, not the mother. That original amniotic oneness must be sacrificed. We spend our lives longing to know that feeling again. And you will. You will eventually be dissolved again into the substance of the universe just as you long to be, but you won't know it. You'll be dead.

This little lecture stupefied everyone. It was the surprise, the incongruity, the callousness of it which so shocked them. Käthe stared, unable to comprehend what she had been told, that her 'little Solomon' had been chopped in half, vaporized, and it was necessary that she harden herself to this.

Necessary? How — *necessary*? Käthe's eyes seemed to sink back, like stones into a bog, beneath the dark ruled line of her eyebrows.

As they came to know this Gepetto better such behavior would seem less remarkable. Their Maltese gangster shrugged, we might say philosophically. Ideologues, he repeated, but negligently. Why bother to talk to such people?

Do you not intend to help, then? Rumpel asked, disappointed.

This elicited another shrug, a downturned mouth, a spreading of the hands as if to say — Who knows? Perhaps.

What *will* you take, then? Hänsel seemed a little desperate.

But Gepetto merely laughed, very quietly. Nothing, he said.

What? Nothing?

I don't want anything. I want for nothing.

Stirpa paused, as if startled by some unintentional aptness.

And I may not want to help, he went on. It is unproductive to desire these things.

You will need money, Rumpel said again.

Hah! Hardly that. Your Herr ... Korn — that is not his name, I suppose.

Certainly it is. Hänsel's voice quivered alarmingly.

Deutwert thought it best now to intervene. He partly rose from his seat and touched Herr Stirpa's elbow.

I will tell you what you must know, he said quietly, insofar as I know it. Let me accompany you out. We can talk in the street.

These people are fools, Stirpa remarked roughly as they were going downstairs. How can you work with them?

The wooden treads creaked loudly. They felt their way in the dark. Outside, there was a bright moon. Stirpa looked across the Augarten to the flakturm which stood up, squat and menacing, the stump of Jack's beanstalk and the giant escaped.

What is that thing?

Ah. Deutwert allowed this soft syllable to escape him. Hitler had that built. It's an artillery platform, part of the fortress defense. There are five.

Why aren't they torn down?

Yes, that would be difficult. They are very heavily built, you see. It would require a rather dangerous explosion.

Stirpa looked a bit longer at the cement stump, black even against the night sky.

A pragmatic people, you Austrians, he said sardonically.

Later on, that summer, Deutwert and Rumpel, with Stirpa, took a bus up to the ridge for a view of the city. They intended to walk back through the woods. On the lower slopes a network of unpaved roads would take them through the vineyards, and in the evening they would stop at a heurige in one of the villages for some local wine and perhaps a meal.

It was a fine day. The sunlight was strong but a breeze kept them from getting too warm. After enjoying the view, chatting for half an hour about nothing of consequence, they moved off. Deutwert found the path into the woods just below the public toilets. It followed the ridge for some ways and then plunged down under the trees. The way was dappled, not the stygian sort of trail of northern legend, among chill, twisted oak and louring beech. They did miss the way once and had to go back over their steps, but the right path was not hard to follow and after an hour's stroll they emerged again into the full sun. The city was no longer to be seen; they had dropped too low for any such views.

On either side of the road the vines hung from their wires, heavy with new leaves and promises. The colors were light; later on the leaves would darken to a thick forest shade.

What grapes are being grown here? Stirpa inquired.

Grüner, most probably. That's a white grape. Some Riesling, I imagine.

Rumpel looked about himself but said nothing. He had not dressed intelligently and was uncomfortable. He wore street shoes, now quite dusty, with smooth leather soles which slipped on the small gravel. His trousers clung to his legs, and the one time when he might have used a hat, for protection from the sun, he was bare-headed. The others wore short pants with many pockets, light shirts, and wide-brimmed straw hats.

Being uncomfortable, Rumpel was melancholy. He hardly listened to what the other two were saying. Korn had not been produced, nor the Reichmann's son; nothing had been heard for five months. They were dead for sure, hideously dead, and who knew how many others, and this Maltese clown had done nothing. Rumpel was of the opinion that it was time to move on to other causes where some actual results might be expected. Mournfully he brushed some of the light tan dust from his cuff.

Deutwert and Stirpa had gotten ahead of him and paused to wait. As Rumpel came up, Deutwert swept his arm across the horizon, ending with a little village whose roofs could be seen below the hill, and remarked on the beauty of the scene.

But Signor Stirpa inevitably demurred. Beauty, it seemed, is merely a contingent category in which the memory of some occurrences in the brain can be stored. Feelings, we call them. Pleasurable feelings are only covert expectations, polite disguises for self-interestedness and the possibility of exploitation.

What? Rumpel was astonished, and this took his thoughts abruptly out of himself. What good are feelings, then? Why should we have them? Why should we waste valuable calories on them?

Mere teleology, Stirpa said complacently. The task is to account for what we do in fact experience. I imagine that scenery which we call beautiful, have called at one time or another — these things change with fashion, of course — have ultimately to do with whether food or sex is likely to be found there.

Absurd. What about the sublime, then?

Nostalgia for the amniotic unity, as I said before. Behind every thought is some quite uncomplicated desire which we tart up in philosophical geegaws to hide the insubstantiality of it.

I find that not comforting, Herr Stirpa. Rumpel pushed his head forward, peering at his tormentor like a beset-upon donkey, sadly determined to balk its malign master. But Stirpa only shrugged negligently.

It is not our business to be comfortable, he said. That is a self-defeating strategy.

A mosquito landed on Stirpa's bare arm, which put him in mind of a suitable homily, that was one cannot defeat a swarm of insects by swatting them one at a time. After a while the mosquito flew away, unswatted. Stirpa seemed not to care about bites.

Rubbish, said Rumpel pointedly, and stumped on ahead.

He is an epicure, Stirpa observed.

Deutwert modified this. A sensualist, he said.

Yes, that's the word. Not to be deprived of his comforts.

Deutwert gazed away over the fluttering grape leaves toward a few white clouds which had formed over the ridge. The air was silent save for the sighing of the breeze through the vines.

We should not talk of *sighing*, however. That is an illegitimate, or anyway unfashionable, animism. People have been growing grapes on this slope for a long time. Twenty thousand years, perhaps. Deutwert often speculated on what a pervasive animism might be like. Would a fullness of spirit endow the world with a certain formality, like that of courtiers amid dimly sensed and probably unfriendly objects of fashion and protocol living their own mysterious lives, seeking … what? Something. An animistic world would have no place in it for indifference.

Ah, well, he said more or less to himself. With a motion of his hand he indicated they should walk on.

It was still early by the time they found a small heuriger at the edge of the village but not far from the bus stop which would take them back into the city. There were some tables set up outdoors under the trees and little more. Only one other table was occupied yet, so the three of them could have one in the back where the shade was deeper. It was a simple wooden trestle, unfinished, with two benches. They had not been settled here for long when a middle-aged woman approached, and Deutwert ordered a pitcher of white wine.

Drei glasen, mein Herren?

Stirpa hesitated, as if he might prefer beer, but nodded. Possibly it was too much to say he preferred either, and the hesitation was over whether to drink at all. Drink or not drink, what was there to choose?

The wine was produced, cold and tangy young wine, and half the pitcher was drunk off at once without any conversation. Then Rumpel began to look around.

The food service is in there, he said, pointing out with his empty glass a rather dark doorway into a shed. Inside was a cafeteria line where it was far too easy to ask for more things than one could comfortably eat. Rumpel came out with a bauernschmaus of roast pork, ham, sauerkraut, and cold cooked carrots in a traditional broth of vinegar, chicken stock, and spices. On top he had two crusty whole wheat rolls. He would, he averred, go back afterward for a mohnstrudel he had noticed and perhaps a bit of raspberry linzertorte.

Deutwert had taken a thick slice of beef, apple and horseradish, and a grüste. Stirpa had only a schnitzel.

Traditional food, eh? Stirpa observed when they were settled again and had looked over each other's choices. No pizza or tofu salads.

Best part about these places, Rumple said, unwrapping his knife and fork from their paper-collared napkin. He refilled his wine glass but then got to his feet.

Just let me get another pitcher, he muttered. This one's about gone.

Deutwert and Stirpa ate in silence. Stirpa put down his fork after two bites of schnitzel.

It's not good?

Oh, yes. I'm not quite hungry.

Not long afterward, Stirpa swung his legs to the other side of the bench and stood up. In two words he excused himself and went out, turning on the street in a direction opposite the bus stop.

Rumpel was as usual stupefied. He stared at the uneaten schnitzel as if it were a wig on a plate, or maybe a tortoise which might wander off in search of lettuce.

Curt fellow, he observed.

He chewed reflectively on the strudel.

Rumpel's thoughts lit, mosquito-like, on a suddenly bared difficulty. Why, he asked, do you refer to Signor Stirpa as Gepetto?

Ah. Fellow who carves people out of wood. Craftsman, you know. Brings 'em to life, walks 'em all around. Waves goodbye.

But Rumpel could easily see in the older man's eyes that wasn't all he was thinking.

Here is a man who is free of desire, but he is not wise. And so the story, always already finished, goes on, finished but always incomplete. Painfully immortal, we begin again, reincarnated anew. We remain, like a bus crawling through heavy traffic, on the great wheel — turning, turning. The gulf yet yawns, the surf beats sullenly against us, the great shroud of the sea rolls on as it has for thousands upon thousands of years — rolling, rolling. An infinity of ones and zeros streams behind — we circle the world of being; on and on we trudge, wandering, trailing behind us this thread of computation which is as long as needs until all is proven, which is to say: forever. And so we begin again, yowling with renewed desire, hoping to be this time wise, and be released. But we will never be wise, so long as we wish it, and the great story wheel will go on grinding — around, around, and yet around, as it has done and will do, forever and ever.

www.ingramcontent.com/pod-product-compliance
Lightning Source LLC
Chambersburg PA
CBHW060422030726
47495CB00003B/696